PUFFIN BOOKS

Praise for *Bodyguard: Hostage*

'Bone-crunching action adventure'
Financial Times

'Breathtaking action . . . as real as it gets'
Eoin Colfer, author of the bestselling Artemis Fowl series

'Bradford has combined Jack Bauer, James Bond and Alex Rider to bring us the action-packed thriller'
Goodreads

'Wholly authentic . . . the action and pace are spot on. Anyone working in the protection industry at a top level will recognize that the author knows what he's writing about'
Simon, ex-SO14 Royalty Close Protection

'A gripping page-turner that children won't be able to put down'
Red House

'Will wrestle you to the ground and leave you breathless. 5 Stars'
Flipside magazine

'A gripping, heart-pounding novel'
Bookaholic

Winner of the Brilliant Book Award 2014

Chris Bradford is a true believer in *'practising what you preach'*. For his award-winning Young Samurai series, he trained in samurai swordsmanship, karate, ninjutsu and earned his black belt in Zen Kyu Shin Taijutsu.

For his new Bodyguard series, Chris embarked on an intensive close-protection course to become a qualified professional bodyguard. During his training, he acquired skills in unarmed combat, defensive driving, tactical firearms, threat assessments, surveillance, and even anti-ambush exercises.

His bestselling books are published in over twenty languages and have garnered more than twenty-five children's book award nominations.

Before becoming a full-time author, he was a professional musician (who once performed for HRH Queen Elizabeth II), songwriter and music teacher.

Chris lives in England with his wife, two sons and two cats.

Discover more about Chris at *www.chrisbradford.co.uk*

Books by Chris Bradford

The Bodyguard series (in reading order)
HOSTAGE
RANSOM

The Young Samurai series (in reading order)
THE WAY OF THE WARRIOR
THE WAY OF THE SWORD
THE WAY OF THE DRAGON
THE RING OF EARTH
THE RING OF WATER
THE RING OF FIRE
THE RING OF WIND
THE RING OF SKY

Available as ebook
THE WAY OF FIRE

CHRIS BRADFORD

PUFFIN

Warning: Do not attempt any of the techniques described within the book without the supervision of a qualified martial arts instructor. These can be highly dangerous moves and result in fatal injuries. The author and publisher take no responsibility for any injuries resulting from attempting these techniques.

PUFFIN BOOKS

Published by the Penguin Group
Penguin Books Ltd, 80 Strand, London WC2R ORL, England
Penguin Group (USA) Inc., 375 Hudson Street, New York, New York 10014, USA
Penguin Group (Canada), 90 Eglinton Avenue East, Suite 700, Toronto, Ontario,
Canada M4P 2Y3 (a division of Pearson Penguin Canada Inc.)
Penguin Ireland, 25 St Stephen's Green, Dublin 2, Ireland (a division of Penguin Books Ltd)
Penguin Group (Australia), 707 Collins Street, Melbourne, Victoria 3008, Australia
(a division of Pearson Australia Group Pty Ltd)
Penguin Books India Pvt Ltd, 11 Community Centre, Panchsheel Park,
New Delhi – 110 017, India
Penguin Group (NZ), 67 Apollo Drive, Rosedale, Auckland 0632, New Zealand
(a division of Pearson New Zealand Ltd)
Penguin Books (South Africa) (Pty) Ltd, Block D, Rosebank Office Park,
181 Jan Smuts Avenue, Parktown North, Gauteng 2193, South Africa

Penguin Books Ltd, Registered Offices: 80 Strand, London WC2R ORL, England

puffinbooks.com

First published 2013

001

Text copyright © Chris Bradford, 2013
All rights reserved

The moral right of the author has been asserted

Set in Sabon by Palimpsest Book Production Limited, Falkirk, Stirlingshire
Printed and bound in Great Britain by Clays Ltd, Elcograf S.p.A.

Except in the United States of America, this book is sold subject to the condition that it shall not, by way of trade or otherwise, be lent, resold, hired out, or otherwise circulated without the publisher's prior consent in any form of binding or cover other than that in which it is published and without a similar condition including this condition being imposed on the subsequent purchaser

British Library Cataloguing in Publication Data
A CIP catalogue record for this book is available from the British Library

ISBN: 978-90-017-3525-8

www.greenpenguin.co.uk

Penguin Books is committed to a sustainable future for our business, our readers and our planet. This book is made from Forest Stewardship Council™ certified paper.

For Zach and Leo
May you protect one another through life . . .

HOSTAGE
PROLOGUE

The driver's knuckles turned white as he gripped the steering wheel of the Humvee and planted his foot hard on the pedal. The immense engine roared and the armoured vehicle shot on to the bomb-blasted road.

As the Humvee tore across the potholed concrete that stretched into the distance like the cracked skin of a dead snake, the two passengers in the back could only stare at the hellish images of a war-torn Iraq whipping past their windows. Barren patches of garbage-strewn desert, burnt-out carcasses of abandoned vehicles, crumbling buildings pockmarked with bullet holes, and the haunted faces of Iraqi children scavenging among the rubble.

The younger of the two passengers, a fresh-faced female diplomatic aide with styled blonde hair, wiped away a tear with an unsteady hand. The other, a tall handsome Hispanic man with strong cheekbones and deep brown eyes as sharp as an eagle's, was more composed. Yet his tense grip on the seat's armrest betrayed his deeper unease.

The bodyguard alone remained impassive, strapped into the front passenger seat, his MP5 sub-machine gun across his lap. He'd survived this run many times. Not that it made the drive any easier. Less than 12 kilometres long, this sweeping bend of road was the sole artery that connected Baghdad International Airport to the Green Zone – the fortress-like military and governmental safe haven in the heart of Baghdad. This made Route Irish the most dangerous stretch of highway in the world – a ready-made shooting gallery for terrorists and insurgents. Any attempt to travel the route was little more than a suicidal dash.

And today the stakes are even higher, thought the bodyguard, glancing over his shoulder at the newly appointed US Ambassador to Iraq. Usually the Americans arranged for a helicopter to transport senior officials between the airport and the zone, but high winds and the threat of a sandstorm had grounded all aircraft.

The bodyguard's eyes scanned the terrain beyond the bulletproof glass. In front and behind were three more Humvees thundering down the highway, forming a formidable military escort. These vehicles were armed to the teeth with mounted M2 heavy machine guns and MK19 grenade launchers. As the convoy raced along, the lead Humvee cleared the road ahead, barging civilian vehicles to one side if they didn't move out of the way quickly enough.

An underpass came into view and the bodyguard tensed. This was a prime spot for an attack. The bridge would have been swept for improvised explosive devices the night before. But that didn't mean *all* the IEDs had been discovered. His hand instinctively felt for the key fob in his pocket. He carried it with him everywhere. It contained a photo of his smiling eight-year-old son. Squeezing the talisman, the bodyguard vowed – as he always did – that he *would* survive the journey, if only for the sake of his son.

As they passed beneath the graffiti-scrawled bridge, he kept his eyes peeled for 'dickers' – lookouts who phoned ahead to rebel fighters lying in wait. The call might trigger a vehicle packed with explosives, a roadside IED, a suicide bomber, a drive-by shooting or even a barrage of mortars and rocket-propelled grenades. The bodyguard had witnessed all these assaults at one time or another, and they always ended in tragedy.

Emerging on the other side of the underpass, he heard the driver breathe a sigh of relief as he gunned the Humvee faster towards the Green Zone. The bodyguard resumed his surveillance sweep – scouring for threats among the surrounding traffic, the tree stumps on the central reservation, the housing estates to the south, and the approaching overpass and ramps of the next concrete-jungle intersection.

'This isn't good,' muttered the driver as their convoy began to slow to a snail's pace. In the distance the traffic had ground to a halt.

The HF radio burst into life. '*Tango One to Tango Three. Collision up ahead.*'

From the rear vehicle, the team leader responded. '*Tango One, this is Tango Three. Push on through. Use the central reservation.*'

The lead vehicle approached the hold-up. As it mounted

the kerb, the bodyguard's attention was drawn to a dead dog lying at the side of the road. The carcass, left to rot in the sun, appeared unnaturally bloated.

Then, as their own vehicle drew closer, the bodyguard spotted a man on the overpass, talking into his mobile phone. His instincts kicked into overdrive and he reached across to yank the steering wheel hard right. Startled, the driver gave him a furious look as their Humvee veered off the highway.

A split second later the booby-trapped dog exploded, engulfing the lead vehicle in a ball of flame.

The blast rocked their own Humvee with its intensity. The aide screamed in terror as a wave of hellfire rolled towards them. Keeping his composure, the bodyguard scanned the horizon and, out of the corner of his eye, spotted the telltale flare of a rocket-propelled grenade being fired from a nearby block of flats.

'GO, GO, GO!' he bawled at the driver.

The soldier floored the accelerator and the engine screamed in protest. They shot forwards, but it was too late. The RPG struck their rear end and detonated. Despite the Humvee weighing over two and a half tons, the vehicle flipped into the air like a child's toy. Inside, the occupants were thrown around like rag dolls. The Humvee landed with a tremendous crash upon the driver's side. Instantly the cabin filled with smoke and the acrid stench of burning paint and diesel.

The bodyguard's ears rang as he fought to orientate himself. Wedging himself in his seat, he looked round to check on his Principal. The Humvee had been up-armoured to withstand such attacks, but a direct hit meant the damage was still devastating. The bodyguard also knew a second strike would be the end for them.

'Sir? SIR!' he shouted, waving away the smoke to find the ambassador. 'Are you OK?'

Dazed but conscious, the ambassador nodded his head.

'We have to get out *now*!' the bodyguard explained, reaching back and undoing the man's seat belt. He tapped the driver on the shoulder. 'You take the second Principal.'

But the driver didn't respond. He was dead, having smashed his head against the windscreen on impact.

Cursing, the bodyguard tried to push open the front passenger door. But, even with his full body weight against it, he couldn't budge it. The force of the explosion had twisted the Humvee's heavily armoured construction and the door was jammed shut. They were trapped like sardines in a can.

Grabbing his gun from the footwell, he now prayed the bulletproof glass was one-way, as he'd requested.

'Cover your face!' the bodyguard ordered the ambassador.

Aiming the MP5 at the far corner of the windscreen, the bodyguard fired off several rounds and the glass exploded outwards. He kicked the screen free, the smoke cleared and he crawled through the opening.

Outside a full-on firefight was occurring. Ear-splitting blasts of grenades and the thunder of heavy machine guns mixed with the concussive explosion of mortars. The air was thick with black smoke and the *whizz* of speeding bullets.

Turning back, he helped the ambassador clamber from the Humvee and pulled him into the cover of its chassis.

'Hayley!' the ambassador implored, indicating his aide hanging limp in the back seat.

But the bodyguard had already clocked her condition. The young woman had taken the full force of the RPG. He shook his head regretfully. 'She's dead.'

Sheltering the ambassador from gunfire, he signalled for the back-up team. The rear Humvee driver spotted them and steered in their direction as a white sedan came tearing down the road from behind. Before any evasive action was possible, the rogue car was alongside. A second later it exploded. The Humvee was annihilated in the blast, taking with it the entire crew and any hope of rescue.

The bodyguard needed no further proof this was a carefully coordinated attack. A simultaneous assault of IEDs, RPGs and suicide bombers meant the rebels had known the ambassador's itinerary and were going all-out to assassinate him.

With the operation so jeopardized, the bodyguard decided he had to break protocol if he was to save his Principal's life. Besides, it was only a matter of time before another rocket hit their disabled Humvee.

'We're sitting ducks out here,' said the bodyguard. 'Are you able to run?'

'Won the four-hundred metre dash at UCLA,' replied the ambassador.

'Then stay close and do exactly as I say. We're heading for the underpass.'

He let loose a spray of covering fire. Then, using his body as a shield, he grabbed the ambassador and led him across open ground. As they dashed for safety, the supersonic crack of rebel bullets flew past their heads.

Behind them, an RPG hit their Humvee. The two of them were thrown to the ground by the explosion. Adrenalin pumped to the max, the bodyguard dragged the ambassador back to his feet.

Diving for cover behind a battered BMW, he stopped to assess their situation. The last surviving Humvee was battling to suppress enemy fire. The few Iraqi civilians who hadn't reached the underpass cowered behind their cars. The bodyguard knew most would be innocent civilians, but he kept his gun primed: it would take only one rebel to kill the ambassador.

Peering round the bonnet, he sighted a black SUV with tinted windows roll down a nearby on-ramp. Its passenger window was open, a gun barrel poking out in their direction.

Suddenly the BMW erupted with the pepper of bullets and its windscreen shattered. The bodyguard dropped on top of the ambassador, shielding him from the deadly shots. The car took the worst of the assault as round after round rattled its bodywork. Then the barrage ceased as the surviving Humvee's machine-gunner turned his sights on the rebels' SUV, forcing them to change target.

'We can't get pinned down here,' the bodyguard grunted, rolling off the ambassador.

Staying low, they weaved between the cars towards the underpass, a hail of bullets following close on their tail. As soon as they were beneath its shelter, the bodyguard hunted for a car that wasn't blocked in by the obviously prearranged accident. He spotted a silver Mercedes-Benz near the front of the pile-up.

The blast of a machine gun and terrified screams echoed through the underpass.

'They're following us!' exclaimed the ambassador, glancing over his shoulder in alarm.

Pushing his Principal ahead, the bodyguard returned fire, ensuring he was between the ambassador and the gunmen at all times.

Zigzagging through the cars, they were almost at the Mercedes when the ambassador came to a dead stop.

'Keep going!' urged the bodyguard.

Then he too saw the man standing before them.

Dressed in jeans and T-shirt, his face hidden behind a red-and-white headscarf, the rebel held an AK47 assault rifle aimed directly at the ambassador.

He fired.

Instinctively the bodyguard leapt in front of the ambassador, knocking him aside. The ambassador could only watch as his saviour was thrown back by the blaze of bullets, then crashed to the floor – lifeless.

The bodyguard had made the ultimate sacrifice to save him.

But it would all be in vain. The rebel strode over and

planted the smoking barrel of the AK47 in the ambassador's face.

'Now *you* die, infidel!' snarled the rebel.

'You can murder me, but you won't murder hope,' said the ambassador, staring defiantly back at the insurgent.

By all rights, the bodyguard should have been killed instantly, but his bulletproof vest had protected him from the worst of the assault. Barely conscious, only his deeply ingrained training allowed him to react. He'd lost hold of his MP5, but pulling a SIG Sauer P228 from his hip, he shot the rebel at point-blank range.

Before the man had even hit the ground, the bodyguard was struggling to his feet. His limbs felt as heavy as lead and there was a worrying coppery taste in his mouth.

'You're alive!' exclaimed the ambassador, rushing to his aid.

Staggering over to the Mercedes, the bodyguard yanked the door open. The driver had already fled for his life, leaving the keys in the ignition.

'Get in and stay low,' he instructed the ambassador, gasping for breath.

Fumbling with the keys, he begged the car to start first time as the back window imploded from a strafing of bullets. The engine kicked into life, the bodyguard slammed his foot on the accelerator and they shot out on to Route Irish. A hail of gunfire rained down on them from the bridge above. Weaving to avoid it, the bodyguard powered down the road, swerving round potholes, until the thunder of battle receded into the distance.

'You're seriously hurt!' said the ambassador, noticing the driver's seat was dripping with blood.

The bodyguard barely acknowledged him as he focused the last of his strength on carrying out his duty. Approaching the blast-walled safety of the Green Zone's first checkpoint, he slowed the Mercedes. The sentries would have no idea he was carrying the ambassador and would more than likely shoot first. Stopping short of the barrier, he got out of the car with the ambassador and walked the final stretch.

Still scanning for threats, the bodyguard stumbled, blood now soaking through his combats.

'We must get you to a hospital,' the ambassador insisted, taking his arm.

The bodyguard looked absently down at himself. Only now with the adrenalin fading did the pain register. 'Too late for that,' he grimaced.

United Nations soldiers rushed out, surrounding them in a protective cordon.

'You're safe now, sir,' said the bodyguard as he collapsed at the ambassador's feet, a small bloodstained key fob clutched in his hand.

HOSTAGE
CHAPTER 1

Six years later . . .

The fist caught Connor by surprise. A rocketing right hook that jarred his jaw. Stars burst before his eyes and he stumbled backwards. Only instinct saved him from getting floored by the left cross that followed. Blocking the punch with his forearm, Connor countered with a kick to the ribs. But he was too dazed to deliver any real power.

His attacker, a fifteen-year-old boy with knotted black hair and a body that seemed to have been chiselled from stone, deflected the strike and charged at him in a thunderous rage. Connor shielded his head as a barrage of blows rained down on him.

'GO, JET! KNOCK 'IM OUT!'

The shouts of the crowd were a monstrous roar in Connor's ears as Jet pummelled him. Connor ducked and weaved to escape the brutal onslaught. But he was boxed in.

Then the ding of the bell cut through the clamour and the referee stepped between them. Jet glared at Connor, his advantage lost.

Connor returned to his corner. Fourteen years old, he sported spiky brown hair, green-blue eyes and an athletic physique – the benefit of eight years' martial arts training. Spitting out his gumshield, he gratefully accepted the water bottle Dan held out for him. His kickboxing instructor, bald-headed with narrow eyes and a flattened nose that had been broken one too many times, didn't look happy.

'You have to keep your guard up,' Dan warned.

'Jet's so quick with his hands,' gasped Connor between gulps of water.

'But you're quicker,' Dan replied, his tone firm and unquestionable. 'The championship title is yours for the taking. *Unless* you persist in offering up your chin like that.'

Connor nodded. Summoning up his last reserves of energy, he shook his arms and breathed deeply, trying to shift the stiffness from his burning muscles. After competing in six qualifying bouts, he was tired. But he'd trained hard for the Battle of Britain tournament and wasn't going to fall at the last hurdle.

Dan wiped the sweat off Connor's face with a towel. 'See the guy in the second row?'

Connor glanced towards a man in his late forties with silver-grey hair trimmed into a severe crew cut. He sat among the cheering spectators, a tournament programme in one hand, his eyes discreetly studying Connor.

'He's a manager scouting for talent.'

All of a sudden Connor felt an additional pressure to succeed. This could be his chance at the international circuit, to compete for world titles and even earn sponsorship deals. Besides his own ambition, he was keenly aware that his family could do with the money.

The bell rang for the third and final round.

'Now go win this fight!' Dan urged, giving Connor an encouraging slap on the back.

Popping the gumshield into his mouth, Connor stood to face Jet – determined to win more than ever.

His opponent bobbed lightly on his toes, seemingly as fresh as in the first round. The crowd whooped and hollered as the two fighters squared up beneath the white-hot glare of the ring's spotlights. They stared at one another, neither willing to show the slightest sign of weakness. As soon as their gloves touched, Jet launched straight into his attack – a blistering combination of jab, cross, jab, hook.

Connor evaded the punches and countered with a front kick. The ball of his foot collided with Jet's stomach and his opponent doubled over. Keeping up the pressure, Connor trapped Jet against the ropes with a torrent of punches. But Jet refused to back down. With the ferocity of a cornered tiger, he blasted Connor with multiple body blows. Each strike weakened Connor a little more and he was forced to retreat. As he stepped away, Jet caught him with a crippling shin kick to the thigh. Connor buckled, opening himself up to another hook punch. Jet threw all his weight behind the attack. At the last second, Connor ducked and the fist glanced off the top of his head.

Realizing he'd been lucky to escape the hook this time, Connor now knew Jet was gunning to knock him down with *that* punch.

Like two gladiators, they battled back and forth across the ring. Sweat poured from Connor's brow, his breathing hard, his blood pumping, as the punches and kicks came thick and fast. Connor felt his energy ebbing. But he couldn't give up now. There was too much at stake.

'Stay light on your feet!' bawled Dan from his ringside corner.

Jet launched a roundhouse to the head. Connor double-blocked it with his arms and countered with a side-kick. Jet leapt away then immediately drove back in, fists flying. The crowd was now going wild at the epic to-and-fro of combat. Connor's name was chanted to the rafters by his friends from the Tiger Martial Arts Dojo: 'CON-NOR! CON-NOR!'

Jet's supporters screamed back with equal ferocity. The shouts reached fever-pitch as they entered the closing seconds of the bout. Connor realized if he didn't knock Jet down, his opponent would likely win on points. But exhaustion was getting the better of him.

'Don't drop your guard!' Dan screamed at him in frustration from his corner.

Jet spotted the gap in Connor's defence and went for it. Jab, cross . . . *hook!*

But Connor had been feigning the weakness to draw his opponent in . . . and Jet had taken the bait. With lightning speed, he sidestepped the attack and thrust in a jab, stunning his opponent. Then, whipping his rear leg round, he executed a spinning hook-kick. Jet never saw what hit him as Connor's heel connected with the side of his head. Jet's black gumshield shot out of his mouth and he crashed to the deck in a heap. A second later the bell rang to end the fight.

A dazed Jet staggered to his feet, helped by the referee. Connor bowed his respect to his opponent, who gave a begrudging nod in return. The presiding judge stepped into the ring. Clasping a microphone, he announced: 'The UK title for the Under Sixteens Battle of Britain Kickboxing Tournament goes to . . . CONNOR REEVES!'

The crowd roared in celebration as Connor was presented with the trophy, a silver figure of a kickboxer atop a column of white marble. Connor felt a wave of elation and raised the prize high above his head in acknowledgement of his supporters.

Dan gripped him round the shoulders. 'Congratulations, Champ!' he said, grinning. 'Your father would be so proud of you.'

Connor looked up at the glittering trophy and at the cheering spectators. He dearly wished his dad could have been by his side to share this moment. His father was the one who'd encouraged him to start martial arts in the first place. It had been his passion – and it was Connor's too.

'I have to admit, you had me worried there for a second,' said Dan.

'Feign and fight,' replied Connor. 'You taught me that trick, remember? So you deserve to hold this as much as me.'

Passing Dan the trophy, he glanced towards the second row and was disappointed to see the silver-haired man had gone.

'Wasn't the manager impressed then?'

'Oh, I wouldn't worry about him,' Dan admitted with a playful wink as he brandished the trophy. 'I've no idea who that man was. I just wanted you to fight at the top of your game – and you did!'

HOSTAGE
CHAPTER 2

A chill wind hit Connor as he emerged from the ExCel Centre in the London Docklands and headed for the bus stop on Freemasons Road. The grey February sky was unforgiving, the tail end of winter refusing to loosen its grip. But not even the dismal weather could dampen Connor's spirits. He was the UK Kickboxing Champion and had the trophy in his kitbag to prove it. He couldn't wait to show his gran – she was his biggest fan, after all.

Pulling up the hood of his sweatshirt, Connor shouldered his kitbag and crossed the bridge spanning the Docklands Light Railway. He dodged the traffic on the opposite side and was passing a row of boarded-up shops when he heard a cry for help.

Halfway down a littered alley, he spotted a smartly dressed Indian boy surrounded by a gang of youths. It was obvious that a man heading for the train station had also heard the cry. But, averting his gaze, he hurried past the scene.

Scared of being knifed, thought Connor. *And who'd blame him?*

But Connor couldn't walk away. *The strong have a duty to protect the weak*, his father had taught him. That was the reason his father had joined the army. And why he'd encouraged Connor to take up martial arts. He never wanted his son to be a victim.

The gang leader shoved the boy against the alley wall and began to rifle through his pockets.

'Leave him alone!' shouted Connor.

Almost as one, the gang turned to face their challenger.

'This ain't got nothing to do with you, mate,' said the leader. 'Leg it!'

Connor ignored the warning and strode towards them. 'He's a friend of mine.'

'This loser ain't got no friends,' the boy said, spitting at his victim's feet, clearly not believing Connor's bluff.

Drawing level with the gang, Connor eyeballed the leader. Dressed in baggy jeans and a Dr Dre T-shirt, the lad was a good few inches taller than him and well built. With a broad chest, bulging biceps and fists like hammers, the boy could easily play front row in the school rugby team. *If he still goes to school*, Connor thought.

The rest of the gang – two boys and a girl – were less intimidating but still dangerous as a pack. One boy in Converse trainers, baggy jeans and a grey hoodie held a skateboard, his face pockmarked with spots. The other wore carbon-copy baggy jeans, a puffer jacket and a red Nike baseball cap, tipped at a 'too cool for you' angle on his bleached blond hair. The girl, who was Chinese with a jet-black bob and a piercing through her nose, wore dark eyeshadow, emo-style, and Dr Marten boots. She shot Connor a hard stare.

'Let's go,' said Connor to his new friend, keeping his voice low and even. He didn't want to show how nervous he really was. He might be trained in kickboxing and jujitsu, but he wasn't looking for a fight. His jujitsu teacher had drilled into him that violence was the last resort. Especially when outnumbered four to one – *that* was just asking for trouble.

The Indian boy took a hesitant step towards him, but the gang leader planted a hand on his chest. 'You're going nowhere.'

Frozen to the spot with fear, the boy looked to Connor in wide-eyed desperation.

A tense stand-off now ensued between Connor and the gang. Connor's eyes flicked to each gang member, his kitbag at the ready to protect himself in case one of them pulled a knife.

'I said, leave him alone,' he repeated, edging between the gang and their victim.

'And I said, mind your own business,' replied the leader, launching a fist straight at the boy's face.

As the terrified boy let out a yelp, Connor moved in and deflected the punch with a forearm block. Then he took up a fighting stance, fists raised, defying the gang to come any closer.

Glaring at Connor, the leader broke into a mocking laugh. 'Watch out, everyone! It's the Karate Kid!'

Don't laugh too soon, thought Connor, unshouldering his kitbag.

The leader sized up Connor. Then he swung a wild right hook at Connor's head. With lightning reflexes, Connor ducked, drove forwards and delivered a powerful punch to the gut in return.

The unexpected strike should have floored the gang leader, but he was much stronger than he looked. Instead of collapsing, he merely grunted and came back at Connor with a combination of jab, cross and upper cut. Connor went on the defensive. As he blocked each attack, it became blindingly obvious the lad was a trained boxer. Having underestimated his opponent, Connor rapidly reassessed his tactics. Although Connor was faster, the gang leader had the advantage of power and reach. And, without gloves, this fight had the potential to be deadly – just one of those sledgehammer fists could land him in hospital.

The bigger they are, the harder they fall, thought Connor, recalling how in jujitsu a larger opponent could be defeated by using their strength against themselves.

As the gang leader let loose a vicious roundhouse punch to his head, Connor entered inside its arc and spun his body into his attacker. Redirecting the force of the strike, he flung the lad over his hip and body-dropped him to the concrete. The leader hit the ground so hard all the breath was knocked out of him. The gang stared in disbelief at their fallen leader, while the Indian boy could barely suppress a grin of delight at seeing his tormentor squirm in the dirt.

'Get . . . him!' the leader wheezed, unable to rise.

The boy with the Nike baseball cap charged in, executing a flying side-kick. Connor leapt to one side before realizing his new friend was right behind him. With no time to spare, Connor shoved him out of the kick's path.

Nike's foot struck the wall instead. Incensed, he turned on Connor and launched a furious succession of spinning kicks. Surprised at the boy's skill, Connor was forced to retreat. As he backed away, only instinct – born from hours of sparring – warned him of a simultaneous attack from behind. Glancing over his shoulder, he saw Hoodie step forward and swing the skateboard at his head.

At the last second, Connor ducked. The tail of the deck missed him by a whisker and struck Nike full in the face instead. The boy fell to his knees, semi-concussed.

Hoodie, horrified at his mistake, was now an open target. Connor took advantage and shot out a side-kick. But the boy reacted faster than Connor expected and held up his deck as a shield. Having broken wooden blocks to pass his black-belt grading, Connor knew the right technique. Gritting his teeth, he drove on through – the board shattering rather than his foot. From there, it took Connor a simple palm strike to floor Hoodie.

With all three boys out of action, the girl now advanced on him.

Connor held up his hands in peace. 'Listen, I don't fight girls. Just walk away and we can forget all about this.'

The girl stopped, tilted her head and smiled sweetly at him. 'How nice of you.'

Then she punched Connor straight in the mouth, splitting his lip. With barely a pause, the girl followed through with a kick to the thigh, her heavy Dr Martens giving him a dead leg exactly where Jet had struck him earlier in the bout. He crumpled against the wall.

'I fight boys, though!' she said as Connor, stunned and hurting, tried to recover his balance.

The girl went to kick him again, but rather than retreat Connor moved in and caught her leg in mid-swing. Struggling to free herself, she struck for his neck with the edge of her hand. But Connor grabbed hold of her wrist and twisted her arm into a lock, forcing her to submit. The girl squealed in pain.

'LET THAT GIRL GO!'

Connor glanced back down the alley. Two police officers – a tall black man and a slender white woman – were hurrying towards them. Connor reluctantly released the girl, who promptly kicked him in the shin before running off in the opposite direction. The rest of the gang followed close on her heels.

Connor went to go after them, but the policeman seized him by the scruff of the neck. 'Not so fast, sonny. You're coming with us.'

'But I was trying to save this boy,' Connor protested.

'What boy?' questioned the policewoman.

Connor looked up and down the alley . . . but it was deserted. The boy had gone.

HOSTAGE
CHAPTER 3

The officers escorted Connor across Freemasons Road and down a side street to an imposing red-brick building. As they neared the entrance, the traditional blue lamp of the Metropolitan Police came into view. Below this was a sign in bold white lettering declaring: CANNING TOWN POLICE STATION. They climbed the steps, passing a poster warning *Terrorism – if you suspect it, report it*, and entered through a set of heavy wooden doors, the blue paint chipped and worn.

The station's foyer was poorly lit and depressingly drab, the walls bare, apart from a cork noticeboard promoting a local Neighbourhood Watch meeting. The sole pieces of furniture were a bench and a glass reception booth, manned by a single bored custody officer. As the three of them approached, he looked up and tutted upon seeing Connor's split lip and the splashes of blood dotted across his sweatshirt.

'Name?' the custody officer asked him.

'Connor Reeves.'

'Age?'

'Fourteen.'

He noted this down on a ledger. 'Address and contact number?'

Connor gave his home in Leytonstone.

'Family?'

'Just my mum and gran,' he replied.

As this was added to the ledger, the policewoman explained the reason for detaining Connor and the custody officer nodded, seemingly satisfied.

'In there,' he said, pointing with his pen to a door labelled INTERVIEW ROOM.

Connor was marched across the foyer. The policeman stayed behind to log the contents of his kitbag with the custody officer.

'After you,' said the policewoman, ushering him through.

Connor stepped inside. In the centre of the room was a large desk with a single lamp and a couple of hard wooden chairs. A single fluorescent strip buzzed like a mosquito, casting a bleached light over the depressing scene. There was a musty smell in the air and the blinds were drawn across the window, giving an unsettling sense of isolation from the rest of the world.

In spite of his innocence, Connor's throat went dry with apprehension and his heart began to beat faster.

This just isn't right! he thought. He'd tried to stop a mugging and *he* was the one being arrested. And what thanks had he got for stepping in? None. The Indian boy had disappeared without a trace.

'Sit down,' ordered the policewoman, pointing to the chair in front of the desk.

Connor reluctantly did as he was told.

The policeman rejoined them, closing the door behind him. He handed his colleague a thick folder. The female officer stepped behind the desk, flicked on the lamp and sat opposite Connor. In its glare, Connor watched the policewoman lay the folder on the table and, next to this, place a notepad and pen. To Connor's growing unease, the folder was stamped STRICTLY CONFIDENTIAL.

He started to sweat. He'd never been in trouble with the police before. *What could they possibly have on him?*

The officer carefully undid the folder's string fastening and began to inspect the file. The towering policeman took up position next to his colleague and stared unflinchingly at Connor. The tension became almost unbearable.

After what seemed an age, the policewoman declared, 'If that girl files a charge against you – for assault – it would be a matter for the courts.'

Connor felt the ground beneath him give way. This was turning out to be far more serious than he could have ever imagined.

'So we need to take a full statement from you,' she explained.

'Shouldn't I call a lawyer or something?' Connor asked, knowing that's what was always said in the movies.

'No, that won't be necessary,' replied the officer. 'Just tell us why you did it?'

Connor shifted uneasily in his seat. 'Because . . . there was a boy being mugged.'

The police officer made a note. 'Did you know this boy?'

'No,' replied Connor. 'And I never will. The ungrateful kid ran away.'

'So why decide to get involved in the first place?'

'They were calling him names and about to beat him up!'

'But other people walked on by. Why didn't you?'

Connor shrugged. 'It was the right thing to do. He couldn't stand up for himself. It was four against one.'

'Four?' repeated the police officer, jotting down more notes. 'Yet you took them on alone.'

Connor nodded, conceding, 'I know a bit of martial arts.'

The officer flicked through the files. 'It says here you're a black belt in kickboxing and jujitsu. I don't call that just "a bit".'

Connor's breath caught in his throat. *How come the officer has this information to hand? What else do they know?*

'That's . . . right,' he admitted, wondering if this would count against him. His instructors had always warned him to be careful using his skills outside of the dojo.

'So let's get the story straight,' said the policewoman, putting down her pen and looking Connor squarely in the eye. 'You're saying you put your life at risk for a complete stranger.'

Connor hesitated. *Am I about to plead guilty to an offence?*

'Well . . . yes,' he confessed.

A hint of a smile passed across the policewoman's lips. 'That takes guts,' she said approvingly.

Connor stared in astonishment at the policewoman's unexpected praise. The officer closed her file, then looked up at the policeman and nodded.

He turned to Connor. 'Well done, you've passed.'

Connor's brow furrowed in bewilderment. 'Passed *what*?'

'The Test.'

'You mean . . . like a school exam or something?'

'No,' he replied. 'Real-life combat.'

Connor was now even more confused. 'Are you saying that gang were a *test* for me?'

The policeman nodded. 'You displayed instinctive protection skills.'

'Of course I did!' he exclaimed, feeling his frustration rise. 'The gang attacked me –'

'That's not what we mean,' interrupted the policewoman. 'You showed a natural willingness to defend *another* person.'

Connor got up from his seat. 'What's going on here? I want to call home.'

'There's no need,' she said, offering a friendly smile. 'We've already informed your mother you may be running a little late.'

Connor's mouth fell open in disbelief. *What on earth are the police up to?*

'We've had our eye on you for some time,' revealed the policewoman, rising from her chair and perching on the side of the desk, her manner becoming more relaxed and informal. 'The attack was set up to test your moral code and combat skills. It had to be authentic, which meant we couldn't warn you. That's why we used trained operatives for the assignment.'

Trained operatives? thought Connor, nursing his split lip. *No wonder they were so skilled at fighting.*

'But why?' he demanded.

'We needed to assess your potential to be a CPO in the real world.'

Connor blinked in surprise, wondering if he'd heard right. 'A what?'

'A Close Protection Officer,' explained the policeman. 'By placing yourself in harm's way to protect another, you proved you have the natural instinct of a bodyguard. You can't teach that. It has to be part of who you are.'

Connor laughed at the idea. 'You can't be serious! I'm too young to be a bodyguard.'

'That's *exactly* the point,' replied a voice from behind in a clipped military tone.

Connor spun round and was shocked to find the silver-haired man from the tournament standing right behind him.

'With training, you'll make the *perfect* bodyguard.'

HOSTAGE
CHAPTER 4

'My name is Colonel Black,' the man said, introducing himself with a curt nod of the head. Dressed in pristine chinos, polished black boots and a khaki shirt, the sleeves rolled up to the elbows, his appearance conveyed a life spent in the forces. Up close, Connor could see the man had craggy features and a strong chiselled jaw. His demeanour was at once disciplined and authoritative, his flint-grey eyes never wavering from Connor's face. And although he looked to be in his late forties he possessed the physique of a man ten years younger – broad-chested with tanned, muscular forearms. Only a ragged white scar cutting a line across his throat detracted from this flawless image, no doubt the result of active service.

'I was most impressed with your performance today, both in and out of the ring,' he stated. 'You displayed true grit. Even when the odds were stacked against you, you didn't give up. I like that in a recruit.'

'Thank you,' replied Connor, too bewildered to say anything else. Then the colonel's words hit home. 'What do you mean, *recruit*?'

'Take a seat and I'll explain.'

His invitation wasn't quite an order, but Connor felt compelled to sit down anyway. The colonel walked round to the other side of the desk and took over the proceedings from the two police officers.

'I head up a close protection organization known as Buddyguard.'

'*Buddy*-guard?' Connor shrugged. 'Never heard of it.'

'Few people have. It's a highly secretive operation,' the colonel admitted. 'So, before I continue, I must stress this information is classified in the interests of national security and not to be repeated – to *anyone*.'

The stern expression on the colonel's face left Connor no room for doubt that there'd be grave repercussions if he ever did. 'I understand,' he replied.

The colonel took him at his word and continued. 'In today's world, there's a demand for a new breed of bodyguard. The constant threat of terrorism, the growth of criminal gangs and the surge in pirate attacks, all mean an increased risk of hostage-taking, blackmail and assassination. And, with the overt media coverage of politicians' families, the rise of teen pop stars and the new wave of billionaires, adults are not the only target – children are too.'

'You mean like that French movie star's son?' interrupted Connor. The story of the boy's kidnapping while on a sailing holiday had been splashed all over the news.

'Yes, they ended up paying a million dollars for his safe return. But it needn't have happened in the first place – if the family had employed a close-protection team. And my organization provides just such a service. Yet it differs from all other security outfits by training and supplying only *young* bodyguards.' Colonel Black looked directly at Connor as he said this. 'These highly skilled individuals are often more effective than the typical adult bodyguard, who can easily draw unwanted attention. Operating invisibly as the child's constant companion, a buddyguard provides the greatest possible protection for any vulnerable or high-profile target.'

The colonel paused to allow everything he'd said to sink in.

'And you want *me* to become a buddyguard?' said Connor, dubious at the idea.

'You've got it in one.'

Connor laughed uneasily and held up his hands in objection. 'You've made a mistake. You must have the wrong person.'

The colonel shook his head. 'I don't think so.'

'But I'm still at school. I can't be a bodyguard!'

'Why not? It's in your blood.'

Connor gave Colonel Black a baffled look. Then the colonel said something that completely threw him.

'You'll be following in your father's footsteps.'

'What are you talking about?' shot back Connor, suddenly going on the defensive. 'My dad's dead.'

The colonel nodded solemnly. 'I'm aware of that. And I was very much grieved when I heard the news. Your father and I were close friends. We fought together.'

Connor studied the man before him, wondering if he was telling the truth. 'But my dad never mentioned you.'

'That's understandable. In the SAS, we try to keep our personal and professional lives separate.'

'SAS? My dad was in the army, Royal Signals,' Connor corrected him.

'That was his cover job. Your father was actually in the SAS Special Projects Team, responsible for counter-terrorism and VIP close protection,' the colonel revealed. 'One of the best.'

This new knowledge unsettled Connor, who thought he'd known his father pretty well. 'Then why did he never tell me that?'

'As a member of Special Projects, your father had to keep his identity secret. To protect himself, you and the rest of your family.'

'I don't believe you,' said Connor, gripping the arm of his chair for support. His whole world seemed to be shifting sideways as the long-held memory of his father was brought into question.

The colonel removed a photo from his breast pocket and handed it to Connor.

'Iraq, 2004.'

Five soldiers in combat fatigues and carrying sub-machine guns stood before a barren patch of desert scrub. In the middle was a younger Colonel Black, his distinctive scar visible just above the neckline of his body armour. Next to him was a tall tanned man with dark brown hair and familiar green-blue eyes – Justin Reeves.

Connor was speechless. Gripping the photograph with a trembling hand, he fought back the tears at seeing his father's face so unexpectedly.

'You can keep that if you want,' said the colonel. 'Now, on to your recruitment into Buddyguard.'

'What?' Connor exclaimed, events moving too fast for him. 'But I haven't agreed to anything.'

'True. But hear me out and you will.'

Connor tentatively put his father's photo down on the desk, reluctant to let it out of his sight.

'First, your school will be informed of your transfer to a private school.'

'*Private* school?' queried Connor. 'My family doesn't have that sort of money.'

'You'll be funded by a special scholarship scheme. Besides, we need an official cover for your relocation to the Buddyguard training camp. We must maintain the secrecy of our operation. No one can *ever* know.'

'Relocation?' challenged Connor. 'I'm sorry, but I can't leave my mum. You'll have to find someone else.'

'We're aware of your situation,' said the policewoman with a reassuring smile as she placed an envelope on the table for him. 'We've made all the necessary arrangements to ensure she's well looked after. And all the costs are covered.'

Connor stared at the mysterious envelope, then at Colonel Black. 'What if I don't want to become a bodyguard?'

'It's entirely your decision. You're free to go home, but I think you'll regret it.'

A truth suddenly dawned on Connor. 'So I'm not under arrest?'

'Whoever said you were?' replied the colonel, arching an eyebrow.

Connor turned to the two police officers, then realized neither of them had read him his rights or *officially* arrested him. They'd only asked him to accompany them to the station.

'I'll leave you to think about my offer,' said Colonel Black, laying a business card on top of the envelope. The card was black as night with an embossed silver logo of a shield sprouting wings. Below it was a single telephone number – and nothing else.

The colonel nodded goodbye, then disappeared out through the door, the two police officers in tow.

Connor was left alone in the room. He stared at the card, his mind whirling with the events of the past hour. His life had been spun on its axis – one moment he was being crowned UK Kickboxing Champion, the next he was being recruited as a bodyguard. He stared at the envelope, both intrigued and a touch afraid of what it might contain. He decided to leave it for later. He had other matters to think about first.

Picking up the card, envelope and his father's photo, Connor stood and headed for the door. When he opened it, he thought he'd made a mistake and gone the wrong way. The lights in the foyer were all off, the reception booth deserted, the building silent as a grave.

'Hello? Anyone there?' he called. But no one answered.

He spotted his kitbag on the counter. Stowing the envelope and photo next to his trophy and pocketing the colonel's business card, he made his way to the main entrance. His footsteps echoed through the empty foyer. As he passed the noticeboard, he saw the Neighbourhood Watch meeting was for two years ago and briefly wondered why the announcement was still up. Pushing open the heavy double doors, he stepped outside into the grey evening light. Relieved to escape the tomb-like atmosphere of the station, he looked down the street for Colonel Black. But neither the colonel nor the police officers were in sight. Then, as the double doors slammed shut behind him, he noticed the terrorism poster had been taken down. An official blue-and-white sign was now visible:

THIS IS NO LONGER A POLICE STATION.
The nearest station is 444 Barking Road, Plaistow.

Connor stared at the sign, stunned. The *whole* operation had been a set-up!

He felt in his pocket and pulled out the one thing proving the encounter had even occurred – the black business card with the silver winged shield . . . and a solitary telephone number.

HOSTAGE

CHAPTER 5

'You're late, Hazim,' growled the brooding man in Arabic, through a mouthful of green khat leaves. The man, who boasted a thick bushy beard, a hooked nose and sun-blasted skin the colour of the deep desert, bared a row of brown-yellowish teeth in displeasure.

'I'm sorry, Malik, but the plane was delayed getting in,' replied Hazim, bowing his head in deference to the man who sat like a king at the far end of the rectangular whitewashed *mafraj* room.

Malik tutted in irritation, yet nonetheless waved him over to sit by his side. Hazim, a young man of Yemeni origin with dominant eyebrows and an angular face, almost handsome if not for his downturned mouth, nervously took his place among the other members of the Brotherhood.

The room was full of men dressed in ankle-length *thawb*, their white cotton robes providing relief from the heat of the day. Some were bareheaded, others wore red-and-white chequered headscarves. They reclined on large cushions, left leg tucked underneath, right arm upon the right knee, and the left arm supported by a padded armrest. Before each was a pile of green stems from which they picked leaves to chew as they engaged in animated conversation.

As was tradition in a *mafraj* room there were two rows of windows, the upper set decorated in stained glass through which the late-afternoon sun scattered shards of rainbow colours across the thickly carpeted floor. The lower clear windows were pushed wide open to allow a cool breeze to waft in. Not accustomed to the country's intense heat, Hazim turned towards one of the openings in relief. From the topmost floor of the house, he was able to admire the magnificent vista of Sana'a, the capital city of Yemen. The flat sun-dried rooftops of the myriad white and sand-coloured houses stretched into the distance, where they met the awe-inspiring Sarawat mountain range.

'So where's your khat?' demanded Malik.

Hazim held up his hands in apology. 'Sorry, I was more worried about the CIA trailing me than shopping in the souk.'

'Tsk!' Malik spat, batting away his excuse. 'I won't tolerate lateness or lack of respect to our traditions. Understand?'

Hazim nodded, shifting uncomfortably under the man's fierce gaze. Then, like quicksilver, Malik's harsh expression switched to a genial smile and he clapped Hazim on the back.

'No matter this time, Hazim. You were right to be cautious. Kedar, give him some of yours,' he ordered a man to Hazim's left. 'A true Yemeni should never be without.'

Kedar, a man of Herculean build with a wiry beard,

offered Hazim a handful of green stems. Chewing khat was the social norm in Yemen. All men gathered together at the end of the day to sit down, chew khat and put the world to rights, just as Americans met in Starbucks for coffee and the English enjoyed a pot of tea – except the intoxicating effect of chewing khat was the equivalent of several strong espressos in a row.

Nodding gratefully to Kedar, Hazim pulled a few leaves from a stem and popped them in his mouth. As he bit down, the bitterness of the khat's juices hit his taste buds.

'Do you have a Coke?' he asked, trying not to grimace.

Malik threw up his arms in exaggerated outrage and turned to a man with thinning hair and rounded scholarly glasses. 'This is what I mean, Bahir! The poison of America seeps into his bones. There's fine Yemeni water over there,' he muttered, indicating a large ceramic jug on a round wooden table. 'The only and *proper* way to enjoy khat.'

Selecting the choicest leaves from his bundle, Malik stuffed several into his left cheek at once. He chewed slowly, carefully studying Hazim as the young man poured a glass for himself. 'He doesn't even have a beard!' he snorted.

Sipping on his water, Hazim self-consciously put a hand to his shaven face and glanced round at his bearded brethren. The other men all eyed him guardedly.

'He looks like a newborn,' commented Bahir. 'Hey, everyone, it's Baby Hazim!'

The group burst into raucous laughter. Hazim flushed in humiliation and cast his eyes to the floor. But the jesting was ultimately good-natured, for all in the room knew the truth. Hazim had been invited into the inner circle of the Brotherhood precisely because he'd shown he *was* able to integrate effortlessly into American life.

Malik patted Hazim reassuringly on the shoulder. 'Enough! Now we're all here, we can begin,' he announced.

The laughter of the other men died quickly, all conversation coming to a halt.

'My brothers,' he began, opening his arms wide. 'Our organization has hidden in the shadows long enough. The time is ripe for a nightmare attack against our enemy. The toppling of the Twin Towers struck at the heart of America. Now I intend we destroy its soul!'

Malik fingered his prize *jambiya* as he spoke. The curved dagger was thrust into his leather belt, positioned in full view of everyone. The semi-precious stones adorning the wooden sheath glistened in the evening's fading light and, with its handle of rare rhinoceros horn, no man would question his status as leader. While for most Yemeni men the *jambiya* was purely a symbol of masculinity and usually blunt, Malik kept his blade sharpened, having used it to slit many an enemy's throat.

'We must hit America where it hurts the most,' he continued, his fervour building. 'A wise man once said, "Kill a few, hurt many, scare thousands." But in this attack, we need only kidnap *one* infidel.'

He paused, relishing the moment of power as his men leant in, mesmerized by his words.

'Who's the target?' breathed Bahir.

'The President's daughter.'

A round of gasps met this revelation. Not from disgust, rather from admiration at the audacity of the plan.

But Hazim couldn't hide his scepticism. 'You seriously intend for us to *kidnap* the President's daughter? One of the most protected families in the world.'

'Yes,' said Malik smugly. 'The plan may be bold, but it'll be as devastating and effective as a thousand bombs. Once we have her, we'll demand the release of our brothers and force all infidels to leave our lands.'

The men cheered at this news, pumping their fists in the air. Hazim tried to get himself heard over the hubbub. 'The United States doesn't negotiate with those they label terrorists. What makes you think the President will bow to our demands?'

Malik removed his *jambiya* and inspected the gleaming blade. 'What father wouldn't if you held his own flesh and blood hostage?'

HOSTAGE
CHAPTER 6

Connor's thumb hovered over the Call button of his mobile. The telephone number glowed steadily in the display, but he couldn't quite bring himself to ring it.

Was he doing the right thing?

He could hear his mum shuffling around downstairs, making them breakfast. Connor wondered if she'd manage on her own. The TV was on in the sitting room, the volume a notch too high for Connor's comfort, to compensate for his gran's failing hearing. But no one complained; their neighbours were just as old, and only the three of them lived in the house.

Spread out on his bed were the contents of the envelope. A company brochure promoting high-quality live-in carers for the elderly and chronically ill, plus a letter detailing Colonel Black's offer. Connor knew exactly what it said. And each time he read the letter, the more sense it made.

His mum suffered from multiple sclerosis. On a day-to-day basis, he looked after her, helped by his gran. But when he was at school or martial arts training he couldn't be around. And recently there'd been a couple of incidents that had worried him – the dropping of a pan of boiling water, then a painful fall down the stairs that had resulted in a broken wrist. As his mum's condition worsened, she'd soon need full-time care. On top of that, he'd noticed his gran was finding it harder to cope. While her mind was still sharp as a tack, she was getting old and less mobile. As a family, they'd once discussed the idea of care homes. But his gran had been adamant it would be the death of her. The little terraced house was full of happy memories of her life with his grandad and father and she was determined to stay. For his mum's part, she was more worried what would happen to her son if she was forced to go into a nursing home. Being a minor, Connor couldn't remain in the house alone. And without any close relatives his choices seemed limited to foster care or entering a children's home himself – prospects that appealed neither to him nor his mother.

Their ideal solution was a live-in carer. But there was no way they could afford one.

Until now.

Connor had spent the past week deliberating over the decision. He dearly loved his mum and gran and didn't want to leave them. Yet by joining Buddyguard he would guarantee their well-being. And he considered it his duty to look after them, just as they'd looked after *him* when his father had died.

He glanced over at the photo on the bedside table of his father in Iraq. Six years had gone by, but there wasn't a day when Connor didn't think of him. His memories were now like snapshots in a dusty family album – playing football in the park, games of hide-and-seek in Epping Forest, sparring in their back garden. And with each passing year these snapshots faded a little more. Connor was worried that one day he wouldn't be able to recall his father at all.

But Colonel Black and his father had been friends. He could fill in the missing pieces. And Connor desperately wanted to know more about his father's secret life – what it was like being in the SAS and working as a bodyguard in hostile environments. He also needed to understand why his father had devoted himself to such a job, one that took him away from his family for such long periods. Connor realized he could never get his father back, but by following in his footsteps he *might* come to know him better.

Connor pressed the Call button.

It rang once before being answered in that familiar clipped tone.

'Glad you've decided to join us,' said the colonel. 'One of the team will collect you Monday at 0900 hours sharp. Be ready.'

'But . . . I-I still haven't agreed to anything yet,' Connor stuttered.

He sensed a smile at the other end of the line.

'Connor, you wouldn't be calling *unless* it was to say yes.'

HOSTAGE
CHAPTER 7

The following Monday a blacked-out Range Rover pulled up outside the house: 0900 hours sharp.

Bags packed, Connor hugged his mum goodbye. 'I'll be back during the holidays,' he promised.

'Now, don't you worry about me,' she said, kissing him tenderly on the cheek. 'You go have a good time. I'm so proud of you.'

She squeezed his hand. To Connor, his mother always seemed at her most energized and pain-free when she was concentrating on him.

'And I'll be here 24/7,' reassured Sally, a jolly, middle-aged woman who was to be his mum's live-in carer.

The morning after the phone call, Sally had dropped by their house. Over a pot of tea, she'd explained the in-care arrangement and that the costs were being covered by Connor's 'scholarship programme'. His mum had immediately warmed to the idea, proud her son's talents were being recognized. By the second cup of tea, the three women were swapping stories and laughing like old friends. Reassured by this, Connor knew his mother was in good hands and that he'd made the right decision for her.

And it had the double benefit that his gran would also be cared for in her own home. This news had initially pleased his gran. But, not one to miss a trick, she had questioned him in private about the 'scholarship programme'. Despite Colonel Black's warning, Connor had told her the truth – as he always did with his gran. She'd immediately tried to dissuade him. But, seeing the determination in his eyes, she'd resignedly shook her head and said, 'You're your father's son. Always putting others before yourself.'

So it was agreed Buddyguard was to be their secret and Connor had no doubt that she'd keep it. As he went to say goodbye, his gran gripped him with surprising strength.

'Stay safe,' she whispered, and for a moment he didn't think she'd let him go.

With a final hug for his mum, Connor picked up his bags and strode over to the Range Rover. The driver got out, a slender woman with dark brown shoulder-length hair and olive eyes that were good-natured yet watchful.

Connor smiled in wry recognition. 'You're not going to arrest me again, are you?'

The former policewoman laughed. 'Only if you don't pay attention in class!' She offered her hand. 'I'm Jody, one of your instructors. Now get in, we've a long drive ahead.'

Tossing his bags in the boot, Connor clambered into the passenger seat. With a last wave to his mum and gran, he heaved the door shut and the Range Rover pulled away. As they drove out of London, they passed the Tiger Martial Arts Dojo. Connor felt a twinge of regret and a nagging doubt returned. The club was almost a second home to him. He'd just made his mark as a national kickboxing champion. *Am I throwing it all away?* His instructor hadn't thought so. Although dismayed to lose his most promising student, Dan had only wanted the best for him.

'The time to strike is when the opportunity presents itself,' Dan had said, giving him a friendly tap on the chin with his fist. 'So good luck – and remember: if you get into trouble, *hit first, hit hard, then hit the ground running.*'

The Range Rover turned a corner and the club disappeared from view. Burying his doubts, Connor now felt an undeniable thrill at what lay in store for him as a bodyguard. 'So where are we going?' he asked eagerly.

'Wales,' replied Jody.

'Oh.' Connor tried to hide his disappointment. He'd been expecting somewhere a little more glamorous. 'Why there?'

'You'll find out soon enough,' she replied. 'Until then, I'd advise getting some rest while you can. The weeks ahead will be demanding.'

Leaving London, they headed west on the M4. While Jody drove, Connor asked her about the Buddyguard organization – a search on the internet had drawn a blank, apart from a news clipping mentioning Colonel Black as the team leader of a high-profile hostage rescue in Afghanistan several years before. But Jody politely evaded this line of questioning. 'All will be answered in good time,' she replied. After his fifth attempt to extract information, she flashed him a steely look and he backed off. However, Jody did reveal that she was an ex-Met police officer of some fifteen years' service. Rapidly promoted up the ranks, she'd moved to CO19, the police's specialist armed unit, before being transferred to SO14, Royalty Close Protection.

'So did you ever protect Prince William and Kate?' Connor asked.

Jody's manner became guarded again. 'That would break client confidentiality, I'm afraid.'

Finding it was like getting blood from a stone, Connor decided to take her earlier advice and tried to sleep.

Three hours later, they crossed the Severn Bridge into Wales. When they eventually came off the motorway, Jody took so many minor roads that Connor lost his bearings completely. But judging by the craggy mountains and endless fields they were in the middle of nowhere.

It was late afternoon by the time a pair of iron gates came into view. Atop the black wrought-iron design was a subtle but distinctive winged shield. Levelling with an entry port concealed in the bushes, Jody pressed an infra-red sensor on the dashboard and the gates parted. As they drove through, Connor spotted a discreet CCTV camera following their progress. The Range Rover crunched up a long gravel driveway, open fields on either side. Cresting a rise, an old granite building appeared, not visible from the road. The size of a country mansion, it was tucked into its own valley with a small lake and dense patch of woodland. Squared battlements and narrow windows gave the impression of a fortified castle.

'This used to be a private school in the 1800s,' explained Jody. 'But the facilities have been updated for our purposes.'

To Connor, the school still looked as if it belonged in the nineteenth century and he struggled to see much improvement beyond a large satellite dish on the roof.

The Range Rover drew up outside the main entrance. Connor jumped out and retrieved his bags from the boot. When he turned round, he almost dropped them. Standing in the arched doorway was the *last* person he expected to see.

HOSTAGE
CHAPTER 8

'Welcome to Camp Buddyguard!' said the Indian boy enthusiastically, helping Connor with his bags. 'My name's Amir.'

'So this is where you ran off to,' remarked Connor.

Amir offered a ready smile. 'Yeah, sorry I didn't get a chance to thank you, but I thought Jody was about to arrest me for late coursework.' He shot the instructor a mischievous wink.

'Show our new recruit to his room,' Jody ordered, apparently immune to his charm.

Amir performed an overzealous salute. 'Yes, ma'am.'

Shorter than Connor and with a lean frame, Amir bounded up the steps into the school's entrance hall. His exuberant manner reminded Connor of a meerkat's – playful yet always on the alert. He was a totally different person from the cowering victim Connor had come across in the Docklands.

'And Amir,' Jody called after them, her tone stern, 'I want that threat report on my desk by 0800 hours.'

Groaning at the deadline, Amir turned to Connor. 'Let's go before she makes it any earlier.'

He led Connor through a grand entrance hall and up a wide sweeping staircase. Old paintings in antique frames hung from the walls and the last of the sun's rays filtered through a bay window on to the polished parquet flooring.

'So you're a buddyguard?' said Connor as they climbed the stairs to the third floor.

Amir nodded. 'Trainee. I've not been on any assignments yet, so I haven't earned my wings.' He pointed to a silver lapel badge on his jumper, the familiar shield and silhouette absent of its guardian wings. 'But hopefully it won't be long. Just depends on who the next Principal is.'

'*Principal?*' asked Connor.

'The person you're assigned to protect,' explained Amir, turning right along a corridor. 'It could be a politician's son, a member of a royal family, the daughter of an oil baron . . .' He nudged Connor with a conspiratorial elbow. 'To be honest, I'm hoping for a film star. Now that would be cool. All those red carpet events!'

He pointed to an open door on their left. 'That's my room, by the way.'

Connor glimpsed an unmade bed with clothes strewn everywhere and a small desk upon which sat a gutted laptop. 'What happened to your computer?' he asked.

'Nothing. Just updating the hard drive and installing a new multi-core processor,' Amir replied, as if such a task was as easy as replacing a light bulb.

He stopped by a door marked with a number seven.

'This is your room,' he announced, inviting Connor to go in first.

The bedroom was small and basic, comprising of a desk, chair, lamp, single bed, washbasin and an old wooden wardrobe. Connor dumped his bags on the bed. 'I thought Jody said the school had been modernized.'

Amir laughed. 'It's what you *don't* see that's impressive.' He flicked open a panel on the desk to reveal an internet port. 'The whole place is wired with fibre-optic broadband. It's a closed system so no one can access it externally.' He pointed to the window. 'The glass has shock detectors in case someone tries to break in. Outside, there's covert CCTV, thermal-imaging cameras and pressure pads at every entry and exit. And beyond that there are perimeter alarms surrounding the school grounds.'

Connor looked out across the open fields, deserted apart from a flock of windswept sheep. 'Why the high-tech security? This isn't exactly a thriving metropolis.'

'There's no point protecting others if we can't protect ourselves,' replied Amir. 'That's one of the basic rules of bodyguarding. Also, only a handful of people know about Buddyguard's existence – that's one reason why we're so effective – and Colonel Black wants to keep it that way.'

Stuck in the middle of Wales, Connor wondered if the colonel wasn't being a little paranoid. 'Then we should watch out for those terrorist sheep!'

Amir responded with a dry chuckle. 'Just wait till you start training. You'll be stunned at what lengths the enemy will go to.' He glanced at Connor's backpack. 'Have you brought a laptop?'

Connor shook his head. He only had an old battered PC at home.

'Don't worry, I'll sort one out for you tomorrow.' A mobile phone pinged in Amir's back pocket. 'That means dinner's served. You must be starving after the journey.'

Making their way downstairs, they headed through to the dining hall. Fifteen or so boys and girls were gathered at one end, sitting at circular tables, chatting and eating. To their left was an open serving area, steaming with freshly cooked food. Passing Connor a tray, Amir grabbed a large plate and helped himself. Connor's mouth watered at the impressive spread of pasta, chicken, curry, rice and even steak.

'This is *nothing* like school dinners,' he remarked, shovelling a mound of chips to go with his rib-eye and mushrooms.

'The colonel believes an army marches on its stomach,' Amir replied, taking a pineapple juice from the chiller. 'And, trust me, you'll need the energy!'

With plates piled high, Amir led Connor over to a table nearest the window, where four other recruits sat.

'You remember Jason?' said Amir, arching an eyebrow at Connor.

A broad-chested lad turned round. With dark tousled hair and an anvil jaw, Connor couldn't forget his face . . . or his fists.

'G'day!' said Jason, an Aussie twang now noticeable in his speech. He offered one of his hammer-like fists in greeting. Connor took it and was subjected to a bone-crushing handshake.

I'm off to a great start here! thought Connor, trying not to wince. 'You're Australian then?'

'He sure is! But don't hold that against him,' teased the Chinese girl perched next to Jason and half his size. She'd lost her emo make-up and was now dressed in jeans, pumps and a red sleeveless T-shirt. 'I'm Ling. How's the leg?' she asked with an impish twinkle in her half-moon eyes.

'Fine,' said Connor, releasing himself from Jason's iron grip. 'How's the arm?'

Ling smirked. 'Not as bad as you'd have ended up, if Jody hadn't saved you.'

'Saved *me*?' Connor responded, remembering the situation differently, but Amir cut in.

'I wouldn't argue with Ling. She *always* wins her fights.' He sat down beside the boy with bleached blond hair. 'This is Marc; he's from France.'

Marc had replaced the gang fashion with a more stylish Ralph Lauren shirt and white jeans. Dark shadows circled his eyes, the after-effect of his bruising encounter with the skateboard.

'*Bonsoir*,' he greeted, then with only the trace of a French accent asked, 'How was the journey?'

'Long!' remarked Connor. As he took his place next to Amir, his eyes were drawn to the girl sitting opposite him. Perhaps a year older than the others, with tanned skin, sun-kissed blonde hair and a radiant smile, she looked like she'd just stepped off a Caribbean beach. She wore a black halterneck top with a winged-shield badge in *gold*.

'I hear you beat Jason,' she said in a soft American accent like honey. 'That's a first.'

'I held back,' Jason growled in protest. 'Didn't want to hurt the newbie.'

The girl gave a noncommittal nod. 'Of course you did!' she smirked.

In an effort to smooth over his rocky start with Jason, Connor interjected, 'Well, to be fair ... he did telegraph that first punch.'

'Exactly,' agreed Jason, a little too quickly.

The girl glanced at Connor, her sky-blue eyes appraising him. Seeing straight through his white lie, the corner of her mouth curled up into a knowing smile. 'I'm Charlotte. But everyone calls me Charley.'

Connor smiled back, hoping the flush in his cheeks wasn't noticeable. He was usually fine around girls. But, for some reason, this one made him feel a touch self-conscious. Opting for a safe opening question, he asked, 'Where in the States are you from?'

'California,' she replied. 'Buddyguard gathers recruits from around the world.' She pointed to the other tables. 'For example, José is from Mexico, Elsa from Germany, David from Uganda, Luciana from Brazil.'

Connor glanced around the hall, the tables only half-full. 'Are these *all* the buddyguards?'

Charley shook her head. 'Most are on assignment. But no more than twenty of us are usually here at any one time.'

'So where's the skater boy who attacked me?'

'Richie's in Ireland,' Amir replied, through a mouthful of rice.

'*Bonne chose aussi*,' mumbled Marc, massaging the bridge of his nose.

'Sorry, what was that?' said Connor, wishing he'd paid more attention in his French lessons.

'Good thing too,' Marc repeated. 'I might have forgiven him by the time he gets back.'

'So that means, Connor, you'll be joining us in Alpha team,' Charley announced. 'By the way, the colonel wants us all in the briefing room at 0800 hours. After fitness training.'

Marc let out a heavy sigh. 'I hate six a.m. cross-country runs.'

Connor raised his eyebrows at this remark. He didn't mind running, but he agreed with Marc – not *before* breakfast.

'And I've still a threat report to complete!' Amir complained, stabbing his chicken with a fork.

'Best get on with it then,' suggested Charley, offering little sympathy.

'I warn you, Connor,' said Marc, picking up his tray to go, 'Buddyguard is *no* holiday camp.'

The others stood to leave too. Apart from Charley. She rolled back her wheelchair before heading for the door.

Taken by surprise, Connor couldn't help but stare.

Amir noticed his eyes following Charley's exit and whispered, 'She was injured on an assignment.'

'How?'

'I don't know the details. And Charley prefers not to talk about it.'

That evening Connor didn't feel like unpacking. He lay on his bed, listening to the wind whistling outside. His thoughts turned to Charley and the shock of seeing her confined to a wheelchair. The reality of what he'd agreed to hit home. Being a bodyguard was no game. The risks were real. *Dangerously real.*

HOSTAGE
CHAPTER 9

'Do you understand what I've tasked you with?' questioned Malik, sitting cross-legged beneath the shade of an olive tree in his courtyard garden on the outskirts of Sana'a. Laid out on a cloth before the leader was a large bowl of *saltah* stew, a plate of *aseed* dried fish with cheese, boiled rice, *malooga* flatbread and a pot of black tea.

Hazim nodded. 'I'm honoured to be entrusted so.'

Malik smiled the thin grin of a snake. 'You've been chosen, Hazim, because of your rather unique position. No one among the Brotherhood can get as close to the President's daughter as you. But nothing can be left to chance. Our planning must be meticulous and our methods discreet.'

'I understand.'

'You must tell no one of your true purpose. Especially your family.'

'I won't,' assured Hazim, 'although *you're* family, Uncle.'

Malik barked a desert-dry laugh. 'And that's why I trust you, Hazim. You're like a son to me.'

Hazim beamed with pride. 'You've always shown me

favour, Uncle. It was you who encouraged my studies at the mosque in the first place. And that's why I won't let you down.'

'I trust not,' said Malik, all traces of humour vanishing from his face. 'The role you play will be vital. And you'll be provided with all the surveillance resources and back-up you need. Bahir is to be responsible for communications and technology, and Kedar for managing our defensive requirements. Now, do you have any questions?'

Malik paused to take a sip of black tea from a small china cup, giving Hazim the opportunity to speak.

'You say money's no object,' began Hazim, 'yet how can the Brotherhood fund an operation like this?'

'You need not concern yourself with that,' said Malik, his tone hardening. 'It doesn't matter what it costs when the prize is so great.'

Selecting a piece of flatbread from the plate, Malik scooped up a helping of *saltah* and shovelled the meat stew into his mouth. He chewed slowly as he studied Hazim. 'All that's important is you're willing to do what's necessary for the purpose of achieving our goal.'

His coal-black eyes bored into Hazim's as he searched for the slightest evidence of doubt, any flicker of cowardice.

Hazim held Malik's stare. 'I'm well aware of the dangers, Uncle. And I'm resolved to my calling.'

Malik grinned in satisfaction, licking the stew from his yellow-stained teeth. 'Excellent.'

HOSTAGE
CHAPTER 10

'Bodyguards are the modern-day samurai warriors,' declared Colonel Black, clicking up an image of a Japanese swordsman on the overhead projector. 'Like these ancient warriors, the bodyguard's duty is to protect their Principal above all else.'

Connor sat with Alpha team in the briefing room, a windowless chamber at the heart of the school building. Kitted out with HD flatscreen projectors, state-of-the-art computers and ergonomic high-backed lecture chairs, it was unlike any classroom Connor had ever been in.

'These warriors followed the code of *bushido* – a set of virtues that shaped the samurai's training and attitude to life. Today, a professional bodyguard adheres to the same principles of Loyalty, Honour and Courage.'

'You're making us sound like heroes!' jested Marc.

'You are,' replied the colonel, his gaze briefly falling on Charley sitting in her chair at the front. 'But you'll be unsung heroes. Connor, you must forget the Hollywood image of the muscle-bound bouncer in a suit barging a path for some starlet through a screaming crowd. Or a secret service 007-type in dark shades, talking into his sleeve, hand inside his jacket ready to draw a gun at the slightest threat. The best bodyguards are the ones that *nobody* notices.'

The next image on the screen showed a restaurant scene. A family of four sat at a table surrounded by other diners.

'So where are the bodyguards in this picture, Connor?'

Connor searched the image for clues. 'The obvious one is the big man in the suit standing by the window, but you just said it *can't* be him.'

'Correct. He's the restaurant's doorman. The actual protection team is here.' The colonel shone a laser pointer at a couple having a seemingly romantic meal. 'And also here.' The red beam now shone on the young girl at the family table. 'She's one of our buddyguards. And that's why *you've* all been chosen. To blend into the background. To become the unassuming friend. By not drawing attention to your Principal, you reduce the risk of making them a target.'

'So why do celebrities always use the Hollywood type?' asked Connor.

'As a deterrent,' replied the colonel, picking up a coffee mug and taking a sip. 'If the Principal is a film star, for example, high-profile protection will keep any fanatical followers at bay. And, in these cases, generally the bigger and uglier the bodyguard appears, the easier it is for them to do their job.'

'Makes Jason perfect for the role!' remarked Ling out of the corner of her mouth.

Jason flicked his pen lid at her. 'Careful I don't step on you, mini-mouse!'

She caught the lid in mid-air without looking. 'You'll have to be quicker than that to get me.'

'Ling!' barked the colonel, bringing a swift end to the frivolity. 'I realize Alpha team knows much of this already, but this session is designed to bring Connor up to speed and the revision is beneficial for you too. So tell me, what's the key to effective security as a bodyguard?'

'Constant awareness,' Ling replied, her expression turning studious.

The colonel slammed his palm on the lectern. Amir almost leapt from his chair in fright at the sudden noise.

'What did Ling just say, Amir?'

'Erm ... constant ... awareness,' he replied, stifling a yawn. The combination of working late and rising early had clearly taken its toll.

'And you'd do well to remember that,' warned the colonel. 'If you're aware, you're less likely to be taken by surprise. And that could mean the difference between life and death for both you and your Principal.'

'Yes, sir,' said Amir, sitting up straight.

'Now explain the relevance of the Cooper Colour Code.'

Amir swivelled in his chair to face Connor. 'According to Marine Lieutenant Colonel Jeff Cooper, the most important means of surviving a lethal confrontation isn't a weapon or martial arts skills but the correct combat mindset. He identified four levels of awareness – White, Yellow, Orange and Red. Code White means being totally switched off. This is where ninety-five per cent of people spend ninety-five per cent of their time – living in their own bubble. Like when you're on a mobile phone and you cross the road without looking.'

Connor nodded, having been guilty of this himself many a time and once almost getting run over.

'Code White is no place for a bodyguard to be,' emphasized the colonel. 'If you're suddenly attacked, you'll get a massive surge of adrenalin that your body won't be able to cope with. It'll trigger a state of *fight, flight or freeze*. This sensory overload will hinder you from protecting your Principal, who's probably in the same state of shock. You need to be thinking straight, making lightning-fast decisions and taking the appropriate actions to get your Principal out of danger.'

The colonel's steely grey eyes fixed on Marc. 'So, what state of mind should a bodyguard always be in?'

'Code Yellow – relaxed alertness,' replied Marc. 'There's no specific threat, but you're aware that the world's a dangerous place and you're prepared to defend yourself and your Principal, if necessary. You use all your senses to scan the surroundings in a relaxed yet alert manner.'

'What's the problem with Code Yellow, Jason?'

Jason looked up from his laptop. Tapping his pen on the lecture chair's writing tablet, he thought for a moment. 'Erm ... while it's simple enough to "switch-on" and become alert, the difficulty is in maintaining that state. You can easily drift back into Code White without even realizing it.'

The colonel raised his eyebrows pointedly at Amir to ensure he got the message. 'But with practice you can "live" in Code Yellow on an indefinite basis. Now, Charley, explain to Connor the last two states of awareness.'

'Code Orange is a specific alert. Having noticed a potential threat, you evaluate your choices. Run, fight or wait and see, depending on how the situation develops,' she explained fluidly. 'Code Red is the trigger. The threat has escalated into a hazardous situation. Having made your decisions in Code Orange, you're now acting on them.'

'Exactly,' said Colonel Black, pleased with her response. 'You haven't jumped from Code White to Code Red in a single leap, resulting in potential "brain-fade". Since your mindset is already in a heightened state of awareness, your body can handle the rush of adrenalin. This means you can run faster, hit harder, think quicker and jump higher than you could seconds before.'

The colonel directed his gaze towards Connor. 'In short, the Colour Code helps a bodyguard to stay in control and think clearly in a life-threatening situation.'

HOSTAGE

CHAPTER 11

Connor was now glad of that early-morning run. His brain was just about 'alert' enough to take this information in. As Connor made notes on the laptop Amir had provided, the colonel forwarded the presentation to a silhouette of a young boy surrounded by four concentric circles. Each ring was marked with a different acronym from the outside in: RST, SAP, PES and BG.

'In the majority of assignments, you'll work as part of a larger adult close-protection team,' explained Colonel Black. His laser pointer flicked to the outermost circle, RST. 'The Residential Security Team, as the name implies, manages the physical security of anywhere your Principal's family might stay – for example, a house, a hotel or a yacht. They'll perform searches, monitor CCTV and check every visitor in and out. In theory, this *should* be the safest place for you and your Principal. On the other hand, being a fixed and known location, a residence is the most obvious target for an attack.'

The red beam moved into the SAP circle.

'The Security Advance Party provides the next layer of

protection. They travel ahead of the family, checking that routes and venues are safe. This may happen months in advance, say for a holiday – or minutes, in the case of an impromptu visit to a restaurant. Many potential attacks have been foiled by an observant SAP team. So good communication with them is essential – you don't want any surprises when you're out and about.'

The PES circle was now highlighted. 'The Personal Escort Section provides a crucial layer of defence when the family is on the move. Depending upon the situation, their function may be to provide additional protection or to eliminate a threat and give you time to escape with your Principal.'

The colonel's laser pointer spiralled in through the circles once more to reinforce their importance.

'Each of these groups forms a cordon of defence round the Principal and their family.' His beam stopped at the smallest innermost circle labelled 'BG'. 'But as a buddyguard you'll be the *final* ring of defence. It's your ultimate responsibility to shield your Principal from danger.'

The colonel directed everyone's gaze to the large silver shield and wings hanging over the door of the briefing room. 'Hence our logo.'

He highlighted three words etched into the burnished metal: *Praedice. Prohibe. Defende.*

'Charley, enlighten Connor with our motto.'

'*Predict. Prevent. Protect*,' she recited. 'Predict the threat. Prevent the attack. Protect the Principal.'

'This isn't a mere saying, Connor,' reaffirmed Colonel Black. 'This is our method of operation. By identifying a source of danger early, we can minimize the risk of it happening. If we put in place counter-measures, then the Principal will be better protected. Hopefully, we'll avoid the threat entirely. For example, if your Principal is a famous young TV star, what threat could she face?'

'A crazed fan?' suggested Connor.

'Very likely. Now, say this crazed fan poses a risk of stabbing to your Principal. How can we prevent this?'

'Body armour,' volunteered Amir.

'Effective, but for your Principal to wear this all the time is unrealistic and impractical.'

'Put a surveillance team on the suspected fan,' Ling suggested. 'That way you can track their movements and keep the Principal at a safe distance.'

'Good. But what if the surveillance team loses the fan?'

'Then the buddyguard keeps an eye out and provides protection to the Principal,' said Jason.

'Exactly. And that's why you need to remain constantly aware – in a Code Yellow mindset. You have to be continually assessing people who come close enough to harm you or your Principal. Is the person in the crowd reaching for a knife or a gun? Or an innocent mobile phone? Have you seen them before? Do they appear unusually nervous? These are the sorts of questions you need to ask yourself.'

The colonel paused to take another sip of his coffee.

'Here's a different scenario: your Principal is on a skiing holiday, there's a demonstration outside her hotel. What action would you take to ensure her safety?'

Connor thought for a moment. 'Stay inside until the demonstration moves on.'

'That's one option,' conceded the colonel, 'but your Principal has to meet friends in the next thirty minutes.'

Unsure what to suggest, Connor looked to the others for help.

'You could use the PES team to form a protective cordon,' said Amir.

'Not ideal,' replied the colonel. 'Any contact with the demonstration *greatly* increases the risk to your Principal.'

Jason put his hand up. 'I'd leave by a rear exit.'

'Good,' Colonel Black agreed. 'But your Principal's still ended up in hospital.'

'Why?'

'She slipped on the icy step of that rarely used exit.'

Jason threw up his hands. 'How could I predict *that*?'

'You should be on the lookout for *all* dangers,' replied the colonel. 'This is what I like to call "salting the step". When it comes to analysing the threats against your Principal, leave no stone unturned.'

Colonel Black gestured towards Charley.

'As Alpha team's operations leader – and the most experienced buddyguard among you – Charley will help you predict and prevent any threats against your Principal,' he explained. 'But it will be down to you *alone* to protect them. And over the coming weeks you'll learn the necessary skills to do just that – unarmed combat, anti-surveillance, body-cover drills and anti-ambush exercises, to name but a few.' He directed his attention at Connor. 'Alpha team have already completed the introductory lessons, so you've a lot of catching up to do. But your martial arts experience should help.'

Draining his coffee mug, the colonel switched off the projector and gathered his papers together.

'I'll see everyone after break for our next session.'

Alpha team rose in respect as the colonel departed the briefing room.

Connor shut down his laptop with relief. '*Phew* ... there's a lot to take in,' he remarked.

'You've barely scratched the surface,' replied Marc. 'Your brain will be fried by the end of the month.'

'That's if he's got a brain!' cracked Jason.

'Leave him alone,' said Ling. 'Just because yours still needs to evolve!'

Jason made a grab for her. Ling sidestepped him and danced down the corridor. As the others headed towards Alpha team's common room, Connor hung back. Walking over to Charley, he bent down to pick up her bag.

'I can do that,' she said, neatly flipping it on to the back of her wheelchair.

'Sorry, of course you can,' replied Connor, feeling awkward at his presumption. He followed her into the corridor.

'Something on your mind?' she asked.

Not knowing how to broach the subject directly, Connor said, 'What made you decide to become a buddyguard?'

Charley laughed. 'Colonel Black.'

Connor gave her a puzzled look.

'You've experienced his recruitment methods,' she explained. 'He's not a man who expects no for an answer.'

'But you still had a choice.'

Charley nodded. 'And I jumped at the chance.'

'But why?'

Charley sighed. 'A friend of mine was kidnapped. She was never seen again. I've always thought that if I'd known how to protect her, I could have saved her.'

'But what do your parents think about you doing this?'

'They died in a plane crash three years ago.'

Connor felt his heart go out to her. 'I'm sorry to hear that.'

'It's all right,' she replied, her voice flat and unemotional. 'I've kinda come to terms with it now.'

But Connor recognized the brave face she put on as the same one he used when someone asked about his dad. She couldn't conceal the deeper grain of sadness in her eyes.

They passed through the entrance hall in silence. As they neared the bay window, a shaft of sunlight glinted off the badge on Charley's top. In an attempt to change the topic, Connor asked, 'Tell me, why's your shield gold?'

Charley glanced down at the badge. 'These are awarded for outstanding bravery in the line of duty.'

Intrigued, Connor asked, 'What did you do?'

Charley rolled to a stop by the window and looked out at the mountains in the distance.

'As buddyguards, we hope for the best, but plan for the worst,' she said softly. 'Sometimes, the worst happens.'

She chewed her lower lip pensively and went silent on him.

Wishing he'd kept his mouth shut, Connor decided not to push the subject any further. Charley seemed to appreciate this. She forced a smile and her face brightened. 'But don't worry, Connor. As ops leader, I'll make certain that never happens to you.'

HOSTAGE
CHAPTER 12

Descending the darkened staircase to the basement level, Hazim walked along a short corridor, lit only by a bare bulb, and looked inside an empty windowless white-walled cell. In the room opposite, Bahir glanced up from a circuit board that he was soldering.

'Malik's asked me to check on progress of the holding cell,' explained Hazim. 'He wants to know if it'll be one hundred per cent secure?'

'When I'm finished,' Bahir stated, the glowing tip of the soldering iron reflecting in his metal-rimmed glasses, 'a spider won't be able to get in or out!'

He pointed to the narrow door Hazim had just peered through. 'That's the only access and it has a reinforced lock.'

'What about electronic communications?'

Bahir indicated a mobile phone on his desk. 'See for yourself, no signal whatsoever.'

Hazim glanced at the display – the aerial icon flashed *searching*.

'I've installed a wide range of electronic jammers,' Bahir

quietly boasted, indicating his spaghetti junction of wires and boxes on the table. 'All operating on different bandwidths. Each jammer has a back-up in case of failure. The system will block against every cellular network – even the newer phones which hop between different frequencies.'

Hazim nodded, as if understanding the complex array of technical equipment before him. 'What about bugs and transmitters?'

Bahir snorted in disdain. 'Useless. *All* radio signals are disrupted.' He gave an oily smile. 'I've employed subtle jamming too. No distortion or erratic tones – that would be too easy to detect. Instead any listener will just hear silence, although everything will seem superficially normal with their equipment.'

'That's pretty impressive,' said Hazim.

'Of course it is,' said Bahir, returning to his work with a grin.

Hazim coughed politely for Bahir's attention. 'Malik's also concerned about thermal-imaging scanners. What should I tell him?'

Without looking up, Bahir pointed to the ceiling and walls. 'A combination of aluminium layers and Plexiglas in the construction will foil any attempts to scan this room for body heat – even if there was a full-blown fire, they couldn't detect it.'

'Right,' said Hazim. 'And what about *our* communications?'

Putting down the soldering iron, Bahir took off his glasses and rubbed the bridge of his nose, clearly irritated at being interrupted yet again. 'The reach of the jammers is about nine metres, so we'll still be able to operate outside this zone. For internet access, I've piggy-backed the neighbouring property's telephone line and installed a re-router.'

'Isn't that risky?' gasped Hazim. 'Won't it reveal our location?'

Bahir gave him a hard stare as if insulted by the mere suggestion. 'Not at all. The connection is bounced between a dozen random servers worldwide, plus it's protected by a few tricks of my own. There'll be no way they can trace the signal back here.'

'And you're *absolutely* certain this room is soundproof?' Hazim asked.

'On my life. Now let me get on with my work,' replied Bahir, replacing his glasses and picking up the soldering iron. 'For all intents and purposes, this room is invisible to the eyes and ears of the US government. In essence, it does *not* exist.'

HOSTAGE
CHAPTER 13

Marc had been right. After a couple of weeks, Connor's brain was turning to mush. He had never envisaged the need to know so much to become a bodyguard. There had been lectures on the law – Common, Civil and Criminal. How to produce a threat assessment. The basics of operational planning. Conflict management. Etiquette at formal functions. And even how to get safely in and out of a car: the technique being to sit backside first, instead of stepping in with one foot. Then if the car sped away in an emergency you simply lifted your legs – rather than being dumped unceremoniously on the pavement as the vehicle shot off without you.

And this was just the start. He still had ten weeks of *basic* training ahead. On top of that, they were expected to attend normal lessons too! Maths, history, English and all the other subjects Connor had hoped to escape by joining Buddyguard. But Colonel Black took all aspects of his recruits' training seriously. 'In all but the most extreme circumstances, a professional bodyguard uses brain over brawn,' he explained. 'And that means being educated and informed.'

After another marathon day of non-stop lessons and fitness training, Connor collapsed on the sofa in Alpha team's common room. 'When will we get some time off?' he asked.

Ling, helping herself to a Diet Coke from the fridge, merely laughed. 'You mean, for good behaviour? We might have a trip to Cardiff every so often. But don't get your hopes up. This course is full on.'

She pointed to the next week's timetable pinned on the noticeboard.

'Read it and weep!'

Dragging himself from the sofa, Connor passed Amir, who was busily tapping away on his keyboard. 'Don't you ever stop working?'

'This isn't work, it's programming,' explained Amir, his eyes fixated on the screen. 'I'm creating a bodyguard app.'

'What will it do?' asked Connor, trying to get a look.

Amir tapped the side of his nose with a finger to indicate a secret. 'I'll tell you when it works.'

'Sounds intriguing.'

'Don't get too excited,' smirked Ling. 'Amir's last app fried his phone!'

Amir shot her evils. 'The phone just couldn't handle the sheer awesomeness of my programming, that's all.'

'Whatever,' said Ling, sipping her can of Coke and strolling out.

Connor scanned the timetable. He groaned when he saw double maths was the opener for Monday morning. His eyes skipped over the standard subjects to the bodyguard lessons – which, if the truth be known, fascinated him. Even if they were demanding and pushing him to his limit, he realized this was the sort of training his father must have done.

Foot drills. World affairs. Hostage survival. Route planning. Embus Debus. Vehicle searches. Unarmed combat –

A relieved smile broke across Connor's face. At least he'd be one step ahead of the others in that class.

HOSTAGE
CHAPTER 14

Connor entered the sports hall with Charley and the rest of Alpha team. A group of kids hung around the basketball court. When they spotted Charley, they strolled over.

'Aren't you that surfer girl?' asked a young lad with wavy brown hair. 'Charley Hunter?'

Charley nodded.

'Wow!' he said, eyes widening in star-struck glee. He turned to his friends. 'I told you so. This girl was the Quiksilver Junior Surfing Champion. She conquered the Banzai Pipeline in Hawaii.'

The kids began to crowd round her wheelchair. One of the girls produced a pen and asked for an autograph. Worried that Charley was going to be mobbed, Connor stepped forward.

'Hey, watch it!' snarled a boy dressed in combats and a death-metal T-shirt, his way blocked by Connor.

'Sorry, mate, but you need to give her some space.'

'I just wanted to get her autograph,' mumbled the boy, moodily stuffing his hands in his pockets.

Suddenly Connor caught sight of a blade. 'KNIFE!' he shouted, as the boy thrust for Charley.

Relying on his jujitsu training, Connor grabbed the boy's wrist. He was almost too late, the tip of the blade sweeping a hair's breadth from Charley's throat. The other kids scattered in panic as the two of them fought for control over the lethal weapon. Connor twisted the boy's arm using *kote-gaeshi* technique to drive him to the floor. The boy still refused to let go of the knife. Jason dived on top, pinning the attacker to the ground, while Ling and Amir rushed Charley towards the exit.

A man clapped for them to stop.

'Excellent reactions,' commended their unarmed combat instructor, Steve. Ex-British Special Forces, he was a six-foot-two man-mountain with skin dark as ebony and the muscles of a gladiator. He'd also been the other phoney police officer involved in Connor's recruitment. 'That training exercise demonstrates how difficult it is to foresee an attack. But you handled it well. The Principal was saved.'

He glanced at the red ink line marking Connor's left forearm where the rubber knife had caught him.

'You, on the other hand, are seriously injured.'

Connor grimaced, disappointed with himself for not managing to cleanly disarm the attacker from Delta team.

'Knife attacks are possibly the most dangerous of all close-quarter combat situations. That's why the best way to tackle a threat is not to tackle it at all,' Steve explained as he collected the training weapon. 'Avoidance and escape should always be your first priority as a bodyguard. This is *not* cowardice. Remember, it's far better to make a good run than a bad stand.'

He beckoned for Alpha and Delta teams to gather round.

'However, there will be times when escape is impossible and you must take the threat head on to defend yourself and your Principal. If you're forced to fight, end it fast. It should be over within five to ten seconds. A punch to the face. A knife-hand strike to the throat. A kick to the groin. Whatever it takes.'

Steve slammed a meaty fist into the palm of his hand for emphasis. The class all nodded obediently. They'd spent the first hour of the lesson doing pad work. Drilling jabs, crosses, front-kicks and roundhouses over and over in order to commit them to muscle memory – so that the techniques became instinctive rather than reactive. For Connor, this was already the case. So, while many of the other recruits struggled to master the moves, he relished getting his teeth back into his martial arts training.

'But remember the whole purpose of any defensive action is to escape with your Principal,' continued their instructor. 'You're hitting to buy time. Even in the middle of a conflict you should be looking for the way out.'

He pointed to the green emergency exit sign by way of example.

'But you can't go around punching and kicking every potential threat. First, the person could be innocent with no intention of harming your Principal. Second, you'll end up in court for assault. That's why it's useful to have several non-lethal techniques in your armoury. Ling and Connor, as you're both black belts, I need you to demonstrate.'

They stepped forward. Steve instructed Ling to hold out her arm straight. Then he positioned her middle finger on the bone of Connor's sternum just above his solar plexus.

'Connor, walk towards Ling.'

Since Ling was small and willowy, Connor saw no problem in getting past her. But as soon as he stepped forward there was a sharp pain in his chest.

'Come on!' chided Steve. 'You're a strong lad. It shouldn't be too difficult.'

Connor pushed harder, but the pain only increased. And Ling wasn't even straining as she held him back.

His combat instructor seemed to enjoy the astonished look on his face.

'That's how you keep someone at bay with *just* a finger.'

HOSTAGE
CHAPTER 15

'The single-finger technique's effective only if the person is a mere annoyance to your Principal,' explained Steve. 'But if they're determined and becoming a serious threat you may need to be more *insistent* and use a different PAL technique.'

'PAL?' queried Connor, having never heard of such a martial art style.

'Pain Assisted Learning,' replied his instructor with a wicked grin.

Asking Ling to step aside, he stood in front of Connor. Holding out a muscular arm, he gently fended Connor off with his fingertips.

'Have you heard of Bruce Lee's "one-inch punch"?'

Connor nodded.

'Well, this is the one-inch push.'

With barely more than a flick of his wrist, Steve palmed Connor in the chest. Taken completely by surprise, Connor staggered backwards then collapsed to the floor, gasping for breath. A concussive wave of pain spread through his lungs and his chest felt as if it had imploded.

'Effective, isn't it?' commented Steve, helping him back to his feet.

Rubbing his chest, Connor managed a small grunt of acknowledgement. These skills were on a totally different level from his kickboxing and jujitsu training.

While Connor recovered, Steve explained the workings of the technique. 'Like a coiled-up spring, you drive your body weight through your arm and into the person's chest. This move can be as powerful as a punch, but you appear to be doing hardly anything. So, if your victim complains, what are they going to say?' Steve put on a whiney petulant voice. '*He pushed me, Officer!*'

The class laughed at this. Then, putting on chest pads, they began practising the two techniques on one another. Connor was partnered with Jason.

'That looked like it really *hurt*,' said Jason with the trace of a smile.

'Felt like he cracked a rib,' Connor replied, still rubbing his chest.

'Well, I'd better let you go first then. Give you time to recover.'

Connor got the distinct impression Jason was implying he was weak, rather than making the offer out of any friendly concern. *Just you wait*, Connor thought, holding out his arm to fend off his partner.

Jason strode forward, utterly confident of overpowering Connor. Then he grimaced in pain and frustration as he failed to push past Connor's finger.

'So it really *does* work!' he exclaimed.

'Oh yes, but not as much as this,' replied Connor, copying his instructor's movements for the second attack. Letting his arm flex like a spitting cobra, he one-inch-pushed Jason in the chest.

Even with the protective pad, Jason grunted in shock and doubled over.

'I see . . . what you mean,' he groaned.

'Sorry,' said Connor, surprising even himself with the force of the strike.

'Don't worry . . . mate,' said Jason, standing upright. 'Now it's *my* turn!'

Jason didn't bother with the single-finger technique. He went straight to the one-inch push. Connor flew backwards, barrelling into two students from Delta team.

'I *like* this attack,' said Jason, cracking his knuckles. 'Move over, Bruce Lee!'

Apologizing to the two recruits, Connor returned to face his partner. Although his chest throbbed madly, he tried not to show any pain.

'Not bad,' he wheezed – then one-inch-pushed Jason.

Jason fell flat on the floor. Gasping for breath, his face contorted in fury, he leapt to his feet and immediately took his turn, striking even harder this time. They continued to exchange pushes, their chests becoming more bruised and battered with every attempt to outdo one another. Then, without warning, their training suddenly escalated into a full-blown fight and Connor found himself tussling with Jason on the gym floor.

Two meaty hands seized them by the scruffs of their

necks and pulled them apart. Their instructor lifted them off the ground until they were at his eye level.

'Anger is only one letter away from danger,' Steve warned them sternly. 'Control your anger, otherwise anger will control you and you'll lose focus. As a buddyguard, you want to fight smarter not harder. Do you two understand?'

Chastened, Connor and Jason nodded their heads in response.

'Good. Now shake up and make up,' he ordered.

Still dangling off the floor, Connor offered his hand to Jason. He had no idea who'd started the fight, but he knew the last thing he needed was an enemy in the team. 'Sorry. Looks like we got a bit carried away.'

After a moment's hesitation the other boy shook it. 'No worries. At least we've battle-tested the technique!' he grinned.

With the apologies made, their instructor seemed satisfied and dropped them both to the ground.

'Well, now you've *mastered* the one-inch push,' he mocked. 'We'll finish with one last technique – the head twist.'

This time Steve selected a tall lad from Delta team for his demonstration.

'Again, there is very little to this defensive attack. That's what makes it effective. Lift the chin, twist the head and simply push down.'

Steve grabbed the boy's jaw and, in an effortless push and twist, he collapsed the boy like a concertina.

'Basically, where the head goes, the body follows,' he explained.

Connor was impressed – the move utilized the same principles as jujitsu in exploiting the weaknesses of the human body. With it, he should be able to take anyone down in a few seconds.

'That's fine if you're similar heights. But how's Charley going to manage that one?' questioned Amir, indicating her disadvantage.

Before Steve could answer, Charley rolled her chair over Amir's toes. He squealed in pain. She punched him in the stomach and he doubled over. Then she grabbed his head and twisted him to the ground.

'Very easily,' replied Charley, as Amir lay bowed and defeated at her feet.

HOSTAGE
CHAPTER 16

Connor looked into the sports shop window on the second floor of Cardiff's Queens Arcade. He barely noticed the display of Nike trainers on sale. Instead, his eyes were focused on the reflection in the glass. A steady stream of people was passing behind him. Most, if not all, were innocent shoppers. But among that Saturday crowd *someone* was following him. He didn't know who yet, but he was determined to find out.

Walking on, Connor headed down the escalator to the ground level of the shopping centre. He crossed the polished tiled floor and stopped beside the information sign. Pretending to be lost, he examined the map, then casually glanced around. As his eyes swept the atrium, he scanned the faces of the people descending the escalator: a blonde-haired woman in a green jacket ... a harassed-looking mother clasping her toddler's hand ... two teenage girls plastered with eyeliner and lipstick ... a man on his mobile phone –

Hadn't he seen that face before?

The square jaw. The broad nose. The deep-set eyes.

Although Connor couldn't be certain, he thought he'd noticed the man earlier while browsing in the video-game store.

Connor decided not to hang around. He headed along the central concourse towards the south exit. All the while he kept his eye on reflections in the plate-glass windows. Twice he caught glimpses of the square-jawed man. But was the man actually following him or just innocently leaving by the same route?

To test his hunch, Connor stopped outside a fashion store. After a few paces, the man paused at a newsagent's and began studying the papers. Connor felt his pulse quicken. This could be pure coincidence still, but the man's behaviour seemed increasingly suspicious. He was leafing through the newspapers without really looking at them. At the same time he was mumbling to himself – *or perhaps into a concealed radio?*

Connor now needed to prove beyond a doubt that this individual was on his tail. But he didn't want to alert the man that he suspected anything. That would scare him off – and then Connor might never find out who this person was or why he was following him. He glimpsed a gold stud in the man's right ear and made a mental note of this. Then he headed for the exit.

When he reached the glass doors, he held them open to let a lady with a buggy through, and took this opportunity to subtly check behind.

The concourse was busy with shoppers. But the man was nowhere in sight.

Maybe all this bodyguard training is making me paranoid? thought Connor.

Stepping outside into the bright spring sunshine, he turned right to weave between the hordes of people milling along Queen Street. The air was filled with the shouts of street hawkers and the strumming of buskers. A local bus roared by, sending up a cloud of diesel fumes.

Connor glanced at the time on his mobile phone. He had five minutes before he was due to meet the others. Heading along the road, he couldn't shake off the feeling that he was still being watched. Though he realized that if anyone was following him now, it would be almost impossible to spot them among the crowds. What he needed was a quieter, yet public, area to draw the individual out into the open.

Up ahead, a blue sign pointed towards a car park. Perfect.

Connor checked for traffic, then crossed the road. As he reached the opposite kerb, he heard the blast of a car horn. Glancing over his shoulder, he saw the square-jawed man had narrowly missed being run over. Although Connor's gaze was directly upon him, the man deliberately avoided eye contact by staring at a blonde-haired lady in a red jacket and sunglasses standing at a bus stop. But Connor wasn't fooled. This man was after him.

Quickening his pace, Connor turned right through a pedestrian walkway to the car park. His tail would have to follow him through the narrow alley – and if he did Connor's suspicions would be confirmed.

He was halfway across the car park and still the man hadn't appeared. Just as he thought he'd lost him, Connor spied the man standing by the ticket machine at the car park's main entrance. Clearly out of breath from running, the man was pretending to look in his pockets for change. While he was distracted, Connor whipped out his mobile phone and took a picture of him. With the evidence in his pocket, Connor ducked behind a van, his intention to escape and return to the others. But a stocky man with a head as bald as a bowling ball stepped out and confronted him.

HOSTAGE

CHAPTER 17

The man was chewing slowly on a stick of gum as he blocked Connor's way.

'Did you get a good shot?' he asked.

'Yes,' replied Connor, showing his phone to his surveillance tutor. 'It was the square-jawed man with the gold stud in his right ear.'

Bugsy raised an eyebrow, mildly impressed. 'And what about the woman who was following you? Did you take a photo of her too?'

Connor's brow creased in puzzlement. 'What woman?'

'The blonde in the green jacket.'

Connor vaguely remembered someone fitting that description, but couldn't quite place where.

'What about the one in the red jacket and sunglasses?' asked Bugsy.

'You mean the woman by the bus stop?'

Bugsy nodded.

'No,' admitted Connor. 'That was the first time I'd seen her.'

'They're the *same* person,' revealed his surveillance tutor with a grin. 'Just a reversible coat and sunglasses. It's amazing how a simple disguise can be enough to fool the untrained observer. And a word of warning: women are far better chameleons than men in that regard.'

Charley and the rest of Alpha team appeared from behind the van.

'So how did Connor fare at anti-surveillance?' Bugsy asked them.

'Pretty good. For a first attempt,' said Amir, punching Connor lightly on the arm.

'He kept his techniques covert,' observed Marc. 'Nice use of windows and natural looking around.'

Connor smiled, pleased by his friends' compliments.

'Until he stared right at his tail in the main street, that is,' Jason was keen to point out. 'That was overt. The guy knew he was on to him then.'

Connor hadn't expected praise from Jason – and didn't get any. Their relationship was still pretty frosty after their unarmed combat tussle the week before.

'But loads of people looked,' argued Ling. 'That idiot almost got himself killed.'

'I think Connor was clever to use the alley as a "choke point",' noted Charley.

'Agreed,' said Bugsy. 'If any tail had followed him through, their surveillance would have been exposed. But he still failed to spot the woman.'

He pointed to a blue estate car two rows behind Connor. The blonde-haired lady was behind the wheel. She gave Connor a teasing wave. Beside her sat the square-jawed man with the gold stud.

'You must remember that experienced operatives work in teams. There won't be just one person following you or your Principal. And they'll take it in turns to avoid detection.'

Connor nodded, his lesson learnt. Bugsy had been training Alpha team in anti-surveillance techniques for the past week. He'd explained that any coordinated attack was always preceded by a period of surveillance. If that surveillance was detected early enough, the attack might be abandoned. The problem was spotting the operatives in the first place. And if the enemy was an organized terrorist group, then they would be highly trained and virtually impossible to detect.

'Criminals, terrorists and kidnappers look the same as everyone else,' reminded Bugsy. 'Men, women, young and old, any could be monitoring your Principal. Children – just like *you* – are also used as information gatherers. A skilled operative will be the "grey" person, the one who blends into a crowd – so you have to suspect everyone.'

He popped another stick of chewing gum into his mouth before offering the packet round.

'The key to identifying surveillance is to force multiple sightings and unnatural behaviour,' he explained, chewing voraciously. 'Drop a piece of paper and see whether anyone picks it up to examine it. Frequently change direction – although try to have a reason for doing this, otherwise the technique is quite obvious. Get on a bus and jump off at the next stop.'

'You could use your mobile phone to scan the area for Bluetooth devices,' suggested Amir. 'If the same username pops up in two or more locations, then you've got a ping!'

Bugsy grinned as he chewed. 'Now *that's* a new trick!' he remarked, nodding appreciatively at his student. 'In terms of unnatural behaviour, look for people peering round corners, over stands or through doors and windows. Check for "mirroring" – if you cross the road, who else crosses the road? They'll have some means of communication, so watch out for a clenched fist or mic switch. A vacant expression on a person can be a dead giveaway – they're concentrating on a radio transmission. Fidgeting, talking to themselves or the avoidance of eye contact are all possible signs. Also be vigilant for handovers. If you suspect an individual, watch them closely but covertly. They may identify another operative by hand signals, eye contact or using a mobile phone.'

Connor now realized that the square-jawed man's stare at the blonde-haired lady had been a blatant signal – and he'd missed it.

'Anti-surveillance is sometimes the only way to meet a threat and deter – or even survive – an attack,' Bugsy emphasized. 'So stay in Code Yellow and keep your eyes peeled for repeated sightings. Remember: *Once is happenstance. Twice is circumstance. Three times means enemy action.*'

HOSTAGE
CHAPTER 18

Hazim kept the sub-machine gun tucked into his shoulder as he crouched behind the rusting oil barrel. A soldier with a rifle emerged from behind a building to his left. Hazim squeezed the trigger. His weapon let loose a deafening barrage. The soldier was hit in quick succession by four body shots.

Almost immediately two more soldiers appeared. Kedar, who stood in the shelter of a nearby doorway, raked them with gunfire. Then a woman darted across from the opposite building. Hazim targeted her, but his initial burst of bullets missed. Hurriedly re-aiming, he fired again. The woman was winged twice in the hip before going down.

More enemy popped up. Hazim sprayed them in a deadly hail of gunfire, the sub-machine jarring against his shoulder like a jackhammer. His palms became sticky with sweat and a red haze seized him as the gun thundered in his grip. He spun on a girl standing in a doorway. His bullets ripped through her too. Only too late did he realize his mistake as the teddy bear clasped in her arms was shredded into tatters.

'Cease fire!' barked Kedar.

Hazim took a trembling finger off the trigger. His breathing was rapid and the air was tainted with the smell of burnt gunpowder and hot metal.

'Good shooting,' commended Kedar, slapping Hazim on the back.

'I'm sorry, I didn't mean to kill the girl,' replied Hazim. 'I lost control.'

Kedar grinned. 'It's easily done. With one of those guns in your hand, you can feel invincible. But you must remain focused.'

Kedar reset the cardboard targets on the private shooting range and turned to the other men in the group.

'The Secret Service agents will be well armed and highly trained,' he warned them. 'That's why we must be capable of holding our own in a gun battle.'

He raised his compact sub-machine gun aloft. 'But don't worry, we'll possess equal firepower and meet force with force.'

Kedar aimed at the furthest target on the range and planted a bullet straight between the figure's eyes, before obliterating the target's head entirely.

HOSTAGE
CHAPTER 19

The *crack* of a gunshot shattered the peace of the valley, sending a flock of startled birds into the sky.

'RUN!' bawled Amir into Connor's ear.

Roughly seized by the shoulder, Connor was spun round and shoved in the opposite direction to the shooter. Amir was directly behind him, holding his body close to shield Connor from the threat. Like some mad three-legged race, they sprinted across the field for the safety of a stone wall.

'Keep going,' ordered Amir, gripping him tight.

As they neared the wall, Connor spotted a burning fuse amid the grass.

'Grenade!' he cried.

Amir's eyes widened in panic and he attempted to alter their course. But their feet became tangled up by the sudden change in direction. They both tumbled to the ground, landing face first in the dirt. The grenade exploded inches from their heads. There was a blinding flash. An ear-splitting blast. Then a shower of red sparks rained down on them.

'That was close,' remarked Amir, laughing nervously as the firecracker burnt out.

Connor dislodged Amir from his back and glared at him. 'Not as close as this sheep muck!'

Amir stifled a snigger as Connor wiped off a dark brown smear of dung from his face with his sleeve.

'Gross,' said Amir, but his amusement was brought to a swift end when he heard the angry shouts of their instructor.

'A-C-E,' said Jody despairingly, as the two of them rejoined Alpha team on the school's front lawn. 'Amir, have you forgotten what that means?'

Amir shook his head. 'Assess the threat. Counter the danger. Escape the kill zone.'

'Then why didn't you assess your escape route? It's no good running with your Principal if you're heading in the wrong direction. Or worse – towards the threat itself!'

Jody was teaching Alpha team the concept of 'body cover': how to effectively shield a Principal from an attack. They'd spent all day doing 'action-on-drills': grabbing their Principal from sitting, standing, walking and running positions, and covering them against various assaults from the front, rear, left, right and even from above. Through constant practice, the aim was to make A-C-E as instinctive as ducking.

'Whenever there's an apparent danger, you must assess the situation *before* you react,' Jody reminded them. 'This might take a millisecond or ten seconds, but it's vital to your survival. The threat – whether it is a punch, a knife, a bullet or even an egg – determines your response. Then, once the assessment is made, you cover your Principal, placing yourself between them and the threat. For example –'

She grabbed Marc, stepped in front of him and shouted, 'STAY BEHIND ME!'

The demonstration took less than a second, but was effective.

'You need to control the Principal both physically and verbally,' she explained, still holding on to Marc's arm. 'The shock of the attack might have caused *fight*, *flight* or *freeze*. This could mean the Principal is either functioning with you or has brain fade. Whatever the case, you need to stay in control and ensure they don't hamper the evacuation.' Jody held up her right hand. 'Leave your strong arm free to punch and defend. And, when you do evacuate, the body cover must remain on. As you've just witnessed with Connor and Amir's spectacular bellyflop into the sheep dung, this isn't easy. Which is why you need to *practise*.'

She released Marc and asked Connor to step forward.

'Punch Marc,' she instructed.

Marc looked shocked. 'But he's a kickboxing champion!'

'And I'm your bodyguard,' replied Jody with a wink.

Obeying his instructor, Connor swung a fist at Marc's face.

'GET DOWN!' screamed Jody, leaping forward and driving her hip into Marc. He was shoved so violently sideways that he was thrown several metres. But he was no longer under any direct threat and Jody now engaged with the attack. Effortlessly blocking it, she countered with a hook punch that stopped just short of Connor's jaw.

'You see, by *suddenly* moving your Principal, the

assailant doesn't know where to look: at his original target or at you, his new threat.'

Jody lowered her fist and patted Connor on the shoulder. 'Remember to block next time,' she said with a grin.

'Isn't the technique a bit *aggressive*?' commented Connor, as Marc stood rubbing his bruised hip. 'You could hurt the Principal.'

'In a life-threatening situation, this technique needs to be aggressive,' Jody replied. 'The Shove, as I like to call it, will save your Principal from any direct attack – a punch, a knife or even a bullet.'

'We're expected to take a *bullet* for someone else!' exclaimed Amir.

Jody's expression became solemn. 'Hopefully, with your training, it won't ever come to that. And even if it did you should be wearing your issued body armour. But when you're on assignment you take on the very same danger your Principal faces. You are their shield. That's why bodyguards are sometimes known as *bullet-catchers*.'

HOSTAGE
CHAPTER 20

The waves rolled towards the shore, long white lines that peeled in perfect curls. Bobbing on the sea's surface like eager seals, local surfers waited to catch their ride and follow the surge in. Along the three-mile stretch of golden sand, a few families dotted the shoreline but otherwise the beach belonged to Alpha team. After twelve weeks of basic training, they'd finally earned some proper time off and Steve had driven them to the Gower Peninsula to relax. Now it was June, the sun was warm, the sky cloudless and the day perfect for a barbecue on the beach.

Jason prodded the sausages and slapped on a couple more burgers.

'These should be done in a minute,' he announced, swigging from a can of Coke.

Ling lay on her beach towel, soaking up the sun's rays. 'Did you keep my veggie kebabs separate?'

'Of course,' said Jason, quickly shuffling Ling's food to one side and sharing a guilty grin with Connor and Marc. Now that training was over, the rivalry between them had relaxed a little. Although their relationship was still fractious, Connor had come to realize Jason wasn't a bad lad in himself. Just neither of them wanted to be second best.

For Connor, the past twelve weeks had flown by and he now felt a completely different person. When a geography lesson was paired with survival in hostage situations, a physics class with fire training, and cross-country running with anti-ambush drills, the mix was mind-blowing. It was as if he now wore special lenses that identified every threat surrounding him on a daily basis. Connor no longer classed this as 'paranoia' – he was simply *aware* of the world, living in Code Yellow. When he walked down a busy street, passers-by seemed to be in a perpetual, and worrying, state of half-sleep. *Did they notice the security camera above the shopping centre entrance recording them? Did they have a clue where the fire exit was in an emergency? Had any of them spotted the suspicious individual hanging near the cash point?* As a direct result of his training, Connor instinctively picked up on these details. And though he was alert to more danger he paradoxically felt safer, since he was now prepared to deal with any trouble that might occur.

Connor wondered if his mum or gran would notice the difference in him when he returned to London for the summer holidays. Despite the intensity of the training, he'd managed to call home every week. His mother always sounded upbeat and eager to hear news of his progress, although he could tell by the edge in her voice that she was often in a great deal of pain. He had to gloss over the details of his bodyguard training, but she was pleased he was learning new subjects as well as continuing his martial arts. His gran seemed happy too, and particularly glad he was paying attention to his 'other' studies. Sally was proving a great help around the house and she'd taken them to local garden parks and on day trips out of London, something the two of them never could have managed before. Any doubts Connor had about joining Buddyguard were dispelled each time he heard about the care they were receiving. Whatever the commitment in becoming a bodyguard, the sacrifice was worthwhile.

Connor watched a surfer catch a wave and ride it all the way in.

'So could *you* do it?' asked Amir.

'Surf like that?' said Connor. 'No chance.'

'I mean . . .' Amir dug his foot into the sand '. . . take a bullet for someone else?'

Connor glanced at his friend. Ever since their body-cover lesson, the spectre of being a 'bullet-catcher' had hung over them. No one really talked about it, but Connor had thought long and hard over the matter. Was this a risk he was willing to take? Had his father made such a sacrifice? He'd never been told the full story. And, if his father had, did *he* have the guts to throw himself in the line of fire?

'Perhaps,' replied Connor. 'If I cared enough about the person.'

'But as a buddyguard you won't know the person at first,' said Marc.

'And worse – you might not even like them!' added Jason, flipping a burger and glancing in Connor's direction.

Ling pulled out her headphones. 'I wouldn't worry about it, Amir. Jody says such a situation rarely happens.'

'Rarely doesn't mean *never*,' replied Amir. 'And who's to say another person's life is worth more than mine?'

'I suppose it's about standing up for what is right,' said Connor. 'The strong protecting the weak.'

'That's easier said than done,' Ling pointed out. 'And Charley should know.'

Charley had rolled down the beach to the point where the last gush of the waves fingered the shore. The sea rushed around her wheels and her feet were lost in the swirling white waters.

'Is Charley all right down there?' asked Connor.

Ling glanced from beneath her shades and nodded. 'She likes to get close. Reminds her of her competition days.'

Connor thought back to their unarmed combat scenario. 'So Charley actually *was* a pro-surfer?'

Jason laughed. 'Do koalas live in trees? Charley was awesome! Youngest Quiksilver Champion ever.'

Connor looked at Charley, constrained by her wheelchair. He could only imagine the frustration she was experiencing at being unable to surf – if he couldn't practise martial arts, he'd go mad. 'I'll go tell her that food's ready.'

Grabbing a drink from the cool box, he wandered down to the shoreline.

'I thought you might like a Diet Coke?' he said, offering Charley the ice-cold can.

She accepted it and offered him a brief smile.

'There's a good swell today,' she said wistfully. 'Nothing like LA, but the breaks are clean and long.'

Connor nodded as if he knew what she was talking about. He wished he had more knowledge of surfer speak. The icy cold sea washed up his legs, soaking his shorts, and he jumped back.

Charley didn't move. 'I just love the feel of the waves. Their power. The overwhelming rush as the surf seizes you. Nothing in the world compares to riding a wave.'

Connor studied her face, bathed in the golden sun, her bright eyes keenly following a surfer. He noticed that in her hand she clasped the gold Buddyguard badge.

She's certainly brave, he thought, *but was the sacrifice worth it?*

HOSTAGE
CHAPTER 21

'Mr President, here are the files on the organization you enquired about.'

'Thank you, George,' said President Mendez, taking the folder marked CONFIDENTIAL from his White House Chief of Staff.

Leaning back in his leather chair in the Oval Office, he studied the winged shield on the first page, then read the opening summary. After a thoughtful pause, he glanced over to a broad-chested man dressed in full military attire.

'You can vouch for this Colonel Black, General?'

'One hundred per cent, Mr President,' replied General Martin Shaw, Chairman of the Joint Chiefs of Staff and the highest-ranking military officer in the United States Armed Forces. 'Colonel Black and I go back a long way. Kuwait, Iraq, Afghanistan. I'd trust him with my life.'

'What about your child's?' remarked a tall man pointedly, who sat ramrod straight on the Oval Office's cream upholstered couch. With premature grey hair and stress lines around his eyes, Dirk Moran, the Director of the Secret Service, was far less enthusiastic about the current issue on the agenda.

The general nodded. 'If you met the colonel, you would too.'

'But we're not talking about him, are we?' replied Dirk, pushing his objection further. 'We're considering a *child* protecting the President's daughter.'

'They're teenagers actually,' corrected the White House Chief of Staff. 'And this Buddyguard organization has an impressive track record.'

'So does my son on sports day, but I'm not considering *him* for the Olympics!' said Dirk, standing up as he struggled to control his frustration. 'A child bodyguard is a joke! Trained or otherwise, they're simply not in the same league as a Secret Service agent.'

'That's true. They're in an entirely *different* league,' observed the general, raising an eyebrow. 'No one would ever suspect a teenager to be a bodyguard. A buddyguard would provide an "invisible" ring of protection around the President's daughter. He or she can go where your Secret Service agents can't.'

Dirk turned to the President, whose dark brown eyes followed their discussion with interest.

'Mr President, you have at your disposal the finest and most dedicated close-protection force in the world,' he implored. 'Are you convinced this is necessary?'

The chief of staff stepped forward and interrupted with a polite cough. 'Dirk, you can't deny that there have been a few holes in the Secret Service net recently.'

Dirk's jaw tightened. 'Granted, but they have been *plugged*.'

'I have complete faith in your team, Dirk,' assured President Mendez. 'But, considering the severe threat level the Director of National Intelligence has advised us of, a buddyguard seems like a sensible extra precaution.'

'I've read Karen Wright's report. All the more reason to *tighten* security. Not to introduce a weakness. We need only double the Secret Service team,' suggested Dirk.

'You know my daughter won't stand for any increased protection,' replied the President, holding his hands up in resigned despair. 'That was the source of the problem in the first place.'

'We can function *low* profile. There's no need to resource externally –'

'Dirk, I understand your concerns. But I must consider every option when it comes to my family's safety. Let me examine the profiles first. If none prove suitable, we won't pursue the matter any further. Is that acceptable?'

Dirk reluctantly nodded his agreement and sat back down.

When it came to serious decisions, President Mendez always kept his cards close to his chest. Therefore he hadn't disclosed the similar doubts that he shared with his Secret Service Director. It seemed unbelievable that he was considering entrusting the life of his daughter into the hands of a young teenager! The buddyguard in question would have to be truly exceptional to deserve his approval.

He studied each of the profiles in turn, his forefinger

rubbing at his temple as he read. The list of potential candidates was short but impressive, their credentials and training equal to any professional close-protection officer.

Dirk watched as the President turned over each page, setting none aside. When the final profile was reached, he allowed himself a satisfied smirk. At last he could put this absurd proposal back into his filing cabinet where it belonged and get on with his job of protecting the President and his family.

'I cannot believe this,' uttered President Mendez under his breath.

'I'm glad you agree, Mr President,' said Dirk, shooting a subtle but triumphant glance at his associates. 'However, you can be assured that my department will maintain impenetrable security round your daughter.'

But President Mendez wasn't listening. He held up the last sheet and handed it to his chief of staff.

'Contact Colonel Black immediately,' he instructed. 'Tell him that we'll be requiring his organization's services.'

Dirk leapt from the sofa to look at the profile in George's grasp. As he scanned the President's choice, his expression crumbled into one of sheer disbelief. 'But this buddyguard hasn't even completed a single assignment yet!'

The President closed the file and replied with complete conviction. 'He's the one.'

HOSTAGE
CHAPTER 22

Hazim sat alone in the study of the large rented house. The residence had come partly furnished and he tapped his fingers impatiently on the mahogany desk as he watched the clock on the wall, its second hand ticking by. It was two minutes to seven.

His mobile phone rang and Hazim snatched it up from the desk. 'Hello?'

'Hazim, it's your mother,' said the voice at the other end of the line. 'Are you still coming over for dinner?'

Sighing, Hazim rubbed his eyes in exhaustion. 'Sorry, Mother, I have to work late. Perhaps tomorrow.'

He clicked on the internet auction site on his computer and began browsing the 'Sporting Goods' section.

'Again?' she protested. 'This new job of yours might pay well, but they're overworking you.'

'I have to make a good impression.'

He glanced up at the clock. It was one minute to seven. Ten seconds to go.

'But I'm worried for your health. It's no good working all hours. You need to rest too –'

'I recently had a holiday,' interrupted Hazim, his mouse hovering over the bike category. The minute hand flicked to 19:00.

'Yes, and the family are desperate to know how your trip went. Your sister and brother are missing you. Please come over. Your father will be most disappointed if you don't . . .'

As his mother ranted on, Hazim selected the category filters: *Men's, Mountain Bikes, Used, 20-inch frame, red colour*. Five postings were listed. The last of the bikes was in a terrible state, its frame dented and chipped, the front wheel bent, a pedal missing: starting price $200. No sane person would bid for such an item. Nonetheless, Hazim clicked on the link and the image of the bike popped up with a basic description. The auction was set for a day – twenty-three hours and fifty-eight minutes were remaining. But Hazim had no interest in placing a bid.

'Are you still listening to me?'

'Yes, Mother.'

'So, can you pick up your sister next week?'

'Of course,' he replied, groaning as if being put upon by the request, but at the corners of his mouth flickered the faintest of smiles.

Using a specialized download helper, Hazim extracted the image of the bike from the browser to his desktop. Then he dropped the file into an application called Scrub. The program opened up automatically and the bike appeared in a fresh window. The image immediately began to disintegrate.

'Hazim, promise to join us for dinner tomorrow,' pleaded his mother. 'It's the weekend.'

'Promise,' he replied, and put the phone down.

The decrypting program had finished its work. The mangled bike was replaced by two lines of text that had been digitally embedded within the image:

KINGFISHER LANDING 1030, STAFFORD, 3 DAYS.
BEGIN SURVEILLANCE OF EAGLE'S NEST.

HOSTAGE
CHAPTER 23

'What's going on?' asked Connor as he hurried down the corridor and caught up with Amir and Marc. He'd been in his room packing to go home for the summer holidays when his mobile had pinged with a message from Colonel Black:

Alpha team. Briefing room. ASAP.

'Maybe he wants to wish us a happy holiday,' suggested Amir.

'If only,' replied Marc. 'I reckon it's far more serious than that.'

Jason and Ling joined them and they entered the briefing room. Charley was already there, deep in discussion with the colonel. A nervous anticipation gripped Connor when he caught sight of Charley's stunned expression. Whatever the colonel had to say, the news had evidently taken her by surprise.

Hurriedly they found their seats. Colonel Black finished talking with Charley and turned to them. His face wore a rare smile.

'Alpha team's leave is postponed,' he announced, not even bothering to soften the blow.

A groan of disappointment escaped Amir's lips.

The colonel disregarded this and continued, 'Buddyguard has received a top-priority assignment. And a member of *this* team has been selected.'

'Who?' asked Ling, perching on the edge of her seat in excitement.

The colonel's steel-grey eyes fell on Connor.

'Me?' said Connor, almost breathless. As the realization sank in, he was unsure whether to be thrilled or terrified at the prospect of his first assignment.

'Yeah, why Connor? He's the newbie,' argued Jason, puffing up his chest. 'Next to Charley, I'm the most experienced. It should be me.'

'I admire your eagerness, Jason,' replied Colonel Black tactfully. 'But, as with every assignment, it's not simply about an operation being available; it's about the buddyguard fitting the operation. This assignment is by order of the President of the United States. He chose Connor personally.'

Connor was speechless. Surely he'd misunderstood. 'He chose me *specifically*. Why?'

'That information wasn't disclosed,' replied the colonel. 'It'll be up to President Mendez to reveal his reasons, if he so wishes.'

'It's probably because of your martial arts credentials,' Charley suggested.

'Well, it certainly can't be for anything else!' mumbled Jason.

Connor let the comment pass, appreciating that Jason was crestfallen at not being chosen himself.

'So who's Connor protecting?' asked Marc.

The colonel looked to Charley to respond.

'Alicia Rosa Mendez,' she revealed. 'The President's daughter.'

Marc whistled through his teeth in awe. 'Rather you than me, Connor.'

'Yeah,' agreed Ling. 'You're going in at the deep end!'

Connor thought there had to be some sort of mistake. 'They're right, Colonel. I haven't even done a test operation yet.'

The colonel looked him in the eye. 'I won't lie to you, Connor. This is the highest-profile assignment Buddyguard has ever been involved in. For us, we're taking a huge gamble. For you, it will be a baptism of fire. But I've watched your progress closely. You possess your father's ability to think on your feet. And, with any luck, his sixth sense to foresee danger too.'

Connor was taken aback by the unexpected comparison to his father. Their course had been so full-on he'd not had the opportunity to talk with the colonel about his father's past life. But clearly Colonel Black had been noting the similarities. It was a boost to his confidence, but Connor couldn't help feeling a new pressure on his shoulders of having to live up to the colonel's high expectations.

'Operation Hidden Shield will commence forthwith,' declared Colonel Black. 'Charley, I want a full profile on the Principal by 0900 hours tomorrow. Amir, prep a

Go-bag with all the appropriate tactical kit. Ling, Marc and Jason, you're responsible for compiling the operation folder. I want maps of all primary locations, threat assessments, sit reps on known hostiles, key personnel and any other relevant information that might help Connor in his task. Connor, come with me for further briefing.'

For a moment, Alpha team sat stock still in their chairs, caught like rabbits in the headlights.

'What are you waiting for?' barked the colonel. 'You have your orders.'

At his command, they rushed to their stations in the briefing room. Alpha team had run through operational planning situations in training on countless occasions. But this time there was an urgency to their actions. This time it was for real.

HOSTAGE
CHAPTER 24

Connor hardly slept all night. *What reason could one of the most powerful leaders in the world have for selecting me to protect his daughter?*

His martial arts skills couldn't be the only justification. Jason was an equal match to him – in fact, Connor had learnt that his rival had once been the Australian Junior Champion. There had to be another reason. But Connor couldn't think what it was. Aside from his twelve weeks of training, he had no real-world experience of being a buddyguard and this deeply worried him. Connor wondered if it was a case of mistaken identity and that the President actually believed he was choosing *someone else*.

But the colonel assured him that there'd been no mistake. He was to work alongside the US Secret Service, the Homeland Security department responsible for the protection of the First Family. He would be reporting direct to its head, Dirk Moran, while maintaining a line of communication with Buddyguard in the UK in case he needed additional support. His mission was to ensure the safety of the President's daughter at all times, particularly those instances when Secret Service agents couldn't be immediately at hand. The threat level for the operation was deemed to be 'Category 1 Life-Threatening'.

Connor's mind whirled with the possibilities – angry mobs, long-range snipers, knife-wielding assassins, exploding car bombs ... the danger list went on and on. And *he* was to be the hidden shield between those threats and the life of the President's daughter. The sheer scale of the task ahead was almost paralysing. He wondered if his father had ever felt like this before any of his assignments. Or did a seasoned bodyguard get used to the pressure? Perhaps it was like a constant trickle of electricity running through their veins, so they felt, yet suppressed, their fears.

And Connor's greatest fear was that he would fail. That at the moment of an attack he would react too late – or, worse still, not react at all.

HOSTAGE
CHAPTER 25

At 9:00, Connor, bleary-eyed and groggy from lack of sleep, joined Alpha team in the briefing room. They looked equally shattered from their late-night research.

'As you know, your Principal is Alicia Rosa Mendez,' said Charley, beginning her presentation as soon as Connor was seated. She clicked a remote to display the photo of a young girl on the overhead screen. 'Fourteen years old of Mexican-American descent, she is the only daughter of Emilia and Antonio Mendez, the current President of the United States.'

Connor studied the photo. Alicia had chocolate-brown eyes, a butter-wouldn't-melt-in-her-mouth smile and a mass of dark curly hair that fell past her shoulders. She looked like any other young teenager. It was hard to imagine her as a target for assassins and kidnappers. But that's exactly what she was.

'According to my research and press reports, Alicia is fun-loving, headstrong and possesses an impulsive streak. She has slipped her Secret Service protection on several occasions. And, as I understand from the colonel, that is the main reason the President has requested a buddyguard.'

Colonel Black nodded in confirmation. 'It's your job, Connor, to stick to her like glue.'

Connor briefly wondered how he'd manage that without becoming an annoying hanger-on.

'Alicia attends Montarose School in Washington DC where you're now enrolled on a student exchange programme for the last two weeks of term,' Charley explained. 'Her grades are good, if not outstanding. Favourite subjects appear to be art, photography and dance. She's generally fit –'

'Most definitely,' said Marc with a rakish grin.

'I mean healthy,' corrected Charley, shooting him evils. 'Alicia enjoys track and field, and is the captain of the school team. She holds the fastest time for the four hundred metres. So, Connor, you'll be thankful for all those early-morning runs.'

Connor and Marc exchanged sideways glances and smirked at one another. Marc had found a short cut on Alpha team's running route, knocking a good couple of miles off the training. Connor now wished he'd done the full circuit. He was going to suffer for it if he had to keep up with his Principal.

Charley clicked to a new slide titled 'Medical History'.

'Known medical issues include mild hay fever and a history of childhood epilepsy.'

'Does that mean she might have a fit?' asked Connor, concerned.

Charley gave a noncommittal shrug. 'According to the doctor's reports, her epilepsy seems to have stopped naturally in the last year or so. But it's still something to be aware of. Factors like emotional stress, sleep deprivation and flashing lights have the potential to trigger a seizure.'

'I've put some information on epilepsy in the operation folder,' Ling interrupted, handing Connor a small USB drive. 'There's an action-on sheet explaining how to handle a seizure.'

'Thanks,' replied Connor, plugging the drive into his laptop.

'The files are all encrypted,' she explained, 'and accessed by fingerprint recognition.' She indicated the thumb-sized scanner built into the body of his laptop. 'I've already programmed it to accept yours. There are also files on Washington DC, Montarose School, the White House staff you'll meet and a hot list identifying the potential threats she faces.'

'It's a *long* list,' said Jason, yawning widely. 'I should know. I was working on it right through the night.'

'Perhaps then you'll give Connor a summary of the key groups that pose a risk,' suggested Charley.

'Sure,' he replied, getting up from his seat and joining her at the front. He took a deep breath and offered Connor a pitying look. 'Well, the leader of the free world certainly has some enemies and Alicia, as his daughter, faces the same dangers. The problems in Yemen, Afghanistan and Pakistan mean that fundamentalists are a major threat. Al-Qaeda and the Taliban are just two of the extremist groups who have the United States and its President in their sights. But it's unlikely they'll target our Principal directly, since their usual methods of attack are bombings, sabotage and scare tactics. Then closer to home, but no less fanatical, are the white supremacists, who dislike having a Latino man as a President. They're a real and present danger. Next, we've got the potential for stalkers and lone-wolf assassins – these are almost impossible to identify before they strike and you'll have to rely on Secret Service intelligence. And, finally, there are the mentally ill, who according to the Secret Service, account for three-quarters of known threats made against the President and his family.'

Jason put on a cheery smile for Connor, whose expression had dropped at the seemingly endless list of threats.

'So to put it simply, mate, the world's your enemy.'

HOSTAGE
CHAPTER 26

'Here's your Go-bag,' said Amir, dumping a sleek charcoal-coloured backpack on the table. 'It contains all you need to run this operation effectively.'

He pulled out a super-slim mobile from the front pocket.

'Next-generation smartphone,' he said, admiring its sleek elegant form. 'Bugsy enhanced this specifically for your assignment. First, fingerprint identification to protect access.' He pressed his thumb to the screen, the phone came to life and Buddyguard's gleaming winged shield rotated in 3D on the retina display. 'I'm currently programmed in as well as you. But the operating system is firewalled and any critical breach of it will wipe the hard drive. But don't worry – all stored data is wirelessly backed up to our servers.'

His index finger selected an app in the top corner. A crystal-clear bird's-eye view of the Welsh mountains appeared, a small green dot pulsing inside a building that Connor recognized as Buddyguard Headquarters.

'Advanced Mapping app, accurate to the metre with pinpoint GPS,' explained Amir. 'In addition, all the Washington maps are preloaded, plus internal layouts for key buildings such as the White House – at least, those we've got access to – the National Air and Space Museum and the Kennedy Center. Whatever happens, you won't get lost. Nor will your Principal.'

He passed Connor a stylish red Armani-branded phone case with a butterfly logo.

'Thanks, but it's a bit girly for me,' said Connor, handing it back.

'The case isn't for you,' Amir replied. 'It's your gift to Alicia and contains a miniature homing beacon. The encoded signal is linked to this Tracker app.' He touched a green target icon on the smartphone's screen. The map reappeared, now overlaid with a grid and a flashing red dot beside the blue. 'It'll locate the case anywhere within fifteen kilometres and calculate the quickest route from your position. Bugsy recommends to keep this feature secret – it's for emergency use only.'

Amir held up the phone and pointed to the tiny lens on the back. 'Ten megapixel camera with optical zoom, high-definition video, night-vision and instant face-recognition software. Film or photo a crowd and it'll ping an individual that it's seen before at a different location. If it records multiple occurrences, the app will highlight the suspected face in red. But Bugsy says *don't* rely on this app. The Mark One eyeball is always your best piece of surveillance kit.'

Amir winked and Connor laughed. Bugsy often referred to his eyes as 'Mark One'.

Opening a small fabric pouch, Amir now handed Connor a tiny flesh-coloured earpiece.

'For when you want to communicate covertly,' he explained. 'It has a vibrational mic that will pick up your voice. The smartphone acts as your transceiver. Just remember the battery life of the earpiece is limited. Eight hours tops before a recharge is needed.'

His finger flicked across the smartphone's screen. 'There are a whole bunch of other apps, like Mission Status, Threat Level and SOS – that's my *own* program,' Amir said proudly.

'So it worked!' remarked Connor. 'Can you *now* tell me what it's for?'

'Real emergencies,' Amir replied, his expression serious. 'Even when you don't have a phone signal, the SOS app can send a short burst of location data to a GPS satellite which is bounced back here to headquarters. Works *anywhere* in the world. Drains the battery like crazy, mind. I'm still trying to fix that. But you can explore all these apps when you're on the plane. I've also added the latest Angry Birds game in case you get bored.'

'Not much chance of that!' replied Connor.

Amir laid the smartphone gently on the table, seeming almost reluctant to let it go. Connor knew his friend was a bit of a tech-head and was dying to keep it for himself.

'That's the showpiece,' Amir sighed, returning to the bag. 'The other items I've prepped include a basic medical kit, mini-halogen torch, prepaid credit cards and this set of clothes for high-threat situations.'

Alongside the rest of the gear, he laid a baseball cap, a pair of sunglasses, a black T-shirt, a cream-coloured fashion shirt and a styled leather jacket.

'Jody promises me that they'll fit. Why not try them on for size?'

Connor slipped on the jacket. The cut was perfect, the quality equal to top-brand Italian leather, but the weight was odd.

'Feels a little . . . heavy,' he remarked.

'That's because it's bulletproof,' explained Amir. 'Both this and the shirt can stop a handgun at close range. The jacket's stab-proof too, as is this T-shirt.'

Connor took a moment to inspect the clothes more closely. His fingers felt the thick cotton-like fabric of the collared shirt. 'Are you certain this will stop a bullet?'

Amir nodded his head with the utmost conviction. 'You can ask Jody, but I wouldn't recommend it.'

'Why not?'

'When I did, she shot me.'

'*What?*' exclaimed Connor, not sure he'd heard right.

Amir lifted his shirt to reveal a purple bruise across his chest. 'She got me to wear one. It's constructed from a hi-tech woven fabric that "catches" the bullet and spreads the impact over the whole torso rather than in one specific area. So I can guarantee you – on my life – that the shirt works.'

'I bet that hurt, though,' said Connor, grimacing in sympathy as Amir re-covered his bruised chest.

'I'd be lying if I said no. It felt like a battering ram. But at the time I was more worried about the contents of my pants! She scared me half to death. I'm *never* going to hand in homework late again.'

Amir began to repack the bag for him.

'It's all right. I've already got my own backpack,' said Connor.

'Not like this one you haven't,' he replied. 'This backpack could save your life too.' He tapped the rear panel, then flexed it. 'State-of-the-art liquid body armour. The jacket and shirt are only effective against handguns. This backpack will shield you from high-powered assault rifles and machine guns like the MP5.'

'That's reassuring to know,' said Connor, hoping he wouldn't be confronted by that sort of firepower.

'Colonel Black spares no expense on our safety equipment,' explained Amir, showing Connor how the panel folded out to double its coverage. Then he resumed packing the bag.

Connor was astonished by the gear at his disposal. State-of-the-art phones, bulletproof clothing, anti-ambush backpacks. 'I feel like James Bond,' he said, picking up the snazzy pair of sunglasses with dark mirrored lens. 'So what do these do?'

Connor was hoping for a 'heads-up' display with augmented reality like the heroes used in the movies.

'Now these are *really* clever – one hundred per cent anti-radiation, anti-glare devices,' explained Amir, slipping them on and grinning. 'They keep the sun out of your eyes!'

HOSTAGE
CHAPTER 27

The Gulfstream jet touched down on the runway and taxied to the small private air terminal. As its engines wound down, the passenger door opened and the steps automatically unfolded. An immaculately presented air stewardess checked the exit was clear before ushering the sole passenger from the plane.

'Thank you for flying with us,' she said with a well-practised smile of service, then added in farewell, '*Ma'as-salama.*'

'*Allah ysalmak,*' replied the man in his native Arabic, his amber eyes admiring the attractive stewardess one last time. Stepping on to the tarmac, he felt a wave of heat that was pleasant, but by no means comparable to the arid warmth of his own country.

An airport official greeted him. 'Sir, if you'd like to follow me.'

They walked the short distance to the terminal building. A pair of glass doors slid efficiently open and they were met by a blast of cold conditioned air. Once inside, the doors closed behind, sealing out the noise of the whirring jet engines. The lobby was virtually deserted, only a few employees milling about. A large flatscreen TV on the wall was running CNN in the background, the news coverage following the increased tension in the Arabian Peninsula over the recent oil blockade.

Crossing the thickly carpeted floor, the man was escorted over to Passport Control. A lone US Customs and Border Protection officer sat in his cubicle, his face fixed with a courteous but aloof expression.

'Passport,' he said in a detached monotone.

The traveller handed over his documentation and the officer swiped it into his computer. He inspected the monitor. 'Welcome, Mr Khalid Al . . .'

'Khalid Al-Naimi,' helped the man.

'And today you've come from . . . ?'

'Saudi Arabia,' he replied, wondering why travellers were required to fill such details out on an I-94 form if the passport officials never looked at them.

'What is the purpose of your visit? Business or pleasure?'

'Business,' he replied. 'Although, with any luck, it'll be pleasurable too.'

The officer's dour expression failed to register the good-natured reply.

'And how long do you intend staying?'

'No more than a month.'

The officer swivelled a webcam to focus on the man's face. 'Please look into the camera.'

An image of a late middle-aged Arab man with a silver-grey beard and amber eyes filled the screen. The officer took a photo, then gestured towards a black and green box fixed to the cubicle. 'Now place your fingers on the scanner.'

Putting down his briefcase, the man laid his right hand across the green plastic. Then his thumb.

The officer re-examined the details that appeared on his monitor. 'What type of business are you in, Mr Al-Naimi?'

'Oil.'

The officer nodded, the answer seeming of no interest to him despite his eyes flicking to the newscast. For a brief moment, he appeared reluctant to authorize the visitor's entry visa. But then he stamped the passport and returned the documents. With the formalities complete, he waved him through. 'Welcome to the United States. Enjoy your stay.'

The Arab smiled. 'I intend to.'

He passed the inspection station and baggage collection without further security screening. His luggage had already been transferred and his driver was waiting for him. Stepping outside into the bright sunshine, he was guided towards a blacked-out limousine by the chauffeur. The driver held open the rear passenger door and the man slid into the plush leather seat. Once the door was closed, he was plunged into air-conditioned, shaded privacy.

With a casual yet careful look round the airport car park, the driver got behind the wheel and pulled away from the terminal.

'Pleasant flight, sir?' asked the driver, as they joined the highway heading north to Washington DC.

In the back, the Arab was peeling off the first layer of skin from his right hand. The micro-thin latex parted to expose the man's real fingerprints.

'Yes, Hazim,' replied Malik, now removing the coloured contact lenses and returning his eyes from amber to their natural coal-black. Later he would wash the silver dye from his beard too and trim it back. 'And Bahir was right – security is relaxed at this private airport.'

HOSTAGE
CHAPTER 28

The black limousine passed the manned checkpoint and rolled along Pennsylvania Avenue. The grandiose, grey-granite Eisenhower Executive Office Building gave way to tall trees and an oasis of green that was Lafayette Square. Ahead, tourists wandered the wide leafy avenue, mostly ignoring the tiny encampment of peace protesters on the kerb. Rather, their attention was on a stately building set back from the road by a run of iron railings. The modest palisade appeared to be the only barrier to the most famous address in America: the White House.

But Connor knew different. As he peered through the limo's tinted window, his observant eye immediately spotted the snipers hidden on the roof. During his operational briefing, Colonel Black had informed him that these gunmen could hit a target accurately at over a thousand yards. Connor was only a few hundred away and, with such shooting skill, he was the equivalent of a sitting duck.

Yet these weren't the only security measures in place. Although the White House appeared open and welcoming to the public, it was actually an impregnable fortress. All the windows were bullet-resistant. Guard stations controlled every entrance and exit. Vibration alarms beneath the lawn warned of fence jumpers and infra-red sensors above ground detected any unwanted intruders. Then there were the teams of Secret Service agents patrolling the gardens. Often out of sight but always on the alert, these dedicated emergency-response units packed semi-automatic pistols, shotguns and even sub-machine guns.

With this level of protection, Connor wondered why the President needed him in the first place.

As the driver pulled up to the gated entrance of the White House, it was a surreal moment. Connor had seen the place countless times on TV and it was almost as familiar as Big Ben or the London Eye. But he'd never imagined that one day he'd actually be visiting it, let alone working there. Barely twenty-four hours ago, he was in London saying goodbye to his mum and gran. They'd been told he was going on a summer exchange programme in recognition for his outstanding school grades. His mother had been delighted, the news seeming to give her a new lease of life. His gran was more reserved. She just whispered, 'Be careful, Connor.'

The gates parted and the limo eased along the curving driveway towards the magnificent white-pillared entrance of the White House residence. But shortly before it the car bore right to arrive at the West Wing, the building that housed the official offices of the President of the United

States. Pulling up beneath the roofed portico, the driver unlocked the doors and the Secret Service agent in the front passenger seat got out. With swift efficiency, he opened Connor's side.

'Welcome to the White House,' he said. 'The driver will see to your bags.'

Connor stepped out, still a touch overwhelmed at his ceremonious welcome. He'd been flown business class, collected by stretch limousine and treated with the utmost courtesy. He felt more like a distinguished guest than a prospective bodyguard.

A single US Marine stood sentry outside the main doors. Still as a statue, he was dressed in full regalia, his boots polished like mirrors, his gloves spotlessly white. With regimented grace, he greeted their arrival and opened the doors to the lobby.

Connor followed the Secret Service agent inside. The white marble-floor entrance turned to plush carpet as they passed through a second set of double doors into the West Wing's official reception room. Furnished with red leather chairs and a pair of richly upholstered couches, the room was both elegant and intimate like that of a top-class hotel. It boasted a collection of eighteenth-century oil paintings and an antique mahogany bookcase that took pride of place along the main wall.

'If you'd kindly wait here,' instructed the agent. 'I'll inform them of your arrival.'

Connor was left in the room with another nameless agent, who stood silent but attentive next to a glass-topped reception desk. Several people passed through the lobby. The majority were too engrossed in their work to pay Connor much attention. But a couple raised eyebrows at the young teenager loitering in reception.

Connor also began to wonder what he was doing here. The initial thrill of his arrival in America had faded and the underlying doubt in his abilities returned. Looking round the West Wing's luxurious reception room, he realized he was completely out of his depth. The truth was he was just a kid from the East End of London – albeit one with a kickboxing title to his name and twelve weeks of basic close-protection training. But surely that didn't qualify him for the responsibility of protecting the President's daughter. At some point, the powers that be were bound to discover he was a bodyguard in name only. That he was a *fraud*. And the consequences of his failure would be unthinkable. Not only would Colonel Black's Buddyguard organization be discredited, but he could put Alicia Mendez's life in real danger.

Just as he was considering making a bolt for the exit, a panelled wooden door opened and an elderly woman in a plaid suit and steel-rimmed glasses appeared.

'The President will see you now.'

HOSTAGE
CHAPTER 29

Connor stepped into the Oval Office. For a moment, he was convinced he'd walked on to a movie set, the scene instantly recognizable from so many films. The ellipse-shaped room with its three floor-to-ceiling windows. The two ceremonial flags – the Stars and Stripes and the President's blue coat of arms – stationed like dutiful guards either side. The polished oak and walnut floor covered by the iconic oval-shaped rug that proudly bore the presidential seal. And taking main stage, in front of the bow windows, was the famous ornately carved wooden desk at which the President of the United States sat.

Upon coming face to face with the man himself, Connor could only stare. His natural presence seemed to fill the room. Blessed with bronzed skin and well-defined cheekbones, President Mendez maintained a youthful yet worldly-wise look. His dark brown eyes were at once alert and deeply intense, giving Connor the impression that the President rarely missed much. He wore a crisp blue suit with a burgundy silk tie, and when the President stood he was much taller than he appeared on TV.

'It's a pleasure to meet you, Connor,' said President Mendez in a voice smooth as honey.

He extended his hand in welcome. Connor accepted it and found his own enveloped by the heartfelt handshake.

'Thank you ... Mr P-President,' he replied, stuttering for words. 'It's good to meet you too.'

On the short walk through the West Wing's corridors, the President's secretary had instructed him on the correct form of address and encouraged him not to be afraid to speak up, the President being a good-natured and gracious man. In the small waiting area just outside the office, a Secret Service agent had asked him to hand over his mobile phone as a security precaution before allowing Connor to enter.

'Please join us for coffee,' said the President, gesturing towards three men standing between a pair of velvet upholstered couches. 'This is George Taylor, my White House Chief of Staff. He's responsible for pretty much running the show here.'

A man with a trimmed white beard and glasses stepped forward. He greeted Connor with a smile. 'It's good to have you on the team.'

'And this is General Martin Shaw, who originally recommended your Buddyguard organization.'

Connor shook hands. 'Colonel Black sends his regards.'

'Why, thank you,' replied the general in a thick Texan accent. Big as a bear and impeccably turned out in his olive-green uniform, he displayed the same military bearing as his English counterpart. 'It's just a shame the colonel couldn't join us.'

The President introduced the remaining member of the group, a thin man with grey-flecked hair and crow's feet spreading out from his steel-blue eyes. 'And, finally, the Director of the Secret Service, Dirk Moran.'

'Pleased to meet you,' said Connor, offering his hand. 'I've been told I'm reporting to you.'

'That's right,' the director replied. His handshake was brief and cool, and Connor got the feeling he was being appraised right from the start.

They all sat as the chief of staff poured out the coffee. Although he didn't actually like coffee, Connor accepted a cup out of politeness.

'Is this your first time in the States?' asked President Mendez, dropping a lump of sugar into his drink.

Connor nodded. 'But I like what I've seen so far.'

'And what would that be?' asked Dirk.

'Well, the White House. It's certainly well protected,' replied Connor and, wanting to impress, added, 'Snipers, bullet-resistant glass, hidden cameras, infra-red sensors . . .'

The general raised a wry eyebrow in Dirk's direction. 'The boy's done his research.'

'In fact, I was surprised I wasn't searched on arrival,' finished Connor.

The President looked to his director for an explanation of this apparent lapse in security.

'That's because you were scanned discreetly as you passed through the lobby,' explained Dirk. 'You don't know *all* our security measures, young man. No one ever does.'

'Sometimes not even the President himself!' laughed President Mendez, putting down his coffee cup. 'President Eisenhower once said, "America is best described by one word: freedom." And that is true. But Thomas Jefferson, our third President and Founding Father, also observed that "the price of freedom is eternal vigilance". Unfortunately, in this day and age, vigilance isn't only a byword, it's a way of life. Especially for the President and the First Family. We need constant, round-the-clock protection from the Secret Service.'

He sighed, the weight of office momentarily seeming a burden rather than an honour.

'This can be hard to live with, day in, day out. Which is why my daughter has taken exception to such imposing protection. And why Buddyguard's services have been requested.'

No longer able to contain the burning question that had been on his mind ever since his selection, Connor put down his un-drunk cup of coffee and asked, 'Why did you choose *me*?'

President Mendez clasped his hands almost as if in prayer. 'I would have thought that was obvious. Your father saved my life.'

Connor's jaw dropped. '*When? How?*'

The President sat back, surprised at his reaction. 'Has no one ever told you this?'

'No,' admitted Connor. 'I was just told my dad was killed in an ambush in Iraq and that he died a hero.'

'That's correct. He gave his life to rescue *me*.'

The President then recounted his trip to Iraq six years previously as US Ambassador. How the British and American forces were working together to secure peace and that an SAS detachment had been assigned to help protect high-profile visiting diplomats. He spoke with passion about his miraculous escape from the attack on their convoy and how Connor's father had risked all to ensure his safety.

Connor listened rapt. This was the first time he'd heard the details of his father's heroic act. But it now explained the Soldier's Medal – the one embossed with the American Eagle – that was among the possessions his mother kept in the 'memory box'. She'd always been too distraught to talk about his father's death, and as he'd grown older he'd stopped asking about it. But, at last, he knew the whole story.

As the President came to the end, he slid a small scratched key fob across the coffee table to Connor.

'I kept this to remind myself of the true meaning of sacrifice,' he explained. 'To ensure that I lived a life of sacrifice for my country as their President. Your father held this in his hand as he died. And now I return it to you.'

Connor stared down at his father's talisman. From beneath the plastic, a picture of a familiar eight-year-old boy smiled up at him.

'In my eyes, Justin Reeves was a very courageous, loyal and noble soldier,' said President Mendez earnestly. 'And you have his blood running through your veins. Which is why I'd only trust my daughter's life with a Reeves buddyguard.'

Connor was speechless, choked with emotion and grief at the account of his father's selfless bravery.

Seeing the impact his words had, the President said, 'I'll perfectly understand if you feel you can't accept this role, Connor.' His expression was kindly and sincere, yet at the same time hopeful. 'But I would sleep more soundly in my bed knowing Alicia is truly safe – not only protected by the Secret Service, but by you.'

Connor stared at the key fob. His *dad's* key fob. Losing a father was a pain no one should have to bear. But, in his father's case, could it possibly be deemed 'worth it'? He'd saved the life of a man who went on to become the President of the United States. A leader who was being hailed as a new dawn for America, according to what Connor had read about him. A visionary who could steer the country to peace and prosperity. And all this was possible *only* because of his father. Connor felt an immense sense of pride in him.

Gripping the key fob in his hand, Connor said, 'I can assure you, Mr President, I'll do my best to protect your daughter.'

'That's all I ask of anyone,' replied President Mendez, smiling warmly.

'Now, Connor, remember your assignment is to be kept confidential,' explained the White House Chief of Staff. 'Aside from us in this room, a few key Secret Service agents and the First Lady, no one will know your true purpose.'

'And Alicia, of course?' added Connor.

Dirk intervened, 'No, you'll be introduced to her later as

a special guest of the President on an exchange programme. The White House have done such exchanges before so it won't raise suspicion.'

'So Alicia won't know I'm guarding her?' queried Connor.

'Hopefully not,' replied the President. 'With any luck, she'll think she's looking after *you*.'

HOSTAGE
CHAPTER 30

'Over ten thousand death threats a year are made against the President and his family,' stated Dirk Moran, as he led Connor down another windowless and indistinguishable corridor.

After his meeting with President Mendez, Connor had been driven with the director to an unmarked building in downtown DC. Although it looked like any other office in the street, it actually housed the headquarters of the Secret Service. Having been issued with a security pass, Connor was then escorted by the director deep into the labyrinthian complex.

'That's *thirty* potential attacks every day,' Dirk emphasized in a grave tone. 'Each and every one has to be investigated.' They passed a busy office to their left. 'In there, our Intelligence Division are tasked with differentiating between those who make threats and those capable of carrying out such threats. Then the agency's job is to prevent any viable threat becoming a full-blown attack.'

They came to an unmarked door and the director stopped.

'Before we go any further, Connor,' he said, his expression hardening, 'I need you to understand something.'

Reaching into his jacket pocket, Dirk pulled out a slim black leather wallet.

'Our mandate is to *Protect the man. Protect the symbol. Protect the office.* And the Secret Service's Presidential Protective Division is the last line of defence,' he explained.

With a flick, he snapped the wallet open in front of Connor's face. Inside was a golden badge with an eagle on the top. At its centre was the American Stars and Stripes, the miniature flag surrounded by a five-pointed star. Above and below the star were emblazoned the words UNITED STATES SECRET SERVICE.

'This badge represents years of training, dedication and experience in the service of the President. As the Director of the Secret Service, I do *not* gamble with the lives of the First Family.' His voice was taut with barely constrained fury. 'And no young upstart – whose only qualifications are a few weeks' training and a bodyguard for a father – will jeopardize our mission!'

Connor was taken aback by the unexpected tirade. 'If you don't want me here, why did you invite me in the first place?'

'I didn't,' replied Dirk through clenched teeth as he pocketed his badge. 'I consider you a liability. But I have to obey the President's wishes. Be warned, though, if you make a *single* mistake that compromises the safety of the First Daughter, you'll be flying home quicker than you can say "Secret Service". Do I make myself clear?'

Although intimidated by the man's hostility, Connor

was determined to prove the director's assumptions wrong. 'Perfectly clear.'

'Good. Point made,' said Dirk, regaining his professional composure and offering a thin smile. 'Now if you're to work alongside us, you need to know *how* we work.'

Sliding a key card through an electronic slot, he pushed open the door to reveal a large room humming with state-of-the-art equipment. There were wall-to-wall monitors, two massive overhead screens, a digital banner displaying a constant flow of live data, and several black cubicles, each with their own terminal and communications port. A small team of agents worked quietly and efficiently, processing the incoming information.

'The Joint Operations Centre,' declared Dirk with some pride. 'This is where we track the movements of the President and the First Family. It contains information so sensitive that only a select few are allowed access. So feel privileged.'

Following the director inside, Connor passed a row of monitors displaying multiple views of a familiar white building and large garden. Two men were stationed at desks, analysing the images.

'The White House is under constant surveillance,' explained Dirk. 'Every entrance, every approach and every exit are covered. Even the air around the White House is monitored twenty-four hours a day.'

They headed over to the first cubicle. The agent manning the desk nodded respectfully at the director. 'Sir.'

'Agent Greenaway here is responsible for tracking the First Lady.'

The agent gestured towards a street map displayed on his screen. A green dot traced a route along one of the roads. 'The First Lady often goes on diplomatic and humanitarian trips abroad,' Greenaway explained. 'Her car has just left the hotel and is heading south-east on the Champs-Élysées in Paris.'

A message flashed up on the monitor:

NIGHTOWL ARRIVING AT BLUE 1.
FIVE MINUTES.

Connor gave the agent a questioning look. 'Is "Nightowl" her call sign?'

The agent nodded. 'To maintain secrecy with radio communications, all the First Family are assigned code names.'

'What are the others?' asked Connor.

'Code names are kept confidential,' said Dirk pointedly. 'If and when the press get wind of them, they're changed with immediate effect.'

'But surely I need to know them in case I have to report any problems?'

Dirk gave a begrudging nod. 'I suppose so. Currently President Mendez is known as "Ninja", for his love of old martial arts movies. The First Lady is "Nightowl", because she stays up late. And Alicia's call sign is "Nomad".'

'*Nomad?*' repeated Connor.

'Well, she's always wandering off!' laughed Agent Greenaway.

The director cut short the agent's amusement with a sharp disciplinary look.

'We've also given you a call sign, Connor,' Dirk revealed.

'Really?' said Connor, looking hopeful.

'Yes, to reflect your role in our operation.'

'What is it?'

'Bandit,' he replied with a smirk.

Connor was coming to realize that, while Dirk wouldn't actively prevent him from doing his job, he certainly wouldn't be helping him either. He'd have to tread very carefully with the director if he was going to succeed in this operation.

Dirk directed him over to a central bank of monitors. 'In the event of a crisis, the standard operating procedure is to ensure every protectee is moved quickly and safely to a secure site – a safe house. These will depend upon your location at the time of the crisis.' He pointed to one of the screens. 'This is a feed from the National Terrorism Advisory System. It's a two-tier alert listing credible threats. These are either classified as *Elevated* or *Imminent* and are accompanied by a summary of the threat and the actions recommended to be taken. Along with the information from the Intelligence Division, this dictates our protection protocol for the First Family.'

Connor studied the scrolling list of alerts. 'There seem a lot of them.'

'We've al-Qaeda to thank for that,' replied the director

bitterly. 'Although America has dealt with terrorism throughout its history, 9/11 changed everything. We're now up against a modern strain of the threat, one that has no boundaries. Attacks can be violent, indiscriminate and crippling. It's very hard to defend against an enemy who lives by the code "The Gates of Paradise are under the shadows of the swords".'

His finger tapped the screen pensively as threat after threat scrolled by.

'Terrorists are like the mythical beast, Hydra – you cut one head off and two grow in its place. The threat constantly looms. Someone, somewhere, always wants to kill the President or his family.'

HOSTAGE

CHAPTER 31

Hazim checked his watch as two black Cadillac limousines rolled up to the school gates: 14:48.

The security guard in the kiosk waved them through. With rehearsed precision, they followed the driveway and stopped outside the main building just as the school bell sounded: 14:50.

A broad-shouldered man in a suit and dark glasses stepped out of the front passenger seat. Tucked behind his left ear was the telltale curly wire of a two-way radio. With a brief yet thorough scan of his surroundings, he headed for the glass doors of the main entrance. Meanwhile, three more men exited the rear vehicle and took up their stations round the front limo – two at the nearside corners and one on the road facing out, so that all the observation arcs were covered.

The Not-So Secret Service! thought Hazim drily, the agents standing out like sore thumbs among the other arriving parents. A slight bulge on each man's right hip hinted at the concealed SIG Sauer P229 pistol that they all carried as standard issue. And on the lapel of their suits gleamed the small but distinctive hexagonal badge with its five-pointed star of the Secret Service.

Hazim took note of all these details from behind his sunglasses while he searched for weaknesses in the functioning of the protection team. Malik had told him that arriving or leaving a location was the most vulnerable point in any security operation – even more so for the daily school run. The timing of arrival and departure was always known. The drop-off and pick-up point always the same. And whatever route the limos took to and from the White House they had to end or start at the Montarose School. It made this the most likely snatch point.

The first of the students began spilling out of the entrance, a few walking home, most being collected by car. The agents kept a wary eye out for strangers. But this didn't concern Hazim as he continued his covert surveillance.

At 14:53, a dark-haired girl – the one they'd *all* been waiting for – walked out of the glass doors with a group of friends. Three girls. They chatted and giggled on the steps for a minute or so. Then, waving goodbye, Alicia Mendez made her way to the front limo.

Two paces behind on her right followed the first Secret Service agent. As soon as she was safely inside the limo and the door closed, the agent jumped into the front passenger seat and the driver pulled away. The escort vehicle quickly moved forward, collected the other agents and sped after them: 14:55.

The whole embarkation process from door to car had

taken less than sixty seconds. Hazim realized the window of opportunity was very small. Possibly too small. But that was for his Uncle Malik to decide.

Hazim's eyes followed the lead limo as it pulled out of the school drive and turned left on to Wisconsin Avenue. The two vehicles merged with the Washington traffic: 14:56.

Hazim didn't make any attempt to pursue them. He simply thumbed a coded text on his mobile:

> Eagle Chick flying south.

A few moments later his phone pinged in reply, a message flashing on the screen.

> Gamekeeper has the eyeball on
> Eagle Chick.

HOSTAGE
CHAPTER 32

Alicia sat on the leather chair, kicking her heels against the soft beige carpet of the President's outer office. She absently surfed the internet on her smartphone, then sent several text messages to her school friends. Glancing up at the clock on the wall, she sighed with boredom.

From behind her neatly arranged desk, Mrs Holland, the President's secretary, offered an apologetic smile. 'I'm sure your father won't be much longer, Alicia.'

'You tell me that *every* time,' Alicia replied, though not unkindly. Mrs Holland, while fiercely loyal to the President and protective of his schedule, had become almost a surrogate grandmother to her within the confines of the White House.

'And I'm never wrong, am I?' said Mrs Holland, peering over her steel-rimmed glasses, as the door to the Oval Office opened and a tall woman with long dark-blonde hair stepped out. She was dressed in a sleek blue business suit and carried a wafer-thin touchscreen computer. Alicia recognized her as Karen Wright, the newly appointed Director of National Intelligence and her father's principal advisor on all matters related to the security of the United States.

'Thank you for the update, Karen,' said President Mendez, appearing in the doorway. 'Keep me informed of any developments.'

'Of course, Mr President, you'll be the first to know,' replied Karen. Turning to leave, she smiled warmly at Alicia. 'Hello, Alicia.'

'Hi, Karen,' she replied as the director disappeared down the corridor.

President Mendez now faced his daughter. 'Sorry to keep you waiting, honey.'

'Don't worry, I'm used to it,' Alicia replied, picking up her school bag and following her father inside.

Feeling a twinge of parental guilt, President Mendez put an arm round his daughter and kissed the top of her head. 'But *this* is the meeting I look forward to the most every day,' he insisted.

Alicia's lips tightened as she bit back the urge to say, *Is that all I am to you . . . a meeting?*

They sat down together on the sofa. Alicia both enjoyed and hated these moments with her father in equal measure. She understood he was extremely busy as President and appreciated that he *always* made time for her in his hectic schedule. Yet their 'meetings' were all too short and often felt like a duty rather than a relaxed personal moment between father and daughter.

'How was school?' President Mendez asked. 'Has your protection team backed off?'

'I suppose so,' she replied with a shrug of her shoulders. 'They still hang around at breaks, though.'

'Well, that's their job,' he replied, his tone firm yet sympathetic. 'Did you have dance class today?'

Alicia nodded. 'Yeah, we're learning how to salsa.'

President Mendez smiled warmly as a fond memory washed over him. 'Your mother's a great salsa dancer. It's a shame she's not here to teach you a few moves.'

Alicia glanced up at him hopefully. 'When's she getting back?'

'Still at the end of the month, I'm afraid.'

Groaning, Alicia slumped back against the cushions of the sofa. 'She's been gone *ages*.'

'Hey, believe me, I'm missing her too,' said President Mendez, pulling his daughter into a hug. 'But I've a surprise to keep you company in the meantime.'

Alicia visibly perked up at this. She'd been begging her parents for a puppy dog for weeks and looked expectantly up at her father.

'We've a special young guest coming to stay for the summer, maybe longer,' he announced.

The hopeful look on Alicia's face faded as fast as it had appeared. This wasn't any puppy dog. Far from it.

'Not *again*!' she exclaimed, recalling the last 'special guest' that had visited on an exchange the previous year – a vain and morose girl of some visiting French dignitary. Despite Alicia's numerous attempts at making friends, the girl had remained aloof and constantly complained about everything from food to fashion to the weather. It had been even more painful to have her in the same class and hanging around with her friends. When the girl had finally returned home, Alicia couldn't have been happier.

President Mendez gave his daughter a stern look. 'I'm sure I needn't remind you, Alicia, of your obligation as the President's daughter to welcome guests to our country.'

'Yeah, but not babysit them!' she retorted, crossing her arms in defiance.

'Well, if you're not keen, I can always cancel the visit,' said the President nonchalantly. 'I just thought having a guy your age around the White House would make a nice change.'

Alicia struggled not to let her jaw drop open in shock. *A boy? Her age?* That was most unusual. Typically, her father was over-protective when it came to the subject of boys.

'No ... it's OK,' she backtracked, her interest now piqued. 'So, who is he?'

'The son of an old and trusted friend who I knew from my time in Iraq.'

'He's an Iraqi?'

'No, he's English. His father was a soldier.'

Trying hard not to appear too keen, Alicia began to inspect one of her fingernails for imaginary dirt. 'When do I get to meet him?'

'As soon as you're ready. He's waiting for you in the Diplomatic Reception Room.'

'*What?*' exclaimed Alicia, jumping up from the sofa and looking at her school clothes in horror. 'I can't see him like *this*!'

President Mendez tried to suppress a smile as he watched his daughter dash out of the Oval Office towards the main residence to get changed. Diplomacy was one thing he excelled at, especially when it came to convincing people that certain decisions were their own.

HOSTAGE
CHAPTER 33

Connor waited nervously in the large oval reception room on the ground floor of the White House. He was alone, apart from a discreet Secret Service agent, who stood stock-still and silent by a set of double doors like he was part of the furniture. The soft gold and blue decor of the stately room did little to alleviate Connor's worries. Despite the distraction of the stunning panorama of American landscapes that circled the entire room, Connor couldn't help but feel apprehensive about his first encounter with the President's daughter.

How should I act? Formal or casual in my manner? Or should I just be myself? What am I going to say? And what if Alicia takes an instant dislike to me? How am I going to do my job then . . .

As all these concerns whirled through his mind, the double doors opened and President Mendez stepped through, followed by his daughter and two Secret Service agents.

'Connor, welcome to the White House,' greeted the President, warmly shaking his hand. 'I'm so glad we could arrange your stay. Please allow me to introduce my daughter, Alicia.'

For a moment, Connor was speechless. Alicia was even more attractive than the photos had suggested. Dressed in a striking sunflower-yellow frock, her bronze complexion seemed to almost glow, and he found himself mesmerized by her deep brown eyes . . .

Connor pulled himself together. These weren't the thoughts of a professional bodyguard. He wasn't here to admire his Principal. He was here to protect her.

'Hi . . . I'm Connor,' he finally managed to blurt out and, for some reason, bowed.

'Pleased to meet you too,' Alicia replied with an amused smile. 'But there's no need to bow.'

'Well . . . you are the President's daughter.'

'True, but I'm not royalty!'

Connor's cheeks flushed a little with embarrassment at his mistake in etiquette.

President Mendez glanced between them both and waited for either to say more. When neither did, he prompted, 'Well, now that you've met, I suggest, Alicia, you give Connor a tour of our home.'

Alicia nodded dutifully.

President Mendez turned to Connor and shook his hand. 'Sorry I can't join you. I have to get back to running the country! But I do hope all goes well during your stay with us,' he said, shooting Connor a knowing wink.

'Thank you, Mr President,' Connor replied as the great man took his leave, the two agents remaining behind.

Once her father was gone, there was a moment of awkward silence. Connor exchanged a strained smile with Alicia as they each sought for something to say.

Then Alicia began. 'So ... this is the Diplomatic Reception Room.'

Her hand swept round the decorated walls.

'Ermm ... Jacqueline Kennedy had this pictorial wallpaper put up in the sixties. That's Niagara Falls over there ... New York Bay ... Boston Harbor. And this old fireplace is where President F. D. Roosevelt broadcast his famous fireside chats.'

Connor nodded politely. While he'd never heard of Roosevelt's broadcasts, he was more than happy for Alicia to take him on a guided tour, since it gave him the opportunity to get to know her. As a bodyguard, it was important to quickly assess a Principal's character and manner so that one could work efficiently and agreeably with them.

'In the past, this room housed a furnace and boiler,' she explained, 'and before that it was used by servants for polishing the silver.'

Maintaining the formality of the occasion, Alicia guided him next door to the China Room and showed him its priceless displays of ivory and burnished gold china. Next, they moved on to the Vermeil Room with its extensive collection of silver-gilt tableware; the wooden-panelled Library with its unusual lighthouse clock; and, to Connor's great surprise, a bowling alley in the basement. Then they climbed the Grand Staircase up to the State Floor. The first point of call was the East Room – a magnificent ceremonial hall with long gilded drapes, a marble fireplace and antique glass chandeliers hanging above a Steinway grand piano. As they traipsed through the furniture displays in the Green, Blue and Red Rooms, Connor was struggling to maintain his interest. Impressive as the White House was, there was only so much antiquity and artwork he could take.

Alicia noticed his eyes glazing over and stopped talking.

'Sorry,' said Connor, attempting to stifle a yawn. 'Must be jet lag.'

But, rather than take offence, Alicia grinned at him. 'Shall we skip the boring bits?'

Connor nodded eagerly. 'If you don't mind.'

'Not at all,' she said, visibly relaxing in his presence. 'To be honest, I hate doing these official tours. I just thought that was what you expected as an official guest.'

'No, I'd prefer to do what *you* want,' Connor replied.

'Cool,' said Alicia, smiling. 'Then I hope you don't scare easily!'

HOSTAGE

CHAPTER 34

'You mean, he could be watching us *right now*?' said Connor, unnerved by Alicia's story. The two of them had headed for the infamous Lincoln Bedroom on the second floor. He scanned the room and looked out through the window at the slowly setting sun.

Alicia nodded, her face drawn into a mask of fright. 'Don't you feel his *presence*?' Her voice was almost a whisper, her dark eyes wide as she pointed a trembling finger towards the door. 'I think . . . that's him . . .'

Connor could see a faint shadow moving along the narrow gap at the foot of the wooden door. Silently, he crept across the plush emerald-green carpet. His fingers clasped the brass handle; it was cool to the touch. The movement outside ceased. With a quick twist, Connor yanked the door open and a startled Secret Service agent leapt away in shock.

'That's not Abraham Lincoln's ghost!' Connor exclaimed with a grin.

Alicia laughed as the agent recovered his wits. 'No, but it could have been. Over the years, numerous sightings have been recorded. President Reagan's first daughter said she saw Lincoln standing at that window peering out across the lawn. Harry Truman, the thirty-third President, once wrote in a letter that he heard footsteps up and down the hallway at night, as well as knocking on his door, when no one was there. Winston Churchill even refused to sleep in this room after coming face-to-face with Lincoln's ghost. The White House is *definitely* haunted.'

'Aren't you scared?' asked Connor.

'A little,' admitted Alicia. 'But he's a friendly ghost . . . I think.'

Connor examined a holograph copy of the Gettysburg Address, President Lincoln's most well-known speech, displayed on a desk by the window. 'It must be amazing to live in the White House,' he remarked.

Alicia smiled proudly. 'Yes, and the Mendez family are now part of its history.'

Then she lowered her voice to a conspiratorial whisper so that the Secret Service agent wouldn't overhear outside in the hallway. 'But, to be honest, Connor, sometimes I hate it. It's a museum, not a home. I'm almost too scared to touch something in case I break it! And thousands of people come through the house on tours every month. It's not like I can leave my things anywhere I want.'

She glanced towards the agent.

'And there's no privacy either. A Secret Service agent is stationed in almost every room. Sometimes I think *they're* the ghosts – haunting my every step.'

Connor smiled sympathetically. 'It must be hard,' he

said. Although he realized that if anyone was a ghost, then *he* was – as her secret buddyguard.

'You don't know the half of it. It's like living in a cross between a reform school and a convent!' She laughed weakly at her comparison. 'Just going to meet my friends in a coffee shop is a mission in itself. Literally *anything* I want to do outside the White House requires advanced planning by the Secret Service.'

Alicia sighed, then shrugged in a what-can-you-do-about-it way.

'Sorry, you don't want to be hearing all this,' she said, perching herself on the end of the Lincoln bed.

'No, it's fine,' replied Connor.

'It's just I don't often have many people my own age around here and . . . you seem pretty easy to get along with. I do realize how fortunate I am. I mean, the White House has its own cinema, bowling alley and swimming pool. And I get to meet some truly amazing people – kings and queens, heads of state, famous musicians and movie stars! I have to pinch myself at times. I once even met the Dalai Lama. He told me, *Happiness is not something ready made. It comes from your own actions.*' Alicia quickly cheered at the thought. 'And there are a *few* rooms in the White House where I can be left alone. Come on, I'll show you my favourite.'

She led Connor out of the Lincoln Bedroom and up the stairs to the third floor, the agent discreetly following behind. This level, as Connor already knew, was where the First Family relaxed and also where the guest bedrooms were housed, a maid having shown him to his room earlier.

As they turned left up a ramped hallway, the agent stopped shadowing them. The two of them entered the solarium, a private chill-out space with comfy sofas and glass walls that offered unbroken views of the Washington skyline.

'Welcome to the fishbowl!' announced Alicia. 'This is about as free as it gets.'

Opening a patio door, she stepped out on to the rooftop terrace. She took a deep breath and opened her arms.

'FREEDOM!' she cried.

But Connor only saw the high stone balustrade that shielded the terrace and solarium from general view. Glancing up at the apex of the roof, he caught a brief glimpse of a black-uniformed sniper. Then he peered between the thick white pillars of the balustrade at the expanse of south lawn. From his vantage point, he could spy the Secret Service agents patrolling the grounds and the boundary fence where swarms of tourists gathered in the hope of spotting the First Family.

Connor began to understand Alicia's plight. The White House was as much a prison as a home. No wonder she was desperate to escape the perpetual shadow of the Secret Service. She was like a bird trapped in a gilded cage.

HOSTAGE
CHAPTER 35

Connor had never arrived at school in such style. Cushioned by soft leather seats and comforted in air-conditioned luxury, he and Alicia were driven through the Washington downtown traffic right up to the steps of Montarose School's main building. After a brief surveillance sweep by Secret Service, the limo doors unlocked and he and Alicia were ushered from the car like movie stars.

'We'll collect you at 1500 hours,' said the broad-shouldered agent with a courteous smile.

'As always, Kyle,' Alicia replied, waving him goodbye.

Kyle, as Connor had discovered, was the primary bodyguard in the First Daughter's protection team. He was also one of the few select agents to be aware of Connor's role – and, surprisingly, the most receptive to it. Upon being introduced, Kyle had taken the time to explain the team's key security procedures and action-on drills. He'd even covered details such as the small hexagonal lapel badges all Secret Service agents wore. These were a security measure; their colour routinely changed to reduce the likelihood of infiltration by an outsider.

As Connor stepped from the limo, Kyle gave him a subtle nod as if to say, *Over to you now*.

Connor knew he wasn't being left entirely alone in his close-protection duties. The grounds of the private school were security-patrolled and cordoned off with high fences. Also the Secret Service agents would be stationed just a short distance away throughout the day. But, that said, Alicia's immediate safety was now in his hands.

Connor followed Alicia up the steps into the main foyer. The corridors were packed with students.

'Alicia!' cried a voice and three girls came running over, just as Connor finished signing in at reception.

They all embraced and kissed each other's cheeks.

An African American girl with a bundle of frizzy hair and a diamond-white smile glanced over Alicia's shoulder. 'Is that the English boy you were talking about last night?'

Alicia nodded.

'Cute,' she whispered to her friends and they giggled.

Connor offered an embarrassed smile. 'Hi there.'

'Oooh,' sighed a girl with cheerleader looks and long blonde hair tied up in a ponytail. 'Say something else.'

Connor frowned in puzzlement. 'Like what?'

'Anything.'

Connor shrugged. 'It's nice to meet you. What's your name?'

The girl clapped her hands in delight. 'I just *love* that English accent,' she cooed. 'I'm Paige. You can talk to me like that all day.'

'And I'm Grace,' said the black girl, dazzling him with her smile.

Alicia urged her other friend forward. 'This is Kalila,' she said, introducing an Arab girl with olive skin and almond eyes, who wore a light purple hijab headscarf.

'Hello,' she said, her voice soft as a breeze.

'Hi,' replied Connor. 'Are you all in Alicia's class?'

The girls nodded.

'Connor's joining our class for the rest of term,' explained Alicia.

'Cool!' said Grace. 'You can sit next to *me*.'

Alicia's eyes flashed her friend a good-natured warning. 'Connor can sit where he wants.'

'But there's a spare seat right beside me,' replied Grace innocently.

Connor looked to Alicia. 'Erm, where will you be sitting?'

'I'd be right in front of you.'

'Well, that sounds fine,' he replied casually. In fact, the positioning was perfect. From the perspective of a bodyguard, he could protect her back if necessary, observe any threat approaching from the front and easily grab her to provide body cover or escape in the event of an emergency.

Alicia's school bag buzzed and she pulled out her mobile to read the text message.

'Hey, that's a neat phone cover!' said Paige.

Alicia grinned, pleased that one of her friends had noticed. 'It's a present from Connor.'

'Lucky you, that's a limited edition Armani!' Grace exclaimed, admiring the red butterfly logo.

The girls crowded round to have a better look.

'Just a thank-you gift,' explained Connor, worried they'd read too much into it. But the girls were more interested in comparing phone covers and lucky charms.

The school bell rang for class.

'Come on,' said Alicia, grabbing her bag and looking at Connor. 'First lesson's history. If you can survive this, you can survive anything!'

HOSTAGE

CHAPTER 36

History wasn't one of Connor's favourite topics, but the lesson was made even more challenging by the double life he was leading. Protecting the President's daughter meant he had to be on constant alert – Code Yellow. But that was hard to maintain when a teacher was asking questions and there was class work to be done. It was only his first day and Connor already felt like he was performing a constant juggling act with his attention.

The open window. The teacher. The other students. Alicia. The unanswered workbook on his desk. The person passing in the corridor . . .

As the bell went for lunch, after the first three periods of history, Mandarin Chinese and maths, Connor was glad to be able to concentrate on just one role – that of being a buddyguard.

Alicia and her friends collected their bags and headed for the refectory with Connor in tow. As they wandered down the corridor, Connor kept a careful eye out for potential threats. Although it was tempting to relax – since they were within the relatively safe confines of a private school – Colonel Black had reinforced in him during training that 'assumption is the mother of all screw-ups'. A bodyguard could *never* assume that an area was totally safe or an individual not a threat. Vigilance was required at all times. This meant that while the Secret Service would have vetted any people in direct contact with Alicia there was always a chance one shark could slip through the net. This could be a teacher, an office clerk, one of the catering staff, the cleaners, the groundsmen, a delivery driver or even a fellow student. *Everyone* was a suspect.

But the threat need not be an assassination. As Alicia's buddyguard, Connor was to protect her from all forms of harm – from everyday bullying to a simple accident. So although he didn't expect there'd be any potential assassins among the students, if Montarose School was anything like his own in East London, there'd certainly be a bonehead or two.

As if on cue, two lads strolled up to their group as they waited in line for food. One was well-built with dark wavy hair, a square jaw and a confident swagger. He looked like a young Clark Kent who'd forgotten to put on his glasses and was still Superman. His friend was bigger – a bulldozer of a boy with a short crew cut and size twelve Converse trainers.

'Hey, Alicia!' drawled Superman. 'What's up?'

'Hi, Ethan,' she replied, smiling coyly as her friends gathered to one side to give them space.

'Ethan, this is Connor from England,' introduced Alicia.

The boy gave a brief nod in Connor's direction. 'Right!'

Then he turned his attention back to Alicia before Connor had a chance to reply.

'So, what you doing at the weekend?' he asked.

Alicia glanced sideways at her giggling schoolmates. 'My father's asked me to take Connor to the National Mall on Saturday. Fancy joining us?'

'Nah, it's just a bunch of old museums and monuments,' snorted Ethan. 'Anyway, I've got baseball practice.'

'Ethan's the top hitter for the school team,' Grace whispered to Connor, handing him a dinner tray. 'He's also the school star quarterback.'

Connor nodded. Judging by the boy's attitude, he certainly thought himself a star.

'Are you going to the Summer Prom?' Ethan asked casually.

'Maybe,' replied Alicia, twirling a lock of her dark hair round her finger. 'Depends who's asking.'

'I am.'

Alicia pursed her lips. 'I'll think about it.'

'*Think about it?*' exclaimed Ethan, his stunned expression suggesting he never expected 'no' from a girl – even the President's daughter. 'It's only two weeks away.'

'Yeah, but I need the Secret Service to check you out first. Got to confirm you're no "threat",' she said, raising her eyebrows teasingly.

'But I'm a senator's son!' he replied, clearly not getting Alicia's joke. He walked off in a huff, muttering, 'Well, don't take too long about it.'

The girls regrouped round Alicia.

'I don't believe you!' said Paige, her blue eyes wide. 'Ethan asked you to the Prom and you didn't say *yes*.'

'He's got to work a bit harder than that,' replied Alicia.

'Treat 'em mean, keep 'em keen, eh?' sniggered Grace.

'No, the guy needs some style first. He needs to impress me. I mean, he asked me in the lunch queue, for goodness' sake!'

As the girls stood gossiping, Connor became aware of someone staring intently at Alicia through the glass pane of a door marked NO ADMITTANCE. He couldn't make out the man's features clearly, since the glass was obscured. But the man's eyes were magnified by it and his attention was definitely fixed on Alicia.

Connor's awareness shot up one level to Code Orange. As he evaluated the potential threat, the man noticed Connor looking in his direction, and suddenly disappeared.

'What's behind that door?' Connor asked Kalila.

'Just the kitchens,' she replied, helping herself to a Caesar salad from the food bar.

'We'll sit over there, Connor,' Alicia called, pointing to a table by the window.

'Right behind you,' Connor replied, quickly selecting a sandwich and a soft drink. He hurried over to ensure he got a seat beside Alicia. He allowed his alert level to drop to Code Yellow again. But for her safety he wanted the best position to view the refectory and NO ADMITTANCE door – just in case the watcher made a second appearance.

HOSTAGE

CHAPTER 37

During his afternoon lessons of English and geography, Connor pondered the face at the glass. If not for his bodyguard training, he doubted he'd have noticed the man in the first place. There was no real reason to suspect anything more than a curious member of the catering staff. The face never reappeared and could simply have been a chef checking the length of the dinner queue, or a new kitchen hand who'd had his first sighting of the President's daughter. But something about the intensity of the stare unsettled Connor. Perhaps it was the way the eyes were magnified by the rippled glass, or the fact that the gaze was directed at Alicia alone and nobody else.

The school bell rang, interrupting his thoughts.

'Remember, I want your assignments on my desk by Friday,' said Mr Hulme, their geography teacher, over the scrape of chairs and thumping of bags.

Connor wished he'd been paying more attention. He hurriedly scribbled down the assignment from the whiteboard as the students piled out of the classroom, eager to go home and enjoy what was left of the day's sunshine. Alicia waited for Connor and they headed for the main foyer with her friends. At the end of the corridor, he held the door open for them.

'Thank you,' said Alicia, surprised by his courteous gesture.

'Aww, English boys are so polite,' said Paige, skipping through after her with Grace and Kalila.

Before Connor could follow, Ethan barged past. 'Good work, doorman.'

His friend, whose name Connor had discovered was Jimbo, also muscled his way through with no more than a grunt of acknowledgement. Connor held himself in check at their rudeness. He didn't want to get on the wrong side of *any* of Alicia's friends – even the most obnoxious. At the same time, he wasn't going to be pushed around.

'Next time leave a tip!' he cried, keeping his voice light and humorous.

Neither Ethan nor Jimbo bothered to reply.

Letting the door swing shut behind him, Connor instinctively checked over his shoulder. He noticed a man with black hair, glasses and a dark complexion standing at the far end of the corridor. He was staring intently in Alicia's direction. *Could this be the face behind the glass?* But the man wasn't dressed in catering clothes. He wore light-coloured chinos, a shirt and a striped blue tie.

'Who's that?' asked Connor.

Alicia glanced back down the corridor. 'Oh, that's Mr Hayek, the new IT teacher. He must be on hall duty.'

Connor let his guard down. He realized he was being *too* paranoid. If he continued to suspect everyone and anyone who merely looked at the President's daughter, he'd be a nervous wreck by the end of the week. He made a mental note to study the photos of the teachers and school staff that Ling had compiled in his operations folder. That way he need only be suspicious of strangers and any staff doing something out of the ordinary.

They congregated in the foyer to say goodbye.

'So who's up for the National Mall this weekend?' asked Alicia.

Grace smiled. 'Sorry, seeing my grandparents.'

'Catch you later for shopping maybe,' said Paige.

'You *always* want to go shopping,' laughed Alicia.

'Hey, it's my favourite hobby. And I'm already meeting a friend for lunch.'

'A friend or a *friend*?' enquired Grace.

'A *friend* called Steve,' Paige replied with a cheeky smile.

'You go, girl!' said Grace, high-fiving her. 'See you all tomorrow.'

She waved goodbye and Paige followed before Alicia had a chance to question her any more about her lunch date.

'What about you, Kalila?' asked Alicia.

'I'll have to ask my father first,' she replied with a timid smile.

'Of course,' said Alicia. 'I understand. I have to get my father's permission to do *anything*!'

Kalila glanced towards a sleek silver Mercedes Benz in the car park. 'Sorry, I'd better go – my brother's waiting for me.'

Connor followed her gaze and spotted a young man in the driver's seat, looking in their direction and impatiently checking his watch.

'Bye, Connor, it's been lovely meeting you,' said Kalila, smiling shyly at him, before hurrying down the steps and over to the car.

'We should go too,' said Alicia. 'Otherwise Kyle will start getting edgy.'

As Connor followed Alicia, he looked back at the silver Mercedes and remarked, 'Kalila seems nice.'

'Yes, she's one of my best friends,' Alicia admitted. 'Her father's a foreign diplomat, so she's not fazed by the fact I'm the First Daughter.'

'What do you mean?' asked Connor.

Alicia considered him a moment, then seemed to decide to trust him with her thoughts. 'Having a father who's President can affect friendships. When my father came to power, some of my friends dropped away, worried they'd appear to be cosying up. Others, who'd never spoken to me before, tried to squeeze into my supposed "inner circle". But Kalila, she just stayed the same.'

'It's good to have friends like that,' said Connor, thinking of Charley and Amir back in the UK. He hoped he would get a chance to speak to them during his evening report.

As they headed down the school steps, Kyle subtly appeared from behind and guided them towards the waiting limo. He opened the door for Alicia. On the other side, another agent held the door for Connor.

'I trust you had a good first day, Connor?' asked Kyle as he shut Alicia's door.

'Tiring, but otherwise uneventful.'

'That's *exactly* how it should be,' he replied with a wink.

HOSTAGE
CHAPTER 38

The two black limos turned down a side street just as a woman with a baby stroller walked out into the middle of the road. The driver of the lead limo put on his brakes, slowing to allow her to cross. But when the mother was halfway she reached into the stroller and drew out a large black gun. Aiming the muzzle at the limo's grille, she pulled the trigger.

Nothing happened *apparently*.

There was no bang. No sound of a bullet or projectile hitting the limo. Just a tiny mechanical *click* and a frisson in the air, like just before a bolt of lightning is about to strike.

The driver floored the accelerator. But the limo failed to respond.

Unseen by the human eye, an intense electromagnetic pulse had been unleashed. Channelling through the metalwork of each car, the massive energy surge fried all the internal circuitry. Both engines died. Power-assisted steering failed. So did the headlights, along with every other electronic system that the handheld EMP weapon had knocked out – including radios and mobile phones. In an instant, the two armour-plated limos were rendered useless hunks of metal. Without power or control, they simply hit the kerb and juddered to a halt.

A second later, several armed men, their faces concealed by bandanas, broke from the cover of the side alleys. Keeping their weapons trained on the two immobile limos, they surrounded their targets and closed in.

Realizing they were sitting ducks, the agents jumped out of their vehicles to engage with the enemy. But snipers on the nearby roofs took each of them down before a single shot was fired in retaliation, their muffled long-range rifles sounding no louder than a whisper to ensure the ambush wasn't heard in the adjacent streets.

In fact, the entire attack was executed in sinister silence.

Inside the front limo, the remaining occupants were cocooned within the armoured box of the passenger section. No way in – but no way out for them either.

Kedar rushed forward and crouched beside the rear door. Pulling out a circular metal device from his backpack, he fixed it to the reinforced glass window.

'Keep clear!' he warned, sheltering behind the limo's bumper. Then he pressed a button.

A high-pitched whirring quickly built in intensity. Just as the sound reached the limit of human hearing, the sonic charge shattered the bulletproof glass. Chunks, like cracked ice, fell to the ground. As soon as the security of the limo was breached, Kedar was at the window with his gun.

'Out!' he growled.

Malik's face appeared, a crooked smile on his lips. He checked his watch.

'Not bad, Kedar,' he said. 'The technology works. But your team needs to shave off another eight seconds.'

He opened the limo door and looked around the disused industrial estate. The downed "agents" were getting to their feet, rubbing their chests where their bulletproof vests had taken the impact of the snipers' "simunition" rounds.

'Drill your men again,' Malik ordered. 'This ambush has *only* a sixty-second window of opportunity. I intend to seize it.'

HOSTAGE
CHAPTER 39

Connor collapsed on his bed in the White House guest room. His head aching, he closed his eyes for a moment, while he waited for his laptop to boot up. Maybe it was jet lag or the strain of his first day on protection detail, or a combination of both, but he felt utterly drained. Colonel Black had insisted that Code Yellow became easier with practice. Connor seriously hoped that was the case, otherwise he'd likely burn out from exhaustion in the coming weeks.

He picked up his father's key fob from the bedside table. He'd overlaid the photo of himself with his father's, cut from the picture Colonel Black had given him. Squeezing the talisman in his hand, he wondered how his father could have done this job day in, day out. While the training had been tough, Connor had never expected actual close protection to be so demanding – and nothing had really happened apart from going to school. But there was always an underlying pressure that came with the responsibility of protecting someone. He may be the last ring in the Secret Service's defence, but if any attacker did get through *he* would be the one held accountable for Alicia's life ... or death. And that weighed heavily on his mind.

His laptop buzzed and the Buddyguard logo flashed on the screen. Unlocking the device with his fingerprint, he clicked the Answer button. Charley's smiling face appeared. She looked fresh and vibrant, despite the time being 1 a.m. in the UK.

'Catch you sleeping, did we?' she teased, seeing Connor rub the tiredness from his eyes.

'Almost,' he admitted, yawning.

'Don't worry, your body will adjust to the time zone in a couple of days. When I was on assignment, it took me at least a week to get used to the new routine. How's your Principal?'

'Fine,' replied Connor. 'Alicia obviously dislikes having the Secret Service everywhere, but there's no sign of that impulsive streak you mentioned.'

'Once she gets to know you, she may open up a bit more and show her true colours,' said Charley.

Marc leant into the camera's view.

'Is she as –' he raised his eyebrows meaningfully – 'as she looks in the photos?'

Connor couldn't help smiling at Marc's off-assignment question. If he was honest, he'd been concentrating so much on protecting his Principal that he hadn't considered that aspect since their first meeting. He couldn't deny Alicia was very pretty. And in different circumstances he may have paid her looks a lot more attention. But that sort of thinking could become a dangerous distraction. Colonel

Black had very clearly stated that a buddyguard's role was to protect. Any involvement beyond friendship was a line *never* to be crossed when on assignment. It could cloud one's judgement and potentially endanger the protectee. Nonetheless, Connor grinned and nodded in reply to Marc.

'Well, don't get too cosy,' said Charley sharply. 'You're there to do a job. And, judging by the increased chatter on the internet and our communications intercepts, your role is more vital than ever.'

'Has a threat been made?' asked Connor, sitting up.

'Not directly. But there are indications of a number of terrorist attacks being planned against the United States. Nothing concrete, but the CIA and Secret Service are certainly twitchy. You should ask Dirk Moran for an update.'

Connor gave a strained smile. 'I'll ask, but he's not exactly welcoming me with open arms.'

Charley nodded, immediately grasping the situation. 'This often happens at the start of an operation. There's always someone who doubts the capability of a buddyguard. You'll have to gain the director's trust. Until then, that's what we're here for. I'll ask Amir to email you an encrypted threat update.'

'Thanks,' said Connor. 'At least I'll know what to watch out for.'

'So, do you have anything to report?'

Connor shook his head. 'Not really. It was a normal school day – or as normal as it can be for a buddyguard! At first I suspected everyone from students to teachers. But that can't last, so I'm going to study the staff list tonight. The drop-off and pick-up by Secret Service is tight, as would be expected. Other than that, I learnt how to say "Where's the toilet?" in Chinese – *Cèsuǒ zài nǎli?*'

'*Hěn hǎo*,' complimented Charley, yet again surprising Connor with her hidden talents. 'Well, it's a good day when nothing happens. Let's hope it stays that way.'

HOSTAGE
CHAPTER 40

'Are you sure you want to join this class?' asked Alicia, raising a doubtful eyebrow at Connor. 'You don't have to do *everything* I do, you know. Most of the boys have opted to play baseball.'

'No, it's fine,' said Connor. 'I've always wanted to learn to dance properly.'

Connor hoped he sounded convincing. He'd never considered dance class before in his life, but he needed to stay close by Alicia to do his job. As they entered the school gymnasium, Connor discovered, to his dismay, he was one of only three boys in the entire class.

'Hey, over here!' called Grace, beckoning them to join her and Paige on a side bench. As they approached, Grace gave him an odd look. 'I wouldn't have thought this was your sort of thing, Connor.'

'You English boys are full of surprises,' giggled Paige, slipping on a pair of glittery dance shoes. 'Have you done salsa before?'

'No,' replied Connor, beginning to feel nervous at the

prospect. 'The closest I've ever got to salsa is some sauce with a bag of tortilla chips!'

Despite the weakness of his joke, the girls all laughed. But they stifled their amusement when an elegant elderly lady appeared and clapped her hands for their attention. Connor recognized the woman from the staff photo file as Miss Ashworth, a former professional ballroom dancer who had toured the world several times.

'Class, we'll continue with the Cuban-style salsa step from the previous lesson,' she announced, her tone clipped and precise. 'Alicia and Oliver, would you please demonstrate?'

Alicia joined a young blond boy in front of the theatre stage and Miss Ashworth pressed Play on a CD machine. A lively, percussion-filled, horn-heavy dance track filled the gym hall and Oliver led Alicia through a series of seemingly complex moves. Connor watched in growing awe as they danced energetically to the music. Alicia was a natural mover, her hips swaying, her arms flowing and her feet shimmying across the floor in a dazzling, twirling display. Her ability was matched only by her enthusiasm. She literally threw herself into the music and seemed to come alive under its influence.

Miss Ashworth paused the CD. 'Not bad,' she conceded. 'Just be careful where you put the break step. Now, everyone, find a partner.'

Having seen what was expected, Connor stayed sitting where he was.

'That includes you, young man,' said Miss Ashworth, noting his presence.

Connor smiled politely. 'I'll just watch for the time being, if that's OK.'

Miss Ashworth gave him a stern look. 'No, it's *not* OK. If you're in my class, you dance. No exceptions.'

Seeing Connor's trepidation, Alicia came over. 'Don't worry, I'll partner you.'

'It's *you* who should be worried. I don't have much experience at this,' he admitted, not wanting to embarrass Alicia – or himself.

'It's all right, I'll lead you,' she assured him.

'Well, on your feet be it!' he said, throwing caution to the wind.

They stood opposite one another in line with the other students. Alicia instructed him to take her right hand in his left and place his right hand on her upper back, while she put hers on his shoulder.

'Now look at me,' she said. 'It's important we stay in eye contact during the dance . . . and you need to come much closer.'

Connor stared at her, feeling slightly awkward at being *so* close to his Principal.

'Don't look so nervous,' she smiled. 'It's just a dance.'

To you it might be, thought Connor, wondering what Colonel Black would make of all this.

Miss Ashworth restarted the music and the Latin American track once more filled the hall. Alicia instinctively found the beat and began moving to the rhythm. Connor attempted to follow Alicia's fluid steps, but quickly ended up looking like a malfunctioning puppet.

Alicia laughed good-naturedly. 'No, like this,' she said above the music, gently guiding him through the sequence. 'You have to start on the third beat of the musical bar,' she explained, clicking her fingers to the track. 'One . . . two . . . now break forward with your left foot. Good! Rock back on your right. Step back left. Now shift your weight to that foot. Step back right. Rock forward on to your left. Step forward right. Then shift your weight on to your right foot – and repeat. It's that simple.'

'Simple!' exclaimed Connor, his mind whirling with the multiple directions as he stared down at his clumsy feet.

'No, look at *me*,' encouraged Alicia. 'Just let your body feel the music.'

Connor continued to shuffle round, willing his mind and feet to function as one. But he couldn't quite get the two to meet. He stepped on Alicia's toes and she cried out.

'Sorry,' he said, moving away. 'I think I must have two left feet.'

'No, you haven't,' chided Alicia kindly. 'You just need a bit more practice, that's all. Get the steps right, then everything else will follow.'

If only it was that easy, thought Connor, mentally repeating the moves over and over in his head.

As the other students whirled effortlessly round the gymnasium, Miss Ashworth noticed him struggling to master the steps and came over.

'Stay light on your feet,' she instructed.

Connor was struck by her words. Dan, his kickboxing instructor, had often drilled the same phrase into him during training in the ring. Connor decided to switch mindset. And as soon as he began to think of the salsa moves as a martial arts *kata* he quickly latched on to the combination and found the rhythm.

'That's more like it,' said Alicia, stepping along with him to the music's groove.

At last they began to *really* dance and Alicia's face lit up with delight. 'See, I told you. You're actually not that bad.'

Connor smiled at her praise and was beginning to get into the swing of things when his eye caught movement on the stage. The theatre drapes were twitching. As he spun round with Alicia, he tried to focus on the gap in the curtains. There appeared to be someone peeking through ... and Connor got the distinct feeling that he and Alicia were the ones being watched.

Suddenly Alicia switched direction in the dance. Distracted by the suspicious observer, Connor mistimed his step and his feet got mixed up with Alicia's. They both stumbled and went crashing to the floor, landing entangled in each other's arms. The whole class stopped and giggled in amusement. Miss Ashworth switched off the music.

'Are you two all right?' she asked.

'Yes,' wheezed Alicia, 'but only just!'

'I'm so sorry,' said Connor, quickly getting up and helping her to her feet. 'I hope I didn't hurt you.'

'No, not at all,' she replied, brushing herself down and

now laughing at their fall. 'But you should come with a health warning!'

'Young man, you need to concentrate more on what you're doing,' scolded Miss Ashworth, turning back to the CD player. 'Now, let's go from the top.'

As the music struck up again, Connor snatched a glance towards the stage. The curtains were now still. The mysterious watcher – if there ever was one – had gone.

HOSTAGE
CHAPTER 41

The first week at Montarose School flew by. Following further advice from Charley, Connor had begun performing "dynamic" risk assessments – changing his level of alertness depending upon the situation. In class, he could allow himself to relax more, knowing they were in a controlled environment, overseen by a vetted teacher. During breaks and lesson changes, when the situation was more unpredictable, he heightened his awareness – staying in Alicia's vicinity and scanning for potential threats. By doing this, he could better manage his concentration levels and wasn't so exhausted by the end of a day.

In the evenings, he was allowed some downtime, since the White House was deemed a safe zone. Each night, after an hour of fitness and martial arts training in the gym, Connor delivered status updates to Bodyguard HQ. He called in even when there was nothing new to report, simply enjoying the chat with Charley and the chance to truly be himself. Afterwards, he would check his emails, dutifully replying to his mother, who reassured him that all was well with her and Gran back in England.

By the end of the week, Connor had become accustomed to the routine and was actually enjoying his protective role. He liked Alicia and felt he was becoming her friend. There had been no real incidents, he'd made no apparent mistakes and he began to wonder if the assignment was going to be easier than he'd first thought. With all the Secret Service protection in place, so far the greatest threat to Alicia at school was dying from boredom in a history lesson.

Having survived the Friday morning period, Alicia and her friends headed over to the edge of the school playing field to sunbathe away the lunch break.

'You mean to say, you still haven't said yes!' gasped Paige.

'Ethan hasn't asked me properly . . . yet,' replied Alicia.

Connor sat behind them on a picnic bench, pretending to read a book. From behind his sunglasses, he kept one eye on the open playing fields, conscious Alicia was positioned in a highly exposed area.

'But we're only a week away from the prom,' reminded Paige.

'You should think yourself lucky,' said Grace. 'No one's asked me yet.'

'Or me,' admitted Kalila.

'Boys our age are always shy to come forward,' said Paige, pushing herself up on her elbows. 'Why is that, Connor?'

Connor glanced up from his book. 'Sorry?' he replied, pretending not to have heard.

'Boys are scared to ask girls out. Why?'

Connor thought about his own experiences. 'Probably because they think the girl will say "no".'

'He's got a point,' agreed Grace. 'There's only *one* boy I'd say yes to.'

'Who's that?' Paige asked eagerly.

'Oh come on, we all know she's got the hots for Darryl,' said Alicia.

'Is it *that* obvious?' cried Grace, mortified by the public declaration.

'I thought it was Jacob,' said Kalila.

'That was last month,' laughed Alicia, standing up and dusting the grass from her skirt as Paige began to interrogate Grace. 'Back in a minute. I need the restroom.'

'I'll join you,' said Kalila.

Connor stayed where he was. There were *some* places he couldn't follow Alicia and, as they were on the school campus, he considered the increase in risk was minimal. Still, as Alicia and Kalila strolled off together, he checked his watch and made a mental note of the time. Then he performed another subtle surveillance sweep of the playing field and surrounding buildings.

As the two girls entered the side entrance of the science block, Connor noticed a man emerge from behind a tree and head towards the glass doors. He was wearing a green uniform and a baseball cap, its peak pulled low to shade his eyes . . . or possibly to hide his face.

Connor subconsciously raised his alert level from Code Yellow to Code Orange.

'Who's that?' Connor asked, nodding in the man's direction.

Grace looked up from her phone and squinted. 'Umm . . . must be one of the groundsmen. Why?'

The man followed Alicia and Kalila through the doors.

'Just wondering,' Connor replied, alarm bells ringing inside his head. *What business did a groundsman have within the science building?*

He excused himself and headed over to the science block. Hurrying, but not quite running, he cursed himself for leaving such distance between himself and his Principal. When he reached the doors, he quietly slipped inside. The corridor leading to the girls' toilets was deserted, apart from the suspect man who was bent over near the toilet entrance.

With caution, he approached the man from behind. Connor wanted to get close enough to identify him, to find out whether he might be the same person as the one behind the kitchen door.

When Connor was a few feet away, the man looked up, startled, water dripping from his stubbled chin. His face was grimy, rough and lined by the sun. He had a large bent nose, as if it had once been broken in a fight, and a pair of hound-dog eyes that were ringed with dark shadows, indicating lack of sleep. *Was this the same face?* The eyes possessed a similar unsettling intensity. But Connor couldn't be certain. He did, however, vaguely recognize the man from the ground-staff roster.

'Sorry, I know I shouldn't be here, but I needed a drink,' the groundsman said in a thick accent. 'Please don't report me. I've been digging all morning and was very thirsty.'

Wiping his mouth with the back of his hand, he turned off the water fountain attached to the wall and quickly made his way out of the science block. Connor watched him go. He realized now that he'd probably overreacted to the man's behaviour, but told himself it was better to be safe than sorry.

'Hanging around the girls' toilets?' sneered Ethan, approaching from behind. 'Is that what English boys do for a hobby?'

Jimbo stood beside his friend, sniggering.

'Not every day,' replied Connor. 'Otherwise I'd always bump into you.'

Ethan scowled at the comeback. 'I've been watching you,' he declared, stabbing a finger at Connor. 'You follow Alicia around like some faithful puppy dog. Even attending her dance classes! What's going on between you two?'

'Nothing,' said Connor, now realizing who the mysterious watcher might have been. 'I'm just finding my feet, that's all.'

'Well, find them somewhere else.'

He pointed to a poster on the wall – a silhouette of a couple dancing against a glittery purple background that announced the forthcoming Summer Prom.

'*I'm* taking the President's daughter,' he stated, puffing out his chest, 'and I don't want any dork getting in the way and spoiling my chances. Understand?'

Connor shrugged off the insult. Ethan might be the school's sports star, but, considering how arrogant he was, he didn't deserve to be Alicia's date.

'I said, do you understand?' repeated Ethan, taking a step closer. 'Or do I have to get Jimbo here to beat it into you?'

Connor suddenly found himself boxed in on both sides. The two lads towered over him, the situation rapidly escalating towards a fight.

'Listen, I don't want any trouble,' said Connor, holding up his hands in peace.

'Who said anything about trouble,' sneered Ethan as Jimbo closed in.

Deciding it was time for a touch of Pain Assisted Learning, Connor targeted the middle of the boy's chest with his fingertips.

'Oww!' cried Jimbo, stopping his advance.

Ethan glared at his friend. 'What's the problem? You're an offensive guard in the football team. Steamroller him!'

Almost half his size, Connor judged the massive American football player would flatten him if he didn't put in first strike. Snaking his arm with a hefty flick, Connor one-inch-pushed Jimbo in the chest. It was like trying to shove an elephant, but the self-defence technique was still powerful enough to send the boy staggering backwards. Jimbo struck the wall behind and crumpled against it, gasping for breath.

'What on *earth* did you do?' exclaimed Ethan, stunned by the ease with which Connor had downed his friend.

'I only pushed him,' declared Connor innocently.

Ethan wound up to let loose a punch. Connor dropped into a fighting guard.

'Hey! What's going on?'

Ethan stopped mid-swing as Alicia and Kalila emerged from the restroom. His scowl transformed into a beaming smile and his punching arm wrapped round Connor in a friendly hug.

'Just ... err ... explaining to my friend here how to throw long in football as a quarterback,' he replied.

Alicia gave them both a doubtful look. 'What's the matter with Jimbo?'

'I think ... he's suffering an asthma attack,' replied Connor breezily.

'Well, aren't you going to help him up?' asked Kalila with concern.

'Of course,' said Ethan. He patted Connor on the shoulder, rather too heartily. 'Now bear in mind my advice for the prom and you should have a great night,' he said, before walking off with Jimbo in tow, the boy wheezing like a steam engine.

Connor doubted that very much. Having made enemies of them both, the prom was going to be a nightmare. He'd already anticipated there'd be a tricky balance securing Alicia's safety while allowing her the freedom to enjoy herself. Now somehow he'd have to find a way to protect Alicia ... without getting himself into a fight.

HOSTAGE
CHAPTER 42

'This is the spot, on August twenty-eighth, 1963, where Dr Martin Luther King Jr, the black civil rights leader, delivered his famous "I Have a Dream" speech,' the tour guide explained to the group gathered on the steps of the Lincoln Memorial. Behind them stood the awe-inspiring monument itself, a white-marble cenotaph with towering Greek columns built in honour of America's 16th President. 'The political march that day and Dr King's speech helped facilitate the landmark Civil Rights Act of 1964, which outlawed discrimination throughout America.'

Connor, Alicia and Kalila sat on the steps nearby, listening to the tour guide's talk.

Kalila leant close to Alicia. 'I bet Dr King never dreamt that less than fifty years later there'd have been an African American president.'

'Or a Latino one,' replied Alicia, smiling at her friend. 'America's truly the Land of the Free. *Anyone* can be President – even my father!'

'Over a quarter of a million people attended the event,' continued the tour guide. 'With crowds stretching down the mall as far as the eye could see, thus making it, at that time, the largest gathering of protesters in Washington DC's illustrious history.'

'Talk about one massive rock concert!' Connor remarked as he gazed east across the impressive treelined expanse of the National Mall and tried to imagine such a number. There were no protests today, just flocks of tourists enjoying the sunshine beside the Reflecting Pool. In the distance, the Washington Monument speared the sky like a giant rocket ready to take off. The huge marble obelisk, the symbol of America's capital, shimmered in the pool's sky-blue waters and gave the illusion that the monument was twice its normal height.

'Wonderful, isn't it?' remarked Alicia.

Connor nodded in agreement, although in his mind he was actually thinking this was the *worst* possible place to be on a Saturday morning. Not because the view wasn't stunning but because Alicia was so vulnerable on the open steps. She was literally a sitting target. There was no cover if some madman took a potshot at her. No place to hide if she was attacked. Hundreds of tourists milled around and *any* one of them could be carrying a knife or a gun.

Connor almost wished he'd never done his bodyguard training. It would be far easier to sit there in blissful ignorance of the countless hidden dangers surrounding them. At least then he could relax. But his assignment meant that he had to remain on constant alert, his nerves wound tight as a guitar string. Connor looked across at a slim blonde-haired woman wearing sunglasses and carrying a pocket tourist guide. She too seemed to be enjoying the view. But every so often she'd glance in their direction.

But Connor wasn't alarmed. He recognized her as Agent Brooke, one of several women on Alicia's PES team. Other agents, including Kyle, were dotted around the Lincoln Memorial steps and along the edge of the Reflecting Pool, all within sight line of the President's daughter and each keeping a low profile so as not to draw attention to her presence. But Connor knew the strain the agents must be under because he was feeling it too – the unpredictability of the situation, the uncertainty of the environment, the constantly changing dynamics of the crowd. No wonder the Secret Service had a hard time walking the thin line between the need for protection and the need for their Principal's privacy.

'Let me take a picture of you,' Alicia suggested to Connor. 'This is *the* tourist spot.'

'Why don't I take it?' offered Kalila. 'Then you can both be in the photo.'

'Good idea,' said Alicia, jumping to her feet and waving Connor over.

Connor grinned. It would be pretty cool to have a photo of him with the President's daughter. At the very least, it would make Amir and Marc envious! Unlocking his mobile's screen and clicking the camera app, he handed his phone to Kalila. Then he and Alicia posed on the steps of the Lincoln Memorial like every other tourist.

'Get closer, you two,' said Kalila, lining up the shot.

As she took several photos from different angles, Connor

began to notice a low buzz of excitement among the tour group. He glanced over and saw that several people were no longer listening to the guide. Instead they were staring in their direction. Or, to be more accurate, in Alicia's direction.

'Is it really *her*?' a large lady whispered to her equally bulbous husband.

'Looks like the President's daughter to me,' he replied, holding up an image on his phone's web browser and comparing it with the dark-haired girl on the steps.

An Italian man, overhearing their conversation, plucked up the courage to take a sneaky photo of Alicia, while poorly feigning a shot of the Reflecting Pool behind. Connor instinctively began to shield Alicia from their attention.

'Shall we go?' suggested Connor as a Japanese man now joined in, targeting his lens on the President's daughter's face with zero subtlety.

'What's the hurry?' Alicia replied, still looking towards Kalila and oblivious to the rapidly growing interest. 'You haven't seen Lincoln's statue yet.'

'I can come back another day.'

By now the tour group had all turned towards the President's daughter and were drawing nearer for a better shot. A tall man in a baseball cap and sunglasses was at Alicia's side in an instant.

'It's time to move on,' said Kyle, his statement not quite an order, but leaving no room for argument either.

Alicia now saw the reason and smiled apologetically at the tour group. 'Sorry, I've got to go!'

As word spread and the crowd began to thicken, Secret Service agents seemed to materialize out of nowhere. They drew into a 'closed box' formation, creating a fluid cordon of protection round Alicia. Connor was by her side as the agents swiftly escorted her and Kalila down the steps and along the paved avenue towards the waiting limo. By the time they reached the car, the steps of the Lincoln Memorial were swarming with tourists, all attempting to catch a final glimpse of the President's daughter.

HOSTAGE
CHAPTER 43

Secure within the confines of the limo, Alicia sat fuming on the back seat.

'Are you OK?' Kalila asked as the car and its escort vehicle pulled away from the gathered crowd.

Alicia didn't reply for a moment. She just stared through the darkened window at the passing traffic.

Then through clenched teeth, she said, 'The Secret Service drive me up the wall! I mean, those people were *only* taking photos.'

'I'm sure Kyle had a good reason for asking us to leave,' defended Connor, glancing at the agent who sat on the other side of the glass privacy screen in the front passenger seat. He knew the Secret Service were used to dealing with crowds, so Kyle must have been alerted to another potential threat. In fact, he was *certain* something more than just a mob of tourists had spooked the agent.

'But I have to put up with this *all* the time!' Alicia cried, her frustration turning to anger. 'At the slightest sign of . . . something . . . I don't know what . . . I'm whisked away. Usually, just as I'm starting to relax or – God forbid – enjoy myself. But how can I, when agents are *always* around me, dictating my movements, controlling my social life? Ironic, isn't it, Connor? I'm the First Daughter in the Land of the Free but I'm really a prisoner!'

'The Secret Service are there for your protection,' reminded Connor.

Alicia gave a weary sigh. 'I know that, but why do they have to be so paranoid?'

'I suppose it's their job to be. So you – and your parents – don't have to worry about your safety.'

'But they're robbing me of any life!'

'Isn't that a little extreme?' Kalila said gently.

Alicia shook her head furiously. 'Not at all! Can you imagine spending every waking moment under surveillance? Seven days a week, twenty-four hours a day. I can't just walk out of the door, meet up with my friends and go shopping. Everything has to be planned in advance. And forget about having a *boyfriend*. If I stay out later than my father approves, he orders the Secret Service to bring me home! And you try saying goodnight to a boyfriend at the door of the White House with the glare of floodlights and a Secret Service agent by your side. There's not much you can do except shake hands. And what sort of basis is that for a relationship? In fact, I'm amazed my father even let Connor stay in the White House!'

Connor offered Alicia an awkward smile, hoping she wouldn't press the matter any further. He'd worked hard not to expose his role as her personal buddyguard. But he needn't have worried; Alicia was too upset to read anything more into the situation. Her eyes began to glaze over with tears and Kalila put a comforting arm round her friend.

'You think that's bad, then you clearly haven't met my brothers,' she said, her voice gently soothing. 'They're as overly protective as your Secret Service – and I have to put up with them for life!'

Alicia attempted a smile. 'Sorry,' she mumbled. 'I didn't mean to get angry with you.'

'I know,' said Kalila, finding her a tissue from the seat's side pocket.

'It's just . . . so unbearable. Last month I wasn't allowed to leave the White House for a whole week due to some threat or other that came to nothing. And I missed out on Grace's sleepover.'

'She understood. We all did.'

Alicia took a deep breath. 'But I feel I'm *always* missing out.'

'Then try not to let it ruin the rest of this weekend,' said Kalila. 'You've been given permission to be Connor's tour guide and there's still loads more of Washington to explore – the Capitol Building, the Washington Monument, the Air and Space Museum.'

Alicia nodded and dried up her tears. 'Sorry, Connor. You must think I'm a spoilt princess.'

'Of course not,' he replied genuinely, having witnessed firsthand her claustrophobic life. 'It must be tough having no privacy. But, at the same time, I can understand why you need Secret Service protection.'

'But that doesn't make their presence any easier,' she

said, glancing bitterly towards Kyle, then gazing out of the window at the pedestrians wandering freely about their business. 'Sometimes I wish I could be someone else for a day – just disappear.'

HOSTAGE
CHAPTER 44

Connor stopped browsing the National Air and Space Museum's gift shop, suddenly aware Alicia was no longer with him. 'Where's Alicia gone?' he asked Kalila.

'She said she'll be back in a minute,' replied Kalila, inspecting a soft toy monkey in a blue astronaut suit from the souvenir rack. 'I can't believe NASA used monkeys to test the biological effects of space travel! That's so cruel.'

Connor's eyes swept the gift shop as he absently picked up a cuddly bear in a white satin space suit and helmet. 'Looks like they sent bears up too!' he joked, finally locating Alicia in the checkout queue. He also spotted Kyle near the exit of the gift shop, pretending to be a father simply waiting for his family. Agent Brooke was posted at the entrance, another agent at a door marked PRIVATE, while a fourth browsed the vast array of souvenirs like a typical tourist. With all exits covered, there was no way Alicia could just 'disappear'.

'Found anything else for your family?' asked Alicia, returning with a small foil bag in her hand.

Connor shook his head. He'd already bought a silk scarf

for his gran and a Navajo feather bracelet for his mum from the American Indian museum. But with his assignment open-ended he had no idea when he'd be able to give them the gifts personally.

Alicia handed him the bag. 'I thought you might like to try this.'

'Thanks,' said Connor, examining the packaging. There was a picture of NASA's space shuttle taking off, with the words *Mission Pack: Freeze-dried Ice Cream*. He looked at Alicia. 'Are you serious?'

Alicia offered a wry smile. 'Supposedly, the early *Apollo* astronauts ate it for a snack.'

Ripping open the foil, he pulled out a multicoloured block of Neapolitan 'ice cream' that was bone dry and as light as Styrofoam. With trepidation, he bit off a chunk.

'Not bad. Tastes like ... solid candyfloss,' he said through a mouthful of the crumbling dehydrated dessert.

Since the incident at the Lincoln Memorial, Alicia and Kalila had taken him on a whistle-stop tour of the best sights along the National Mall. At the Museum of American History, he'd been shown the tattered red, white and blue flag that had inspired the US national anthem, 'The Star-Spangled Banner'. In the Museum of Natural History, he'd stood at the foot of a sixty-five-million-year-old Triceratops nicknamed 'Hatcher' and gazed upon the 45-carat Hope Diamond once owned by Marie Antoinette – the jewel having even more security than Alicia. Then, passing via the Museum of the American Indian, the three of them had finally ended up at the Air and Space Museum with its displays of spy planes, sound-barrier-breaking fighters and historic spaceships. To top it off, he'd had his photo taken in front of all the key landmarks, including the Washington Monument, the Capitol Building and even, for a joke, the White House.

Connor had been the ultimate tourist, while Alicia had tried her best to be his enthusiastic host. But the shadow cast by her ever-present Secret Service had dampened her spirits. Although she willingly joined him in the photos, her smile no longer quite reached her eyes.

'How about we go shopping?' suggested Kalila.

Although shopping wasn't high on Connor's list of favourite activities, the suggestion seemed to perk Alicia up.

'I suppose that's one benefit of the Secret Service,' she said, managing a smile. 'We've always a taxi to hand.'

Leaving the Air and Space Museum, they jumped into the limo.

'Take us to Dupont Circle,' said Alicia.

The driver nodded and headed northwest up Pennsylvania Avenue.

'But I thought you preferred the fashion stores in Georgetown?' said Kalila.

'I do, but I've heard there's a fantastic new boutique opened up just off Connecticut Avenue,' Alicia explained, and both girls began to get quite excited at the prospect.

Connor noticed Kyle talking rapidly into his wrist mic, no doubt instructing his advance team to scope out the intended clothes store before their arrival.

The SAP team didn't get long to do their sweep. The car journey only took ten minutes.

As the three of them entered the boutique, Connor recognized the watchful face of a Secret Service agent loitering near the entrance. As soon as Kyle's team had deployed themselves, he made a subtle exit with the rest of the SAP agents.

The store itself was a top-end boutique with wall-to-wall fashion from Europe, as well as unique garments from New York, LA and San Francisco. Alicia seemed to be in her element as she browsed the racks of designer clothes.

'What do you think of this?' asked Alicia, pulling out a sheer gold dress.

'It's gorgeous,' gasped Kalila. 'Are you thinking for the prom?'

Alicia nodded. 'For you.'

'No,' she protested. 'I couldn't get away with wearing that. Besides, I wouldn't be allowed to. It's far too short. But you could –' Kalila's phone beeped. She looked at the message and sighed. Texting a reply, she explained, 'Sorry, I have to go home.'

Alicia tried to hide her disappointment. 'Do you want us to drop you off?'

'Thanks, but my brother's picking me up.' Her phone beeped again. 'Wow, he's parked just round the corner. I told you they're my own Secret Service!'

Alicia laughed and the two girls hugged each other goodbye.

'See you on Monday, Connor,' said Kalila.

Connor waved farewell as she hurried out of the store.

'Well, it looks like *you'll* have to be my clothes judge,' declared Alicia, selecting a couple more glamorous dresses from the rail. 'I'll just try these on, then we'll grab a bite to eat.'

Connor watched Alicia make her way to the changing rooms and smiled to himself in bemused amazement. Never would he have imagined that one day he'd be shopping with the President's daughter, let alone giving advice on what she should wear.

'How's it going?' asked Kyle, appearing at Connor's shoulder.

'Fine,' replied Connor. 'But I think you're doing all the work.'

Kyle shook his head. 'There hasn't been one moment when you weren't aware of your surroundings. Seems to me, you're a natural at this game.'

Connor smiled at the compliment – the first he'd received from Secret Service. 'What happened back at the Lincoln Memorial?'

'One of the team pinged a man on our threat list. Rather than cause a scene or alarm Alicia, I decided to simply avoid contact.'

Alicia popped her head out of the changing-room cubicle and waved Connor over.

'Good luck!' Kyle remarked as he wandered off, to all intents and purposes appearing the bored husband waiting for his wife, rather than a Secret Service agent protecting the President's daughter.

Connor headed over to Alicia and stood beside her cubicle.

'Fancy joining me on a little adventure?' whispered Alicia, a mischievous grin on her face.

'What do you mean?' asked Connor.

Alicia glanced towards an emergency exit at the back of the store.

Immediately grasping her intentions, Connor replied, 'I *don't* think that's a good idea.'

'Oh, don't be such a killjoy! Even a soldier's son must have broken the rules.'

'Your father wouldn't be happy.'

'I don't *care* what he thinks,' she shot back. 'Besides, what's the worst that could happen? I get recognized and asked for an autograph or photo.'

Connor could imagine a whole host of other possibilities and none of them good.

'Anyway, if there's real danger, I've a panic alarm in my bag,' Alicia insisted.

'I still think it's too risky,' said Connor.

Alicia scowled. 'Fine. Then don't come with me. I just thought it would be a bit of fun.'

She beckoned the shop assistant over. 'I think that lady over there might be a shoplifter,' she whispered, pointing to a blonde-haired woman browsing a nearby rack. 'I'm sure I saw her put something in her bag.'

'Thank you, I'll call security,' replied the assistant, taking Alicia at her word.

Connor looked over his shoulder at the shoplifter, only

to discover the accused was Agent Brooke. A few moments later, a burly security guard approached her and asked to inspect her bag. While the agent was distracted, Alicia made a bolt for the emergency exit.

Connor realized he had to alert Kyle. It was his duty. But, if he did, Alicia would know and she'd no longer confide in him as a friend. He'd lose that essential connection that enabled him to be an effective and covert buddyguard.

Caught between a rock and a hard place, Connor had no choice but to follow her.

HOSTAGE
CHAPTER 45

Bursting out of the back door into an alley, Alicia was off like a shot. Connor was on her tail, but he was left for dust as she sprinted past some dump bins and disappeared round a corner.

'Wait!' cried Connor, realizing now why Alicia was the captain of her school team.

He pursued her down a deserted side street. But Alicia was still pulling away.

'Keep up!' she called, giggling at the thrill of her escape.

Glad of all his fitness training, Connor put on a burst of speed. His trainers pounded the tarmac as he followed her left on to the main road. Then lost her . . .

The sidewalk was thronged with shoppers and there was no sign of Alicia. Connor threw his hands up in despair. He was her sole bodyguard now and he'd already lost track of her within the first minute. Just as he was about to shout her name, a hand grabbed him from behind and pulled him into a shop doorway.

'Careful, they might spot you!' Alicia whispered, her eyes full of rebellious delight.

Connor realized Charley had been right. Only now was Alicia showing her true colours. And the President's daughter had never looked happier. Like a bird freed from its cage, she was all aflutter with excitement.

Alicia snatched a quick peek up and down the street.

'Not a Secret Service agent in sight!' she laughed.

And she thinks that's good news, thought Connor. The real pressure of protection was now on his shoulders – and his alone.

Oblivious to Connor's worries, Alicia opened up her bag and pulled out a short platinum-blonde wig and a large pair of dark sunglasses. Pinning up her hair, she popped on the wig, then slipped on the Jackie Onassis-style glasses. In an instant she was transformed from President's daughter to . . . anybody.

'How do I look?' Alicia asked.

'You planned this!' Connor exclaimed.

'Yes,' she admitted with a half-guilty smile. 'President Johnson's daughter used to wear a disguise to dodge the media. I thought I could do the same to escape the Secret Service.'

Connor was astonished at the lengths Alicia was willing to go to for some personal space.

'Come on, let's go,' said Alicia, joining the stream of pedestrians.

'Where to?' asked Connor.

'U Street. It has some hip places to shop and eat.'

Connor stayed close by Alicia's side. If anything did happen, he wanted to be within arm's reach and able to react fast. From behind his mirrored sunglasses, he scanned their surroundings just as Bugsy his surveillance instructor had taught him. His eyes flicked between the faces of approaching people, making snap decisions on their intentions. He watched the passing traffic for any suspicious vehicles, while noting any nearby alleyways in case someone was concealed there. In the highest state of Code Yellow, he had to be alert to *anything* that could materialize into a threat. The good thing was that Alicia was no longer identifiable as the President's daughter. That reduced the risks, but didn't eliminate them entirely. Every city had its fair share of crime, violence and accidents – and Washington DC was no exception.

Alicia's mobile phone rang. She glanced at the screen, tutted, then turned it off.

A second later, Connor's phone buzzed with equal urgency. Pulling it from his jeans pocket, he saw CALLER ID WITHHELD but knew exactly who it would be – Kyle. As his thumb hovered over the Answer button, Alicia snatched the phone from his grasp.

'Give that back!' said Connor.

'Later,' she said, offering him a playful wink.

Connor made a grab for the phone, but she danced away. 'I should at least reply, so they know we're OK.'

'What are you so worried about? Let them sweat a bit.'

Alicia switched off his phone before dropping it in her bag. Then she trotted off down the street.

Connor sighed in frustration. He didn't wish to make a scene. That could draw unwanted attention to the

President's daughter, so he resigned himself to letting her have her own way – for the time being.

Quickening his pace, he caught up with Alicia. Every so often he glanced behind, checking for trouble but also secretly hoping to spot an agent in pursuit.

'Relax,' insisted Alicia, taking his arm. 'Just let me enjoy myself for once. I'm the one who'll get into trouble later.'

That's what you think, mused Connor. Then it dawned on him that this was exactly what he'd been hired for. To protect Alicia in moments when the Secret Service couldn't. Colonel Black had specifically instructed him 'to stick to her like glue'. He wasn't supposed to stop Alicia living her life – just protect her.

With that thought in mind, he allowed himself to relax a little. But he kept his awareness at Code Yellow.

They turned off the main street and headed north on 13th. Upmarket apartments gave way to rundown rowhouse blocks, which alternated randomly with fancy condos recently built as part of the city's redevelopment effort. The strange blend of new and old, rich and poor made Connor uneasy. The mix of people walking the streets became more diverse and unpredictable. There was a palpable tension in the air, magnified by the summer's heat radiating off the sidewalk.

'Are you certain this area's safe?' Connor asked.

'Of course,' replied Alicia, casually strolling along. 'During the day, definitely.'

That statement didn't reassure Connor. Although he could handle himself in a situation, there were places in the

East End of London that he wouldn't wander into – day or night. And this area possessed a similar undercurrent of menace.

HOSTAGE

CHAPTER 46

The mobile phone emitted a short buzz and Bahir snatched it up from the table in the front room. He waited an impatient second for the message to decrypt. Then his eyes widened in astonishment.

'You won't believe this, Malik,' he said, holding up the phone to his leader. 'Eagle Chick has flown the nest!'

Malik stopped sharpening his *jambiya* and smirked to himself. 'It's almost as if she *wants* to be taken hostage.'

The phone buzzed again and Bahir read the message out loud. 'It's from Hazim – *Sparrows in a panic*. It appears Secret Service are having trouble locating her!' he laughed. Bahir turned excitedly to his leader. '*This* could be our chance.'

Malik laid the curved dagger in his lap. His right hand trembled slightly and he reached out to a small bundle of khat. As he chewed the intoxicating leaves, he mulled over the new turn of events.

'Yes, it's an opening,' he agreed. 'But an unplanned one. Not all the preparations are in place.'

'But this seems too good an opportunity to miss,' insisted Bahir.

'The situation isn't in my *direct* control,' pointed out Malik. 'And we've the added complication that Secret Service are *actively* looking for her at this time. That greatly reduces our chances of an undetected escape.'

'True, but if we took her now, alone, we wouldn't risk our lives in a gun battle.'

Malik pondered this. 'Do either Gamekeeper or Birdspotter have the target in sight?'

Bahir rapidly typed a message and pressed Send. Almost a minute passed before his mobile vibrated twice in response. He read both messages, then grimaced in disappointment. 'Not yet, but Gamekeeper is on the hunt.'

Malik rested the tip of his knife on his bearded chin, reconsidering his options. Then a sly grin slid across his face, revealing his arc of yellowing teeth. 'Bahir, I have an idea.'

He explained his plan, then asked, 'Is such a thing possible?'

'Yes,' replied Bahir. 'I could do it in my sleep!'

'Then get to it,' ordered Malik.

As Bahir hurried out of the room, Malik returned to honing his *jambiya*, the curved steel blade gleaming razor-sharp.

HOSTAGE
CHAPTER 47

With every step, Connor was becoming more and more anxious. He was about to suggest that they turn back, when Alicia swung right on to U Street and the neighbourhood suddenly improved. Ethnic restaurants, bars, music clubs and the occasional church lined the busy road. Connor was reassured to spot several groups of tourists wandering the route too, but he didn't allow his alert level to drop.

Alicia stopped outside a red and white building with a neon sign flashing OPEN in the window. Above the door, a billboard proclaimed: DON'S DOGS – THE BEST CHILLI DOGS IN DC.

Connor noticed Alicia was staring intently at the flashing sign as if mesmerized.

'Are you all right?' he asked, recalling her history of epilepsy from his Buddyguard briefing.

Alicia blinked and refocused her gaze on Connor. 'Yes, of course. Why?'

'I thought . . . you might be about to have a seizure,' he replied, indicating the flashing light.

'How do *you* know about my epilepsy?' demanded Alicia, suddenly defensive.

Connor realized he'd made a mistake. 'Erm ... your father mentioned it.'

Alicia scowled at this. 'I'm *over* that now. I wish he'd stop bringing it up.'

'Sorry,' said Connor. 'He's probably just concerned, that's all.'

'My father's always worrying about me,' sighed Alicia. 'Anyway, this is the place I was looking for. Supposedly, their hot dogs are seriously *hot*.'

Connor peered in through the smeared window. A white formica counter stretched the short length of the fast-food joint. On the wall behind, a menu displayed its combo meals and specialities in unappealing backlit photos. Red plastic stools stood in contrast to the off-white tiled floor, some of the seats clearly straining under the weight of their well-fed customers. Opposite the counter were four booths, with only one occupied by two large men in cement-stained construction clothes.

The food had better be good to make up for the decor, thought Connor.

Holding the door open for Alicia, a waft of fried meat and cooking fat assaulted Connor's nostrils. Behind the counter and through a hatch, a sweaty, African American cook served up piles of cheese fries and massive hot dogs slathered in mustard, chilli sauce and onions. He gave a nod in their direction, indicating with a grunt for them to take a booth. Slipping into the second one along, Connor made sure that he sat facing the entrance. As dictated by his training, he wanted to know exactly who was coming and going.

While Alicia studied the menu – which unsurprisingly consisted of various combinations of hot dog – he took the opportunity to check out the restaurant. It was crucial to locate any exit points in case of trouble. Looking over his shoulder, he spotted a door leading to a communal toilet, which he guessed would likely be a dead end. Through a hatch behind the counter, he saw a red emergency exit sign pointing to the back of the kitchen. If anything did happen, Connor decided that would be the route he'd take with Alicia.

'What are you going to have?' asked Alicia as the waitress came over.

'Umm . . . whatever you're having,' he replied, not even looking at the menu.

'Two chilli dog specials with large Cokes,' said Alicia.

With a tired smile, the waitress took their order, then went back to the hatch and handed it to the chef.

Connor glanced along the counter. An old man in a brown polo shirt sat eating a hot dog. Next to him a young African American in ripped jeans and a white T-shirt was picking at a tray of fries. As he dipped several in the ketchup, he casually eyed Alicia's Prada handbag lying on their table. Connor realized that, although Alicia might be able to disguise who she was, she couldn't disguise her wealth or social status. It was obvious they didn't belong in this establishment.

Leaning forward, Connor whispered to Alicia, 'I'd keep your bag beside you.'

She took his advice without protest. And Connor relaxed a little when the young man directed his attention back to his food. The waitress returned and dumped two hot dogs drowning in mustard and chilli, along with a pile of cheese fries and two bucket-sized Cokes. Connor was slightly taken aback at the size of the hot dog – it was well over a foot long.

'Enjoy!' said the waitress, almost as if it was a command rather than a wish.

The two of them tucked in. After just one bite, Connor had to admit that it was the best hot dog he'd ever tasted . . . then the roof of his mouth was almost blown off by the heat of the chilli.

Alicia laughed as she saw tears streaming down his face. 'I warned you they were hot!'

Spluttering, Connor grabbed his Coke and chugged down several mouthfuls.

Once he'd recovered enough to speak again, Alicia began to quiz him on his life back in England – where he lived, which school he went to, his parents, which countries he'd been to, whether he'd met the Queen and so forth. Connor gave his answers as truthfully as possible without revealing his double role. He didn't like deceiving Alicia, it wasn't in his nature, but he understood why it was necessary.

Finishing off their meal, they both leant back in the booth and gave a contented sigh.

'That was an awesome hot dog!' said Connor. 'Even with the chilli.'

Alicia nodded in agreement and wiped her lips with a paper serviette. 'And do you know what's even better?'

Connor shrugged.

Alicia lowered her voice. 'This is the first meal I've had outside the White House with no one looking over my shoulder.'

At that moment, the door opened and two Latino youths entered. Dressed in baggy jeans and white sneakers, with tattoos up their arms and red bandanas around their heads, they appeared to be local gang members. One of them, boasting a gold front tooth, stared hard in Connor's direction. Connor immediately averted his gaze. He didn't want to antagonize them in any way. But as they took two stools at the counter Connor kept them in his line of sight. The other gang member, sporting a crew cut, eyed up Alicia with an appreciative sneer before turning to place his order.

Troubled by their presence, Connor suggested to Alicia, 'Let's make a move.'

'You mean go back?'

'It might be a good idea. Kyle and the others must be going crazy by now.'

Alicia groaned. 'Not yet. I'm enjoying myself too much. Let's go up to Meridian Hill Park. It has a great view of DC and every weekend there's a drumming circle.'

She waved to the waitress for the bill. Connor reached for his wallet.

'No, I'll pay,' Alicia insisted, pulling a Platinum American Express card from her purse.

The waitress raised an eyebrow in surprise. 'No cards,' she said, thumbing towards a scrappy sign above the till stating CASH ONLY.

Alicia sifted through her purse and pulled out a 100-dollar bill.

'Don't you have anything *smaller*?' asked the waitress.

Alicia shook her head. 'Sorry.'

With poorly concealed irritation, the waitress took the money. While they waited for their change, the two youths at the counter sipped on their Cokes but didn't order any food. Connor's sense of unease grew.

The waitress returned and managed her first genuine smile when Alicia left a hefty tip.

'Come back soon,' she called.

Unlikely, thought Connor as they stepped on to U Street.

Turning right, Alicia headed north again on 13th. But they'd only gone one block when Connor had the distinct feeling they were being followed. Pretending to watch a car pass by, his eyes swept the road and sidewalk. Among the scattering of pedestrians, he instantly recognized the Latino youth with the gold tooth walking several paces behind, nonchalantly slurping on his Coke. Connor told himself it could be pure coincidence. The lad probably lived nearby. But, to leave no doubt, Connor decided to employ some anti-surveillance techniques.

'Let's cross the road,' he suggested to Alicia. 'Stay out of the sun.'

'Sure,' said Alicia.

At the next junction, they switched to the other side. Connor snatched a look over his shoulder.

Gold Tooth had crossed the road too. Connor felt his heart rate increase. 'Mirroring' was one of the key signs. But this could still be an innocent matter of circumstance.

'Hold on, Alicia, my shoelace has come undone,' said Connor, bending down.

As he pretended to retie his lace, he glanced behind. Gold Tooth had also stopped, appearing suspicious as he hung around a parked car. But then he finished his Coke and dumped it in a trash can.

'Not far now,' said Alicia, oblivious to their tail. 'It's left here. Then just two blocks down on the right.'

They stopped at a crosswalk on the junction of 13th and W Streets. For Connor, this was the moment of truth. If Gold Tooth followed them towards the park, he knew they were in serious trouble.

HOSTAGE
CHAPTER 48

The seconds counted down with excruciating slowness as Connor waited with Alicia for the pedestrian signal to turn green. A few metres behind, Gold Tooth loitered on the corner, yabbering into his mobile phone. Connor's alert level had rocketed to Code Orange and he was ready to react at the slightest threatening move from the gangster.

The signal turned from red to green and Connor followed Alicia across the road, ensuring he was between her and Gold Tooth at all times. On the far side they bore left and made for the park. There were no pedestrians on the sidewalk ahead, so Connor risked a glance back. Gold Tooth still had his ear clamped to the mobile phone and was walking on past the junction.

'Have you listened to anything I just said?' asked Alicia.

'Sorry,' said Connor, allowing his awareness to return to Code Yellow.

'The Meridian Hill Park is nicknamed "Malcolm X Park". It has a thirteen-step waterfall –'

Alicia came to a sudden halt as a youth stepped out from behind a van and blocked their path. Connor cursed himself for letting his guard down. He'd been so focused on Gold Tooth, he'd forgotten about the other gang member with the crew cut. The lad was a good foot taller than Connor and his arms not only boasted tattoos, but vicious scars from numerous knife fights.

In the second that followed, Connor instinctively applied the A-C-E procedure from his training.

Assess the threat: gang member, high probability of carrying a knife or gun, one hundred per cent certainty of an attack.

Counter the danger: priority one – provide body cover for the Principal, then . . .

Escape the kill zone: evacuation options (A) fight way through the threat but risk injury; (B) turn round and retreat but danger of exposing back to knife or gun attack; (C) take side street to next busy road and find safety in numbers.

Grabbing Alicia by the shoulder, Connor took option C and pulled her towards the side street.

'RUN!' he shouted, keeping himself between her and the gangster.

Alicia was too stunned to do anything but obey. Yet no sooner had they begun to flee when Gold Tooth jumped out from a nearby alley and cut off their escape route.

'Where *you* going so fast!' he said, grinning to reveal his gleaming tooth.

Connor spun to take Alicia back the way they'd come. But Crew Cut was bearing down on them from behind.

'Yo, girl, give us the bag,' Gold Tooth demanded.

Connor looked around. There were no other people in

sight to call for help, the two gang members having picked their mugging spot carefully. Panicking, Alicia became frozen to the spot and Connor recognized the symptoms of 'brain fade'. He, on the other hand, was already pumped with adrenalin and able to think straight.

'Do as he says,' urged Connor, hoping that would put an end to their predicament. It was far better to lose a fancy bag than an invaluable life.

Alicia moved as if to comply, but as she unshouldered the bag she dived her hand in. Gold Tooth grabbed the Prada bag and wrenched it from her grip.

'No tricks, girl,' he spat. 'You ain't using no mace spray on me. That'll cost you your necklace.'

'No,' Alicia protested, her hand going protectively to the silver chain. 'It was my grandmother's.'

'Well, it's mine now.'

Gold Tooth snatched for his prize. Connor instinctively stepped in to protect Alicia. But Gold Tooth got his fingers round the chain. Alicia jumped back, her wig and glasses dislodging as she fought to free herself. Her long dark locks tumbled out and Gold Tooth, taken by surprise, let go.

'What the –?' he yelled. Then his eyes widened in recognition. 'I know you –'

Seizing on the distraction, Connor made his move. The situation demanded an all-or-nothing approach and he drove the edge of his hand into Gold Tooth's throat. The sudden attack cut off the gangster's air supply. Gold Tooth's eyes bulged as he fought to breathe. He dropped Alicia's bag, its contents spilling across the tarmac.

Connor immediately followed up with a hook punch to the solar plexus, then a lightning-fast upper cut to the jaw. There was a bone-jarring crunch and the gangster's gold tooth flew from his mouth. Over in less than five seconds, the final punch knocked the former Gold Tooth unconscious and he collapsed to the sidewalk in a heap.

Alicia dropped to her knees, scrabbling for her bag's discarded contents.

'Leave it,' said Connor, his priority her escape.

'Behind you!' cried Alicia as Crew Cut now charged in.

Connor spun to face the other gang member. In Crew Cut's hand flashed the ominous steel glint of a switchblade. Alicia screamed as she saw the knife plunge into Connor's side.

HOSTAGE
CHAPTER 49

Connor felt a sharp stab of pain in his ribs as the blade hit its mark. But the adrenalin blocked out the rest of the damage. Battling now for his own survival as well as Alicia's, Connor fought with the fury of a tiger. He palm-struck Crew Cut in the face, stunning and weakening his opponent. Then, grabbing the gang member's hand that held the knife, he spun himself under Crew Cut's arm. The whole series of joints from wrist to shoulder twisted against themselves. The effect was instantly crippling. Crew Cut's elbow hyper-extended until it snapped out of joint with a sickening pop. Crew Cut bawled in agony and dropped the switchblade. Kicking the knife away, Connor then finished off the gang member with a strike to a pressure point at the back of his skull. Crew Cut ceased screaming and crumpled to the ground.

Ensuring there were no other immediate threats, Connor pulled Alicia to her feet.

'Are you hurt?' he asked.

'Me?' gasped Alicia, panting from the shock of the attack. 'I should be asking *you*.'

'I'm fine.'

'But I could have sworn he stabbed you.'

Lifting his black T-shirt, Connor inspected his ribs. There was a small round bruise forming, but the knife hadn't penetrated his skin. He thanked his lucky stars for the stab-proof T-shirt Jody had given him.

'Just missed me,' he said, quickly lowering his shirt so she didn't question his miraculous survival.

They turned their attention to the two gang members who lay unconscious on the road.

'I can't believe it,' said Alicia, studying Connor in a new light. 'Where did you learn to fight like that?'

'I've trained a bit in kickboxing,' he admitted.

Alicia gave an astonished laugh. 'A bit? You're more deadly than Secret Service!'

'Look, we have to get out of here,' replied Connor. 'There may be others.'

Hurriedly gathering the contents of Alicia's bag, including his mobile, he noticed the panic alarm was already clasped in her hand. So *that* was why she'd been so determined to retrieve her belongings.

As they turned to go, three black limos screeched to a halt at the end of the alley. In a matter of seconds Secret Service piled out, guns at the ready. They cordoned off the area, three agents immediately surrounding Alicia. Two others began inspecting the comatose gang members and handcuffing them.

'What happened?' demanded Kyle, his eyes sweeping the alley for further danger.

'We were mugged,' explained Connor.

'I can see that. I mean . . . back at the clothes store.' He glared at Connor, clearly wanting to say more. But he held his tongue, realizing he couldn't blow Connor's cover.

'It's my fault, Kyle,' said Alicia boldly. 'I wanted a little adventure. On my own.'

'Well, you certainly got it,' he replied, struggling to maintain his professional composure. 'You could have been *seriously* hurt.'

Alicia shook her head. 'Not with my knight in shining armour by my side,' she replied.

Smiling, she took Connor's arm and strode off towards the waiting limo.

HOSTAGE
CHAPTER 50

'What were you trying to prove?' Dirk demanded, his steel-blue eyes boring into Connor. 'That you're some sort of hero?'

'I was just doing my job,' replied Connor, sitting on the opposite side of the conference table in the Roosevelt Room. As soon as they'd returned to the White House, he'd been summoned to the West Wing by the Director of Secret Service for a crisis meeting. Kyle had already been grilled by the director and now it was his turn.

'Your "job" is to inform Secret Service *immediately* of her intentions.'

'I'd have broken Alicia's trust if I'd done that.'

Dirk gave a hollow laugh. 'Trust is the last thing you should be concerned about. Your very presence is a deception.'

'That wasn't my choice,' replied Connor, shifting uncomfortably in his seat. 'But, if Alicia's going to run away, isn't it better that I'm with her?'

'Not if you introduce her to city gangs!' he snapped, hammering the mahogany table with his fist. 'You put

Alicia's life at great risk, boy. As you well know, your appointment was against my better judgement. And I've been proved right. You're a tragedy waiting to happen, Connor Reeves.'

Before Connor had a chance to defend himself, there was a knock at the door and the President's secretary popped her head round.

'Dirk, the President will see you now.'

The Director of Secret Service shot Connor a withering look. 'I hope you've got a thick skin, because you're about to be flayed alive.'

Connor swallowed nervously. He thought he'd done the right thing. And he *had* protected Alicia when it mattered most. But now he questioned his judgement. Even he realized that they could have avoided trouble if he'd just pre-warned Kyle. But it was too late to change that. He had to live with his decisions. Bracing himself to be sent home in shame, Connor followed the director and Kyle into the Oval Office. President Mendez was standing by the window, his back to them. The White House Chief of Staff, George Taylor, was also present. He greeted them with a strained smile.

'So what happened?' asked President Mendez, his expression grave as he faced them.

Dirk stepped forward and gave his report. 'First and foremost, your daughter is safe and unharmed,' he began, before proceeding to deliver an account that was more or less accurate, although Connor's actions were not presented in a favourable light. 'So you see, Connor's lack of communication and disregard for protocol resulted in your daughter being placed unnecessarily in harm's way. Fortunately, as soon as the panic alarm was triggered, my Secret Service team secured her safety,' Dirk concluded.

'Why couldn't you just track Alicia's position like the last time?' asked George.

'She switched off her cellphone,' explained Kyle. 'Alicia's got wise to our tricks.'

'Short of implanting a GPS tracker, there's not much we can do about that,' Dirk said. 'The panic alarm pinpoints her position, but only when *she* triggers it.'

President Mendez frowned and sighed. 'I take your point. And she certainly won't accept any further invasion of her privacy. Once again I must apologize for my daughter's wayward nature. Like her mother, she needs her freedom. But there's one matter I need clarifying. Who actually tackled the two gang members?'

Dirk was slow to answer, clearly reluctant to give Connor any credit. But Kyle spoke up.

'The two threats were eliminated *before* our arrival, Mr President,' he replied. 'By Connor, in fact.'

Connor looked over at Kyle in surprise. He'd not expected the agent to back him up, especially with his boss present. Nor apparently had Dirk, whose jaw fell open in disbelief.

President Mendez gave a satisfied nod, as if he'd almost expected that answer. Striding over to Connor, he laid a hand on his shoulder. 'Well, Connor, you've certainly lived up to my expectations. I knew I could trust in a Reeves bodyguard. Keep up the good work.'

'Aren't we all missing the point here?' interjected Dirk. 'We were lucky this time, but we can't risk this happening again. *Ever.*'

'Perhaps the shock of the mugging will convince Alicia of the necessity for Secret Service?' suggested George. 'Maybe she won't be so eager to fly the nest now.'

'I sincerely hope so,' Dirk replied. 'But we can't guarantee it. And we can't have *anyone* on the team going along with her escapades.'

The director stared at Connor, making it known that he blamed him for the fiasco.

'But, Dirk, this is precisely the reason we hired Connor in the first place. He should be congratulated, not criticized,' said President Mendez. He held up his hand to prevent any further protests from the director. 'Let me have *another* word with Alicia. And hopefully this will be the end of it.'

With a weary shake of his head, he walked back to the window and gazed out at the Rose Garden.

'Sometimes, I think bringing up a teenage daughter is harder than governing the country.'

HOSTAGE
CHAPTER 51

That evening Connor pounded the punch bag in the White House gym. Now that the adrenalin rush from the attack had faded, the harsh reality of what had happened hit home. Only with hindsight did he realize how close he'd come to serious injury and even death. He may well have dealt with both gangsters and protected Alicia, but he'd still got stabbed in the process. And he found himself agreeing with the Director of the Secret Service – next time he might not be so lucky or be wearing his stab-proof shirt.

That thought made him train harder. He pummelled the bag. *Jab, cross, jab, hook!* His hands began to tremble under the effort. But he had to ensure his combat skills were up to scratch. From now on, he vowed to do extra martial arts training every morning. Not just for his own safety, but for Alicia's too.

His phone rang. Pulling off his punch mitts, he picked it up and saw the Buddyguard logo flashing for a video call. He pressed his thumb to the screen and Charley's concerned face appeared.

'Are you all right, Connor? You missed your report time,' she said.

'Just overshot on my training, that's all,' he replied, wiping the perspiration from his brow with a towel.

Charley saw straight through his attempt at bravado. 'I know what happened, Connor. Secret Service got in contact when they were trying to locate you and Alicia. Next time, don't switch off your mobile. I can't find you otherwise.'

Hearing the edge of concern in her voice, Connor said, 'Sorry, my fault. I made some serious mistakes today.'

He sat down on the weight bench and retold his version of the events: his decision to follow Alicia and not to inform Secret Service; allowing her to take his mobile and switch it off; his stupidity in forgetting the second gangster; and his failure to defend himself properly.

'Don't be so hard on yourself,' said Charley, trying to comfort him with a smile. 'You should be proud of what you achieved. The bottom line is Alicia's alive and unharmed thanks to your quick reactions. And Colonel Black issues body armour precisely for those moments when we're overwhelmed or taken by surprise.'

Connor felt better hearing this from Charley. Since she was the most experienced member of the team, he valued her opinion. So he decided to bring up the other issue that had been gnawing away at him since the start of the operation.

'I'm getting to like Alicia,' he admitted, then saw Charley's lips tighten in disapproval. 'As a friend,' he hastened to add. 'Which is why I'm finding it hard not letting her know who I really am.'

'It's for her own safety, Connor,' Charley reminded. 'You've just proved today how valuable your presence is.'

'But doesn't this go against the very principles of being a bodyguard? Colonel Black's always stressing how important integrity and honesty is to our job.'

'Yes, it does,' admitted Charley. 'But sometimes due to the nature of an operation, a buddyguard has to remain covert – even to their Principal. Your role is to protect Alicia, but it is the President who is our client. We're required to comply with his instructions, and that means concealing your true purpose.'

'But I can't hang around Alicia forever without her eventually suspecting something.'

'Colonel Black's well aware of that possibility,' Charley admitted. 'And we'll have to cross that bridge when we come to it. In the meantime, stay on guard. I fear there may be a storm coming.'

Connor sat up straight. 'Have you intercepted more threats?'

'No, exactly the opposite. It's gone quiet.'

HOSTAGE
CHAPTER 52

'They literally came out of *nowhere*,' revealed Alicia to her friends, who sat transfixed on a picnic bench in the schoolyard. 'One moment we were walking to the park, the next these two gangsters jumped us.'

Not exactly out of nowhere, thought Connor, recalling their carefully planned assault.

'I bet that was terrifying,' said Kalila.

'Too right!' Alicia replied. 'But Connor wasn't scared. He leapt straight into action, even though one of them had a *knife*.'

The girls all gazed at Connor in awe.

'You're *so* brave,' remarked Paige.

'It was nothing,' replied Connor, wishing to play down his role. 'Anyone in my shoes would have done the same.'

'No, they wouldn't,' protested Alicia. 'Connor, you took them *both* down in seconds. You were truly amazing!'

'Serves them right too,' said Grace.

'But where were the Secret Service?' asked Kalila.

Alicia offered a guilty smile. 'We'd given them the slip.'

'Yeah, but who needs Secret Service when you've got Connor!' laughed Grace, striking a fighting pose. 'He's a ninja warrior!'

Nudging Kalila, Paige whispered, 'If I didn't already have a date for the prom, I know who I'd want to take me.'

'Hands off, Paige, he's mine!' said Grace, putting a possessive arm round Connor's shoulders.

Alicia gently pushed her friend away. 'Hey, you've already got a date with Darryl.'

'Darryl *who*?' replied Grace innocently and the girls laughed.

Although flattered by the attention, Connor hoped it would soon die down. If any of the girls actually *did* take a fancy to him, this might compromise his ability to protect Alicia. There was even the risk one of them might guess his true role.

As the girls pressed Alicia for more details of Connor's heroism, Connor glanced at his new watch – a gift from the President for protecting his daughter. He'd felt awkward at accepting it, but the President had insisted. Surprisingly, Dirk Moran had also encouraged his acceptance, afterwards instructing Connor to wear it night and day. It was then that Connor discovered the watch had been implanted with a micro-GPS tracker by the director. The Secret Service had also been granted access to his mobile-phone locator. Dirk was taking no more chances with him – wherever he went, the Secret Service would know.

'I wish I'd come along now,' said Paige. 'It sounds so exciting.'

'Next time I'll call you, so you don't miss any of the action,' joked Alicia.

'That reminds me,' said Kalila, rifling through her bag. 'My eldest brother bought me a new cellphone.'

'Lucky you!' said Grace. 'The most my brother's ever given me is his old console.'

Kalila pulled out a slim touchscreen phone. 'I'd better give you my new number.'

Finding their mobiles, the girls bumped phones and transferred contact details.

'What about Connor?' Paige suggested. 'You never know when you might need his protection.'

'Well . . . OK,' said Kalila, turning shy at the idea. 'But if you do call me, Connor, I'll have to put your number under a girl's name, just in case any of my brothers happen to see.'

'No problem,' said Connor, unlocking his mobile. 'You can put me in as Daisy if you want!'

Giggling at the suggestion, Kalila bumped phones and Connor accepted the incoming vCard containing her contact details.

'So this is where the tough guy hangs out?' said Ethan, swaggering over to their picnic bench. 'With the girls!'

Behind Ethan, Jimbo glared at Connor, doing his best to intimidate him. Connor groaned inwardly at their appearance. Clearly, word of Alicia's mugging was spreading through the school like wildfire.

'Not jealous, are we?' goaded Grace.

Ethan snorted. 'Me? He only beat up a couple of street

bums. I've hit more home runs this season than any batter in the state. There's no contest!'

'But Connor *saved* Alicia's life,' said Kalila.

'Well, if *I'd* been with Alicia, those bums wouldn't have got within spitting distance in the first place.' He turned to Alicia and puffed out his chest. 'Next time you want to go out in DC, stick with me.'

Connor couldn't believe the boy's arrogance. And he very much doubted whether Ethan would have even noticed the gangsters approaching, let alone have had the courage to stand and fight.

'Speaking of which, Alicia,' continued Ethan. 'Have you come to a decision yet?'

'About what?'

'The prom!' he cried in exasperation.

Alicia looked thoroughly unimpressed by his second clumsy attempt at asking her.

'Sorry,' she replied and faked an apologetic smile. 'I'm already spoken for.'

Connor glanced over in surprise. This was news to him. And judging by the reaction of her girlfriends, news to them too.

'*What?*' exclaimed Ethan, disbelief written all over his face.

Alicia looped her arm through Connor's. 'My knight in shining armour is taking me.'

HOSTAGE
CHAPTER 53

Ensuring he was alone in the rear kitchen, Malik switched on the untraceable mobile phone he'd acquired from his contact. Then he dialled the number he'd committed to memory. Answered on the fourth ring, there was a burst of high-pitched squealing and electronic chatter as the scrambled signals synchronized with one another.

A digitally enhanced robotic voice spoke. '*Answer?*'

'All war is deception,' replied Malik, quoting the Chinese philosopher Sun Tzu, as dictated by his contact instructions.

'*Proceed with your update.*'

Malik had no idea of the identity of the person on the other end. Nor did he ever want to know. Anonymity was critical for the isolation of each cell – and even more so for the central cell. *They* had contacted him first. *They* had proposed the plan. And *they* had given him the means to carry it out. But *he* would be the one to receive all the glory. He would be seen as the leading light. And the rest of the Brotherhood need never know of their existence or the part the central cell had played. That had been the deal.

'The egg has been laid in the nest and is ready to hatch,' replied Malik. 'All units are set to go.'

There was a pause on the end of the line.

'*Has the operation been compromised in any way?*' asked the robotic voice.

'No,' stated Malik with absolute certainty. 'The sleeper has not awoken.'

'*Then execute operation without delay.*'

Malik's hand holding the phone began to tremble in anticipation. The time had come to make history.

'One question,' he said, sensing the receiver about to hang up. 'My final payment?'

Another pause. '*When the operation succeeds, you'll be justly rewarded.*'

Malik grinned at the thought.

'*Is that all?*' said the voice, a trace of impatience detectable in its manipulated tone.

'Yes.'

'*Then this will be our last communication.*'

HOSTAGE
CHAPTER 54

All eyes turned towards Connor and Alicia as they made their entrance into the school prom. It was the first time Connor had worn a tuxedo and black bow-tie and he was enjoying the James Bond look. It seemed appropriate for a bodyguard. Next to him, Alicia looked truly stunning in a flowing red silk dress, her long dark hair adorned with a cascade of miniature roses. And Connor couldn't help feeling a sense of pride as he walked across the school gymnasium with the President's daughter on his arm.

The gym hall had been transformed into a glittering ballroom, festooned with purple and white streamers, flashing spotlights, lasers and a huge disco ball that dazzled like a diamond in the centre of the room. On stage a live band was playing and the dance floor was already abuzz with students celebrating the end of term. Around the edge, tables were laden with food for a buffet.

'You look gorgeous,' gushed Paige, welcoming Alicia and Connor to their table.

'So do you,' replied Alicia. She stepped back to admire her friend's champagne-coloured gown.

'This is Steve,' said Paige, introducing her date, a tall handsome boy with cropped black hair and a chiselled jaw. 'He's from Sidwell Friends School.'

Alicia smiled warmly. 'So *you're* the Steve that Paige has been hiding from us.'

'Must be,' he replied with a laugh. 'Unless she's hiding any others?'

Paige playfully bashed him on the arm with her purse. Then she leant close to Alicia's ear and with an impish grin revealed, 'Steve's in the *senior* year!'

Alicia raised an eyebrow both in surprise and approval.

Connor nodded in greeting to the older boy and introduced himself. Steve was just one of many new faces in the hall, the prom being open to student guests. This fact in itself presented an additional security problem for Secret Service, especially since the school principal had deemed it inappropriate to search attendees on arrival.

Already seated round the table were Grace and Darryl, a laid-back boy from their year whose father was the ambassador for Barbados. He raised his hand in respectful acknowledgement of Connor, while Grace hugged Alicia. Kalila sat next to them with her date – another face Connor didn't recognize – an older Arab lad with sleepy eyes and a sour expression suggesting he didn't want to be there at all.

As Alicia and Kalila kissed cheeks, Connor heard them whisper.

'So who's your date?' asked Alicia.

'Fariq,' Kalila replied. 'A friend of the family and the *only* one my father would approve.'

Connor went over to say hello, but after a few attempts at conversation he gave up with the monosyllabic guest. Connor pitied Kalila. She deserved a better date than this bore.

The band began to hot up and more students joined the party.

'Come on, let's dance!' suggested Grace, grabbing hold of Darryl's hand.

As Darryl was dragged somewhat unwillingly from his chair, Steve and Paige rose to join them. Alicia turned expectantly to Connor.

'Are you sure you want to risk it again?' said Connor.

'Don't worry, I can handle a little danger,' she assured him with a toying smile. 'And I *know* you can.'

'OK,' agreed Connor. 'But be prepared to take your feet to hospital!'

Alicia glanced over at Kalila and her date. 'How about you two?'

Fariq seemed decidedly uncomfortable at the idea.

'Maybe later,' said Kalila, offering a strained smile.

Reluctantly leaving them alone at the table, Connor and Alicia made their way over to the others on the dance floor. The music was pumping and everyone was swaying and jigging to the beat. Alicia immediately got into the rhythm, her flowing movements making her appear like she was dancing on air. By comparison, Connor appeared awkwardly stilted, but as soon as Alicia took his hand and reminded him of some of the salsa steps his movement became more natural.

'That's more like it,' beamed Alicia, stepping away and beginning to lose herself in the music.

Dancing alongside Alicia, Connor momentarily forgot his role as a bodyguard and began to properly enjoy himself for the first time since arriving in America. He hadn't fully appreciated how stressful the past fortnight of covert protection had been. There hadn't been a single moment in Alicia's presence when he hadn't been thinking of her safety. That constant alertness eventually took its toll. So, all things considered, he felt he deserved a short break. Besides, after preventing the attempted mugging by the two gangsters, he was feeling more confident in his role. He'd proved he was up to the task.

As the dance floor grew more crowded, Connor's enjoyment was rudely interrupted by a sharp elbow in the ribs. Then another. Harder this time. Cursing himself for being in a state of Code White, Connor turned round to discover Ethan right behind him.

'Sorry,' said Ethan harshly. 'I didn't see you.'

Connor doubted that, especially when a few moments later he was knocked into again.

'Watch it!' Ethan snarled as if it had been Connor's fault this time.

Realizing the boy was trying to goad him into a fight, Connor moved away. But he was bumped into from the other side by the mass bulk of Jimbo. Blocked in, Connor was unable to avoid Ethan's fist, disguised as a bad dance move. It struck him in the kidneys and he almost buckled under the blow.

'Are you all right?' asked Alicia, suddenly noticing Connor's pained expression.

Ethan and Jimbo had danced away into the crowd.

'Fine,' he replied through gritted teeth.

But, as soon as Alicia turned away, Ethan and Jimbo moved in for another attack. Connor didn't want this to escalate into a full-blown fight. That was a sure way to get thrown out of the prom, embarrass Alicia and, most importantly, prevent him from protecting her.

But he had to end their bullying tactics. There and then.

Still appearing to dance, Connor spun on the spot, stepped on Ethan's toes, then drove his shin into his attacker's lower leg. Pushing against the joint, Ethan's knee locked up and, with Connor's foot pinning his toes to the ground, Ethan lost all balance. Connor's subtle jujitsu attack went unseen. But Ethan went sprawling across the dance floor in full view of everyone.

'What's he doing?' asked Alicia, as the school's baseball star took out two dancers and Jimbo on the way down.

'Not sure,' replied Connor, edging them away from the scene. 'I *think* he was attempting to breakdance.'

HOSTAGE
CHAPTER 55

'*I'm FREE to do what I WANT!*' sang Alicia along to the band's music, as she pirouetted on the dance floor.

Connor grinned at her gleeful performance. She'd hardly stopped dancing all night, only pausing for the buffet. With no Secret Service agents permitted within the gym hall itself, Alicia had felt able to spread her wings and truly let go. Connor knew Kyle and his protection team were standing post around the school grounds, securing the perimeter. But there was no one *directly* looking over her shoulder – that she knew of, at least.

Following the previous incident, President Mendez had requested that Secret Service give his daughter more freedom. In return, Alicia promised not to run off again. Dirk Moran wasn't convinced about the idea of relaxing security arrangements. But the President had argued that Connor's presence meant there was less need for agents in close proximity, especially during social engagements like the prom. The director had finally submitted to the President's will on the proviso that Connor wore his covert earpiece. With so many non-vetted guests attending the prom, he wanted Connor to remain in radio communication with Kyle on a secure channel. Consequently, every so often Connor would hear a burst of radio chatter in his ear as each Secret Service post reported in.

'*Bravo Three to Bravo One. All clear.*'

'*Ten–four,*' acknowledged Kyle. '*Bravo Four, send update –*'

'I thought it would be a real drag looking after yet another summer exchange guest,' admitted Alicia, as Connor suddenly became aware she was talking to him. 'But you're like no other boy I've met . . .'

She was dancing closer, her deep brown eyes gazing into his. With the prom in its final hour, the band had slowed the pace and several couples were already dancing hand in hand. As Alicia swayed nearer to him, Connor sensed her intentions might be heading in the wrong direction. *Or is it the right one?*

He certainly enjoyed her company and to say Alicia was attractive was an understatement. But such feelings were close to the line no bodyguard should cross. Indeed, Colonel Black had threatened dismissal of any buddyguard who entered into a relationship with their Principal. It was a matter both of security and of client confidence.

The President's daughter was now dancing toe-to-toe with him. Connor could smell her perfume and, with each passing moment, he found his resolve weakening. He could be mistaken, but there was every indication Alicia wanted to become more than just friends. Whether that was because of his valiant defence of her the previous weekend, or because she genuinely liked him, or simply because he was the first boy her father apparently trusted around her, the situation presented a problem. Connor had been concerned that Alicia would find out he was a buddyguard, whereas the real danger was her falling for him. *And me for her...*

The song came to an end. They stood awkwardly opposite each other, both unsure what the next move should be.

Connor broke the tension first. As the band counted in another slow number, he asked, 'Would you like a ... drink?'

'Sure,' she replied, her hesitant smile unable to disguise what she'd really hoped he'd ask. 'I'll ... um ... go see how Kalila's getting on with her "date".'

Connor watched Alicia walk away. As she reached the edge of the dance floor, she glanced back over her shoulder at him, a fond look in her eyes. He offered what he trusted was a reassuring smile, then headed to the punchbowl table. He was halfway there when he noticed Ethan and Jimbo having an intense discussion at a nearby table. Their two dates sat with them, ignored and appearing as though they wished they'd never come.

Deciding it was best to avoid another confrontation, Connor diverted his course and stepped out through the gym's main doors. He judged that it would be OK to leave Alicia for a short while. She was among her friends and Secret Service were patrolling the grounds outside the building.

Passing the restrooms, Connor turned left to pace a dimly lit corridor and ponder his dilemma over Alicia. *Who could blame me for liking her?* She was fun, gorgeous and the daughter of the *President of the United States*! Such a combination would be hard for any teenager to resist. Especially when *she* was the one showing the interest. Under any other circumstances, he'd have jumped at the chance.

No! Connor told himself. He'd made a promise to President Mendez – on his father's memory – to protect Alicia. And he couldn't do that if he got involved with her. Besides, as soon as anyone found out, he'd be transferred back to England – that is, *if* he survived the wrath of her father first. Then Colonel Black would boot him out of Buddyguard and all the care provided for his mum and gran would be taken away.

With regret, Connor knew he'd have to harden his heart and maintain a respectful distance. The easiest solution would be to say he had a girlfriend back in England ... Charley, for instance. That would also help explain the international calls he kept making. As he resigned himself to his decision, Connor became aware of a figure at the far end of the corridor. Presuming it was one of Kyle's agents, Connor raised a hand and said, 'How's it going?'

Without a word, the figure turned away and disappeared round the corner.

His suspicions aroused, Connor hurried after him. But the adjoining corridor was empty. Connor walked back to where the figure had been standing. There was a row of lockers. One of them was numbered 235 – Alicia's locker.

It didn't appear to have been tampered with, but Connor was taking no chances.

He pressed a finger to his covert earpiece.

'Bandit to Bravo One,' he whispered, using his designated call sign.

Kyle's voice immediately responded. *'Bandit. Go ahead.'*

'I spotted a suspect in the east corridor but lost him. He was looking at Ali–' Connor corrected himself – 'Nomad's locker.'

'I'll send an agent to investigate. Stay with Nomad. Bravo One out.'

'There you are!' cried a voice.

Connor spun to see Darryl walking towards him.

'Who were you talking to?' he asked, looking around the deserted corridor.

'Err . . . just myself,' Connor replied.

Darryl gave him a dubious look. 'They're about to announce the Prom Prince and Princess and Alicia's asking where you are. You haven't seen Fariq, have you? Kalila said he went to make a phone call and isn't back yet.'

Connor shook his head.

'What a weird guy he is!' remarked Darryl, as they made their way into the hall and over to Alicia and the others. The students were all gathered in a mass before the stage. The band had stopped playing and the principal was addressing the school.

'By popular vote, this year's Prom Prince and Princess are . . .'

'*You got here just in time,*' Alicia whispered to Connor, not seeming to notice that he'd forgotten the drinks.

The principal fumbled with an envelope. The students grew quiet in anticipation and the drummer began a crescendo drum roll.

'. . . Connor Reeves and Alicia Mendez!'

The room erupted with applause and Alicia hugged Connor in delight.

'My knight has become my prince!' she laughed.

Connor was taken aback by the tribute. He hadn't even known what a Prom Prince or Princess was until this evening.

Grace winked at Connor. 'Nothing like a bit of superhero action to win the vote.'

Paige threw some confetti over them and whooped, 'Congratulations!'

'You deserve it,' said Kalila, her face lighting up for the first time that night.

'Now if you'd like to come up on stage,' said the principal, beckoning to the honorary couple.

The crowd parted, creating a corridor on the dance floor for Connor and Alicia. The band launched into the classic 'Celebration' by Kool & The Gang and the two of them danced their way towards the stage. On either side, students clapped and hollered. Alicia beamed with joy, clasping Connor's hand tight. Connor was also caught up in the infectious atmosphere as party poppers went off and a large *bang* triggered a cascade of silver glitter, streamers and balloons from the ceiling.

His earpiece crackled into life. '*Bravo Four to Bravo One. No intruder in east corridor. Just a couple of kids necking in the locker room. Continuing search . . .*'

Then, out of the corner of his eye, Connor glimpsed the muzzle of a gun.

HOSTAGE
CHAPTER 56

For a brief split second, Connor's mind froze. Time seemed to grind to a halt. Amid the cheering crowd, falling glitter and tumbling balloons, the ominous black barrel of a handgun poked out between two oblivious students. Targeted on the Prom Princess, the deadly weapon seemed to grow in size as Connor focused all his attention upon it. The roar of student applause faded like a rapidly receding wave until he heard only his heart beating... *THUMPthumpTHUMPthumpTHUMPthump*...

The moment of truth had come.

Deep within him, he heard Jody's voice bawl, '*A-C-E!*'

Assess. Counter. Escape...

Suddenly time speeded back up as his bodyguard training kicked into gear. Within a matter of milliseconds he'd assessed the threat and decided on his course of action.

'GUN!' shouted Connor, grabbing Alicia and shielding her with his body.

At first, the crowd looked bemused, uncertain they'd heard right.

Then a girl spotted the barrel too and started

screaming. Like the spread of wildfire, the crowd panicked and fled in all directions. There was a *BANG* and Connor tensed, expecting a bullet to hit him. When none did, he crouched low, holding Alicia to him, and ran as fast as he could.

'This way!' he yelled, heading for the nearest exit.

Alicia, utterly bewildered by the sudden turn of events, had no option but to obey.

Two more *bangs* went off. Total chaos ensued. Tables were knocked over. Drinks spilt. Glasses shattered. People collided and began falling over themselves. Connor kept a firm grip on Alicia as he barged a path through the hysterical students. But his first choice of exit had become blocked as too many people tried to escape through the narrow doorway.

Connor directed Alicia behind an overturned table to reassess his options.

'Where's the gunman?' she asked, her voice trembling with fear.

'Stay down,' Connor instructed, trying not to make her a target. It was impossible to see where the shooter was hiding among the frantic crowd. Their closest exit was now at the rear of the stage. But that meant going up the steps and exposing themselves to the gunman.

At that moment, Secret Service burst into the gymnasium. Weapons armed and at the ready, their foreboding appearance created even more panic and sent the students scattering. But the highly trained agents kept a level head as they scanned the hall for the threat.

'DROP IT!' shouted an agent on the far side, aiming his SIG Sauer P229 at a figure in the crowd.

Surrounded on all sides by Secret Service, the gunman threw his weapon to the floor.

'Don't shoot me!' cried a stunned and terrified Ethan, holding his hands high above his head. 'It's a water pistol . . . just a water pistol!'

CHAPTER 57

The hall's main lights came up and the school principal, who'd dived off stage at the first 'shot', now attempted to restore calm over the microphone. Secret Service agents had Ethan pinned to the floor. The rest of the students hung around in shocked silence or spoke in hushed tones as they watched their classmate being frisked for further weapons.

'It was meant to be a joke,' blubbed Ethan, as his hands were cuffed behind his back. 'Tell them, Jimbo, tell them.'

Connor cautiously rose from behind the table to confirm the danger was truly over. Secret Service had the gymnasium locked down and no else appeared to be a threat.

'Can I get up now?' asked Alicia, still crouched in his shadow.

'Yes, it's safe,' said Connor, helping her to her feet.

Kyle spotted them and came running over.

'Are you hurt, Alicia?' he asked, noticing an ominous dark patch on her ballgown just below her chest.

Alicia shook her head. Then she looked down at herself and groaned, 'Aww, but my dress . . . it's ruined.'

She inspected the stain on her bodice and a tear where someone had stood on the hem during their attempt to flee.

'That can be replaced – unlike you,' said Connor.

Alicia sighed, 'It's actually a one-off. But you're right, I suppose it could have been a *lot* worse.'

An agent approached Kyle. 'Looks a bit like a Glock 17, but it's a kid's water pistol all right,' he confirmed, handing Kyle the evidence. 'That idiot filled it with ink for a prank. Said something about wanting to pay the English boy back . . . for stealing his date!'

Kyle raised an enquiring eyebrow in Connor's direction and saw a matching ink stain on his jacket. Connor gave a strained smile.

'So what about the gunshots?' Alicia asked, her cheeks flushing at the disclosure of her date.

'His accomplice burst some balloons,' the agent replied, pointing to the remains of one on the floor.

Letting the matter of their supposed date pass, Kyle showed Connor the 'gun'. In the full glare of the gym lights, it was obvious that the weapon was a plastic toy.

'Sorry, I *thought* it was real,' said Connor, feeling an utter idiot. At the same time, he was glad it hadn't been. Judging by the stain on Alicia's dress, he'd have reacted too late to save her from a real bullet.

'Easy mistake to make in the heat of the moment,' replied Kyle. 'Many of our agents have been fooled one time or another. You did the right thing by calling it in.'

'I'm *so* angry with Ethan –' began Alicia, glaring in his direction. Then she frowned. 'What did you just say? Connor *called it in*?'

'Erm ... it's just an expression we agents use,' Kyle replied, quickly trying to backtrack.

Alicia glanced between the two of them, sensing there was something more to it than that. Then she noticed a tiny piece of skin-toned plastic protruding from Connor's left ear. Her eyes widened in recognition. 'Is *that* what I think it is?'

Connor discovered his covert earpiece had become dislodged during their escape. He pushed it back in and offered a sheepish grin.

'What are you? My *bodyguard*?' said Alicia, half-joking.

Connor said nothing. But she saw the truth in his eyes and her jaw dropped in disbelief.

'You ARE!' she exclaimed. 'The son of a soldier ... martial arts expert ... your reactions to the gun ... all this is starting to make sense ...'

'I can explain,' said Connor. 'It's not what you think –'

Alicia held up her hand, stopping him.

'I don't want to hear. If this is true, then everything you've said to me is a *lie*.' Tears of fury welled in her eyes as her anger at Ethan was now redirected towards Connor. 'You've deceived me. Betrayed our friendship. Can't I trust *anyone* in my life?'

Her lower lip quivered and she began to cry. Connor reached out to her, wanting to explain that out of anyone *he* could be trusted. With her life.

'*Don't* touch me!' she said, pushing him away. She turned to Kyle. 'Take me home, right now.'

And, with not so much as a glance back in Connor's direction, Alicia stormed out of the gym hall.

HOSTAGE
CHAPTER 58

'A *buddy* guard? Don't make me laugh!' said Alicia, curled up on the sofa in the Oval Office, surrounded by discarded tissues. 'The Secret Service have gone *too* far this time.'

'It was actually my idea,' admitted President Mendez, sitting beside his daughter trying to comfort her.

'*WHAT?*' exclaimed Alicia, her hands balling into fists as she glared at her father. '*You* hired Connor?'

'Please, honey, there's no need to shout.' He glanced towards his secretary's door, hoping she couldn't hear.

'No need! I thought you of all people would understand. That's what you've been saying anyway. Now I find out *you're* the one behind it.'

'A buddyguard is for your personal safety,' President Mendez explained, recognizing his wife's fiery nature in their daughter. 'In light of your recent escapades, the nightmare scenario is you getting kidnapped or shot at by some terrorist, criminal or crazed individual. So it was either that or upping the Secret Service protection. And I knew you wouldn't want that.'

'I didn't ask for any of this,' Alicia said, waving her

hand dismissively around the Oval Office. 'This is *your* dream.'

'And you are an important part of that dream – my *inspiration* to make this a better world,' insisted the President, taking her hand in his. 'We've always said family comes first. And that's true. But we're the First Family too. And with that comes the necessity for Secret Service. I admit, it's a real pain at times. But no price is too high to protect my family – especially you, my only child.'

Alicia pulled her hand away. 'So you send someone to spy on me instead!'

President Mendez sighed. 'Connor isn't spying. He's protecting you. As he's proven tonight and last week when you ran into those low-life gangsters.'

Alicia bit her lip as she sought a suitable reply.

'Don't you realize he's risked his life for you – *twice*?'

'Yes,' admitted Alicia, unable to meet her father's eye. 'But that's not the point. I'm entitled to live a *normal* life.'

President Mendez nodded sincerely. 'And I want you to have your freedom and your youth. I want you to have everyday experiences with friends your own age. But as *my* daughter that is a privilege, not a given.'

Alicia turned to him. 'You may rule this country, but what right do you have to rule my life?'

'It's true I am the President of the United States, but first and foremost I'm your father.'

Alicia let out an incredulous laugh. 'Sometimes I wonder if you really understand the toll living in the White House has on me. As soon as you took office, you were no longer the father I knew and loved. I mean, I have to make an *appointment* to see you! And with Mother always away on her diplomatic business, I'm a virtual orphan. My school friends are all I have. And now you're even controlling them.'

'I'm glad you consider Connor a friend –'

'Connor, a *friend*? My prom night has been ruined because of him. I've been humiliated in front of my true friends. And now, thanks to you, I don't know which of them I can trust.'

'You can trust Connor,' replied President Mendez. 'I certainly do. His father saved my life.'

'This isn't about you!' snapped Alicia. 'It's about *me*. My life.' She rose to her feet in anger. 'And I *never* want to see that boy again.'

HOSTAGE
CHAPTER 59

Connor stood outside the Oval Office. He could hear the quarrel through the door. It was too muffled to make out precisely what they were saying, but the gist of the argument was clear. He felt dreadful for having deceived Alicia. She lived under the watchful eye of the Secret Service day and night, and she cherished the rare moments away from its scrutiny. Now she'd discovered he was one of them too and there'd been no real privacy after all.

Yet whether she liked it or not, Connor recognized that Alicia *needed* close protection. Aside from the incident with the two gangsters, Ethan's prank demonstrated just how easy it would be for a gunman to shoot her. In the light of that possibility alone, it was clear Connor's role as a covert buddyguard was more than justified.

But did the *right* reason warrant the *wrong* lie?

The door to the Oval Office swung open and Alicia came out, fuming. She saw Connor and tried to avoid him.

But Connor made a move towards her. 'I wanted to tell you the truth, but –'

'I've had enough of you, Connor,' she cut in, her stare

cold and hard. 'I don't want you talking to me or even near me. You were *hired* to be my "friend" – my buddy! And you know the worst thing, I –' a tear ran down her cheek – 'I was actually falling for you.'

The words hit Connor harder than a punch. He realized he'd done more than deceive Alicia – he'd broken her heart. *Sorry* wouldn't be nearly enough to make up for that. But, lost for any other words, Connor could only watch her as she walked away, sobbing.

'Made quite an impression, didn't you?'

Connor spun round to find Dirk Moran standing behind him. He wasn't sure whether the director had heard Alicia's disclosure or not. But judging by the triumphant smirk on his face, Dirk appeared to be savouring Connor's fall from grace.

'After you,' said Dirk, ushering Connor into the Oval Office.

The President was slumped in his chair, rubbing the bridge of his nose to ease a headache. 'Take a seat. George will be with us in a moment.'

Connor perched on the sofa opposite Dirk. No one spoke and Connor felt the tension in the air. It seemed he'd not only upset Alicia, but her father too.

The chief of staff entered and closed the door behind him. 'It's been quite a night by all accounts,' he remarked, sitting down beside Connor.

'The situation was inevitable,' said Dirk, his tone sympathetic rather than scathing. 'Connor's inexperience resulted in an error of judgement and he's paid the price.

Secret Service will miss his presence, but what more can I say?'

Despite his words and manner, the director didn't look too cut up about the situation.

'Come, come, Dirk, we've all made mistakes,' replied George. 'Remember when you thought the Russian ambassador was planting a bomb and it turned out to be his cigar case!'

Dirk shifted uncomfortably at the recollection of that embarrassing incident. Recovering his composure, he responded, 'But now Connor's cover has been blown the only course of action is to return him to the UK.'

'Surely that's an overreaction,' said President Mendez. 'Connor's presence has been invaluable. We can still utilize his skills, can't we?'

The chief of staff nodded in agreement. Dirk was about to protest further, but Connor interjected.

'Mr President, I think the director's right,' admitted Connor, much to Dirk's astonishment. 'I'm sorry. I tried my best, but I can't see Alicia wanting me around any more. I'll pack my bags.'

'No, Connor, this isn't your fault. I take full responsibility,' insisted President Mendez. 'Perhaps if I'd been straight with my daughter from the start we wouldn't be in this mess.'

'Don't be so hard on yourself, Mr President,' said George. 'It was your daughter's exploits dodging Secret Service that forced our hand. And we went through all the options. A secret buddyguard was clearly the best solution.

And Alicia is better embarrassed than dead. Once she calms down, I'm sure she'll see sense and get used to the idea of a full-time buddyguard.'

Dirk coughed politely. 'I don't see the point of a buddyguard now. I mean, Secret Service cover all angles of her security. What advantage does Connor have over one of my highly trained agents?'

'Age,' reminded George. 'Connor can *still* go where your agents can't. Alicia may know the truth now, but no one else is going to suspect him of being a bodyguard.'

'But since Alicia won't accept him around he can't do his job in the first place,' Dirk argued.

'With great reluctance, I'm starting to side with Dirk on this one,' said the President. 'Alicia's headstrong like her mother. I can't see her changing her mind any day soon.'

President Mendez leant forward on his desk, his hands clasped together, and looked Connor in the eye.

'Connor, you've done Alicia and me a great service. And I can say, hand on heart, your father would be proud of you. But I'm truly sorry – I'll have to send you home.'

HOSTAGE
CHAPTER 60

Sitting on his bed in the White House guest room, Connor stared glumly out across the Washington skyline. The National Mall was bathed in bright morning sunshine, but the promising summer day did little to improve his mood.

Operation Hidden Shield had come to an abrupt and humiliating end.

Despite the President's kind words, Connor couldn't help feeling that he'd failed. While Alicia was physically safe and unharmed, he'd hurt her more deeply than any knife or bullet. And it was infuriating that she'd found out about his role by him protecting her from a *water pistol*! That mistake, as Dirk had rightly pointed out, had cost him dearly. Maybe if it had been a real gun, the outcome would have been different. Alicia would have been thankful for his presence rather than resentful. Then again, he reminded himself that he'd reacted too late to the threat, so he'd failed in his duty anyway. And even if she had survived the attack, she would have always felt their friendship had been based on a lie. That he was 'employed' to like her – which in his heart couldn't be further from the truth.

Connor clasped his father's key fob in one hand. Looking down, he studied his father's face.

'I'm sorry, Dad, I hope I'm not a disappointment to you,' Connor whispered. 'Maybe I'm just not cut out to be a bodyguard.'

He clipped the key fob to his backpack of Buddyguard gear, then began throwing the rest of his belongings into his suitcase. He was almost finished when his mobile rang and the Buddyguard logo flashed on the screen.

Connor had been dreading this call – having to explain to Colonel Black why the assignment was over. He knew the colonel had pinned high hopes on him. A successful operation for the United States government would have boosted the reputation of his organization dramatically.

Taking a deep breath, he pressed Accept and Colonel Black's craggy face appeared. Connor braced himself for an earful.

'We've received Secret Service's report,' he growled. 'What's your side of the story?'

Connor related the events of the previous evening.

Colonel Black nodded and rubbed his chin thoughtfully. 'The director's comments do seem overly harsh. And we knew we'd hit this problem sooner or later. It just came a little sooner than any of us expected. Have you tried convincing the President's daughter of the value of a buddyguard? She has more freedom with you than she would ever get under adult agent supervision.'

'There hasn't been the opportunity,' replied Connor. 'And it's a little more complicated than that.'

'What do you mean?'

'Alicia . . .' He sought for the right words. '. . . took a liking to me.'

Colonel Black shook his head in despair. 'Teenage hormones! They'll be the downfall of this organization.'

'But I didn't encourage her or –'

'Listen, Connor, I don't blame you for what's happened. And neither should you blame yourself. Being a bodyguard is one of the toughest jobs in the world. And being a *buddy*guard is even harder. So let's put this assignment behind us and move on. You're to return to HQ for further training.'

'Yes, sir,' replied Connor, relieved he hadn't been entirely chewed up and spat out by the colonel.

'I'm going to hand you over to Charley now. She's made all your travel arrangements.'

Charley appeared, her expression serious and her tone businesslike. 'I've emailed your itinerary and e-ticket. Your flight is at 1600 hours out of Dulles International. A car will pick you up at 1200 hours.'

She glanced off-screen and Connor heard a door close. He guessed Colonel Black had left the room. When Charley looked back, her sky-blue eyes had softened.

'Don't beat yourself up over this, Connor,' she said, keeping her voice low. 'The first assignment is often an ordeal. And I don't need to tell you my last one was a complete nightmare. But we *do* get decent assignments. Jason's currently in the Caribbean working protection on a client's beach holiday. His updates consist mostly of the progress of his suntan!'

Connor managed a weak laugh. 'Lucky for some, I guess. But I doubt the colonel is going to send me on another mission any time soon. And I'm not sure I could face one after upsetting my Principal so badly.'

Hearing the heartache in Connor's voice, Charley replied, 'Look, your flight isn't until this afternoon. Why don't you find Alicia and speak to her?'

'She doesn't want to talk . . . or even be anywhere near me.'

'That was yesterday. Maybe she's cooled off by now. You need to make amends otherwise you'll never forgive yourself. Explain to her what it means to be a buddyguard and why you did it. You never know, she might change her mind. And if not, she'll at least know your intentions were good.'

Connor nodded, knowing Charley was right. He needed closure. He wanted Alicia to know how much her friendship meant to him and that it had been real – not just a part of his job description.

HOSTAGE
CHAPTER 61

Ending the connection to Charley and leaving his bags on the bed, Connor went to look for the President's daughter. But she wasn't in her bedroom. Nor was she in the solarium on the third floor. Nor her favourite getaway – the rooftop terrace. He checked the gym, music room, guest bedrooms and even the linen cupboard. But to no avail.

Spotting a passing Secret Service agent, he asked if he'd seen her.

The agent shook his head. 'Sorry, not part of my detail today.'

'Do you happen to know if she's gone out?'

'No idea,' replied the agent. 'But I can check for you.'

The agent radioed in his request. A minute later, he received a response. 'No, not according to her schedule,' he repeated.

'Thanks,' said Connor, racking his brains to think where she might be.

He headed to the ground floor, reasoning the library would be as good a place as any to escape unwanted company. He passed a tour group on the stairs making their way up from the State Floor. A few glanced curiously in his direction, but most were gazing in awe at the grand staircase with its glass-cut chandelier and portraits of twentieth-century presidents from Truman to Nixon.

Alicia wasn't in the library. But that was no surprise to Connor now he'd discovered the White House was open to tour groups that day. Thinking of all the other places she might be, he tried the cinema, the dining room, then the bowling alley. He looked everywhere he was permitted to go. As the general staff weren't aware of his dismissal yet, none questioned his movement through the White House.

Growing more concerned as to Alicia's whereabouts, Connor went outside to search the grounds. Aside from the expected roaming patrols, the tennis and basketball courts were deserted. So too were the putting green and children's garden. He asked one of the sentry agents if he'd seen Alicia.

'Negative,' he replied.

On Connor's urging, he radioed the other patrols.

'None of the gates report that she's left the premises. Have you checked the swimming pool? Otherwise, she's probably inside the main residence.'

'Of course, the swimming pool!' said Connor, hurrying off.

But Alicia wasn't there either.

Connor finally decided to call her on his mobile. He hadn't tried before since he doubted she'd answer when his number came up. His assumption had been right. His call was diverted straight to voicemail: '*Hi, you've reached me!*

If you're calling this number, you know who I am. So leave a message after the beep . . .'

'Hi, it's Connor, I want to apologize for . . .' He hated answer machines and couldn't think of what to say that wouldn't sound crass or pathetic. 'Look, just ring me back.' He ended the call.

At this point he was on the verge of giving up. Then Connor remembered the tracking device that was planted in Alicia's phone cover. *For emergency use only*, Amir had said. Connor judged that 'Principal missing' qualified as an emergency. Unlocking his mobile, he pressed the green target icon. The phone froze and he had to reboot. But on the second attempt the Tracker app popped up on the screen.

The map zeroed in on Washington DC and his green locator flashed steadily beside the swimming pool. Almost immediately a reassuring red dot appeared within the White House. He zoomed in closer.

Alicia was in the Lincoln Bedroom.

He must have just missed her in his earlier search. The Tracker app outlined the quickest route. Connor hurried back inside and upstairs to the second floor.

Entering the plushly furnished room, he called out, 'Alicia?'

There was no answer.

'Alicia! Are you there?' said Connor as he wandered round the room. He checked the adjoining bathroom, opened the walk-in wardrobe, and even looked under the bed. But she was nowhere to be found.

Connor rechecked the Tracker app. It had frozen again. He tapped the screen, but the phone was obviously malfunctioning.

'So much for Amir's "showpiece",' he muttered, rebooting and dialling his friend's mobile number.

After four long-distance rings, Amir answered. 'Connor! Are you all right? I heard the assignment's nosedived.'

'Yeah,' replied Connor. 'It's not good. But I can't find Alicia to apologize and your super smartphone keeps glitching. The Tracker app won't work.'

'Really?' said Amir, surprised. 'It's probably an I-D-eight user problem.'

'What?'

'I'll translate – an i-d-iot user problem.'

'Ha ha,' said Connor, 'but I'm not in the mood for jokes.'

'Sorry, bud, I'll get Bugsy to take a look,' he replied. 'We can remote access it from here. It may take a while to fix, though. I'll give you a call when it's finished. Just don't switch off your phone.'

'Thanks,' said Connor. 'I'd really like to say goodbye to her before I leave.'

Connor slipped the mobile into his pocket and wandered over to the window. He looked out across the south lawn towards the soaring needle of the Washington Monument.

Where are you, Alicia?

As he turned away, his foot knocked something. Glancing down, he saw the red Armani case with its butterfly logo on the floor. It had been snapped in two and now lay in pieces partly concealed beneath the drapes.

Connor guessed Alicia must have thrown it across the room in a fit of anger.

But then another possibility occurred to him and he felt a knot of dread tighten in his gut. Without wasting a further second, Connor headed straight to the West Wing and down to the in-house Secret Service office.

Dirk Moran was there briefing an agent.

Connor knocked on the open door. 'I can't find Alicia.'

'The President's daughter is no longer your concern,' Dirk replied, dismissing him irritably with a wave of the hand. He returned to briefing his agent.

Connor stepped inside. 'No, I mean, I've looked throughout the White House and she's *nowhere*.'

The Director snorted. 'That's probably because she doesn't want to see you. And nor do I.'

'But what if she's run away again? Or worse – been kidnapped?' pressed Connor, unable to believe the director wasn't taking his claim seriously.

Dirk glared at him. 'The White House is one of the most secure buildings in the world. No one gets in or out without Secret Service knowing. *We* are professionals. Now go and play *buddy*guards elsewhere and stop wasting my time.'

With that, he pushed Connor out and slammed the door in his face.

HOSTAGE
CHAPTER 62

Connor stood outside the north portico of the White House, his suitcase beside him and his backpack slung over one shoulder. His departure was definitely less grand than his arrival. Aside from the obligatory Secret Service agent posted at the door, he waited alone for the car to turn up and take him to the airport. No one had come to say goodbye, the President and chief of staff having done so at the meeting the night before and the Director of the Secret Service wanting nothing more to do with him. He hadn't expected to see Kyle as he was off-duty today with the rest of his shift team. But he had hoped that Alicia might appear.

Connor couldn't stop worrying about her. Whatever Dirk Moran believed, he was convinced that she was no longer in the White House. And, like a storm brewing on the horizon, he sensed something wasn't quite right.

The President's daughter is no longer your concern.

Despite the truth of the director's words, Connor still felt responsible for her. And he really didn't want to leave without confirming she was safe.

But he'd run out of time. In little less than four hours he'd be on a flight back to England.

His phone rang. He snatched it from his pocket, hoping that it would be Alicia.

'We sourced the problem,' said Amir on the other end of the line. 'Your phone was infected with a virus.'

'But I thought you said it had an impenetrable firewall.'

'Yeah, but this virus is cutting-edge,' Amir replied, his tone implying admiration as well as concern. 'A "Cell-Finity" bug drilled through our firewall code. Fortunately, Bugsy had installed a secondary spyware program that blocked it from spreading. The glitching you experienced was the attempt by the virus to break through.'

'What was it trying to do?' asked Connor.

'Bugsy says it allows a hacker – using a secret access code – to connect to the infected phone without the user knowing. The hacker can then monitor all calls, intercept and block texts, and even switch on the mobile's microphone to eavesdrop on private conversations. The phone essentially becomes a silent spy.'

The storm Connor had sensed on the horizon suddenly felt a whole lot closer. 'Who would have planted it? Secret Service?'

'Possibly, but the unusual coding suggests a *foreign* source. And that's not the worst of it,' continued Amir. 'This particular bug sends out a tracer signal. As long as the phone is on, the hacker can track the movements of the user.'

'So you're saying someone's been following me, reading my texts and listening to everything I've said?'

'No,' replied Amir. 'The virus didn't take hold.'

'So my phone's OK now?'

'Yeah, we've reinstalled the entire OS from scratch, but a virus like this is easily transferred via the internet, through an app or even by a simple text message. Our guess is you weren't the intended target and your phone contracted the bug from the person who is.'

'*Alicia!*' gasped Connor. 'I still haven't been able to find her.'

'Well, you can now the Tracker app is working,' reminded Amir.

'No, I can't. I found the phone case smashed to bits. So, while I can't find her, someone else can.'

'That's *not* good.'

Connor waited while Amir related the bad news to Bugsy.

'We might have a solution,' said Amir, coming back on the line. 'Bugsy's going to try to hack into the Cell-Finity program. If he can reconfigure the coding, break the access code and "mirror" the signal, then theoretically we can track the target phone too.'

'How long will that take?' asked Connor.

'He reckons at least an hour.'

'I've a feeling that might be too late.'

'Look, I'll call you as soon as we make any progress. And remember: we don't know for certain if Alicia's the one being tracked.'

'That's not a gamble I'm willing to take,' replied Connor, hanging up.

Knowing that Dirk Moran would refuse to see him, Connor was on his own until Amir could get proof. In that time, anything could happen to Alicia. He had to warn her.

Opening up his contacts, he dialled Alicia's number. But his call went straight to voicemail again. He left another message – more urgent this time.

As he considered what his next move should be, a tour group spilt out of the north portico's doors. Watching them go past and head towards the north-east gate, it dawned on Connor how Alicia might have left the White House undetected.

HOSTAGE
CHAPTER 63

Alicia stuffed her platinum-blonde wig back into her bag. The sweltering summer's day made it too hot to wear. But she kept on her Jackie Onassis-style sunglasses. They were large enough to conceal her features so she wouldn't be immediately recognized.

After leaving the tour group in Lafayette Park, she had darted through a warren of back streets to get more distance between herself and the White House. Now clear of its oppressive shadow, Alicia finally felt able to breathe. She was free of all the surveillance cameras, patrols and restrictions that made her life a virtual prison sentence. She was free of the Secret Service. Free of her father's control. And free of . . . Connor.

After discovering he was her buddyguard, she simply couldn't take it any more. She felt the walls closing in and desperately needed her own space.

Her phone rang. Alicia looked at the screen and saw Connor's name.

'*Why can't you just leave me alone?*' she muttered, stabbing the screen with a thumb and rejecting the call.

A moment later her phone buzzed, indicating a voicemail. Alicia ignored it. She didn't want to hear his voice. It would just make her cry again. She couldn't comprehend how Connor could betray her like that. Pretending to be her friend, while all the time working for the Secret Service. She wouldn't be so upset if she didn't like him so much. But he'd worked his way into her heart and even *now* she was missing his reassuring presence.

'No!' she told herself. 'He lied to me from the start –'

'Watch where you're going!' snapped a suited businessman as Alicia almost collided into him.

Looking up from her phone, Alicia discovered she was at the banks of the Potomac River. She'd had no real destination in mind when leaving the White House beyond simply escaping. But as she wandered along the towpath Alicia realized that, more than her freedom, she desperately needed a friend to talk to. One she could trust.

Alicia thumbed a text into her phone.

> Really need to see you. By river near
> Nat Mall. Can you meet me asap? A x

Her phone beeped a few seconds later.

> Of course. Jefferson Memorial?
> 15 mins. K x

Alicia smiled with relief. She could always rely on Kalila.

HOSTAGE
CHAPTER 64

The phone in Bahir's hand buzzed. He read the message.

> I'll be waiting on the steps. A x

Bahir turned to face Malik in the passenger seat of their blacked-out vehicle.

'Eagle Chick has taken the bait.'

'All according to plan then,' said Malik. 'And you're certain her messages have been blocked?'

Bahir nodded with a self-satisfied grin. 'Absolutely. My Cell-Finity bug gives us *complete* control of her phone. We can falsify all text messages. Govern every in- and outbound call. Even if she tries phoning Kalila now, the line will ring as if engaged.'

'Good work, Bahir,' said Malik. 'You certainly excelled in the task I set.'

He looked over at Hazim in the driver's seat. 'And well done, Hazim, for planting the bug in the first place.'

Hazim managed an anxious smile as Bahir announced, 'Target is five minutes out.'

Bahir showed Malik the tablet PC in his lap, where a red dot traced its way slowly across a digital map of Washington towards the Jefferson Memorial.

'Then it's time,' said Malik, licking his lips in anticipation as he took the prepaid cellphone Bahir offered him.

Hazim started the engine and gripped the steering wheel tight. He looked out through the tinted window at the Memorial with its iconic white marble Greek columns, domed roof and wide stone steps that led down to the water's edge. They had recced the location on several occasions, starting with simple drive-bys to identify perimeter protection, CCTV and access control. Then they'd progressed to on-site surveillance. Disguised as tourists, they'd photographed the Memorial from every angle, observed the patrol patterns of the park rangers, and planned their escape routes. Even the traffic flow around the monument had been monitored. Nothing was to be left to chance.

Hazim pulled out into the traffic and began their slow approach.

'This day the Brotherhood will strike back against the American tyranny over our land and brothers,' Malik declared with zealous pride. 'This day will mark the turning point in our war on the West.'

He flicked open the mobile phone and began dialling . . .

HOSTAGE
CHAPTER 65

Connor stepped through the north-east gate, past the sentry and on to Pennsylvania Avenue. No one questioned him as part of the tour group. Which meant no one would have questioned a *disguised* Alicia either. Connor now realized he'd actually seen her on an earlier tour. She'd been on the grand staircase, her back to him, pretending to study a portrait of President Nixon. But he'd been in such a rush and so focused on finding a dark-haired Alicia that his gaze had shot straight past the unassuming girl in jeans with the platinum-blonde bob.

Standing at the entrance to Lafayette Park, Connor wondered which direction Alicia might have gone. Without the tracker, it would be like searching for a needle in a haystack. But he guessed she'd try to hook up with one of her friends.

Unlocking his phone, he called Kalila. 'Hi, Kalila. It's Connor.'

'Hi . . . err . . . Daisy,' answered Kalila, giving a nervous laugh. 'That was some prom last night. You and Alicia left pretty quickly afterwards. Are you all right?'

'It's a long story,' replied Connor. 'But I was wondering if Alicia was with you? Or had called?'

'No, sorry. Is anything wrong?'

Not wishing to worry her unnecessarily, Connor said, 'Not really . . . can you just let me know as soon as she contacts you?'

'Sure,' replied Kalila.

In the distance Connor heard a deep rumble and wondered what it was. 'Look, I've got to go.'

Hanging up, Connor tried Grace next. Then Paige. But neither of them had heard from Alicia. He was trying to think of who to call next when his phone rang and the Buddyguard logo flashed on the screen.

'Bugsy's had a breakthrough!' said Amir, his voice tense and urgent. 'Alicia's mobile is *definitely* being tracked.'

'Have you told Secret Service?' said Connor.

'That's the problem,' replied Amir. 'We can't get through.'

'What do you mean?'

'All hell's broken loose. Washington DC's being bombed.'

'*What?*' exclaimed Connor, his eyes scanning the park for danger. But everywhere appeared calm and peaceful. Then in the background he heard a second ominous rumble and the wail of police sirens.

'Hi, Connor, it's Charley,' said a voice on the line. 'Intelligence reports a suspected car bomb has gone off at H Street and Ninth.'

'That's near Secret Service Headquarters!'

'We know. The explosion was detonated right outside the entrance. Hang on –' there was a ping of an incoming message and a muffled gasp – 'there's been a *second* explosion, near the Capitol Building this time.'

'I just heard it,' said Connor, the tourists milling around him still oblivious to the impending danger.

'Connor, it's Colonel Black,' said a gruff voice. 'Get off the streets now. That's an order.'

'But I believe Alicia's somewhere in the city,' he replied, '*without* Secret Service protection.'

The colonel grunted. 'Then it's down to you to find her. Amir, has Bugsy managed to mirror the signal yet?'

'Yes,' Amir replied. 'He's patching through the tracer code to Connor's phone as we speak.'

Launching the Tracker app, Connor watched the map home in on Alicia's location. It showed her approaching the Jefferson Memorial.

'I've got her,' he told them.

'Then it's time to do your job,' said Colonel Black. 'Just keep your head down. DC's turning into a war zone!'

'Yes, Colonel,' replied Connor, shouldering his backpack.

'Stay safe!' said Charley quickly. 'I'll send you threat updates.'

Taking the route dictated by the Tracker app, Connor sprinted along Pennsylvania and down 15th Street. The Jefferson Memorial was estimated to be over ten minutes away. Running flat out, Connor hoped he could reach Alicia in half that time. Her life might well depend upon it.

HOSTAGE
CHAPTER 66

Sitting on the top step of the Memorial, Alicia gazed across the glassy waters of the Potomac's tidal basin. Lush cherry trees framed its banks and families cruised about in paddle boats, laughing and splashing one another. She watched the carefree way the tourists wandered along the footpath and the easy enjoyment of the children running to and fro. Bathed in glorious sunshine, the scene was almost picture perfect.

A couple of teenagers walked by hand in hand, stealing the occasional kiss. Alicia's eyes followed them, envious at the couple's freedom to do as they pleased.

'And they would think *I* lived the privileged life,' she sighed.

Alicia glanced at her watch for the umpteenth time, impatient for Kalila to arrive. She had so much she needed to confide in her friend. The whole buddyguard issue, her father's lack of understanding and her feelings for Connor crushed by betrayal. Even thinking about the boy brought tears to her eyes.

Blinking them away, Alicia looked up into the cloudless

blue sky. It was then that she noticed a dark column of smoke rising from central Washington.

Alicia gasped, shocked by what appeared to be a massive fire in the heart of the capital.

Then she spotted a second swirl of smoke to the east. Although the sun shone warm and bright, a cold chill ran down her spine at the sight.

Other people began to notice them too and a murmur of unease spread among the groups of tourists dotted around the Memorial. There was a distant rumble like thunder and a third plume of smoke smeared the sky.

'Oh my gawd, what was that?' exclaimed a woman in a white baseball cap.

'Maybe it's a gas explosion,' suggested the man next to her.

An elderly gentleman with a cane and Vietnam Vets badge squinted into the distance. 'Sounded more like a bomb to me.'

'Ladies and gentlemen, the Memorial's being closed,' announced a park ranger, ushering people from the massive temple-like structure. 'Please vacate the area immediately.'

Bewildered tourists began to file out and down the steps.

'The Jefferson Memorial is *never* closed,' muttered the elderly gentleman. 'This has to be serious.'

He glanced down at Alicia. 'If I were you, young lady, I'd go straight home.'

Beckoning to his wife, he hurried down the steps as fast as his limp would allow.

Alicia looked north in the direction of her home. The

White House suddenly seemed very far away. Alone upon the steps, the President's daughter felt dangerously exposed. And truly scared. Alicia now realized how stupid she'd been to run off. Reaching into her bag, she pulled out her panic alarm.

HOSTAGE
CHAPTER 67

President Mendez's feet barely touched the ground as he was rushed from the Oval Office by his Secret Service detail. They charged through the door to the Rose Garden and across the south lawn to the awaiting helicopter. Marine One's blades thudded loudly and the grass was whipped into a frenzy by the whirling wind. Bundled up the steps, President Mendez just caught a glimpse of his White House staff fleeing the residence. Karen Wright, her dark blonde hair streaming out behind her, was close on his heels. A moment later, she joined him in the helicopter's main cabin. The Director of National Intelligence was swiftly followed by George Taylor and Dirk Moran. The doors shut behind them and Marine One lifted off.

'Tell me what's going on! Is this for real?' demanded President Mendez as he brushed himself down and straightened his tie.

'The White House has been compromised,' Dirk explained. 'We've just received notice of another bomb threat.'

'A bomb in the *White House*!' exclaimed the President. 'How's that possible?'

'We've no idea at this time. But, given the three car bombings, we must assume this is a viable threat.'

'Three?'

'Yes, Mr President,' said Karen Wright, holding on to her seat as Marine One banked left to head towards Andrews Air Force Base where it would connect with Air Force One, the President's official plane and mobile base in a national emergency. 'The FBI Headquarters were hit barely a minute ago. This is a *confirmed* terrorist attack on our capital.'

'Has any group claimed responsibility?'

'Not yet. It's far too early,' she replied. 'But the National Security Directive is being implemented and all key government personnel are being secured.'

'I gave the order to evacuate the White House,' informed George, panting heavily from his dash to the helicopter.

The President looked anxiously through the window at the White House disappearing into the distance. 'Where's my daughter in all this?'

'Do not concern yourself, sir,' replied Dirk, who after five fretful minutes had just got word that Nomad's locator beacon had been triggered. 'Secret Service are en route to escort her to a safe house.'

HOSTAGE
CHAPTER 68

'That should keep them occupied for a while,' Malik said, ending his call to the receptionist at the White House and flinging the prepaid phone out of the car window. He watched it sail over the bridge railing and disappear into the Potomac River.

Bahir checked his tablet PC where large orange dots now blossomed on the screen. 'FBI, Secret Service and US Capitol bombs have all been triggered successfully,' he announced to Malik's obvious delight. 'Early news reports indicate chaos on the streets.'

'Wonderful,' said Malik, almost sighing with pleasure. 'Then it's time to collect our prize.'

A radio crackled into life.

'*Gamekeeper to Hide. Over.*'

Bahir snatched up the receiver. 'Send message: *Eagle Chick is without sparrows*. I repeat, *Eagle Chick is without sparrows.*'

Bahir looked over his shoulder at Malik in triumph. 'Fortune favours us.'

Then his tablet PC sounded an alarm and he cursed out loud.

'What's the problem?' Malik demanded.

Bahir tapped away on the electronic keyboard. 'My scanner's picked up a distress signal. From Eagle Chick.'

'Then block it!'

Bahir feverishly entered more code but shook his head in frustration. 'I can't. It's not coming from her phone.'

Malik's expression grew thunderous. 'Tell Kedar to move in NOW!'

HOSTAGE

CHAPTER 69

His lungs burning, his heart pounding, Connor raced full pelt round the banks of the tidal basin. The Jefferson Memorial was in plain sight. Tourists were spilling out of the domed structure and down the white marble steps. His eyes scanned among them for any sign of Alicia. He couldn't spot her. But according to the Tracker, she was still there.

His phone buzzed. He glanced at the secure message from Charley.

> White House evacuation. Bomb scare.
> Do NOT return. Head to Safe House
> Blue 1.

A blue dot – numbered 686 – now pulsed on the digital map several blocks east of the Jefferson Memorial on E Street SW.

Connor was stunned by the rapid sequence of events. Like a house of cards, Washington DC seemed to be collapsing around him. He'd heard a third explosion rock the capital only a few blocks away as he'd sprinted across the National Mall. People were bunched together, gazing in stupefied awe at the billowing columns of smoke. Some were fleeing in panic; others were too shocked to know what to do.

Connor just kept running.

With three key targets hit, he knew the odds of a tourist site being next were dangerously high.

Crossing the Outlet Bridge, Connor entered the final stretch of path to the Memorial when he noticed a 4x4 vehicle with blacked-out windows speeding along the East Basin Drive. Weaving in between the traffic, it too was headed directly for the Jefferson Memorial.

Connor put on a last burst of speed, his backpack riding high on his shoulders. He fought against the flow of tourists heading the opposite way. The 4x4 disappeared from his line of sight. But Connor was convinced the driver's objective was the same as his – the President's daughter.

He reached the base of the Memorial.

'ALICIA?' he shouted, looking left and right between the countless faces of the passing people.

A head turned in his direction. Connor immediately recognized the dark flowing curls and oversized sunglasses.

'Alicia!' he cried in relief as he bounded up the steps two at a time.

'What are *you* doing here?' she demanded, both baffled and upset by his unexpected appearance.

'My job,' he replied, grabbing her hand and pulling her down the steps.

But Alicia resisted. She tugged her hand free from his grasp. 'Connor, you're *not* my bodyguard.'

'But I am your friend and we have to leave now!' he insisted.

'I've already alerted Secret Service,' she explained, taking off her sunglasses and giving him a defiant stare. 'I don't need your help.'

'They'll be too late.' Connor's gaze swept the Memorial for approaching threats, his alert level firmly at Code Orange. There were fewer tourists now and only a couple of park rangers. The speeding car he'd seen must have pulled up behind the building.

'What do you mean?' asked Alicia, hearing the tension in his voice.

'Your phone, it's bugged. Someone is intercepting your calls and tracking you *now*. And it's not Secret Service.'

A flicker of shock passed across Alicia's face, then she snorted in disbelief. 'Listen, if this is some trick to prove yourself –'

'Far from it,' Connor cut in. He pointed to the skyline. 'See for yourself. Washington is under attack. I'm sorry I couldn't tell you I was your buddyguard before. That wasn't my choice. But my friendship is *real*. You have to trust me.'

He offered his hand again.

Alicia looked him in the eyes, trying to judge his sincerity. Under his gaze, her resistance soon crumbled. 'I do, I do,' she replied, taking his hand.

'Then let's go,' said Connor.

The two of them turned to run, but blocking their path were four men armed with sub-machine guns.

HOSTAGE
CHAPTER 70

'Alicia Mendez, come with us,' said the lead man.

They all wore matching black jackets and mirrored sunglasses. Each carried an FN P90 sub-machine gun and a holstered SIG Sauer P229. Pinned to their jacket collars were identical red badges with the gold five-pointed star of the Secret Service.

'You got here quickly,' remarked Alicia.

'We were in the vicinity,' he explained.

'And who *exactly* are you?' asked Connor, not willing to let his guard down.

'Agent John Walker,' the man replied, flicking open his credentials. 'And *you*?'

Satisfied with the agent's ID, he replied, 'Connor Reeves.'

The agent arched an eyebrow. 'We'd been informed you'd left.' He glanced at the ominous smoke-filled skyline. 'Well, you'd best come with us too.'

He signalled to his men who'd been keeping a close watch on their surroundings.

'Let's move out.'

The four agents swiftly escorted Alicia and Connor

down the steps and round the memorial. They followed a treelined path to the car park. The blacked-out 4x4 was waiting by the kerbside, its engine running. As they approached, Agent Walker keyed his palm mic.

'Delta Four to Control. Nomad recovered. Destination update requested. Over.'

The agent listened a moment, then keyed his mic again.

'Received and understood, Control. En route to Blue One. Delta Four out.' He turned to Alicia. 'We're taking you to a safe house,' he explained.

As he opened the rear passenger door to the 4x4, its engine died. The driver looked over at his team leader with a bewildered expression.

'It won't start. All the electrics have shorted out –'

Suddenly the ground erupted with a spray of bullets and the 4x4's bodywork rattled as if caught in a hailstorm. One of the agents screamed as he was cut down by the gunfire.

'GET IN!' yelled Agent Walker, shoving Alicia into the back passenger seat.

Connor dived in after her, pushing her down into the footwell to shield her from the deadly shots.

'Stay there,' Agent Walker ordered. He went to slam the door shut, but another blast of bullets ripped across the 4x4's bodywork. The agent grunted in pain and blood splattered the interior. He slumped forward on to the seat, jamming open the door.

Connor turned to Alicia and saw blood on her too. 'Are you hit?' he asked.

She mutely shook her head, unable to take her eyes off

the murdered agent. Connor couldn't allow himself to think about the man's sudden and violent death. This was a Code Red situation. He had to focus all his attention on getting Alicia out of the ambush alive.

The gun battle raged on. The driver jumped from the immobilized 4x4 and joined the last of his team in returning fire. Connor risked a glance through the tinted windscreen. The enemy had secured good cover, firing from behind the car park's concrete barriers. The two agents, on the other hand, were in the open, the immobilized bulletproof vehicle their only protection.

Connor ducked as the windscreen thudded under the impact of more rounds. But the bullet-resistant glass held. Then there was an agonized cry as a third agent was downed.

'Radio for back-up!' Connor shouted to the driver.

'Radio's dead,' he replied grimly, firing off another shot. 'And I'm fast running out of ammo.'

'Then we'll have to make a break for it,' said Connor, realizing their chances of survival were dwindling. He didn't know what the enemies' intentions were – kill or kidnap – but he couldn't allow either to happen to Alicia. Peering through the window again, he hunted for a possible escape route. Their only option lay in heading back the way they'd come. But the path was totally exposed for about twenty metres until it reached the treeline. Any escape attempt would be little more than a suicidal dash.

Then Connor remembered his backpack.

'What are you doing?' asked Alicia as he hurriedly removed his pack.

'Making a shield,' Connor explained, unzipping the panel to double its length. 'It's bulletproof.'

'I'll give you covering fire,' said the driver, acknowledging Connor's intention.

'What about you?' asked Connor.

'Just get Nomad to safety.'

Connor gave him a single grave nod in acknowledgement, conscious of the sacrifice this unknown agent was about to make for them. 'We'll head for the trees. Are you ready, Alicia?'

She glanced out of the door. 'We'll never make it,' she said.

'Imagine you're racing to the finish line in the four hundred metres,' said Connor.

Alicia managed a strained smile. 'OK, but I'm never usually shot at!'

She took a deep breath and steeled herself for the perilous sprint.

'On my mark,' said the driver. 'Three . . . two . . .'

Gripping the handle of his backpack, Connor prayed the liquid body armour would do its job.

'. . . one . . . GO!'

HOSTAGE

CHAPTER 71

The driver blasted the enemy with a storm of bullets from his sub-machine gun. Clambering over Agent Walker's body, Connor bolted out of the car with Alicia. He kept the backpack shield high to protect them as they ran. With his other arm he held Alicia close by his side so she was always in his cover. Their feet pounded in unison across the gravel path.

'Whatever happens, don't stop!' ordered Connor.

They were halfway when they heard the driver's gun give out. There was a rapid return of fire and a pained cry.

But Connor daren't look back.

'STOP OR WE'LL SHOOT!' shouted one of the gunmen.

They had just 10 metres to the treeline – 8 . . . 5 . . . The ground beneath their feet spat dirt as a spray of warning fire cut across their path.

Alicia screamed but Connor urged her onwards. They were almost there when a barrage of bullets struck the backpack. The brutal impact knocked Connor off his feet. They stumbled the last few metres before collapsing together behind the trunk of an elm tree.

'Are you all right?' Alicia gasped, realizing he'd taken the full force of the hits.

'Yes . . .' Connor managed to reply. His shoulder felt bruised, but the liquid body armour had stopped the rounds from doing any lethal damage.

Masked gunmen now emerged from behind the concrete barriers and advanced on their hiding place. One of them fired high into the treeline.

'STAY WHERE YOU ARE!' he ordered.

'What do we do now?' asked Alicia.

Connor realized the gunmen intended to kidnap her, otherwise they wouldn't have bothered with warning shots. But they'd equally shown their willingness to use deadly force to achieve their aims, even if it meant wounding Alicia and killing him. Their situation was desperate whatever decision he made.

'We keep running,' he replied, scrambling to his feet.

With the body armour now slung over his shoulder to protect their backs, Connor shepherded Alicia deeper into the cluster of trees. The gunmen gave chase. Connor weaved in between the trunks, hoping to prevent a clear shot. There was a burst of gunfire. Bullets whizzed past, taking out chunks of bark. Splinters rained down on their heads as the two of them powered on. Then, as they approached the main road of Ohio Drive, the trees thinned out and they lost their cover.

'Over the bridge!' shouted Connor.

They raced across. The gunmen were still among the trees. But it wouldn't be long before they had them in their sights again. Connor realized their only hope was to get to the safe house. From what he recalled, he knew it lay somewhere east of the memorial. Searching for the quickest route, Connor spotted an underpass on the other side of the junction of 14th and 15th Streets.

'Through that tunnel!' he directed Alicia.

The traffic was heavy, but with no time to spare they dashed across the highway. Cars swerved round them. A truck blasted its horn as they were almost mown down beneath its wheels. Connor heard gunfire and felt a bullet catch the corner of his backpack, spinning him into the side of a passing car. From behind there was a mighty *bang* and the ear-splitting crunch of metal as several vehicles collided. Horns blared and tyres squealed as the traffic ground to a sudden halt.

Connor kept his grip on Alicia and they darted into the underpass.

'Where are we going?' she asked, breathing hard.

'To the safe house,' said Connor, trying to reboot his phone on the run. But the screen remained blank. 'Is your phone working?'

Alicia pulled it from her pocket. 'No!'

Damn, thought Connor, *but at least she can't be tracked any longer.*

He tried to recall exactly where the safe house was: 6 . . . 8 . . . 6 . . . *E Street SW.*

'How far's E Street South-West from here?'

'Only about four blocks away,' replied Alicia.

'Then let's go.'

Behind they heard the shouts of the gunmen echoing through the tunnel.

Alicia now led the way. They crossed the road, jumping the central reservation, and headed along Maine Avenue. They were about to duck into a side street, when a blacked-out 4x4 screeched to a halt in front of them. A blonde-haired woman wearing a green Secret Service lapel badge jumped out.

'Quick, get in,' urged Agent Brooke from Alicia's PES team.

They dived into the rear passenger compartment. She closed the doors behind them and leapt into the front seat. Flooring the accelerator, she drove off at high speed.

Connor looked through the back windscreen. The gunmen had disappeared from view.

'Are we . . . glad to run . . . into you!' Alicia panted.

'You're a hard one to keep track of,' replied Agent Brooke, arching an eyebrow.

Connor turned to her. 'I thought you were off-duty today, like Kyle.'

Agent Brooke gave him a sharp look. 'Everyone's called in during an emergency.'

'Not that I'm ungrateful,' Connor quickly added.

She turned left on to C Street.

'Aren't we going to the safe house?' Connor asked.

'Yes,' replied Agent Brooke.

'But isn't E Street the other way?'

'There's a roadblock due to the bombings. We have to go round.'

At the traffic lights, she turned left again on to 14th

Street. They headed past the junction to D Street and continued on, joining the main highway that led out of Washington. As the Jefferson Memorial came back into view, Connor began to sense something was wrong. The detour wasn't logical.

'How long until we get to Blue Two then?' asked Connor.

'About five minutes,' replied Agent Brooke.

Connor had called her bluff. The call sign for the safe house was 'Blue One'. It was now that he noticed the colour of Agent Brooke's Secret Service badge. The other agents today had been wearing *red* lapel badges. On his first outing with Secret Service, Kyle had told him the colour-coded badges were an important security measure. Any legitimate agents on a protection detail would be wearing matching badges.

Connor reached for Alicia's hand and squeezed it. *We have to get out of here*, he mouthed to her.

Her brow knitted in confusion. *What?* she mouthed back.

'*She's NOT Secret Service!*' he whispered.

As the traffic slowed, Connor made a grab for the door handle – but discovered it was locked. He threw his shoulder against the door. 'Let us out!'

Agent Brooke spun round in her seat. 'You're brighter than I thought,' she snarled.

Drawing her gun, she shot Connor point-blank in the chest.

HOSTAGE
CHAPTER 72

'I've lost contact!' cried Amir, searching his computer screen for the green dot that represented Connor. But the bird's-eye view of Washington DC was devoid of any tracer signal.

Charley sped over from her central workstation in the Buddyguard operations room. 'It may be just a satellite delay.'

'No, I've run diagnostic checks. The uplink is fine.'

'What about resetting the connection?'

'Already done that. Nothing.'

Charley frowned, a bad feeling starting to creep in. 'So where was Connor when you lost the signal?'

'Near the Jefferson Memorial,' Amir replied, pointing to the location on the screen. 'Judging by his movements, he'd made contact with Alicia and was heading to the car park. Shortly after –' he clicked his fingers in the air – 'gone!'

'What about the Cell-Finity bug on her phone?' she asked. 'We're mirroring the trace, aren't we?'

Amir offered a pained expression. 'That disappeared at the same time as Connor's.'

Charley snatched up the desk phone and dialled Connor's number. The line sounded a continuous dead tone. She put the phone down.

'You don't think ... they've been caught in a bomb blast, do you?' Amir asked fearfully.

Charley's face went pale at the thought. She rapidly typed at the keyboard, requesting an update on the Washington attacks. A few seconds later, a confidential security news feed popped up on the screen. She scanned the page, but there was no report of a fourth explosion ... not yet anyway.

'During a state of emergency, the government can block all mobile communications,' said Bugsy, coming over from his workstation in the corner of the operations room.

'That's not exactly helpful!' remarked Amir.

'There're two very good reasons. One, to stop the spread of panic among civilians. Two, to prevent a mobile phone signal triggering an explosive device. Nowadays, the remote-control IED is the terrorists' first choice of bomb. The group behind this attack wouldn't even need to be in the city, let alone the country, at the time of the attack.'

'So how can we locate Connor and Alicia and find out if they're safe or not?' asked Charley.

'Have you tried the GPS-tracker that Secret Service implanted in his watch?'

Amir shook his head. 'We weren't given access to that.'

Bugsy plumped himself down at his computer terminal. 'Shouldn't be a problem to fix,' he replied, popping a stick of gum into his mouth and chewing hard. 'The tracker will be transmitting on a separate protected frequency.'

His fingers rattled across the keyboard as he quickly gained access to the Secret Service Locator program. Leaning back in his chair to study the data, Bugsy scratched his bald head with bemusement.

'Strange . . . even that's disappeared,' he mumbled, half to himself.

On hearing this, Charley picked up the phone again and dialled a different number. She gave her call sign and typed in her security password. 'Can you give me confirmation of Nomad's arrival?'

After listening to the response, she numbly put the phone down.

'They're not at the safe house,' she informed them. 'We need to update Colonel Black. I fear the worst has happened.'

HOSTAGE

CHAPTER 73

A body lay in the middle of the disused aircraft hangar, a bullet through the head.

'That will ensure her silence,' grinned Malik, lowering his gun.

'But that agent was one of us!' exclaimed Hazim, his face aghast at the brutal execution.

Malik's expression became stony. 'We must tie up all loose ends, Hazim. A double agent can never be trusted.'

'Well, what about all those innocent people killed by our bombs? You never told me about that part of the plan. How can we justify those killings to God –'

'Don't you *dare* question my command, Hazim!' snarled Malik, taking a step closer and looking Hazim in the eye. 'They were infidels. But I'm beginning to wonder if I should be questioning *your* commitment to the cause?'

'No, not at all,' defended Hazim, vehemently shaking his head.

'I hope not,' said Malik, then strode away, leaving Hazim staring at the body of the ruthlessly slain agent.

Malik approached the 4x4 where his men stood guard.

Peering into the rear passenger compartment, he admired his prize. The President's daughter was slumped unconscious on the back seat, a tranquillizer dart piercing her neck.

'When the dust settles, Washington will discover what we've *really* achieved,' he laughed coldly.

Bahir swept a surveillance scanner over Alicia's prone body. A red light blinked on as the device passed over her jeans pocket. Bahir pulled out the bugged phone.

'A job well done!' he said, congratulating himself on his programming skill with the Cell-Finity bug. He extracted the SIM card and snapped it in half, before crushing the phone under his boot.

The scanner flashed again, this time over her bag. He rifled through the contents and pulled out the panic alarm.

'I trust that's not still active?' said Malik.

Bahir shook his head. 'The EMP Kedar fired during the attack at the memorial disabled all electronic equipment in the 4x4's vicinity.' He broke apart the alarm case and disconnected the innards. 'This sweep is just to make one hundred per cent certain.'

Bahir now turned his attention to Connor's body. The scanner immediately found his smartphone. He popped out the SIM card and destroyed it. He went to smash the phone too when he noticed the screen boot up and the graphic of a lock appear.

'That's strange,' he muttered. 'How can its circuitry still be functioning?'

Intrigued by the anomaly, he checked there were no outgoing signals, then pocketed the phone for later analysis.

He continued his surveillance sweep. The scanner blinked rapidly as it passed over Connor's wrist.

'Someone certainly didn't want to lose this one,' he remarked, removing the fancy watch.

'I wonder why that is?' Malik mused, leaning in closer to get a better look at Connor's face.

'He's a special guest of the President on an exchange programme,' Hazim replied flatly as he rejoined the others. 'His name's Connor Reeves. He's English.'

'Well, he's not invited to our party,' said Kedar, drawing his handgun and aiming at Connor's head.

'Hold your fire!' ordered Malik.

'But I thought we agreed no prisoners, apart from the girl.'

Malik pushed Kedar's gun away.

'No, don't kill him . . .' He tugged the tranquillizer dart from Connor's chest. 'Not yet anyway. Having another child hostage might prove a useful bargaining chip.'

HOSTAGE
CHAPTER 74

'The White House is all clear, Mr President,' announced George. 'The bomb disposal team have swept the residence, three times now, and *that* particular threat appears to have been a hoax.'

'A *hoax*? The others certainly weren't,' replied President Mendez, seated at the head of the conference table aboard Air Force One. The past few hours had been some of the worst the nation had known since 9/11 and he was in no mood for practical jokes.

'This was most likely a prank call, inspired by but unconnected to the bombings,' explained Karen Wright. 'We couldn't take that risk, though.'

'It was the right decision, Karen. But I need to get back into the Oval Office and make a statement to reassure the nation. What's the situation at the other locations in Washington?'

The Director of National Intelligence swiped her finger across her touchscreen computer. An updated situation report appeared on the screen.

'All targeted areas have been cordoned off. Official reports indicate structural damage to Secret Service and FBI Headquarters. The US Capitol building has escaped unscathed. There were one hundred and fifty-four casualties at the last count, but mercifully few confirmed deaths. We can thank the swift response of our emergency services for that.'

Karen scanned down the page to the ERT report.

'The Environmental Response Teams have completed initial atmospheric analysis. Apart from the anticipated smoke and fumes, no chemical, biological or nuclear compounds were found in any of the attacks.'

President Mendez breathed an audible sigh of relief. 'A dirty bomb would have been our worst nightmare. So, can we assume the immediate threat is over?'

'It appears that way,' replied Karen. 'But as a standard precaution we've closed all public buildings, diverted traffic out of the downtown area and a block-by-block search for any suspicious vehicles or packages is under way. So far, no further danger has been reported.'

'Then we can inform the public that we are in control of the situation.'

'Yes, Mr President.'

'Excellent. It's important that we display a show of strength against these terrorists.'

'I'm afraid it's not all good news, Mr President,' said Dirk, entering the airborne conference room, his face drawn and haggard following a high-priority call from the Joint Operations Centre. 'As you know, we received confirmation from Delta Four that your daughter was picked up and being taken to a safe house. But –'

'But what?' demanded President Mendez.

'The team never reached the safe house.'

President Mendez blinked, unwilling to believe what he'd just heard. 'And you've only learnt about this now?' He glanced at the clock on the cabin wall. 'It's been over *five* hours. Where is she then?'

Dirk's solemn expression said it all. 'The Secret Service team has just been found dead in the Jefferson Memorial car park. There'd been a gun battle.'

'Alicia too?' he asked, his hands beginning to tremble. As President he was more than capable of handling a national crisis, but as a father the thought of losing his daughter was too much to bear.

Dirk shook his head. 'There was no sign of her.'

'So she's still alive?'

'Yes, in all probability,' replied Dirk. 'I've also been informed Connor was with her at the time.'

President Mendez frowned. 'I thought he'd left?'

'So did I. But Buddyguard uncovered last-minute evidence that your daughter's phone was tapped and being tracked.'

'Then why haven't you found her yet?' asked President Mendez, anguish gripping his heart like a vice.

'Her panic alarm malfunctioned. We lifted the block on mobile calls, but her cellphone's dead too,' explained Dirk. 'With Secret Service headquarters crippled by the bomb blast and the current state of emergency, our teams have been stretched to the limit. If we'd only been allowed to put a tracker on her –'

'Dirk, I don't want excuses. I need results,' President Mendez barked, pounding the table with his fist. 'Land this plane right now. Get me back to Washington. Divert every resource available to *finding my daughter*!'

HOSTAGE
CHAPTER 75

A splitting headache was the first sensation Connor was aware of. Then a deep throbbing ache in his muscles. Followed by an unsettling queasiness in his stomach. As he regained full consciousness, he attempted to swallow, but his mouth was dry as a desert and his throat sore and swollen.

Cracking open his eyes, the light hurt like fire and indistinct shapes swirled before his vision. When it eventually settled, Connor discovered he was lying on a hard concrete floor. In front of him was a battered plastic bottle of water and a featureless wall. Fighting the heaviness in his limbs, he tried to sit up but was instantly hit by a wave of nausea. He lay still until the feeling passed.

With an immense effort, he managed to prop himself up against the wall. His head swam and the sickness returned. Reaching for the water bottle, Connor undid the cap and took a swig. It was warm and slightly bitter, but revived him enough to regain his senses. He had no idea how long he'd been unconscious. It could have been hours or days. But judging by the hunger cramps in his stomach, he'd missed a meal or two.

Looking around, he discovered he was in a small windowless room, a single bare bulb for light. There was a door to his left, flush to the frame and without a handle. To his right lay Alicia, her body discarded like a rag doll on a thin mattress in the corner.

'Alicia!' he croaked.

She didn't respond. Fighting the nausea and pain in his muscles, he dragged himself over to her. Alicia was so still that he thought she was dead. Then Connor noticed a strand of hair across her mouth quivering as she exhaled a shallow breath.

Connor gently shook her shoulder and she groaned, still deep in a drug-induced sleep.

'Alicia, wake up!' urged Connor.

Her eyes wearily blinked open. 'Huh?'

'Drink this,' he said, pressing the bottle to her lips.

Alicia managed a sip.

'I think I'm going to be sick,' she rasped.

'It's just the effects of the tranquillizer, or whatever drug they've given us,' explained Connor.

He gave her time to recover, then helped her into a sitting position.

'What's going on?' she murmured, holding her head in her hands.

'We've been kidnapped,' said Connor, keeping his voice low. There was no one else in the room, but he didn't want their conversation overheard by whoever had taken them. 'What do you remember?'

Alicia tried to think, disorientated by the strange

environment. 'Umm ... you getting shot ... by Agent Brooke. Then she turned the gun on me and it all went dark.' She looked up at Connor, her eyes wide, panic bubbling just beneath the surface. 'I thought I was ... *you* were dead.'

Connor took her hand, trying to calm her. 'No, we were just sedated.'

'How long have we been out for?'

Connor glanced at his wrist, but found his watch had been taken. 'Your guess is as good as mine.'

Alicia looked fearfully round the bare windowless cell. 'Do you know where we are?'

'No idea,' replied Connor, forcing himself to his feet. But he feared they were a long way from home.

Swaying slightly, he made the five short steps across the room to the door. He tried to push it open. Then he tried to get his fingers round the edges and pull the other way. But it wouldn't budge. Pressing his ear to the door, Connor listened for any noise that might give away their location.

He heard nothing. Just deafening silence. It was as if they were cut off from the entire world.

HOSTAGE
CHAPTER 76

The atmosphere in the White House Situation Room was tense and frantic as Colonel Black was shown his seat at the conference table. Already gathered round the long mahogany desk were the key members of the National Security Council and the head of every relevant security and intelligence agency, all pooling their resources to solve the case in hand. National Security staff worked feverishly in the background, analysing incoming data and delivering constant updates.

'Good of you to come,' said President Mendez, acknowledging Colonel Black's arrival with a firm handshake.

To the colonel's eyes, the President had aged dramatically, his renowned youthful vigour weighed down by a terrible burden.

'It's my honour and duty,' replied Colonel Black. 'Don't worry, we will find your daughter.'

And Connor, he promised himself. He'd never lost a buddyguard yet and he didn't intend to now.

The White House Chief of Staff appeared and handed

the colonel a folder. 'This contains a summary of all the information we hold at present, including your organization's report.'

'Thank you,' acknowledged the colonel, immediately scanning the files.

'Is there *any* word yet?' asked the First Lady, who sat beside her husband, pulling at a frayed hankie. Exhausted from her transatlantic flight home, her usual glamorous appearance had all but disappeared under the strain, her make-up streaked with anguished tears.

'I'm afraid not, Mrs Mendez,' replied George. 'But, I can assure you, we're doing everything in our power.'

'Well, it's not enough!' she snapped. 'It's been twelve hours. Alicia could be *anywhere* in the world by now.'

'That's why we've brought the CIA in on this,' informed Karen, offering the First Lady a glass of water that she took in one trembling hand. 'They've put out a worldwide alert to every agent. If they get a sniff of anything, we'll be the first to hear about it.'

'That's reassuring to know,' said Mrs Mendez, sipping at the water and trying to regain her composure.

A blonde-haired woman with frameless glasses leant forward and raised her hand.

'What shall we do about the press?' asked Lara Johnson, the White House Press Secretary.

'Keep a lid on it for as long as you can,' replied George.

'But we could use them to promote a search for the President's daughter,' she suggested.

Karen shook her head vehemently. 'Then we'll have

every Tom, Dick and Harry phoning in. And any possible lead will disappear under a pile of misguided calls. No, concentrate on the containment of the bombings until we have more concrete information.'

'About the bombings,' interrupted General Martin Shaw, walking over and saluting Colonel Black. 'I think we must assume a connection.'

'Why's that?' asked the President.

'The timing for one. The last contact with Delta team and Alicia's disappearance were just minutes after they detonated. I believe these attacks were merely a *distraction* for the main event.'

'A distraction!' exclaimed George. 'The three bombs almost crippled Washington.'

'Exactly. Their targets were designed to disrupt communications and impede the workings of Secret Service. With their attention focused elsewhere, the kidnappers had all the time they needed to escape with the President's daughter.'

'I concur with the general,' said Colonel Black. 'It would certainly explain the planting of the Cell-Finity bug and the coordinated ambush on your Secret Service team. Has any terrorist group claimed responsibility yet?'

'Still nothing,' Karen replied. 'But we're doing an analysis of the most likely candidates –'

'We've got a lead!' Dirk interrupted, coming off the phone.

The Situation Room went silent as he pressed a remote and a live-link flashed up on the central monitor. An auburn-haired man with a rounded pockmarked face appeared.

'Mr President, my name is Agent Cooper,' he declared. 'I'm in situ at a disused aircraft hangar near Stafford Airport. My team have discovered one of our off-duty Secret Service agents, Lauren Brooke, shot dead, execution-style.'

The camera panned to show a body sprawled across the concrete floor, a pool of dried blood surrounding it. The First Lady gasped at the gruesome sight and averted her eyes.

'How does this connect with Alicia's disappearance?' asked President Mendez, a cold sensation creeping into the pit of his stomach.

'My team found the remains of a cellphone that bear her fingerprints.' The camera was angled to display the shattered phone. Then an empty 4x4 came into view, surrounded by three agents analysing the vehicle for further clues. 'They've also just confirmed that hairs on the back seat of Agent Brooke's vehicle match your daughter's.'

'But is there any sign of my little girl?' asked the First Lady, almost dreading the answer.

'No, ma'am,' replied Agent Cooper. 'But that can only be seen as good news. It indicates she's still alive. We also found this at the scene.' He directed the camera to a backpack lying in the footwell of the 4x4.

'That belongs to Connor,' volunteered Colonel Black, recognizing both the design and Justin Reeves' face in the attached key fob.

'Connor, sir?' questioned the agent.

'He's a boy secretly assigned to protect Alicia,' Dirk explained. 'Part of the Buddyguard organization.'

Agent Cooper raised an eyebrow at this revelation but made no direct comment. 'That explains the backpack's unusual construction then. The rear panel's liquid body armour, it shows signs of recent combat usage. But there's no blood, so it appears to have been effective.'

'That means Connor's still with her,' said Colonel Black, feeling relieved that his charge was most probably alive and, at the same time, more optimistic about the survival prospects of the President's daughter. He just prayed that Connor's basic training would be enough to see him through the crisis.

'Looks that way,' replied the agent.

'Then there's hope,' said the President, squeezing his wife's hand.

The First Lady returned a strained smile.

Dirk sighed inwardly at President Mendez's unwavering belief in the boy. 'But, Mr President, it could also mean our problem's doubled . . . if they've *both* been kidnapped.'

HOSTAGE
CHAPTER 77

'This is all my fault,' sobbed Alicia, her entire body trembling with shock. 'I should have listened to Secret Service... if I had, we wouldn't be in this mess. Now I've put you in danger too, Connor. What have I done? I'm sorry... I'm so sorry.'

Connor knelt before her. He was as scared as she was, but he couldn't allow his own fears to spiral out of control. He had to remain strong – for both their sakes.

'This *isn't* your fault,' he assured her. 'The blame lies with our kidnappers. What we need to do is stay calm and focused. Your father, Secret Service, Buddyguard, *everyone* will be looking for us.'

Alicia stared at Connor, her eyes wide and swimming with tears. 'Do you really think so?'

'I know so. We just have to hold out until they come.'

'But what if they can't find us?'

Connor was aware that was a distinct possibility, but replied, 'With all the government's resources, they're bound to sooner or later. We must have faith.'

Alicia fell silent and gazed doubtfully around their tiny

cell. Connor could see she was battling to keep her panic in check. But she bravely wiped away her tears and managed to stop shaking.

'So who do you think has taken us?' she eventually asked.

'Agent Brooke must have been working for those gunmen,' Connor replied. 'And with all the bombings I can only guess that they're terrorists of some sort.'

'So they're going to ... kill us?' said Alicia, her voice fragile and desperate.

Connor gently shook his head. 'If they wanted us dead, that would've happened already.'

'Then what *do* they want?'

Connor heard a bolt unlock and he spun round. 'I think we're about to find out.'

His nerves taut as a wire, Connor stood protectively in front of Alicia as the door swung open. A colossal man in black robes stepped inside, his bulk almost filling the tiny cell. The man's face was obscured by an all-enveloping coal-black headscarf that left only his dark eyes blazing through at them.

'*Ta'ala ma'ee!*' he growled in what Connor presumed was Arabic.

When they didn't respond to his command, he grabbed Connor by the arm and shoved him roughly through the doorway. Connor didn't want to be separated from Alicia and struggled in his grip.

'Let me go!' he protested.

But the ferocious glare from the man warned him not to resist any further.

Their captor treated Alicia more respectfully. He gestured for her to leave the cell and follow Connor.

Numbly getting to her feet, Alicia hurried over to Connor's side. They said nothing as they were marched down a short corridor. Connor kept alert to every detail, just as he'd been trained to do. He noticed their captor wore sandals, his feet were dark-skinned and his style of robes Middle Eastern in origin. There were no windows in the corridor and the air smelt stale and slightly damp, so he guessed they must be underground. In a small room opposite their cell, he'd glimpsed a computer with an array of electronic gadgetry. If connected to the internet, he might be able to send a message for help – that is, if he found out exactly where they were and *if* he ever got the chance.

At the end of the corridor a flight of wooden stairs led upwards into blackness. The temptation to make a run for it was almost overwhelming. Then a second masked man stepped from a doorway, a sub-machine gun in his grasp. The brief flicker of hope Connor had felt was extinguished in an instant.

Their captor shoved them into the end room. Alicia recoiled in horror as they were greeted by three more faceless men. Two carried assault rifles and the third brandished a gleaming curved dagger, its bone handle studded with jewels. As threatening as the guns were, the presence of the knife was even more intimidating.

'Kneel!' ordered the man in accented English, pointing to a spot on the floor with his dagger.

On the wall behind was a large black flag with Arabic

writing in white. Positioned opposite was a video camera on a stand. Connor felt an icy spike of fear.

Their captors hadn't killed them yet, simply because they intended to do so *live* on camera.

HOSTAGE
CHAPTER 78

Connor knelt next to Alicia, who once again was trembling like a leaf. He couldn't blame her; his own heart was thudding furiously within his chest. Neither of them could take their eyes off the vicious-looking knife as it was waved in front of their faces. The man with the dagger seemed to relish their fear and purposefully took his time.

Suppressing his panic, Connor vowed that he wouldn't go down without a fight. However futile the attempt, he'd at least try to save Alicia. It would be what his father would have done in such a situation.

The man, who appeared to be the leader, placed the tip of his knife under Alicia's chin and forced her to raise her head and look him in the eye.

'No need to cry,' he declared. 'We've no *intention* of harming you. You are our guests.'

Overcoming her abject terror, Alicia stared defiantly back at the man. 'That's funny, we didn't get the invite.'

The leader grunted a dry laugh. 'Ah! American humour. How amusing!'

He sheathed his knife then clapped his hands once, the

sudden noise startling Alicia. A moment later, a tray was brought in and laid before them. Upon it were two pieces of flatbread, a bowl of hummus, a jug of chilled water, some rice and a thick meat stew. As it was presented to them, an awful thought crossed Connor's mind. *Our final meal*.

'Please eat,' invited the leader casually, as if they were dining in a restaurant.

Ravenous from the after-effects of the sedative, Connor and Alicia were unable to resist the offer. Tentatively picking up a spoon, Connor dipped it in the stew and scooped some into his mouth. Simple as the meal was, with death so close at hand, the food tasted almost divine. Alicia joined him, tearing off a piece of flatbread and nibbling at it nervously. But, overcome with hunger, she soon dug in and they both momentarily forgot their grim predicament.

As they ate, the leader nodded to one of his men to press Record on the video. The camera's light flashed red and the leader addressed the lens.

'President Mendez, we, the Brotherhood of the Rising Crescent, hold your daughter hostage,' he said with an arrogant pride in his voice. 'We also have her friend, the English boy. As you can see, they're both well and being looked after according to their status.'

He gestured to them with a sweep of his hand and Connor looked up, his mouth half-full. He now realized the meal was purely a show for the camera.

'I'm certain, as a father and the President of your country, you wish for their safe return,' continued their hooded captor. 'Their fate very much lies in *your* hands.'

Both Connor and Alicia stopped eating, the thinly veiled threat killing all appetite. They glanced anxiously at one another, each wondering if the broadcast was going out live.

Connor thought about shouting out or signing a message, but he knew little of their location – except they were possibly somewhere in the Middle East – and he knew even less about their captors that would help Secret Service or Buddyguard rescue them. He briefly considered an escape attempt while the terrorists were distracted. But one glance towards the doorway, where the gunman stood guard in the corridor, soon dispelled any such illusions. They'd be shot down before they even planted one foot on the stairwell. He was utterly powerless.

Yet, just as he felt a cloak of despair settle over him, Connor suddenly realized that he did have two pieces of information he could communicate on camera. He just had to stay sharp and proceed with caution.

HOSTAGE
CHAPTER 79

'Our demands are simple,' stated the hooded leader, his image filling the central flatscreen monitor in the White House Situation Room. 'You have until midnight on the third of July to release every one of our brothers imprisoned on terrorism charges and announce the withdrawal of all American troops from the Middle East. Meet the first demand and the boy will be freed as proof of our word. Meet the second and you'll be reunited with your daughter. These are our terms. For this year, the fourth of July will be *our* Independence Day.'

The picture froze on Alicia's face. Her expression was defiant, but her complexion was pale and her eyes shone with barely restrained tears.

A deathly silence fell over the Situation Room. No one even breathed, too stunned by the inconceivable kidnapping of the President's daughter.

Then the First Lady let out a sob and the Situation Room was motivated into frenzied action.

'At least we know they're both alive,' stated Karen, the Director of National Intelligence trying to offer the First

Lady some comfort. 'The video was time-stamped just fifty-eight minutes ago.'

'Has this gone public?' President Mendez asked, his voice strangely fragile.

'Not so far as we're aware,' replied Dirk. 'The video link was sent direct to your secretary's email account.'

'That's odd,' remarked the press secretary. 'Most terrorists want publicity. I'd have thought they'd plaster this across the entire internet.'

'There's no guarantee they won't,' said George, grimacing, then popping an antacid tablet into his mouth to ease his heartburn. 'It'll all be part of their sick propaganda war.'

'Who *are* the Brotherhood of the Rising Crescent anyway?' General Shaw demanded.

Karen's Middle East Advisor, Omar Ahmed, opened a file on his laptop and linked it with the Situation Room's central monitor.

'They're a fundamentalist group, based in Yemen,' he explained, pointing to the information on display. 'Unrepresentative of the majority of their faith, their stated goal is "To fight every non-believer until victory or martyrdom and to make every American regret their occupation of their lands". The leader is believed to be Malik Hussain.' A grainy picture of an Arab, too indistinct to make out his features, flashed up on the screen. 'Born in Sana'a, the capital city of Yemen, to a wealthy oil family, he was educated in Saudi Arabia before heading to Afghanistan to fight with the Taliban. After that he pops up in Pakistan and Iraq until settling permanently in his homeland.'

Omar closed his laptop.

'Is that all you have on them?' said General Shaw.

Omar nodded regretfully. 'Like many minority extremist outfits, they were under our radar. The CIA simply didn't consider they had the resources to launch a viable attack.'

'Well, they did!' snarled Dirk. The Secret Service Director's jaw was tense with anger.

'Yes, we underestimated this enemy,' admitted Omar. 'But to coordinate bombings and a kidnapping on this scale some *other* organization has to be backing them.'

'Like who?' asked the President.

Omar shrugged. 'These groups function as independent cells. We may never find that out.'

There was a heavy silence round the conference table as they considered the grave implications of this.

'Our first priority must be to locate and safely retrieve the hostages,' said General Shaw decisively. 'Have we sourced the origin of the email yet?'

'Our analysts are working on it as we speak,' replied Dirk. 'And technicians are searching for clues in the transmission itself.'

'We're also checking every outbound flight within the last twenty-four hours,' added Karen. 'Charter, private, commercial and business. That should narrow our search.'

The President thumped his fist on the table in frustration. 'How could these people smuggle my daughter out of the country without *someone* knowing?'

'My poor little girl, she must be terrified,' said the First Lady, fresh tears running down her cheeks.

President Mendez drew his wife into his arms and she wept on his shoulder. 'At least Alicia's not alone in her plight. Connor's been trained to handle hostage situations. Isn't that right, Colonel?'

Colonel Black nodded, although he now seriously wished he'd dedicated more time to it in the Buddyguard syllabus. But he had faith in Connor's resilience. 'Connor will be as crucial to your daughter's survival as your team in finding her,' he assured them.

Dirk couldn't help a dismissive snort. 'Some bodyguard your boy turned out to be,' he muttered, evidently cracking under the pressure.

Catching his comment, Colonel Black spun on him. 'Well, if you hadn't dismissed him so readily, he might have been able to do his job properly,' he retorted. 'And, thanks to Connor's intervention, the last ring of defence hasn't been broken yet.'

Dirk shot him an incredulous look. 'He's a hostage! An *additional* problem.'

'Connor's an asset,' corrected the colonel, and asked for the video to be replayed. 'He's already informed us that they're being held underground and that there are at least five gunmen.'

He paused the video and indicated the screen. 'See here, Connor's pointing a finger down beneath his hand. And here he forms his fingers into the shape of a gun, then opens his hand to indicate five.'

'Are you sure of this?' asked George, scrutinizing the video playback.

'Yes. The movements are very subtle, but he repeats them twice.'

'Still, that's not much help,' remarked Dirk.

'It's a start,' stated Colonel Black. 'And such information could be crucial for any rescue attempt.'

HOSTAGE
CHAPTER 80

Connor had no idea whether anyone would spot his discreet hand signs or even recognize them as signals. But the act itself afforded him a small sense of control over their situation. And this helped fend off his feelings of powerlessness.

After the video recording, their captors escorted them back to their cell and locked the door once more. Alicia, who'd fought so hard to hold back the tears, collapsed on the threadbare mattress and sobbed her heart out. Connor sat down beside her, put his arm round her shoulders and let her cry.

During Hostage Survival class, Colonel Black had told them they would need to control their emotions, stay calm and keep a level head.

Easier said than done, thought Connor, glancing at Alicia and then around their tiny prison cell. If he didn't have Alicia to protect and look after, he'd probably be falling apart himself.

At the time, the colonel's advice had seemed somewhat hypothetical. Being kidnapped was a situation that would *never* occur – or so Connor had believed. But now he and Alicia were held hostage he had to deal with it.

He tried to recall the other vital pieces of advice Colonel Black had given them.

Don't offer resistance ... Say as little as possible if questioned ... try to stay fit and healthy ... keep your mind active ... set goals ... plan on a long captivity to stave off disappointment and depression ... and, most important of all, maintain the will to survive.

Colonel Black had reiterated this last point. Despite all temptation to cave in and succumb to despair, it was essential to believe the situation would come to a positive end eventually. Sustaining hope was the key to survival.

'Don't worry, Alicia, we *will* get home,' said Connor.

Alicia sniffed and looked up at him with eyes red from crying. 'How ... can you be so sure?'

'We're worth more alive than dead to our captors. They'll need to prove we're unharmed to get what they want.'

Alicia nodded, seeing the sense in his words. 'You're right. It's just that knife and the filming were all too much for me.'

'I understand,' said Connor, shuddering himself at the thought of the leader's vicious blade. 'But we need to appear strong to these terrorists. We can't let them think they've beaten us.'

Alicia sat up and composed herself, tying back her hair and wiping her eyes dry.

'I won't give them that satisfaction,' she said, the steel in her voice returning.

'That's more like the Alicia I know,' said Connor, smiling.

She returned his smile but struggled to maintain it. 'I just can't help thinking about my parents. They'll be beside themselves with worry.'

'True,' said Connor, his own thoughts going to his mother and gran. If they'd seen the broadcast, they could be utterly devastated too – and they would have the shock of discovering his double life. 'But just keep in mind your father will be doing everything in his power to negotiate our release.'

HOSTAGE
CHAPTER 81

'The United States Government does *not* negotiate with terrorists,' declared Jennifer Walker, the US Secretary of State, who sat opposite President Mendez at the conference table. She wore a dark green business suit, her auburn hair cut short and her face, icy hard at the best of times, was fixed in a fiercely determined expression.

'But we're talking about my daughter here!' implored President Mendez.

Jennifer's gaze softened a little. 'I'm wholly aware of that, Antonio. And I'm deeply sorry for your predicament. But you know full well our position on such matters.'

The President sank back into his chair and nodded with great reluctance. He realized he was no longer acting like the commander-in-chief. In truth, he was a father out of his mind with worry because his little girl was in some grim basement with a gun at her head. And he would do *anything* to bring her home.

'Can't we even offer them money?' suggested the First Lady, wringing her hands in desperation.

'We could try via an intermediary, but that's not what they're seeking,' said Karen.

'Karen's right,' concurred Dirk. 'If it was only money the terrorists wanted, they'd have selected an easier, less prominent target.'

'Surely every terrorist has a price.' The First Lady looked hopefully round the table for agreement.

Omar shook his head. 'The Brotherhood's motives are purely political. We're dealing here with fanatics, willing to kill or be killed for their cause.'

The harsh reality of the lengths the terrorists would go to numbed the First Lady into silence.

George stepped in. 'Then we have to open a dialogue with this group and stall for time to allow our forces the best chance to trace their hideout. As our initial response, we could ask for the names of the prisoners the terrorists want released and what proof they need.'

There was some consensus round the conference table at this.

'Perhaps even release some of them in return for Connor,' he continued. 'The handover might give us vital information on Alicia's location.'

'That's too steep a price to pay,' argued General Shaw. 'We're talking about men directly responsible for 9/11 and hundreds of dangerous terrorists that our forces have sacrificed their lives to capture. We simply can't contemplate freeing them to wreak more devastation on our nation.'

'As much as I want Connor back, I agree with the general,' said Colonel Black. 'And, given their meticulous planning, they'll avoid any links to their hideout in such a handover.'

'But when this goes public the pressure from the media and the American people to get Alicia back will be overwhelming,' noted the press secretary. 'We might have no choice *but* to negotiate.'

'Absolutely not!' countered Jennifer. 'If we bow to one terrorist organization, we'll open the floodgates and never be able to close them again. We can't allow terrorism to dictate our foreign policy.'

'You're right, Jennifer,' sighed President Mendez. 'Besides, it's inconceivable to withdraw our troops from the Middle East. The delicate balance of nations would likely crumble into a full-blown war.'

'So, you're just going to sacrifice our daughter?' said the First Lady, staring at her husband in disbelief.

'No. We'll find another way to get her back.' He took her hand and squeezed it reassuringly. 'I promise you.'

Colonel Black glanced up at the clock on the wall and coughed for attention. 'Then we've got less than seventy-two hours to find them.'

HOSTAGE
CHAPTER 82

'Connor's in *serious* trouble,' said Amir, staring in disbelief at the overhead flatscreen monitor in the Buddyguard operations room. Colonel Black had forwarded the ransom video via a secure satellite link and Alpha team had viewed it in shocked silence. Charley, Marc and Ling all wore the same distraught expressions, struggling to come to terms with Connor's dire situation.

'Let's just pray the terrorists don't discover who he *really* is,' remarked Bugsy, scrunching up his last packet of chewing gum in frustrated anger and tossing it in the bin.

'Why? What difference would that make?' asked Ling.

'He'd become a threat to them,' explained their surveillance tutor, his tone grave. 'It's rare for a bodyguard to be kidnapped alongside their Principal. They're normally killed straight away.'

Amir exchanged an uneasy look with Charley.

'Then we had better find them *fast*,' said Charley, wheeling herself over to her workstation. 'Bugsy, how can we trace the source of the email?'

The tutor pursed his lips thoughtfully. 'You can try stripping the header info for the original sender's IP address, then run a reverse DNS lookup,' he suggested. 'There's a geo-location tool on our system that'll track down the ISP and provide us with a geographical area that the IP is *believed* to be used in.'

'You don't seem very certain,' remarked Ling as Charley hammered away on her keyboard.

'Such a trail can be easily spoofed,' admitted Bugsy. 'The IP address might be that of an innocent person or organization who's had it hijacked by the terrorists. And I've no doubt they've used a server relay to bounce the signal around the world.'

'You're right,' said Charley, slumping back in her chair. 'The trail dead-ends at a legitimate book publishers in London.'

'Hang on a minute,' said Bugsy, hurrying over to his terminal, a sly grin detectable on his lips. 'I do have a beta program that might be able to trace the ghost image left behind by the real server. It'll take a bit of time, though.'

While Bugsy ran the tracer application, Charley organized the rest of the team.

'Ling, I need you to check the CCTV camera footage around the Jefferson Memorial – before, during and after the ambush. We might pick up some clues – a face or a vehicle reg. Marc, Colonel Black says they found the dead Secret Service agent in a disused hangar near Stafford Airport. Execute a digital sweep of the surveillance satellites we have access to and find out if any were over the vicinity at the time. Amir, I'll need your help analysing the ransom video. Scan its audio track for background noise, accents, anything that might indicate the location of the terrorist's hideout.'

Amir sat down at the terminal next to her and logged on. 'But won't Secret Service be doing all of this anyway?' he questioned.

'Of course, but locating Connor and Alicia will be like hunting for a needle in a haystack,' replied Charley, expanding the video to fullscreen and searching for visual leads. 'There's every chance they might miss a vital clue. So the more eyes, the better.'

HOSTAGE
CHAPTER 83

At least two days had passed ... or so Connor thought. It was difficult to judge the time, trapped in a windowless cell where the light was never switched off. He and Alicia slept fitfully, a razor edge of fear and uncertainty making it impossible to rest for long. Every so often the door to their cell would be flung open and they'd tense in anticipation of what was to come: *humiliation ... torture ... death ... or possibly freedom?*

But any such thoughts of release were quashed each time the shrouded face of one of their captors appeared. Armed with a gun, he'd bring in a small tray of food: some flatbread, a thin stew and more water, but no cutlery, nothing that could be used as a weapon. Connor would make an attempt at conversation, hoping to find out what was going on. He recalled Colonel Black saying it was important to build a rapport with any hostage-taker – *by winning their respect, this reduces their inclination to hurt their victims*. But their captor would say nothing and answer no questions. Just set down the plate and leave. Whether he didn't understand English or purposefully ignored him, the lack of information was almost as torturous as their confinement.

A bucket in the corner, replaced infrequently, was their sole means of a toilet. Connor used the mattress to offer Alicia some privacy at these times. There were no washing facilities provided either and this added to their discomfort, Alicia suffering more than Connor with this indignity.

Early on, Connor had noticed a small camera lens above the door, so they knew they were being watched. And probably overheard too. With that in mind, the two of them had taken the precaution of whispering everything into each other's ears, with their backs to the camera or a hand cupped over their mouths to avoid any possibility of lip-reading.

'Don't you think we should try to escape?' Alicia suggested, looking to the door in the vain hope that one of their guards had forgotten to lock it.

'Only as a last resort,' Connor replied, heeding Colonel Black's advice. The chances of success had to be high or the situation so desperate that it demanded an escape attempt. Otherwise such a move was potentially suicidal. Moreover, escape was merely the beginning. The ability to evade the enemy and survive in a foreign country was the *real* challenge. And, since they didn't know where they were, this would be a leap into the unknown. They could be high in the mountains, in a remote hostile village or in the middle of an endless desert.

'Why haven't they found us yet?' Alicia asked, her tone almost pleading.

'Your father's probably still negotiating, while also playing for time.'

'But what if that fails? Even I realize the terrorists' terms are impossible to meet. Nobody's worth that sacrifice . . . not even me.'

'You mustn't think like that,' said Connor, conscious he had to keep Alicia's mind occupied with positive thoughts. Lack of sleep and enforced captivity were making them both over-anxious. But she was starting to show signs of self-pity and he couldn't allow her to drift into despair.

'Listen, when the rescue occurs, drop to the floor immediately,' he advised. 'There'll probably be a lot of gunfire and smoke from stun grenades. Cover your head with your hands and arms to protect yourself. Let the rescuers know who you are by yelling out your name. And don't make any false moves in case you're mistaken for a terrorist. You don't want to get caught in the crossfire.'

Alicia nodded, gazing at him with admiration.

'I'm sorry,' she whispered.

'For what?' asked Connor.

'For not appreciating you . . .' Alicia seemed to be hunting for the right words. 'At the time I was so upset that you weren't who you said you were. Now I'm glad you *are* who you are. My buddyguard.'

She nestled closer to him, seeking the safety of his embrace.

'There's no need to apologize,' said Connor.

Alicia buried her head in his chest and Connor felt his T-shirt moisten with her tears.

'You might be released soon,' she said, keeping her voice light and joyous. 'That'll be good news.'

But Connor sensed the tight knot of terror in her heart at being left to cope on her own.

'I won't leave you,' he said.

'But you might not have a choice.'

Connor held Alicia close. 'I made a promise to your father that I'd protect you, just like my father protected yours. And I will . . . on my life.'

HOSTAGE
CHAPTER 84

Malik angrily hurled the remote control at the television in the corner of the sparsely furnished front room. It barely missed, shattering against the wall behind. On the screen ran a CNN newsfeed of a blonde-haired woman reporting on the aftermath of the bomb attack on Washington DC. But there was no coverage of the mass pardon for terrorist prisoners that Malik had demanded.

'*Why haven't they released any of our brothers yet?*' he shouted.

Bahir and Kedar exchanged uneasy glances over their leader's unexpected outburst of rage.

'This is the game they play,' Bahir replied softly, putting down the smartphone he'd been tinkering with. 'They say "no negotiation". But they will. Eventually.'

'I wish I had your patience,' remarked Malik, shoving a handful of khat leaves into his mouth and chewing manically. 'First, the US Government tried to stall for time by asking for specific names, which is why I had the list already prepared,' he said smugly, tapping a forefinger to his temple. 'Then the infidels tried offering us money.

A typical American solution to everything, although they didn't have the *respect* to present it to us directly!'

'And now they'll wait until the final hour before contacting us again,' Bahir pointed out.

'That's when our brothers will be freed, right?' said Kedar, trying to back up Bahir and reassure their leader.

Malik shook his head, dark thunder swirling in his eyes. 'No, I bet they'll plead for an *extension* of the deadline.' Fuming at the idea, he spat a gob of green spit on to the floor, just missing Hazim as he entered the room with a tray of food. 'But we won't give it to them!'

With a troubled look at his irate uncle, Hazim timidly approached. 'Do you still want your dinner?' he asked.

'Of course!' snapped Malik, slumping down on a cushion to eat.

As Malik tore off some flatbread and dunked it in a bowl of hummus, Bahir said, 'The Americans' push for delay is understandable, from *their* point of view. They'll be desperate for more time to allow their agencies to pinpoint our location.'

'What!' exclaimed Hazim, his hands now trembling as he poured his uncle a cup of coffee. 'You mean they could find us here?'

'Don't look so worried, Hazim,' laughed Malik, offering a green-stained grin. 'They'll *never* find us. Isn't that right, Bahir?'

Bahir nodded confidently. 'As I told you before, Hazim, all the jammers are operational and the ghost server relays are fully functional. So we should *all* just try to relax. There are still six hours to go to the deadline.'

'But what happens when they don't comply with our demands?' asked Hazim.

Malik unsheathed the *jambiya* from his belt and held the fearsome blade in front of Hazim's face.

'Then we prove our *commitment* to our cause.'

HOSTAGE
CHAPTER 85

'Please tell me that's the *last* press conference I have today,' said President Mendez, rubbing a hand across his haggard face. 'I don't think I can hide my loss much longer.'

'Yes, it can be,' replied Lara, the Press Secretary, checking her schedule. 'I'll ask the Vice-President to cover the remaining two.'

'Thank you,' he sighed. He was worn out, the worry for his daughter leaving a hollow inside so great he felt paper-thin. With trepidation, he made his way down to the ground floor of the West Wing. So far there'd been no success in locating her, or Connor, and he was beginning to despair. But, as he entered the Situation Room, Dirk strode over to him, a victorious gleam in his eye.

'Mr President, I've some good news. We've found them!'

President Mendez was suddenly alert, all tiredness blasted away. 'Where?'

'Yemen,' replied Karen, calling up a satellite map of the Middle Eastern country on the central monitor. 'A private plane flew out of Stafford Airport just two hours after the attacks. The official documentation stated the destination as Riyadh, Saudi Arabia. But a trace of its flight path shows the plane *actually* landing in neighbouring Yemen.'

'The digital trail also ends there,' stated Dirk. 'There were multiple relay servers and spoofed identities, but the email appears to have originated from the capital city of Sana'a. This was confirmed by Colonel Black's surveillance operative.'

Colonel Black now stepped forward. Even though Bugsy had been the first to trace the email, he let this fact pass. There were far more important matters than point scoring against the Secret Service Director. 'My team also scrubbed the video's audio track and identified a "Call to Prayer" sounding in the background.' The colonel replayed the short piece of enhanced recording over the Situation Room's speakers and an echoing chant, barely audible above the hiss and general noise of the video, filled the room. 'This particular one is quite distinctive to the region.'

President Mendez nodded. 'So where exactly do you suspect my daughter is being held?'

'CIA have eyes on the ground there,' explained Karen. 'They report there's been increased activity at a location on the outskirts of the city.'

An aerial view of an arid plain and mud-brick city zoomed in to a large building surrounded by a walled compound. The real-time satellite feed revealed four figures patrolling the perimeter.

'I've a Navy SEAL unit stationed just off the coast of Yemen,' announced General Shaw. 'They can be at the target within twenty minutes by attack helicopter.'

'How certain are you my daughter's there?' asked President Mendez, studying the aerial shot of the building intently, not daring to let hope enter his heart just yet.

'We can't be one hundred per cent,' admitted Dirk, 'but all the indications are strong. An infra-red satellite scan indicated people inside and there were a few suspicious cold spots within the building too.'

George interrupted. 'Shouldn't we allow time for a negotiated release? We've still five hours left. That's surely our best chance of recovering your daughter unharmed.'

'The secretary of state made our position crystal clear on that,' reminded Karen. 'The US Government cannot be seen to negotiate with terrorists. Besides, there's no guarantee they'll honour their side of a deal anyway.'

'More hostages are killed during rescue attempts than from execution by their captors,' George noted. 'We should wait this out.'

'Mr President, if we don't move now, we may never get another opportunity,' urged General Shaw.

President Mendez held up his hand, asking for silence. 'What's the mission's probability of success?'

General Shaw swallowed uncomfortably. 'I won't lie to you. Intelligence estimates a fifty–fifty chance. But this is our *best* hope of rescuing her.'

President Mendez closed his eyes, feeling weighed down by an almost impossible decision – he was literally gambling with his daughter's life.

'The odds are improved by Connor's presence, though,'

stated Colonel Black. 'He'll stand by her side and do all that's necessary to protect her.'

President Mendez considered this, recalling how his own life had been saved by Connor's father. Opening his eyes, he finally declared, 'It's a high-risk strategy, but it's a measure of my desperation. General Shaw, you have my GO for the mission.'

HOSTAGE
CHAPTER 86

The two Black Hawk helicopters swooped low over the desert ridges, phantoms against the moonless sky. The six-man Navy SEAL unit, split equally between the two choppers, remained silent and focused, checking their equipment for a final time.

'One minute out,' the pilot called through their earpieces.

Lieutenant Webber, 'point man' for the operation, clicked off the safety on his assault rifle. Like the other soldiers in his unit, he knew what was at stake and had trained all his life for just such a mission.

In the green glow of his night-vision goggles, the shadowy outline of the compound came into view. He spotted the ghostly face of a sentry peering into the night, hunting for the source of the thudding blades. As they made their final approach, Webber targeted his laser gunsight on the man's head and squeezed the trigger. A split second later the man dropped lifeless to the ground.

Another sentry appeared and fired his AK47 blindly in their direction. A crack-shot from the other Black Hawk took the man out. The two remaining sentries fled their posts and sprinted for the main building. Webber brought them both down a few metres from the doorway. But he had no doubt the alarm had already been raised. His squad now had little more than a minute to locate and extract the hostages – any longer and it would be too late.

As soon as they'd cleared the compound wall, the SEALs fast-roped from the hovering helicopters to the ground below. Touching down on the hard-packed earth, amid swirls of dust, they unclipped themselves and dashed to the central building. A set of metal double doors served as the entrance, but they'd been locked from the inside.

Kneeling by the doorway, Webber waited a few precious seconds while one of his team, a large man from the Bronx nicknamed Sparky, attached an explosive charge.

'Clear!' barked the soldier, retreating a step and shielding his face.

The device detonated, flinging the metal doors back on their hinges. They banged like temple gongs, the blast echoing around the dusty compound. Inside, the building was cloaked in darkness, but the soldiers' night-vision gear revealed a long empty corridor with doors opening off on either side.

As point man, Webber took the lead.

Suddenly there was an eruption of gunfire. Bullets whizzed past, narrowly missing Webber as he dived into the shelter of a doorway. He and his men returned fire.

'Stairwell!' shouted one of the SEALs.

Webber had line of sight and sprayed the landing with 7.62 calibre rounds. A robed man tumbled down the staircase and landed in a bloody heap on the corridor floor.

A turbaned head then peered out from a room on the far right and immediately disappeared back inside as a hail of bullets raked the corridor wall. Ceasing fire, Sparky hurled a 'flashbang' through the open doorway. The stun grenade went off, blinding light and a concussive blast incapacitating the occupant within. Aware they might need the man alive, one of the SEALs cuffed him while the rest of the unit swept the other rooms.

The ground floor was clear; no sign of the hostages.

But under the staircase they found an iron gateway and a set of steps leading downwards. Dividing into two teams, one SEAL unit headed for the upper floor to subdue any remaining hostiles, while Sparky blew the lock on the gate.

Webber descended the narrow stairwell. It was pitch-black and even his night-vision goggles struggled to pick up anything. As he approached basement level, his ears strained for the sound of footsteps or the telltale *clink* of a round being chambered. He was on the last step when he heard the scrape of a sandal and caught the faintest glint of a blade to his right.

Webber dropped and rolled, squeezing off several rounds at the same time. A man screamed in the darkness. More shots rang out, deafening within the confined quarters of the basement. Sparky and the other SEAL discharged their weapons into the room, neutralizing a second assailant toting an AK47.

Scrambling to his feet, Webber took no more chances. He tossed flashbangs into the two final chambers. The basement blazed lightning white and the air shuddered with the thunderclap of detonating stun grenades. But the SEALs encountered no more hostiles.

Webber noticed a door at the far end of the corridor. He directed Sparky to attach a small charge to the lock. As it exploded, he kicked the door wide open.

'Alicia? Connor?' he called.

Storming in, finger primed on his trigger, Webber was greeted by an empty cell.

HOSTAGE
CHAPTER 87

The door to Alicia and Connor's cell crashed open. The black-robed giant, his face still no more than a pair of raging eyes through the slit of his headscarf, barged in and seized them both by the scruff of their necks.

'*TAHARAK!*' he snarled, dragging them through the door.

Connor and Alicia had no choice but to obey as they were shoved along the corridor at gunpoint. Once again they found themselves in the makeshift video room. Two masked terrorists flanked the black flag while the leader stood waiting before the camera, his jewelled dagger in hand.

Connor's heart froze at the sight of the gruesome knife. *The deadline must have passed. The terrorists' demands not met.* He couldn't believe that President Mendez had failed to negotiate *at least a delay*. His throat went dry with panic and he began to hyperventilate. Despite his training, nothing could prepare him for his own execution.

Alicia took his hand, clasping it tight. Connor met her terrified gaze, her eyes brimming with tears at the prospect of losing him forever. Connor then felt a strange calm wash over him. Despite the fear for his own life, a cool logic reasoned that if he was sacrificed *she* could be saved. The US Government would be forced to submit to the terrorists' demands, in some form or other, and Alicia would be freed. His death wouldn't be in vain. He'd have protected Alicia with his life, just as he'd promised to.

A ghost of a smile even passed across his lips as he realized he'd be following in his father's footsteps . . . right to the very end.

'It'll be all right,' he told her as he was pushed towards his fate.

'No, just the girl,' ordered the leader. 'It'll have more impact.'

Connor was stunned by his unexpected reprieve. But his fears quickly turned to Alicia as *she* was forced to kneel before the camera, her back to the foreboding flag. Without thinking of the consequences, Connor flung himself at the leader to grab the dagger. But, before he'd even gone two steps, the giant hammered a fist into his right kidney. Connor buckled to the floor, wheezing from the blow, pain flaring bright within him.

'Let's send the Americans a message they *can't* ignore,' declared the leader, paying no attention to Connor's suffering and gesturing to the man behind the camera.

As the terrorist pressed Record, the leader stood over Alicia with his knife. Alicia became stock-still, her eyes fixated on the gleaming steel blade.

'President Mendez,' spat the leader to the camera,

making no effort to hide his contempt. 'We gave you the opportunity to do the honourable thing. To bow to our demands with your head still held high. But you've broken the terms of our deal by attempting – and *failing* – to rescue your daughter. Worse still, you murdered our innocent countrymen in the process. Now we, the Brotherhood of the Rising Crescent, will broadcast our message to the world – and you will listen and *obey*.'

Sheathing his knife, he pulled a gun from his belt and planted the muzzle against Alicia's temple.

Alicia whimpered softly, shying away from the cold hard barrel that promised her death. Yet somehow she managed to overcome her terror and glare up at her captor. 'My father will *never* give in to you.'

The leader ignored her. 'President Mendez, we're men of our word – but it is *you* who have forced our hand.'

He pulled the trigger.

'NO!' shouted Connor, reaching out desperately to Alicia as she screamed.

But the gun clicked empty.

The leader stared hard into the camera lens.

'Next time, there *will* be a bullet,' he warned. 'You've less than two hours to meet our demands. Do NOT try our patience again!'

HOSTAGE
CHAPTER 88

Charley, Amir, Ling and Marc huddled round the monitor in the operations room, sickened and speechless at the terrorists' ruthless mock execution of Alicia.

'So that's the situation with less than two hours to go,' said Colonel Black gravely over the conference video. 'This crisis has gone public, the rescue attempt has failed, and the President is out of options.'

'But where's Connor?' asked Ling. 'He wasn't in the video.'

Colonel Black's expression darkened. 'That I don't know.'

'Perhaps he's escaped,' Amir suggested, his expression hopeful.

'But we're taught never to leave our Principal,' reminded Ling.

'He could be dead,' said Marc flatly.

'NO,' said Charley, denying even the possibility. 'We don't know anything, so cannot presume anything.'

'Then why isn't he *in* the video?' asked Marc.

'The terrorists are possibly holding him back for the

deadline,' replied Colonel Black grimly. 'I'll contact you if there are any updates.'

As the colonel ended his transmission, Alpha team exchanged uneasy looks with one another, each aware what Colonel Black meant by 'deadline'.

From the corner of the room came a shout. Leaning back in his chair, Bugsy slapped his forehead with the flat of his hand. 'So that's what they've done!' he exclaimed, shaking his head in frustrated disbelief.

'What?' asked Amir.

Bugsy beckoned them over to his workstation. 'These terrorists are using a number of crafty technical tricks to mislead us. I've just digitally compared their two videos and both have a distinctive call to prayer sounding in the background. I extracted them both from the audio. Look at the two wave patterns. They're an exact match!'

On the monitor two graphic sine waves appeared. Using his mouse, Bugsy dragged and dropped one on top of the other. The two patterns were identical.

'So what does that mean?' asked Ling.

'The "call to prayer" has been added in post-production, *after* the recording had been made,' explained Bugsy. 'Whoever their techie is, he's good. He anticipated that we'd search for a location clue in the first video and planted it on purpose for us to discover, making us think they were somewhere else. But he's used the same trick twice.'

Bugsy now pulled up a stream of code on his computer workstation.

'Next, I analysed the two emails the President received.

As we already know, the terrorists misdirected us over the origin of the email, using fake IP addresses and server relays. I thought my beta program had cracked the source. But see this code here.' He pointed to a bewildering collection of numbers and commands. 'This indicates the terrorist programmer set up the equivalent of an "infinity loop" between servers.'

'What's an infinity loop?' asked Marc.

'Like two mirrors opposite one another, this piece of code creates a duplicated signal that bounces between two servers continuously. To my program, this appeared to be a dead end, the "origin" of the email. Whereas in fact it was a "doorway" that only opens on command.'

'So, can you now trace the source?' asked Charley.

Bugsy grimaced and shook his head. 'We'd have to access the mirrored servers at the exact moment the terrorists send another email. The chances of doing that are next to zero. I'm afraid there's no more I can do. Wherever he is, Connor's on his own.'

HOSTAGE
CHAPTER 89

The cell door clanged shut. Connor kicked at it in frustration and fury.

'You gutless coward! You scumbag!' he roared.

He wanted to pound the terrorist leader to a pulp. He was no longer scared. He was angry.

Anger is only one letter away from danger. His unarmed combat instructor's words repeated in his head. *Control your anger, otherwise anger will control you and you'll lose focus. As a buddyguard, you want to fight smarter not harder.*

Giving the steel door one last kick, Connor checked his temper. He knew he had to think clearly and focus on the situation at hand. But their cruel toying with Alicia's life had boiled his blood. In that split-second moment when the masked leader had pulled the trigger, a crushing grief had overwhelmed him, compounded by the realization that he'd failed to protect her. But no thundering blast of gunfire had followed and Alicia had opened her eyes, stunned to discover that she was still alive. At first Connor only felt relief. Then he became concerned for her as she just knelt in a zombie-like trance until the end of the video, before allowing herself to be dragged back to their cell.

Having vented his fury on the locked door, Connor turned to see Alicia slide down the wall and slump to the floor. She pulled her knees to her chest and stared vacantly at the opposite wall.

'Alicia, are you all right?' he asked.

She didn't reply, just continued gazing into the distance.

Bending down, he touched her shoulder gently, worried the mock execution had broken her spirit.

'Alicia? It's OK. I'm with you.'

Alicia mumbled something.

'What was that?'

A single tear rolled down her cheek. 'We're going to die.'

'No, we're not,' countered Connor, although his words seemed to ring hollow. With time fast running out, any hopes of rescue were rapidly dwindling. And the terrorists seemed determined to follow through on their threats. If there was ever a situation for a last resort, this was it. They *had* to escape. Connor looked round the tiny windowless cell. He'd already inspected every inch of it for a weakness and had found none. As he racked his brains for a plan, he noticed Alicia trembling from the effects of trauma-induced shock.

'Stay with me,' he pleaded, trying to get her to focus on his face. 'We'll find a way to escape, somehow. I promise you.'

HOSTAGE
CHAPTER 90

'All hell's broken loose,' said Lara, the Press Secretary dashing in and switching on the TV in the President's private study of the West Wing. 'The story's running on every news channel, worldwide.'

Turning his gaze to the TV screen, President Mendez sank back into his leather chair and braced himself for the media storm. He was joined in his study by the core members of the National Security Council: the White House Chief of Staff, the Secretary of State, the Director of National Intelligence, the Director of Secret Service and General Shaw. Together they watched as a series of news bulletins flashed across the screen.

PRESIDENT'S DAUGHTER TAKEN HOSTAGE!

A clip from the terrorists' video showed Alicia with a gun to her head. Even though he'd already seen it once, President Mendez clenched his fists and shuddered with a combination of cold horror and burning rage. He was one of the most powerful men in the world yet felt utterly powerless to help his own daughter.

The image was replaced with a soundbite of the President addressing a press conference the previous year. '*America stands strong against the threat of terrorism,*' he was saying. '*We don't negotiate with terrorists and never will . . .* '

The strapline running along the bottom of the screen read: WHAT WILL THE PRESIDENT DO NOW?

The segment came to an end and the monitor filled with scenes of outraged crowds in Times Square calling for Alicia's release. Some were weeping, others were angry, while a growing number were baying for blood.

Finally, the bulletin switched to a view of a dusty compound outside Sana'a. Eight bodies were laid out, surrounded by wailing families. The headline ran: ATTACK ON FARMERS' COMPOUND – AN 'INNOCENT' MISTAKE?

The newsreel ended on images of spontaneous protests and the burning of American flags in the capital cities of the Yemen, Pakistan and Afghanistan.

'Those men *weren't* innocent,' growled General Shaw, pounding a fist into his palm. 'They were drug dealers. The SEAL unit uncovered a mass shipment of opium in the compound. That's why it was so heavily guarded.'

'The Yemeni people won't see it that way,' replied Jennifer. The secretary of state stood by the door, her arms crossed, a frown on her face. 'And their government are viewing it as an invasion of sovereign territory. We've got a full-blown international crisis on our hands.'

'That was always going to be the case,' argued Karen. 'The question is how did we get it so wrong? I know the surviving gunman admitted that Malik Hussein was behind the drug-running, but the SEAL team found no evidence of Alicia or Connor *ever* having been at that location.'

'Listen, we'll have more than enough time for analysis and blame another day,' said President Mendez, noticing with dismay that a countdown clock had been posted on the TV newsfeed. 'We've less than fifty-five minutes to meet the midnight deadline. I need to hear your views on what our next move should be. You first, Karen.'

'I think we can all agree these terrorists won't back down. If we don't comply, they'll kill Alicia – or more likely Connor first to prove their point.'

'We don't know that for certain,' said Jennifer. 'They may bluff again.'

'The bombs were no bluff,' reminded Karen.

George held up the list of captured terrorists. 'How about we make a concession of a handful of prisoners? The least significant ones. Then we may be able to stall them – even seek a chance of ending this crisis.'

'It'll make us look weak,' argued General Shaw, taking the side of the secretary of state. 'Release any of them and they'll only push for more.'

'What about just announcing our troops' withdrawal then? We don't have to *actually* withdraw from the countries.'

Jennifer shook her head. 'George, I know you're seeking every possible solution. But such a declaration would send a shockwave through the Middle East. The terrorists know full well that a mere announcement would be enough to create anarchy.'

'But if we don't offer the terrorists some consideration at midnight, Connor could die.'

'Much as I hate to say this,' interjected Dirk, his steel-blue eyes hardening, 'it's his duty to make such a sacrifice.'

'How can you even *think* such a thing?' exclaimed Karen, shocked by her colleague's cold-heartedness.

Dirk shifted awkwardly under her accusing gaze. 'Look, if the terrorists kill Connor and we still hold out against their demands, then they've lost. They'll realize that we can't be forced into submission, even when lives are at stake.'

'But we're talking here of a child's life,' reminded George. 'And how will the world view America then?'

A heavy silence descended on the room and President Mendez looked to his press secretary for her opinion.

'The fact that Alicia and Connor are still children makes this a highly emotive issue,' explained Lara. 'The public and media are split on the matter. Half are calling for your daughter's release under *any* circumstances, while the rest consider an iron fist should be used. If she is . . .' Lara was unable to meet the President's eyes '. . . killed, there's a danger her blood will be on both the terrorists' and the US Government's hands. Whatever decision you make, Mr President, we must be *seen* to have done everything possible to save her and Connor.'

'But we are, aren't we?' queried the President, looking round at his staff.

'Yes,' replied Karen quickly, 'but I agree with Lara on this – perception is everything.'

President Mendez sighed in despair. 'Jennifer, what do you advise?'

'You've an impossible choice,' stated Jennifer. 'Give in to their demands and we set a dangerous precedent – one the nation may never recover from. Hold your ground and we maintain the status quo – the Brotherhood may even *lose* crucial support by using such terror tactics. But you risk losing your daughter. This is a no-win situation. You know my views already, but I'm not the one who has to make the ultimate decision on this.'

President Mendez studied the secretary of state's ice-maiden face. Despite her seeming lack of compassion, she was an excellent stateswoman and he knew she only had the good of the nation at heart. His own heart and mind, however, were torn in two. On the one hand, he was the President who'd made an oath to preserve, protect and defend the United States. On the other, he was a father whose whole world was his daughter and his instinct was to put her first, over everything.

Deep down he knew what *had* to be done. But the choice left a cold spot in his heart, one that would grow like a cancer if either Connor or his daughter died at the terrorists' hands.

The countdown on the TV ticked down to forty-nine minutes.

'Antonio, you may want to see this,' interrupted his wife, poking her head round the door.

With the weariness of a burdened man, President Mendez followed her into the Oval Office and over to the bay windows. The First Lady drew back the drapes to reveal a view across the south lawn. In the darkness beyond the iron railings, ten thousand flickering flames hovered like fireflies all the way back to the Washington Monument. And even through the thickened bulletproof glass the sound of hymns being sung could be heard like a distant choir of angels. Tears welled up in the President's eyes at the sight of the candlelit vigil in honour of their captive daughter.

'At a time like this, we need all the help we can get,' said President Mendez.

'And maybe a little more,' suggested the First Lady, clasping his hands.

Together they sank to their knees and began praying for a miracle.

HOSTAGE
CHAPTER 91

'At last!' exclaimed Bahir, his eyes widening in delight as he broke through the final safeguard on the firewalled smartphone. The screen burst to life and a winged shield rotated in 3D on the retina-display. Intrigued by the strange logo, he pressed the home button and the screen filled with icons – *Advanced Mapping, Tracker, Mission Status, Threat Level, SOS* . . .

'What are all those for?' asked Kedar, who sat beside him in the basement room.

'I've no idea,' replied Bahir, studying the smartphone with growing consternation. 'This phone belongs to that English boy. It survived the EMP blast due to an in-built failsafe device. The operating system was guarded by an advanced firewall, plus a secondary spyware program that threatened to wipe the contents of the drive every time I attempted to disable it. It even had fingerprint recognition access. But I *beat* the system in the end.' Bahir allowed himself a superior grin.

'Congratulations,' said Kedar. 'But what does any of that mean?'

Bahir looked at his associate as if he was stupid. 'That this mobile phone is no *normal* phone – which means our hostage is by no means normal either.'

He pushed Kedar aside to access the computer terminal on his desk.

'What are you doing?' Kedar protested. 'We're still waiting for a message from the Americans.'

'This could be as important,' said Bahir, putting aside the smartphone and launching the computer's internet browser. He typed 'Connor Reeves' into the search engine.

There were too many hits to sift through so he tightened his parameters by inputting BOY as well. Most were still irrelevant links. But convinced he was on to something, Bahir searched through 'images only'. It wasn't until the third page that he recognized Connor's face in a photo. He clicked on the link, opening a website to the *East London Herald* newspaper. The feature was headlined: LOCAL BOY BATTLE OF BRITAIN CHAMPION!

Below the caption was a large picture of Connor Reeves holding aloft a silver trophy.

'*Kickboxing champion?*' remarked Bahir. 'There's more to this English boy than meets the eye.' He rose from his chair and headed for the door. 'Kedar, stay here in case the Americans contact us. I have to go up and speak with Malik.'

'Is there a problem?' Kedar asked.

'Possibly. Just keep watch over the hostages.'

Kedar nodded and took his place in Bahir's chair. After checking the online mail server for any messages, he heard cries for help over the cell's speaker and glanced up at the video monitor. The English boy was jumping up and down and waving his arms in front of the camera. Kedar was going to ignore his desperate plea for attention when he noticed, in the corner of the cell, the President's daughter having convulsions.

HOSTAGE
CHAPTER 92

At ten minutes to midnight, Malik began honing his *jambiya* for the final time. With feverish intent, he ran the whetstone along the edge of the blade, the scrape of steel and stone sounding like fingernails down a chalkboard.

'So you really intend *killing* them?' said Hazim, unable to take his eyes off the glinting steel.

Chewing madly on a mouthful of khat, Malik replied, 'Just one for starters. Both, if the Americans don't comply.'

'We will be condemned by the whole world!' argued Hazim.

'But we will be exalted by our brothers-in-arms!' Malik countered, shooting him an irritable glare. 'Now get the coffee I asked for.'

Hazim could see by Malik's dilated pupils that he'd chewed too much khat. His uncle was becoming manic and out of touch with reality. 'But they're just kids,' he reminded him. 'Alicia's the same age as my sister.'

'She's the offspring of our *greatest* enemy,' snarled Malik. He eyed Hazim dubiously. 'Don't tell me your belief in our cause is wavering, nephew!'

Hazim shook his head. 'No, I don't doubt the cause. But I never thought it would come to this.'

As Bahir ran into the room, Malik gave a thin smile. 'It was *always* going to come to this.'

HOSTAGE

CHAPTER 93

'HELP!' shouted Connor, waving in desperation at the camera lens. 'PLEASE! She's having an epileptic fit!'

Behind him, Alicia was thrashing wildly on the mattress. Her eyes were rolled back into her head, only the whites showing. Her breathing was becoming laboured and Connor could hear wet choking gasps like the sound of a dying fish.

He screamed again at the camera, praying that someone was watching or listening. 'PLEASE! HELP! She could die!'

Just as he was about to give up hope, the cell door opened.

'Thank goodness,' Connor cried as the black-robed giant entered. 'She needs a doctor. Right now. The stress of that mock execution must have caused it.'

Whether the giant understood him or not, he pushed Connor irritably aside and bent over to examine the writhing girl. As soon as his attention was on Alicia, Connor grabbed the man's head, twisted it and drove it downwards. Taken totally off-guard, the terrorist was unable to stop Connor's surprise head-twist attack. His huge mass toppled over. But, rather than guiding the man's head to the ground as he'd been taught in buddyguard class, Connor used all his strength to smash the terrorist's skull into the concrete floor. The giant grunted and went limp.

Alicia immediately stopped fitting and sat up. 'I *really* should be an actress,' she said, managing a smile despite the circumstances.

'You can collect your Oscar when we get out of here,' Connor replied, taking her hand and pulling her to her feet. His plan had worked perfectly.

As they ran for the open door, Alicia stumbled and let out a cry. Connor turned to see the terrorist had seized her ankle. Dazed and disorientated as he was, the man, snarling like a pit-bull, refused to let go.

If you're forced to fight, end it quick, his combat instructor had said.

Spinning round, Connor kicked the man squarely in the jaw. Teeth flew and the terrorist lost his grip.

How's that for Pain Assisted Learning! thought Connor.

But the giant still wouldn't stay down. Spitting blood, he made a desperate lunge for them. Connor shoved Alicia into the corridor as the terrorist bore down on them like a charging bull, his eyes filled with pure rage. Connor threw himself against the cell door. It banged shut and Alicia turned the key just as the door shuddered under the terrorist's impact.

But mercifully the reinforced lock held.

'What now?' she whispered, glancing nervously along the shadowy corridor.

'*Shhh!*' cautioned Connor, putting a finger to his lips and checking the room opposite. It was empty apart from the array of electronic gadgetry and the computer that he'd spotted before. Darting into the room, he wondered if he could send a message. But the keyboard was in Arabic and, besides, he still had no idea where they were. Connor glanced over at a second monitor and saw the giant hurling himself against the cell door, his screams of outrage crackling over the tinny speaker. Connor switched it off. If the other terrorists didn't know about their accomplice's fate, it might give him and Alicia a few more precious seconds to escape. Turning to leave the room, he was astonished to find his smartphone lying on the desk. Grabbing it, he powered it up and pressed his thumb to the fingerprint recognition scanner. The home screen appeared. But any hopes of making an emergency call were quickly shattered. There was no signal.

Alicia touched his arm, urging him to hurry up. Connor nodded and shoved the phone in his pocket. Hopefully, he'd get reception above ground. Silently beckoning Alicia to follow him, he crept along the corridor towards the stairwell, pausing only to check the video room was clear. It was deserted.

There were no weapons either – just the ominous black flag and camera on show. Connor steeled himself to climb the darkened stairs, unarmed.

He took it one step at a time, terrified one of the wooden treads would creak under his weight and alert the other terrorists. Alicia stuck close behind, her breathing loud in the darkness. Neither knew what would await them at the top and Connor feared they'd come face to face with someone before they managed to escape the basement. If that happened, they'd have nowhere to run.

But they reached the top of the staircase undetected. A solid wooden door now blocked their route. Connor grasped the handle and slowly turned it. To his relief – and surprise – the door wasn't locked. Pushing it open a fraction, he put his eye to the crack. Beyond was a bright hallway with several rooms leading off from it and what looked like the main entrance door at the far end. He could hear voices. But otherwise the hallway was empty.

Ready? he mouthed to Alicia.

She nodded.

They slipped out and closed the door quietly behind them. Now dangerously exposed, Connor kept Alicia close as they tiptoed along. They were almost to the first doorway, a kitchen coming into view, when a terrorist stepped out.

HOSTAGE
CHAPTER 94

Connor and Alicia found themselves confronted by a young man in his early twenties. No longer in his traditional Middle Eastern robes, the terrorist wore jeans and a blue office shirt. He was carrying a pot of steaming coffee on a tray and stood stock-still, shocked by the hostages' unexpected appearance.

For a moment, no one moved.

Then Alicia gasped under her breath. '*Hazim?*'

Suddenly aware he was unmasked, the terrorist cast his eyes to the ground as if deeply ashamed.

'You know him?' Connor whispered in astonishment.

Alicia stared incredulous at the young man before them. 'He's one of Kalila's brothers.'

Connor now vaguely recalled him collecting Kalila from school on a few occasions. No wonder Secret Service hadn't picked up on any terrorist surveillance at Montarose School – Hazim would have already been security checked. Connor reckoned Hazim must have been responsible for planting the Cell-Finity bug too, when he gave Kalila her new phone and she forwarded the number to Alicia, himself and all her friends. Yet at that precise moment Connor didn't care *who* the terrorist was. His priority was to escape with Alicia.

'Hazim! What's taking you so long?' barked a voice from the far room.

A conflicted look passed across Hazim's face as he glanced from Alicia to the room and back again. He didn't reply and the man in the room became impatient.

'Bahir, go give him a kick up the backside!'

A man with round steel-rimmed glasses appeared out of a doorway. His eyes widened in shock at seeing their two captives free.

'Hazim, don't just stand there!' he cried, dashing into the corridor. 'Grab them!'

When Hazim didn't react, Connor seized upon the young man's hesitation. He snatched up the coffee pot and threw the scalding contents into the face of the approaching bespectacled man. The terrorist fell back, screaming, his skin blistering. Connor then one-inch-pushed Hazim in the chest. Hazim flew backwards, sprawling on to the kitchen floor. Connor grabbed Alicia's arm and made for the front door.

But they hadn't gone two steps, when a bearded man with a hooked nose leapt like a tiger into their path.

'Not so fast!' he growled, unsheathing the jewelled dagger from his belt.

Confronted by the formidable blade, Connor recalled his instructor's words: *It's far better to make a good run than a bad stand*. But, with nowhere to run this time, a bad stand was the only option Connor had.

He took the terrorist leader head on, crescent-kicking the hand that held the dagger. But the leader was deceptively quick. Pulling back, he slashed with the blade. Connor leapt aside, barely avoiding his stomach being sliced open. As the dagger came in for another attack, Connor truly wished he'd worn his stab-proof T-shirt. Pushing Alicia out of range of the knife, Connor made a lunge forward, seized the man's wrist and twisted it into a jujitsu lock. The leader grimaced in pain, his bones grating, but he refused to let go. The two of them began wrestling for dominance of the knife. They slammed against the wall. The tip of the blade dug into Connor's shoulder. He cried out, losing control of the terrorist's wrist. The leader pinned him by the throat to the wall.

'Who the hell *are* you?' snarled the terrorist leader, as Connor choked in his vice-like grip.

Struggling to free himself, Connor spluttered, 'Alicia's . . . buddy.'

The leader shook his head. 'No, you're trouble,' he replied, raising his dagger and aiming the sharpened tip at Connor's heart. 'Too much trouble to keep alive.'

HOSTAGE
CHAPTER 95

For all Connor's protection of Alicia, it was now she who came to *his* rescue. As the dagger arced down, Alicia launched herself at the terrorist leader.

'Leave him alone!' she cried, landing on his back.

Clinging on for all she was worth, she clawed at his face with her long fingernails, gouging at both his eyes. The leader roared in fury and pain. Releasing Connor, he snatched at the wildcat on his back. He grabbed hold of an arm and flung her off. Alicia flew through the air, struck the opposite wall and landed in a dazed heap, blood trickling from a gash on her forehead.

Seized by a bloodlust, the leader turned on her. Deep red score-marks lined his face and one eye was a bloody pulp.

'You'll pay for that,' he yelled, brandishing his dagger. 'I'll cut *your* face to pieces!'

'NO! UNCLE MALIK, DON'T!' protested Hazim as he ran from the kitchen and stepped between them. 'She's just a girl.'

'She's an infidel,' spat the terrorist leader, glaring at his nephew through his one good eye. 'Now out of my way or I'll go through you to her.'

Connor could see Hazim was trembling with fear, but he held his ground.

Malik appeared to back down. Then with the speed of a striking cobra he drove the dagger into Hazim's gut. Hazim gasped in shock, his eyes bulging, his whole body shuddering.

'I've always questioned whether you had the *stomach* for this mission,' smirked Malik as he drove the blade up to the jewelled hilt and twisted. Hazim screamed, his blood now spilling on to the floor.

Connor seized his moment and rushed over to Alicia. She was still stunned from the blow against the wall. Ignoring the pain in his shoulder, he half-carried her into the kitchen, praying they'd find a back door.

'Bahir, get after them! And where the hell's Kedar?' Malik shouted from the hallway. 'They're escaping!'

Connor's gamble paid off. On the other side of the kitchen was an exit leading on to a wooden veranda. Flinging open the door, Connor and Alicia ran out into a large garden bordered by a high brick wall. A shimmer of moonlight revealed a small shed next to the wall and the silhouettes of tall trees beyond.

'This way,' he said as Alicia, recovering from her attack, found her feet again.

They fled into a warm starlit night, the darkness quickly enveloping them. From the kitchen, Malik's voice barked, 'Get the guns! Search the garden.'

Feet thundered on to the wooden veranda just as Connor and Alicia reached the shed.

'Which way did they go?' said a voice, urgent and angry.

Connor noticed a woodpile stacked beside the shed. Gritting his teeth against the burning fire in his shoulder, he pushed Alicia up. He could feel his top had become slick with his own blood. They clambered on to the shed's roof, from where they could just reach the top of the garden wall.

'Over there!' came a shout.

Connor was caught in the beam of a flashlight. There was a gunshot and a bullet ricocheted inches from his head. He and Alicia flung themselves over the wall, hung on to the tile-capped lip, then dropped down to the other side. The distance was further than either of them had anticipated and they both crumpled to the rocky ground. Alicia let out a cry.

'I've . . . twisted my ankle,' she grimaced, nursing her foot.

This was the last thing they needed. But Connor wasn't going to fail in his duty now. He put an arm under Alicia's shoulder and hauled her to her feet. There was a slim chance the trees might conceal their escape. Hurrying as fast as her ankle and the terrain would allow, they beat a path through the undergrowth and weaved between the trees.

As they fled, Connor pulled his phone from his pocket. Still no signal.

Then he noticed the 'Insert SIM Card' icon flashing at the bottom of the screen.

Cursing, Connor was about to discard the phone when

his phone jogged the screen and Amir's SOS app appeared. In his rush to escape, he'd forgotten all about it. Connor launched the app and pressed Send.

He just hoped the phone had enough battery life to do the job.

HOSTAGE
CHAPTER 96

In the operations room of Buddyguard Headquarters, the atmosphere was tense and agitated. Charley drummed her fingers on the arm of her wheelchair. Marc sat with his head in his hands. Next to him, Ling rubbed her eyes with exhaustion and took another sip of energy drink. Amir was pacing nervously up and down, while Bugsy stared blankly at the monitor of his terminal, defeated by the server source code.

'The deadline's past,' said Amir, glancing up at the clock. 'So why haven't we heard anything yet?'

'No news is good news,' offered Bugsy.

'But the terrorists were pretty insistent on their deadline,' said Ling.

'Maybe the President struck a deal with them?' Marc suggested.

Charley sorrowfully shook her head. 'We'd have heard from Colonel Black by now.'

They all lapsed back into anxious silence. Charley began to bite her nails. She felt partly responsible for Connor's fate. She was the operations leader, after all. An ominous thought passed through her mind. *Perhaps bad karma's following me since my last assignment as an active buddyguard.* Nothing, it seemed, had gone right for her since that fateful day. Connor had been a turning point in her life, or so she had hoped. But now it appeared he would be yet another dead end. Literally.

A computer terminal began beeping incessantly.

'What's that?' asked Ling.

Charley looked over at Amir and they blurted out simultaneously, 'SOS!'

Rushing to the terminal, Amir woke the monitor and his jaw dropped in disbelief.

'If this really *is* Connor, then you're not going to believe where they are . . .'

Charley sped over and stared at the screen in equal astonishment.

'Amir, relay the coordinates to Colonel Black, right now!'

HOSTAGE
CHAPTER 97

Connor and Alicia rushed headlong through the undergrowth, branches and bushes tearing at their faces and clothes. The forest was inky black, the moonlight struggling to penetrate the canopy above, and Connor could only hazard a guess at the direction they were headed. But as long as it was away from the terrorists he didn't care. Behind, he could hear them crashing through the bushes in hot pursuit. Alicia struggled on valiantly, but with her injured ankle, the terrorists were gaining on them fast. Glancing back, Connor could see the lights of their torches sweeping the area for them.

'Leave me,' she panted, leaning against a tree trunk to catch her breath. 'Go and get help.'

'No,' said Connor. 'A buddyguard *never* leaves their Principal. Nor does a friend.'

She managed a weak smile. 'You're one hard date to get rid of!'

Bearing more of her weight, Connor pressed on despite his own injury. Alicia bit down on her lip as pain rocketed up her leg with every step. The shouts of the terrorists grew louder. Several bullets whizzed past, shearing off chunks of bark and sending splinters into their path. Hobbling down a slope, Connor and Alicia burst from the undergrowth and hit a tarmac road. A car zoomed by, horn blaring, as it almost ran them over.

'STOP!' cried Connor, trying to flag the vehicle down.

But the red tail lights disappeared rapidly into the distance.

'Did you see that?' asked Alicia, her eyes wide.

'What?'

'The license plate!'

'No, but keep moving,' Connor insisted, trying to hurry Alicia across the road before the terrorists appeared. But she continued to stare after the car. Then he too was brought to a sudden halt by a road sign . . . in English:

> Rock Creek Park – Beach Drive
> ↺ Maryland
> Downtown DC ↻

'Rock Creek Park?' said Alicia, reading the sign twice and still doubting her eyes. 'We're *still* in Washington!'

Connor couldn't believe it either. The disorientation of their captivity, the terrorists' robes, the constant use of Arabic and the traditional style of food had all convinced him that they were being held in the Middle East. As the truth dawned on him, Connor tried to recall the park's layout from his briefing notes. He knew it wasn't a particularly wide park, a couple of miles at the most, so they'd soon come to the city suburbs. They just needed to keep off the road and out of sight until they could reach help.

The sign clanged, loud and harsh, as a bullet pierced a hole dead centre through the first 'O' of 'Downtown'. Connor spun round to see Malik and his men scrambling down the slope, guns levelled at them.

'Stay right where you are!' warned Malik.

Instinctively protecting Alicia, Connor propelled her towards the bushes on the other side of the road. Gunfire ripped through the night, bullets peppering the road at their feet. They dived for the cover of the trees, landing hard on the rocky ground. As they scrambled back up, Alicia's ankle finally gave way beneath her and she screamed.

'Come on!' cried Connor, his adrenalin driving him on as he lifted her on to his shoulders and ran.

But in those fateful few seconds the terrorists had caught up and Connor found himself confronted by the barrel of Malik's gun.

'Make one false move and I'll put a bullet through both of you,' said Malik, his eye still bloody from where Alicia had clawed him.

Gently lowering Alicia to the ground, Connor stood in front of her – his body, her shield.

'I admire your commitment to the girl,' smirked Malik, revealing a row of yellowed teeth. 'A *boy* willing to make the ultimate sacrifice . . . and so you will.'

The gunshot rang loud through the forest.

HOSTAGE

CHAPTER 98

'Will he live?'

'Unfortunately, it appears so,' replied Kyle as he eyed the wounded terrorist with contempt.

Malik lay handcuffed to a stretcher, a drip in his arm, a mass of bloody bandages wrapped round his chest. Two medics were checking his vital signs and preparing to transfer him into the waiting ambulance.

Connor sat on the back step of a second ambulance, a medic stitching up the knife wound to his shoulder. He could feel the tug of the stitch against his flesh, but the anaesthetic was keeping the pain at bay.

When Connor had been confronted at point-blank range with Malik's gun, he'd thought his life was over. He'd braced himself to take the bullet for Alicia. A final and fatal act of protection. And the only thing, as a bodyguard, he had left to give. But it was Malik who fell to the ground, screaming.

Immediately following the gunshot, the forest had erupted with Secret Service agents. Connor had thrown himself on top of Alicia as there was a furious exchange of gunfire. One terrorist was instantly shot down. The others were subdued in a matter of seconds. Then Connor and Alicia were encircled by an impenetrable barrier of agents, Kyle among them.

'That'll be some battle scar,' Kyle remarked, nodding at Connor's wound when the medic had finished.

Connor smiled; he supposed it would look kind of cool. A badge of honour to show Charley, Amir and the others when he got back to the UK.

As the surviving terrorists were bundled, hands bound, into a windowless armoured van, the Director of Secret Service strode over to Connor.

'How many did you say there were?' asked Dirk.

'Six, that I saw.'

'Well, we've accounted for five,' stated the director, frowning.

Connor looked towards the armoured van. 'I don't see the terrorist with glasses.'

'The one you scalded with coffee?' queried Dirk. Connor nodded and the director immediately got on his radio, circulating the man's description to his team. He turned back to Connor. 'I've two units sweeping the park. With any luck, they should apprehend him. We've also checked out the house and found the terrorist you locked up. There was a dead one in the hall too. Did you do that?'

Connor shook his head. 'That was the leader's work.'

Dirk raised an enquiring eyebrow.

Connor thought of Kalila. She'd be devastated by the news of her brother's treachery – unless he could offer her some comfort through his last-minute act of redemption. 'The guy was Hazim, a brother of one of Alicia's classmates. He had a change of heart and tried to save us.'

Dirk nodded and instructed Kyle to make a note of this.

'What's going to happen to the terrorist leader?' asked Connor as the doors to Malik's ambulance were slammed shut and he was driven away, sirens blaring.

'He'll first be taken to a secure medical facility for questioning, then charged with kidnapping, terrorism and murder,' replied Dirk. 'He'll no doubt spend the rest of his life in a maximum security prison, although he deserves much worse.'

Connor looked over his shoulder into the back of his ambulance. Alicia was laid out on a stretcher, her ankle bound. A medic was tending to the laceration on her forehead and a drip had been inserted into her arm to treat for mild dehydration and shock.

The director noted his concern. 'Don't worry, the medic says she'll be fine ... all thanks to the great job you've done in protecting her.'

Connor looked up at Dirk, dumbfounded by his uncharacteristic praise.

Dirk unpinned the small Secret Service badge on the lapel of his jacket and fastened it to Connor's top. The five-pointed star glimmered in the ambulance's twirling red and white lights.

With a rare smile, he declared, 'You've earned this, Agent Reeves.'

HOSTAGE
CHAPTER 99

4 July

'Today is Independence Day!' declared President Mendez, standing before the microphone on the steps of the Lincoln Memorial. 'Not only for the United States, but for my daughter, Alicia.'

Connor could barely hear himself think as the crowd roared its delight. Bathed in glorious July sunshine, thousands upon thousands of people had gathered to celebrate Alicia's freedom. American flags and pennants were being waved in joyous triumph, a rippling sea of red, white and blue that encircled the Reflecting Pool and stretched as far as the eye could see. Connor thought this was what it must have been like for Dr Martin Luther King, Jr, as he delivered his famous 'I Have a Dream' speech.

'I prayed for a miracle,' proclaimed the President as the crowd quietened down. 'And one was delivered.'

He glanced over his shoulder at his daughter. Just offstage stood Connor in a cream-coloured shirt, baseball cap and mirrored shades. For a brief moment the President looked directly at him, his eternal gratitude apparent.

'But I haven't only God to thank for that,' continued President Mendez, addressing the crowd. 'There are certain people who work tirelessly and endlessly to protect me and my family. And they're the ones responsible for the safe return of my precious daughter. I'm forever grateful to the Secret Service and all the security agencies. I must also thank *you*, the American people, for your support in my darkest hour.'

There was a wave of heartfelt applause.

Connor knew he wouldn't be thanked publicly. Nor would his role in the operation ever be admitted, since the Buddyguard organization had to remain secret to be effective. So it had been agreed that Secret Service would receive all of the credit for Alicia's rescue. However, Connor didn't feel cheated by this. In fact, he had no desire for any such acknowledgement. Just seeing Alicia alive, free and happy was enough for him. He now understood why his father had been so compelled to be a bodyguard. The reward was in the knowledge that a life had been protected and saved. And each day after that was a gift.

'Terrorism will *never* defeat America!' President Mendez thumped his fist on the podium. 'However low they sink, we will never bow to their pressure. For we are a nation of strength, of determination and of love. We are *one* family.'

He beckoned to his wife and daughter to join him in front of the cheering crowd. Alicia glanced at Connor, a beaming smile on her lips meant only for him. Connor returned the smile. They hadn't had much chance to talk since their escape, Alicia being reunited with her family and Connor being debriefed by both Colonel Black and Secret Service. But he knew there was still a great deal to be said between them. And once things settled down he hoped for just such an opportunity.

Caught up in the emotion of the event, Connor felt the urge to take a photo. It was a unique moment and he wanted to share it with his friends back at Buddyguard Headquarters. Slipping his phone out of his pocket, he snapped a picture of Alicia approaching the podium and the flag-waving crowd beyond.

Straight after depressing the button, an icon on the screen began to flash red. Connor thought the battery was dying, then the face-recognition software app launched and a series of thumbnail photos appeared. The first was of him and Alicia on the steps of the Lincoln Memorial; another was at Montarose School prior to entering the prom; and the third was the one he'd just taken. Each photo zoomed in on a red-highlighted face in the background.

Connor felt a cold sense of dread as he too recognized the face.

HOSTAGE
CHAPTER 100

Once is happenstance. Twice is circumstance. Three times means enemy action.

Connor's alert level shot up to Code Orange. He searched the crowd, his eyes scanning the countless faces among the forest of flags and pennants. Quickly referencing his phone for a position, he found who he was looking for.

With a large bent nose and hound-dog eyes, the man was instantly recognizable. He'd been the face behind the glass, the thirsty worker at the water fountain and, in all likelihood, the mysterious figure in the corridor at the prom. On this day, the groundsman from Montarose School was just a spectator. But he appeared agitated and, taking into account the hot day, was oddly dressed in a bulky sports jacket.

Connor pressed his earpiece.

'*Bandit to Bravo One. Suspect spotted* two *o'clock of the podium.*'

'*Bravo One to Bandit. Describe,*' came back Kyle's voice immediately.

'Tall, black hair, large nose, wearing red sports jacket, brown T-shirt with –'

As Connor relayed his description, the groundsman reached into his jacket.

Time suddenly seemed to slow for Connor. The first thing he thought he saw was the butt of a gun protruding out of the man's hand. Connor waited a beat, not wishing to 'cry wolf' again and ruin another celebration. Then a barrel emerged from the jacket and there was no longer any doubt. His mind switched to Code Red.

'GUN!' he barked into his mic.

A fraction of a second later, another agent spotted the threat. But the groundsman was already bringing his weapon round on Alicia. She was oblivious, her gaze directed towards her father. And so were the people in the crowd, who were entirely focused on the First Family. Only the Secret Service agents were paying the man any attention. As two agents rushed to tackle the assassin, Connor launched himself towards Alicia. Each step felt like he was running through thick mud, the distance between them stretching rather than closing.

Agents from the President's Protective Detail were also moving in to secure President Mendez and his family.

Connor levelled with Alicia just as he heard two gunshots. He drove his hip into her and 'the Shove' knocked her sideways. He was about to follow and provide body cover, when the bullets hit him with the force of a battering ram.

HOSTAGE

CHAPTER 101

Malik's eyes flickered open and a grey windowless room swam into view. The harsh neon strip light on the ceiling hurt his one uncovered eye; the other was blessedly shaded by a bandage. Next to his bed was an ECG monitor, softly beeping at a regular pulse. An IV drip hung beside it, the tube attached to a cannula in his left arm. Malik felt maddeningly thirsty and his lungs whistled with every shallow breath he took. He tried to sit up, but it was as if a lead weight had been dropped on his chest. Glancing down, he saw that his torso was swathed in bandages, a patch of blood seeping through. Turning his head slowly, he became aware of a man in a white coat sitting at the end of his bed.

'Who . . . are . . . you?' wheezed Malik.

'I have some questions,' said the man.

'Talk . . . to my lawyer.'

The man ignored his suggestion and took out a mobile computer from his pocket.

'You were paid ten million dollars in advance for kidnapping the President's daughter.'

Malik went still. 'How do you know that?'

'The people I represent paid you that amount. And they want it back for *failure* to fulfil the terms of the deal.'

Malik felt a chill run down his spine. 'B-but I succeeded. That English boy, Connor Reeves, is to blame!'

The man appeared unmoved by his argument. Clutching at the possibility of a deal, Malik said, 'Well, what would I get in return?'

'We can talk about your release after. First, I need your account details and transfer code,' said the man, tapping at the screen of his computer.

Malik considered the offer for a brief moment only. If the central cell was powerful enough to reach inside the US Government, then it was powerful enough to free him. Malik recited the digits from memory. The man typed the account number and code into his mobile. Once the transaction was complete, he returned his attention to Malik.

'Now everything is in balance. Equilibrium, you might say. We can proceed. What does the Brotherhood know about the funding of your operation?'

'Nothing,' replied Malik. 'I never told anyone about the central cell.'

The faintest trace of a smile passed across the man's face. 'Excellent.' He put his hand into his coat pocket and pulled out a large fountain pen. 'So you're the only link.'

The man removed the nib to reveal a long syringe.

'What are you doing?' spluttered Malik, his uncovered eye widening in horror at the sight of the needle. 'You're not a doctor!'

'No,' the man replied, calmly inserting the syringe into the Y-connector of Malik's IV drip. 'I'm your executioner.'

'But I *won't* talk,' promised Malik, a sweat suddenly breaking out on his brow. 'I don't even know who you are!'

The man depressed the plunger on his pen and a clear liquid fed into the drip. A second later, Malik felt a fire ignite in his arm, as if molten iron was coursing through his veins. He tried to scream, but the sheer agony of the poison spreading through his body took all his breath away. Arching his back and writhing, he clawed at the man in a desperate attempt to stop him. The man watched, impassive to his suffering. Then the poison reached Malik's heart and he slumped lifeless on to his bed, the ECG beep turning to a continuous drone.

'And you *never* will talk,' said the man, putting the nib back on his pen and leaving the room.

HOSTAGE
CHAPTER 102

'How's the leg?' enquired Colonel Black, standing beside Connor's bed in the secure wing of the George Washington Hospital.

Connor shifted uncomfortably. He felt as if he'd been run over by a bus and his thigh still throbbed like wildfire.

'Better,' he replied, wincing, his badly bruised ribs making it difficult to breathe.

His life had only been saved by his decision earlier that morning to wear his bulletproof shirt. The first round had hit him dead centre in the chest, resulting in blunt trauma – excruciatingly painful but survivable. The second bullet had struck his unprotected thigh and he'd dropped to the ground, blood pouring from the wound over the white marble steps. Connor had initially felt nothing, the burst of adrenalin masking the pain. And in those few moments of shocked numbness, he'd watched the groundsman being tackled by the two agents and finally disarmed. Alicia had screamed his name as she was evacuated at speed by Secret Service. But only when she was out of the danger zone did Connor relax, then a whiteout of pain exploded in his leg.

Everything after that was a blur of agents, rapid-response medics, ambulances and nurses.

'Excellent,' said Colonel Black, with an approving nod at Connor's manly response. 'Your doctor tells me it's just a flesh wound, so you'll be back on your feet in no time.'

He handed Connor a get-well card.

'You shouldn't have!' jested Connor, surprised by the colonel's thoughtfulness.

'I didn't,' he replied, straight-faced. 'It's from Alpha team.'

Connor smiled. He supposed it was a bit much to expect sympathy from a battle-hardened ex-SAS soldier. Opening the card, his smile widened into a grin when he read the message: *To the Bullet-catcher!*

'Charley's due in tomorrow,' revealed the colonel.

Connor looked up. 'She's coming *here*?'

Colonel Black raised an arch eyebrow. 'I have to return to HQ and she volunteered.'

Connor was delighted by this news. It would be good to have a friend around, especially one who'd understand a little of what he'd been through. The US Government had been quick to suppress media reporting of his true role in protecting the First Daughter. He was just a casualty of the 'crazed gunman' and, due to the baseball cap and shades he'd been wearing, his identity hadn't been revealed. Even his name had been changed on the hospital records. His own mother and gran didn't know the whole story either. They'd been told he was involved in a mountain-biking accident while on his student exchange programme. The colonel had arranged a video call to reassure them. And although Connor didn't like keeping his family in the dark he appreciated the need to do so – just like his father had when working for the SAS.

Connor put aside the card. 'So what's the news on the groundsman? Was he connected to the terrorists?'

Colonel Black shook his head. 'No, it doesn't appear so. Secret Service intercepted the missing terrorist yesterday, a man called Bahir, as he was trying to escape to Mexico under a false passport. The groundsman appears to be a lone wolf. They checked Alicia's school locker on your suggestion and found a note threatening to kill her for "ignoring him". It seems he had a fixation on her.'

Connor shuddered at the thought. If it hadn't been for the water pistol incident at the prom, his original call-in might have been followed up by Secret Service. But at least all the terrorists had now been captured – that was reassuring news for both him and Alicia.

'Tell me, did Secret Service find out any more about that double agent?'

'Dead end,' replied the colonel. 'Agent Brooke's apartment burnt down a few days back. The FBI are investigating. But there's no need to concern yourself with that. Remember, you're a bodyguard, not a spy. Talking of which . . .'

Colonel Black reached into his jacket pocket and pulled out a winged Buddyguard shield.

'For outstanding bravery in the line of duty,' he declared, pinning the badge to Connor's chest and saluting him.

Connor glanced down and saw that the winged badge was *gold*.

HOSTAGE
CHAPTER 103

'I was right to trust my daughter in the hands of a Reeves buddyguard,' said President Mendez, making his personal farewell in the Blue Room of the White House Residence, along with his wife and Alicia. 'You're most certainly your father's son. You've proven beyond doubt that you have his courage, dedication and strength of character.'

Connor smiled gratefully at the President's words. The bruising on his chest had disappeared and his leg, although stiff, was almost fully healed. But now another wound was beginning to heal too – the one in his heart caused by his father's death. Being compared to his father was as close as Connor could get to actually *being* with him again. And that meant a great deal.

'I just did my duty, Mr President,' replied Connor.

'You went way beyond the call of duty,' stated the First Lady, kissing him on the cheek and embracing him. 'There are no words to express how thankful we are for you protecting our treasured daughter.'

'This gift may go some way to helping you in the future,' said President Mendez, handing Connor a dark blue passport.

'In recognition of your services, I've granted you honorary citizenship of the United States. With this, you'll be able to call on any of our government's resources and gain consular protection from our embassies throughout the world.'

'Thank you, Mr President,' replied Connor, accepting the unique and powerful gift.

President Mendez and his wife now stepped aside to allow their daughter to come forward. Wearing a lilac summer dress, her long locks pinned back and a touch of make-up highlighting her natural beauty, Alicia was a far cry from the distraught and terrified hostage she had been the previous month.

'We'll leave you two together,' said the President tactfully, as he led the First Lady out on to the south portico.

Alicia waited until the doors closed behind them, then turned to Connor.

'I suppose this is really goodbye,' she said, biting her lip and blinking back tears.

Connor nodded. He hadn't been looking forward to this moment either. They'd been through so much together and shared a close, seemingly unbreakable bond. It felt wrong to part like this. But now that Alicia understood the necessity of Secret Service protection Kyle and his team could function 100 per cent effectively and Connor's role was no longer required.

'Thank you for protecting me,' said Alicia. 'Without you, I could never have survived being a hostage.'

'Without *you*, I wouldn't have survived either,' admitted Connor.

Alicia gave him an affectionate smile. 'Well, you'll be pleased to know I've accepted my role as the First Daughter. I appreciate that while it offers me many unique opportunities, my freedom is limited – and for good reason. I won't be running away from Secret Service again!'

Smiling ruefully, she glanced in Kyle's direction. Kyle nodded, before discreetly leaving the room. Now truly alone, Alicia took a step towards Connor. She studied his face, seemingly trying to commit it to her memory.

'I know you can't stay . . .' she whispered, 'but this is to remember me by.'

Alicia wrapped her arms around his neck and kissed him full on the lips. Connor's breath was taken away and he became lost in the moment.

Suddenly the door to the room opened.

Alicia broke away. 'Kyle, I asked not to be disturbed –'

'Sorry, I didn't get the message,' replied Charley, wheeling herself in. She glanced at Connor who was guiltily rubbing away a faint smear of lipstick with the back of his hand.

'Our car's here,' she stated pointedly.

Connor nodded, unable to meet her questioning stare.

'*Already?*' said Alicia, almost pleading for more time.

'We've a plane to catch,' Charley replied, breezily pivoting on the spot and heading for the door.

While Charley's back was turned, Connor took Alicia's hand and looked her in the eyes. 'I definitely won't forget you . . . or that kiss!' he promised.

Then, with great reluctance, he hurried after Charley.

At the threshold to the room, he glanced back. Alicia stood silhouetted by the window, gazing out across the south lawn.

'Don't worry, Connor, I'll protect her,' said Kyle, who stood sentry at the door.

Knowing she was in safe hands, Connor headed through the White House's main entrance hall and out on to the driveway of the north portico. Charley was already waiting for him in the car.

'Honestly, I didn't make the first move,' he explained, offering a sheepish grin as he clambered in next to her. 'Besides, I'm no longer *officially* protecting her –'

'It's not important,' said Charley, although Connor could tell that she was annoyed.

'Surely you must've found yourself in similar situations,' he pressed.

Charley gave him a look that he couldn't quite read. Then her expression softened. 'Don't worry, I won't tell the colonel.'

With that she placed a black folder on Connor's lap. The folder was marked CONFIDENTIAL in red lettering and had a silver winged shield embossed on the cover.

'Your next assignment.'

Connor stared at Charley in disbelief. 'But I've barely got out of hospital. Besides, who's to say I *still* want to be a buddyguard.'

'The colonel,' she replied, handing him a scratched key fob. 'He says it's in your blood . . . and he's never wrong.'

As they drove away from the White House, his Principal safe and secure, Connor studied the key fob. His father's face stared back at him and Connor thought he could discern the ghost of a proud smile.

Connor couldn't deny the fact. It *was* in his blood. He was born to be a bodyguard.

HOSTAGE
ACKNOWLEDGEMENTS

Starting a new book is always a challenge, and a new series is even more so. There are countless risks to the ultimate success of the story: from deciding which plotline to follow, which characters to choose and what words to use; to having the time to actually write the book, think without distraction and defeat that self-doubt which plagues all authors. The journey of a book from idea to completion is fraught with many dangers. But thankfully I was able to rely on my own team of 'bodyguards' to protect me in my mission.

These fearless protectors who deserve my thanks are:

My darling wife Sarah, my super-charged Zach and my glorious Leo; my mum and dad who have protected me my entire life; Sue and Simon for their love and support; buddy-guards Steve and Sam; and Karen, Rob and Thomas of 'Rose Security Forces'.

Charlie Viney, my agent, who I believe would actually throw himself in the line of fire to protect my career! Franca Bernatavicius and Nicky Kennedy at ILA, who would be right behind him (probably using Charlie as a shield!) along with Pippa Le Quesne.

My squad of loyal Puffin Bodyguards – my editor Alex Antscherl, operations leader Shannon Cullen, Jayde Lynch, Julia Teece, Wendy Shakespeare, Helen Gray, and Sara Chadwick-Holmes for producing such a fantastic cover.

Trevor Wilson and Sarah Wilson at Authors Abroad for all their hard work in organizing my book tours.

My friends who continue to stand by me in life, including but not exclusive to Geoff and Lucy, Matt, Charlie, Nick and Zelia, Ann and Andrew (my godparents), my cousin Laura and the Dyson clan (especially my god-daughter Lulu!).

The following fans for helping me with the Arabic: Shazaan Nadeem, Jan Murphy, Lee Lalka, Peter Brown, Mus Hertoghs, Zo Zo Harley Clews.

These super-fans who deserve acknowledgement for their unwavering support from Young Samurai through to Bodyguard: Kevin Haex, Tim Hoogstoel, Steve McCormick, Charlie Harland and Aidan Bracher.

A huge thanks must go to all the friends I made on my Close Protection Course with Wilplan Training. These people are *real* bodyguards and deserve true respect. This book is written in honour of them: Mandie, Simon, George, Sarah and Andy, Big Si, Baz, Andy, Jimmy, Sean, Nigel, Alex, Joe, Ronnie, and of course Sam and Mark!

Finally, to my instructors and the staff on the Wilplan Close Protection Course (www.wilplantraining.co.uk) where I learnt the true art of being a bodyguard. Gary, Simon, Claire, Wendy, John, Ray and Pete – thank you for your dedicated instruction, patience and knowledge. Your wisdom is the lifeblood in this book.

Stay safe.
Chris

Any fans can keep in touch with me and the progress of the Bodyguard series on my Facebook page, or via the website at *www.bodyguard-books.com*

TERRORISTS, ASSASSINS, KIDNAPPERS, PIRATES.

THE WORLD IS A DANGEROUS PLACE.

HAVE YOU GOT WHAT IT TAKES TO BE A BODYGUARD?

- **Sign up** to be a Buddyguard and take on email missions
- **Read more** about Chris Bradford's own bodyguard training
- **Download** exclusive extracts
- **Watch** the action-packed trailer
- **Unlock** hidden content (using a secret code)!

Visit **www.bodyguard-books.co.uk** today!

BE READY FOR
B**O**DYGUARD
RANSOM

COMING MAY 2014

Connor's **MISSION**: to protect the twin daughters of an Australian media mogul aboard their luxury yacht.

It should be a **WATERTIGHT** operation, but Connor knows twins mean twice the **TROUBLE!**

ATTACKED in dangerous waters, **PIRATES** demand a $100 million ransom.

As the **DEADLINE** looms, they threaten to KILL the captives one by one.

But the pirates didn't count on **CONNOR REEVES** being aboard . . .